D.D. Johnston mixed a first novel out of years flipping burgers, studying sociology, starting an underground trade union, and chasing the corporate beast around Europe. Brought out by a small anarchist press in the US, *Peace, Love and Petrol Bombs* became a Book of the Year in *The Sunday Herald.* Time moved on. D.D. lodged himself in middle England, where students at the University of Gloucestershire voted him their outstanding lecturer of 2012. His mind chased revolutionary thought and action across the twentieth century as he charted the imbecility of existence in a modern university. His short fiction was shortlisted for the Bridport Prize. This second novel won him his PhD.

ALSO BY D.D. JOHNSTON

Peace, Love and Petrol Bombs

THE DECONSTRUCTION OF PROFESSOR THRUB

D.D. JOHNSTON

Published by Barbican Press in 2013

First published in Great Britain as a paperback original by
Barbican Press
1 Ashenden Road, London E5 0DP
www.barbicanpress.com

A CIP catalogue for this book is available from the British Library

ISBN: 978-0-9563364-6-0

Typeset in Garamond 11.75/15.5 pt by
Mike Gower

Cover image: Lao Tzu Series, 'The Sublimity of the Creative', by
Ian Pollock

Cover Design by Jason Anscomb of Rawshock Design

Printed by Lightning Source, Milton Keynes

LUCY

THE LIFE AND TIMES OF ELSIE ANGELENETTA STEWART: FREE WILL AND DETERMINISM IN THE 20TH CENTURY

PHD

CHELTENHAM UNIVERSITY

2013

Acknowledgements

Examiners, let me say it at the outset: I am grateful to my supervisor. An unexceptional sentiment from a PhD candidate, perhaps, but one I could not have imagined expressing two years ago. You see, Professor Thrub was no ordinary supervisor. He routinely ignored my messages, possibly deleting them unread. To arrange a tutorial it was necessary to accost him in his office (even this was not without difficulties: on one occasion I caught Thrub hiding behind his filing cabinet), and it was not unusual for him to make suicidal gestures during our meetings. At my RD1 meeting, during which Thrub twice called me a cunt, he made a bonfire out of our research degree supervision forms. When the bonfire triggered the smoke detectors and caused the evacuation of the building, he told the campus dean that he suspected I'd been smoking in the toilets. Nevertheless, this project would not have been possible without Thrub's unorthodox guidance.

There are many other people who deserve my thanks: I would have known little about Elsie Angelenetta Steel (née Stewart), the subject of this creative biography, had not her son, George Steel, been courageous and generous enough to discuss his memories. I would never even have heard of Elsie, had not my friend Barry Spence introduced me to this topic. And would I even be here to tell these stories were it not for the nurses, doctors, and auxiliaries at the Maxillofacial Unit in Gloucestershire Royal Hospital? I am grateful to them and to those staff and students at Cheltenham University who supported me during and after my hospitalisation; special thanks are surely due to my office mates – Jez, Obi, and Samuel.

But though I am grateful to all of the above, this project is dedicated to Lempi Bridgette. Lempi was my translator, my muse, my love. During our Great Research Trip, en route to Lausanne,

9

Lempi and I bought ice cones and sat on a pier by Lake Geneva. Pleasure boats slid in silent courses, their engines as quiet as the swans, and on the far bank, the jet d'Eau fountain shot 200 metres high, refracting light with its spray. Lempi said that as a child she'd been obsessed with chasing rainbows. Several times, she said, she had run away from home, convinced she could catch a rainbow. She'd keep running, even after the rainbows faded, even as dusk approached, and finally, exhausted and lost, she'd collapse in tears awaiting rescue. Well, it's the chase that matters, Lempi. I dedicate this thesis to you.

Author Declaration

I declare that the work in this thesis was carried out in accordance with the regulations of Cheltenham University and is original except where indicated by specific reference in the text. The obvious exceptions are the photocopied articles wedged between chapters.

Before chapter one, there is a photocopied page from François Barrot's *La Revolution Libertaire D'Espagne* – the page on which I first encountered Elsie Stewart. Between chapters one and two, you will find an article, by a sociologist previously unknown to me, on Anthony Giddens's attempt to resolve the structure-agency dichotomy. Its obvious relevance to the question of free will and determinism provoked my interest, but it was the article's unexpected shift in tone that persuaded me to include it here. Between chapters two and three I've included an article written by Elsie's son, George, which appeared in *Heritage: Newsletter of the Historical Society of North West Scotland and the Hebridean Islands*. Finally, between chapters six and seven, I have reproduced an article by my supervisor, Professor Thrub. This article, 'Leave our Dicks Alone: the Spectre of the Real in the Market-Stalinist Post-Fordist Academy,' broke the Professor's decade-long publishing silence, and marked his retirement from education.

Any views expressed in the thesis are those of the author and in no way do they represent those of the University – seriously, they couldn't be further removed.

21/12/2012

CLARA THALMANN
NÉE À BASEL EN 1910

CARL EINSTEIN
NÉ À NEUWIED-SUR-LE-RHIN
EN 1885 ET MORT À
LESTELLE-BÉTHARRAM
EN 1940

Dans la colonne Durruti, on
ne connaît que la syntaxe
collective. Les camarades
enseigneront aux écrivains à
changer la grammaire pour la
rendre collective. Durruti avait
eu l'intuition profonde de la
force anonyme du travail.
Anonymat et communisme ne
font qu'un. »

ELSIE ANGELENETTA
STEWART
NÉE À BELFAST EN 1918
ET MORTE À BUDAPEST
EN 1956.

Spain, 1937

1

Ten miles from the French border, they stopped at the lip of a canyon. They approached the drop on hands and knees, lay exhausted in the awful heat, and thought of love and distance. Far below, the river laced turquoise and white in the depth of the gorge. Elsie closed her eyes and listened to the cicadas and dragonflies, the faraway clang of goat bells, the funnelled whisper of the river, and the distant hum of a Nieuport.

At last she said, 'It's absurd, isn't it? ¿Absurdo? ¿Absurda?'

Andriy, her travelling companion since north of Barbastro, laughed at this, as he laughed at most things she said. He was digging the chalky earth with a spoon, gazing into the canyon. Andriy was thirty-seven but Elsie guessed he was fifty at least. In part this was because the young always imagine the future to be bigger than it is; in part it was because time had worked on Andriy's face, cutting and contouring it, as it had worked on the gorge below.

«El mundo est absurdo, ¿no?» she said again.

«¿Absurdo?» He laughed. «Si, absurdo. ¡Absurdo! Elsie, ty mne nravishsya.»

They spoke in fragments of Spanish, inflected with Catalan and Aragonese. He spoke in Russian, with Ukrainian words, and often tried French when the Spanish phrase eluded him, but he had a partial cleft lip that distorted his speech, and sometimes Elsie had no idea what language he was trying to use. When she spoke English, she used Ulster Scots phrases and conveyed meaning with the pitch of her voice. Sometimes she found a word of her mother's Italian floating out of childhood like some castaway thing. They spoke with smiles and gestures and drawings in the ground. Tonight or tomorrow they would cross into France, never see each other again. Chaotic and absurd, she thought.

Noticing the Nieuport, he found the energy to stand and aeroplane his arms, neeeuw-ing circles through the boxwood, kicking clouds around his chalk-dusted trousers. Then he stopped, laughed, pointed: «está Ramón! ¿No?» Ramón, Elsie's lover, her compañero, had volunteered as a translator at an aviation school in Russia (actually Azerbaijan), and when she met Andriy, she had tried to explain this, but had got no further than repeating 'avió' and 'Unión Soviética', so that Andriy imagined Ramón to be a Republican fighter pilot, who at any moment might pass overhead. «¡Está Ramón!» he said again. Elsie didn't know whether he was mocking her or trying to cheer her up. «¡Libertat!,» he shouted. «¡Viva los valientes! Allez-y doucement, Ramón! Ton amour t'embrasse dans la nuit.» He crouched beside her, his laughter sloping away, and then he turned, saw she was crying. «Elsie,» he said. «Yce dobre. Is okay.» It was the last day in August, 1937.

2

In September 2006, a year before I started my MA, and long before I ever expected to write a doctoral thesis, I was reading François Barrot's *La Revolution Libertaire D'Espagne* (an autobiographical account originally published in Paris in 1939, but in 1972 reprinted in Toulouse) during the final – seats upright, trays stowed – easyJet descent to Belfast. We were bumping out of the clouds, angling forward for the landing view (always the same, examiners: a crazy paving of agricultural polygons, buildings, roads, cars), when I glanced back at the book and– there: Elise Angelenetta Stewart.

The book had been given to me, one year previously, by a friend from my undergraduate days, a man with whom I'd shared a flat during my second year at the University of Manchester. While visiting Barry in Belfast, I took care to thank him for this gift, and to demonstrate my interest, I showed him the picture of Elsie. Had he, I wondered, ever heard of Elsie Angelenetta Stewart? Barry took the book from my hands, studied the photograph, and shook his head. He guessed that she had probably been a Tankie – a member of the Communist Party – for she had been in Spain during the Civil War and had died in the Eastern Bloc. While this sounded plausible, I found no mention of her in any histories of Irish Communism – e.g., Mike Milotte's *Communism in Modern Ireland: the Pursuit of the Worker's Republic since 1916* (1984) – and she is similarly absent from O'Connor's *A Labour History of Ireland 1824-1960* (1982) and Patterson's *The Politics of Illusion: Republicanism and Socialism in Modern Ireland* (1989).

3

She was fleeing Fascists, she thought. When Enrique Líster's 11th Division entered Valderrobres, Elsie, who had been dozing in the evening heat, awakened to the noise of tank engines, to curses and screams and breaking glass; she saw people running towards the castle, heard shouting and gunshots, and later, through the slats of her shutters, she saw Ramón's father, the school teacher, his hands on his head, being marched across the Plaza at gunpoint. Fascists, she thought. Don't panic, she thought. She washed her face.

She knew from westerns that in these moments women scream and betray their position, or they run out from hiding, holding their skirts; so Elsie stayed silent, back to the wall.

After a few minutes she thought to gather Ramón's books and newspapers – *El Sol, La Liberta, Solidaridad Obrera, El Heraldo de Aragón* – all the ones she thought were communist, and she hid them as best she could in the suitcase she had brought from England. On top of the books she placed a spare dress and camisole, all the time imagining how she would describe this to Ramón when next they met.

She was most afraid of being raped. Fascists, she knew, raped young women. She folded Ramón's letter into her brassiere; because she was right-handed, she placed it next to her heart.

After an hour or more, she heard shouting from Arturo's house – men, a woman, and children – too fast and run together for her to pick out more than stray words: *detención, fascista, puta*, and she determined then that if she sensed the opportunity, if everything was quiet and the plaza looked empty, she would edge down the wooden steps, right Ramón's bicycle, and pedal out of town.

4

As undergraduates at the University of Manchester, Barry and I had read Politics and History. After seminars we would repair to the Thirsty Scholar, to drink snakebites and discuss Marx until one of us was drunk enough to claim he had read the *Grundrisse*. It's true that after three pints Barry's arguing style became unnecessarily aggressive. Barry had lived as a child on the UDA-controlled Taughmonagh estate in South Belfast. His father was a telephone engineer. This was an unusual background for a student at Manchester, and he felt it entitled him to veto certain arguments as 'bourgeois nonsense' (Hobbes), 'middle class shite' (Rousseau), or (when I once foolishly mentioned Gilles Deleuze) 'some slaver ye learned at public school'.

In fact, examiners, I had attended the local comprehensive, where I was relentlessly bullied; one of the stranger school crazes involved stealing my shoes – specifically mine – and throwing them in the most imaginative place possible: the urinal trough, the electricity generator, strung over the phone lines, above the room D14 ceiling tiles, in the girls' locker room. This last incident is indelibly imprinted on my memory. I tapped the door and called, as politely as I could (at this time my voice was breaking and my every utterance occasioned shame), that my shoes were inside and might someone be kind enough to bring them to the door? To my surprise, one of the girls (from her voice I would guess Tracey Henderson) called cheerfully – one might even say coquettishly – that I should 'come on in'. And so I entered, stood in the softening steam, smelled the clouds of Impulse and the shampoo smells of mango and citrus and honey, and saw – to my incapacitating shock – the girls, standing and sitting, some in bras, some wearing only panties, some with towels wrapped round their breasts and drops of water trickling on their thighs. 'Don't be shy,' said Susan Campbell. And then, as Tracey let her towel slip to the floor, the girls shrieked and screamed, their poorly-acted alarm barely disguising their laughter, until Mrs Strang arrived (Susan even managed to cry at this point), and dragged me, still barefoot, to see the paedophilic head of PE. The paedophilic head of PE referred the matter to the disciplinary committee (watching children naked was, after all, his job), and so it happened that the first time I saw a naked female coincided with the first time that I was suspended from school. Such incidents, combined with my constant unhappiness-induced truancy, saw me classed as an unlikely problem child, to whom the state assigned a social worker, for one hour every week.

No, my upbringing did not, as Barry insisted, involve polo matches, fox hunting, or attendance at a debutantes' ball. My father, a pharmacist, spent his whole life working in other people's businesses, and would not – I'm speculating here – have earned *massively* more than an experienced telephone engineer. But such questions would not have interested Barry at times when he was animated by drink. When sober, Barry could eloquently discuss the extraction of surplus value and economic relations to the means of production; but when drunk, he advanced a class analysis based on his interlocutor's pronunciation of 'oven'.

5

The town from which Elsie fled, Valderrobres, is in the Aragonese province of Teruel. It is built on the banks of the río Matarraña and dominated by a Renaissance castle. This castle, which I visited with my translator, Lempi, during The Great Research Trip, in 1936 was the base for the region's Civil Guard; in response to the military uprising, the Civil Guard declared itself loyal to the Republic, but in deed began to arrest known radicals (Floristan, 1971, p-138). On the night of July 20th, union militants met at the train station between Valderrobres and Cretas (ibid.).

It is easy to see why they chose this meeting spot, for even today there is not another building in view. The line has long been abandoned and the single track is overgrown with St. John's Wort and wild grasses that grow to shoulder-height. Between the station buildings there grows an oak tree. The terracotta-tiles have in places cracked the timbers, crumpling the roof. The steel girders that support the platform canopy have rusted dark brown and rain and time have washed stripes of rust the length of the plastered pastel walls. By the time we had hiked there, our sun-hit skin smelled wild and sweet. I remember this moment especially fondly because it was one of the few times that Lempi and I were left alone, unmolested by Alfredo, a Venezuelan-born American backpacker, who attached himself to us for the duration of our travels. He had gone to visit a college friend in Saragossa, and so, for once, Lempi and I were able to sit together in quiet companionship. The air was heavy with the scent of rosemary, and for some minutes we rested in the shade, listening to the unseen rush-hour of insect life.

Seventy-four years earlier, the militants had hiked overnight to the union-controlled town of Gandessa. There, on the wireless, they heard Garcia Olivier announce the liberation of Catalonia. They joined with an anarchist column marching from Tortosa, and armed with shotguns they entered Calaceite and Villalba de los Arcos. When they returned to Valderrobres, their column was 1000 strong. Here, they expected to face a prolonged battle with the civil guard; instead, upon arriving on the town outskirts, they saw a white flag flying from the castle. Nationalist supporters fled to Saragossa and the trade unionists established a revolutionary committee (ibid.). It was the only authority in Valderrobres until the invasion in August 1937.

This invasion was orchestrated not by Franco but by General Enrique Líster, a member of the Stalinist Partido Comunista de España (PCE). In August 1937, supported by the 27th and 30th Divisions, Líster's troops invaded Lower Aragon to destroy the workers' collectives and subordinate the region to the central authority of Negrín's government. Elsie assumed that the invading troops were Nationalists – that Franco had suddenly and unexpectedly broken through Republican lines. In fact, the Nationalists didn't arrive in Valderrobres until March 1938, and by then the roads towards Catalonia were crowded with refugees.

6

Barry was and still is an anarchist. I won't patronise him by suggesting that his political views developed only as a rebellion against his Loyalist upbringing, for in his sober moments he could expound this ideology with reason and compassion. Yes, Barry was a revolutionary for a thousand righteous reasons: because half the world's population live on less than $2.50 a day; because seventy-three per cent of known flowering plants are in danger of extinction; because at least 80,000 women are raped in Britain every year, and the rape conviction rate is 6.5%; because half-a-million Iraqis died as a result of bombing and sanctions; because each year more people die trying to cross the Gibraltar Strait than died at the Berlin Wall in its entire history; because, for all our technological advances, we work longer hours today than fifty years ago; because 450,000 Britons suffer homophobic crime every year; because an area of rainforest the size of Wales— On and on and on.

I do not share Barry's political certainty, or his admirable commitment to praxis, but he has imbued in me a higher-than-average respect for the tradition of libertarian socialist thought. This tradition has influenced and been influenced by such writers as Edward Abbey, Michael Bakunin, John Berger, Martin Buber, Anthony Burgess, William Burroughs, Judith Butler, Albert Camus, Edward Carpenter, Noam Chomsky, J.M. Coetzee, Gilles Dauvé, Guy Debord, the Marquis de Sade, Carl Einstein, Max Ernst, Dario Fo, Michel Foucault, Charles Fourier, Mohandas Gandhi, William Godwin, Emma Goldman, Jaroslav Hašek, Aldous Huxley, Henrik Ibsen, Ivan Illich, Ba Jin, James Joyce, Franz Kafka, Lewis Grassic Gibbon, James Kelman, Peter Kropotkin, Gustav Landauer, Henri Lefebvre, Ursula Le

Guin, Dambudzo Marechera, Karl Marx, Louise Michel, Octave Mirbeau, Alan Moore, William Morris, Antonio Negri, George Orwell, Grace Paley, Sylvia Pankhurst, Antonie Pannekoek, Elisée Reclus, Rudolph Rocker, Bertrand Russell, Ramon Sender, Percy Shelley, Max Stirner, Henry David Thoreau, Leo Tolstoy, B. Traven, Kurt Vonnegut, Walt Whitman, Oscar Wilde, Gerrard Winstanley, and Howard Zinn. If we imagine these giants as mountains, distant and diverse, then between them there is nevertheless a valley, in which one may trace the thread of a tradition. This tradition – which you may call libertarian socialist, anti-authoritarian, anarchist, or anything else you want – has, it seems to me, as a foremost concern, the tension between individual experience and collective existence: 'We have said,' wrote Michael Bakunin, 'that man is not only the most individualistic being on earth – he is also the most social' (n.d. [1867]).

Like much political thought, the libertarian tradition addresses the relationship between collective obligation and individual freedom; its answer – in so far as it has *an* answer – is not to weigh two independent poles against each other, or to collapse these categories into each other, but to start always with that irresolvable tension itself. The individual and the social are not ontological realities between which a balance can be achieved (as is attempted in the hegemonic discourse of liberal-democratic capitalism) because – as western philosophy has known at least since Hegel – no individual exists primary to her socio-historical moment. There is no individual that transcends society, but – as twentieth-century history so fearsomely reminds us – there is no society that transcends the individual.

7

In Valderrobres and throughout The Great Research Trip, I struggled to conceal my bowel movements from Lempi. The hotel in Valderrobres had a tiny en-suite separated from our twin bedroom by a vinyl accordion door. Not wanting the smell and noise of my shit to fill the bedroom, I had decided to wait for a more private facility. By lunch time, my need was urgent. Leaving the castle, I found a small taberna and suggested we stop for lunch. Having relieved myself, I joined Lempi under the Orangina awning at the one outside table. When the elderly owner emerged with the menus, she was flapping at the air and muttering about the smell I had left inside. Despite this, I persuaded Lempi to ask her if she had lived in Valderrobres during the 1930s; I was determined to find someone who remembered Elsie and the taberna proprietor was the oldest-looking resident I had seen. The conversation did not go well. The proprietor flicked her cigarette at a stray dog and muttered curses as she shuffled back inside. She was, Lempi explained, only fifty-two. When she returned to take our orders, I asked in nonsense Spanish whether there was a vegan option. I didn't understand one word of the proprietor's response, but it was at this point that Lempi suggested we leave.

Since I was unable to find an eyewitness, I am limited in what I can say about Elsie's time in Valderrobres. Like many communities in Aragon, Valderrobres collectivised its agricultural production, but the experience of collectivisation varied greatly from village to village. In some villages, collectivisation was voluntary and spontaneous; in other villages, peasants were pressurised by anarchist militias. In some areas, collective and individual producers maintained cordial relations; in other areas, they drank in separate cafés. Some collectives traded with industrial Catalonia; other collectives strove for self-sufficiency and refused to cooperate with the wider economy. Some communities allocated generous rations of wine (for example, half-a-litre a day in Alcorisa); other communities encouraged temperance. In many collectives women continued to receive inferior wages; in other collectives – e.g., in Monzon and Mirambel – women achieved parity (Acklesberg, 1991, p-80). In some areas the monetary system remained intact; in other areas workers shopped with stamps correspondent to hours spent in productive labour. (For opposing analyses of collective efficacy, see Seidman, 2000; Leval, 1975).

As to Valderrobres specifically, my search for accounts of life before the Stalinist invasion yielded few sources. In *With the Peasants of Aragon*, eyewitness Augustin Souchy Bauer (1982 [1937]) describes newly-painted sky-blue houses and an economy that operated completely free of money. Bauer's writings are propagandist in favour of the collectives and he presents an idealised vision of revolutionary life. However, he does include some interesting details about Valderrobres: fifty per cent of the population was illiterate, and the villagers, according to his account, recruited a new teacher from Tortosa. Although they could pay no salary, the teacher was promised 'all the necessities of life'. Souchy Bauer concedes that a number of peasants asked to leave the collective after two months, but he claims this request was granted without acrimony. In place of money, the collective used a 'worker card' on which the work done each week was recorded. In the union hall there was what Souchy Bauer described as a 'wall newspaper' on which the distribution of clothing was recorded; the idea appears to have been to ensure transparency and to demonstrate fairness. When I think of this wall newspaper, I imagine Elsie Stewart choosing a new top from a trunk of recycled clothing. She holds a shirt across her chest, measuring the fit, checking the stitch work on the patches. It troubles me that this image seems so real.

A more considered and detailed account of revolutionary Valderrobres is presented by Julián Floristan (1971), whose *Comarcal de Valderrobres, Teruel: sus luchas sociales y Revolucionarias* Lempi, Alfredo, and I devoted ourselves to at the Centre International de Recherches sur l'Anarchisme in Lausanne, Switzerland. We learned that the Comarcal of Valderrobres produced grapes and almonds, but the major industry was olive production (p-11). The oil of this region, according to Floristan, is among the best in Spain, and long before the revolution, the people of Valderrobres had driven their prized oil along the treacherously winding road to Tortosa. Significantly, the harsh winter of 1936/7 damaged the olive groves and impacted on the local economy for years to come (p-13). Of course, in 1937 the war effort reduced the commarcal's labour force and increased the demand on its produce. Floristan describes an economy struggling to reconcile libertarian communist principles with the pressures of the situation and the recalcitrance of economic individualists. The Valderrobres committee fixed the price of oil at the pre-insurrectionary level, and since the price had risen, they were able to trade with collectives and businesses across the region; for example, they bartered oil for sugar at the refinery in Monzon and for fertiliser at the factory in Mongat, near Barcelona (p-16). These supplies were then distributed to the individual collectives within the Valderrobres region. When people complained that they were producing more than they were consuming, others replied 'does that forest belong to you?' (p-15), and where the commarcal committee sold oil for money, the profits were used to support the cultural and economic life of the region. In Valderrobres, they established a food cooperative, a transport fund, and a rest home for the elderly (p-140).

Additionally, a local library was stocked with books and periodicals and 'copious daily press' (p-133). I have often read about the enthusiasm for self-education that prevailed in many areas of revolutionary Spain, and I confess the idea seduces me. For example, Soledad Estorach, a Barcelona textile worker, participated in constructing a 'People's University' in an old French convent. She remembered being 'Ecstatic about the books' as she and others stocked the new university library with literature requisitioned from all over the city (interviewed in Acklesberg, 1991, p-71). I cannot help imagining Elsie in the ad hoc Valderrobres library, mouthing Spanish words, slowly moving her finger across the page. Again, this image seems as real to me as does her photograph.

8

Around the time I first saw that photograph, I was working for £10,500 per annum as a Customer Experience Adviser at a coach station in central Manchester. Initially, I had tried hard to fit in; I agreed, examiners, to watch my colleagues' mobile phone clips, even though every clip featured either a man being beheaded by Islamists, or a woman having goldfish inserted into her anus through a cone. I tried to deal tactfully with the racist jokes – coach drivers tell a lot of racist jokes (What's the difference between Leicester and Kabul? Two more years of immigration) – for to state my objection would likely cause offense and see me further ostracised. My solution – and it was somewhat cowardly – was to find something urgent to do as soon as I realised that a joke was likely to be offensive; i.e., at the first mention of a 'towel head' I would pretend to remember some urgent transportation issue and jump to make an imaginary phone call. But sometimes the remaining audience members, pitying me for having missed the punch-line, would repeat the joke's conclusion the moment I had hung up (and one can only talk to silence for so long).

When the buses were late – and they usually were – I was expected to find them. 'How long are you going to be?' I would ask. But when the drivers realised it was me on the phone, rather than admit to being stuck in a traffic jam near Knutsford, they would say something like: 'About five foot ten.' (I always laughed heartily at this.) 'Where are you now, Jim?' 'Behind the steering wheel.' 'Jim, you get me every time. Where's the vehicle?' 'On the motorway.' 'Jim, where on the motorway?' 'The middle lane.'

Then, in August, the week after the cleaner died of throat cancer (an inconvenience that management treated like a Christmas-time holiday request), I had an unusually bad day. A pile up had closed the M6 in both directions, and the M62 was shut following a machete-based road rage incident. Announcing the 12:45 to Bangor, I was subjected to the kind of mass abuse normally reserved for football players taking corner kicks at the away ends of lower league football grounds. The London coach was two hours late and the forty-seven passengers had grown irritable in the heat (our security guard, Steve, had just threatened to start a fist-fight with a family of Hassidic Jews). The situation came to a head with the arrival of a coach, whose destination blind said 'LONDON'. By the time the vehicle was stationary, the passengers, with the organic efficiency typical of crowds, had formed at the gate a throng of wheeled cases and sweating bodies, and as the drivers attempted to disembark, the crowd pressed forward, proffering their tickets. The drivers – two Glaswegians who were evidently infuriated by this reception – saw me struggling through the crowd and called 'We're no London; we're the 538 dupe tae Glasgow.'

'Oh,' I said, the implications dawning on me. 'It says London on your destination blind.'

'Aye? Well it says India on the tyres and we're no going there.'

The crowd's reaction to this can best be understood by imagining a man who has, with tolerable ease, held his urge to urinate for an hour, but who has now found a public toilet, and has raced towards it, psychologically prepared to pee. Upon finding the toilet door locked, the urge, which hitherto had been controllable, becomes utterly irresistible. The passengers threw their cases to the ground and gathered around me, shouting that the situation was ridiculous, the delay disgusting, as I backed towards the control point, gesturing for calm. The Glaswegians, evidently sick of each other's company, followed me to the desk, chatting amiably about the road works on the A74. 'Here,' said one of them, offering me his mobile phone, 'See what this dirty bastard sent me.' The goldfish, I could see, were still in the plastic bag, the cone only now being inserted into the unfortunate woman's anus. 'I'm sorry,' I said, 'I really need to make this phone call. Hello there, Dave, we're eh just wondering how long you're going to be?'

'About six foot.'

That afternoon I gave my notice and applied to do a Master's in Creative Writing.

9

Elsie Stewart fled Valderrobres and travelled north. I imagine her crossing badlands, through days so hot they shook the world. In my version, she slept the first night amid the olive trees. In the morning she rode a cart from La Fresneda to Alcañiz, arguing with the driver, who wouldn't believe she'd seen fascists. He asked her where she was going and she said Fraga. She said she was a refugiada. He asked her why she came here. She said, for love. Of course, he said.

In January, she and Ramón had spent some days in Fraga, breaking their journey south from France, and she thought Ramón would want her to go there. Later, she imagined, she would explain to him how she had considered the situation and decided to escape the occupied village. She knew already that she would exaggerate the story. She'd tell him how she hid roadside from a fascist convoy; how they stopped to pee just beside her; how a half-extinguished cigarette kindled the shrub at her nose; how she dared not breathe.

She rode a XV International Brigade troop truck to Fraga. She met a French Negro. She met an Austrian who played a Harmonica. She met two Americans. One of them was sunburned all over his chest and neck. 'You a nurse?' he asked.

'No, I help in the fields.' He offered her a cigarette. 'Cheers. I'm Elsie; what do they call you?'

'I'm Eddie,' he said.

'Are you escaping the fascists?' she asked.

'There's no escaping the fascists.'

'They took my village: Valderrobres.'

'Where's that then?'

Elsie shrugged and pointed. 'South of here.'

'You hear that, Michael? Franco's in Valdersomewhere.'

'Oh yeah? Where's that?'

'South of here.'

'He'll be in New York by the winter,' said Michael.

'Beautiful country,' said Eddie, gesturing at the scenery.

'Beautiful.'

'You got a boyfriend, Elsie?'

'Aye.'

'Of course.'

When they stopped roadside the Americans took turns on her bicycle.

10

Applying to study an MA in Creative Writing was an impulsive act, the first reckless thing I had done in years. A year later I would be further in debt and even less employable, but my writing career demanded professional help. I had hoped my 14000-word novella, 'The Unbearable Shiteness of Being,' would be the title story of a collection of short fiction on the theme of loneliness, but this piece, and the nine stories that accompanied it, had been rejected by every English language publication from the *Reader's Digest* to *McSweeny's*.

A year earlier I had moved into a bedsit that was so small I sometimes splashed the mattress while warming soup. Now, moving to Cheltenham, I slid further in the property market, letting a single room in a damp basement flat. The landlord had tempted me by promising that I'd share with a beautiful PhD student from Sweden, but, as it transpired, I shared with two anti-social teenagers from the East Midlands (one of them disappeared in March, leaving behind two replica guns, a Scream mask, and a German-language guide to guerrilla warfare).

To avoid returning to the flat, I would sometimes study in Wetherspoon's. On one such occasion, the barmaid, pausing to ask whether I had ordered onion rings, looked at the three translations of *War and Peace* that I had spread open on my table. 'You can't read three books at once!' she said. Her tone was friendly, flirtatious even, but without thinking I answered: 'Oh – oh no, these are all the same book.' She stood for a moment – agape is the word, I think – and then she carried away the onion rings.

War and Peace is the great novel of historical agency. As Georg Lukács put it:

At the heart of Tolstoy is the contradiction between the protagonists of history and the living forces of popular life. He shows that those who, despite the great events in the forefront of history, go on living their normal, private and egoistic lives are really furthering the true (unconscious, unknown) development, while the consciously acting 'heroes' of history are ludicrous and harmful puppets. (1969 [1937], pp-98/99)

In demonstrating the limitations of human agency in historical context, however, Tolstoy's analysis of free will and determinism accepts the freedom of any act that relates to the actor alone. In 'Some Words about *War and Peace*,' originally published in 1868 and reproduced in the Maud and Maud translation, Tolstoy insists: 'In spite of all the materialists may say, I can undoubtedly commit an act or refrain from it if the act relates to me alone. I have undoubtedly by my own will just lifted and lowered my arm' (1997, p-1351). Interestingly, when I advanced the old claim that there is no free will, and, properly speaking, no choice, Lempi refuted me by raising and lowering her arm. Is this a coincidence or is it an indication that even the simplest actions are determined by our biological constitution and our socio-historical context? 'When we start to think like this,' I said to Lempi, 'the boundaries between "internal" and "external" become blurred, and it is difficult to conceive of any act that "relates to me alone."'

11

Elsie found Fraga dying in the heat, flies knocking each other in circles. She wheeled the bicycle through empty streets. She saw teenage soldiers grouped in shade, laughing, calling her beautiful. She stopped to hear a one-legged man play an accordion because his quick happy tune seemed like so much sarcasm here. She saw a card game that almost became a fight. She watched a small man whistle 'Los Cuatro Generales' as he painted a Republican Flag where before had been a mural of the POUM.

She found and didn't find the dining hall where she and Ramón had eaten; she found the building, definitely, and they still served food, but the diners were mostly soldiers, and the servers all women, and she couldn't see one of Ramón's friends. The women no longer wore trousers, and didn't crack jokes as they had before, and she saw that the comida, breadcrumbs fried with garlic and spicy sausage, which Ramón had paid for with a smile and an anecdote (the one about an English woman who said she didn't like garlic because, it transpired, the one time she had cooked with it she had used three bulbs instead of three cloves), were now rigorously accounted for, and purchased with pesetas, or tokens, and there was, she noticed, now no wine. But what most had changed was the way the men looked at her. She was now unaccompanied, it was true, but the atmosphere too was different. What she felt, which she could not define, was loneliness, for the interrogative stares returned her to herself, where seven months ago it had seemed that strangers looked out at the future together. She experienced this loneliness as embarrassment, and since her embarrassment was greater than her hunger, and since she had neither pesetas nor tokens, when the maître d smiled at her she hurried into the high-sun glare.

And realised, as she hauled up the bicycle, that since the soldiers she thought were fascists had entered Valderrobres, she had not once cried. Then, halfway across the río Cinca, as she leant on the bridge rail watching the slim river trickle between dry banks of earth-grey rocks, she heard a polite «perdóneme camarada,» and turned to see two policemen of the National Republican Guard (the first she had ever seen in Spain), who, with much show of apology, asked to see her documentación. Elsie, at this time a member of no political organisation, had arrived in Spain with nothing but a British passport, and in her rush to escape the imagined fascists, even this she had left in Valderrobres. Gesturing regret, the guards invited her to follow them (the smaller guard wheeling her bicycle) back across the river, though the close streets of Fraga, to an office which was busy like nowhere she had seen in months. There were portraits piled not-yet-hung against the wall – Negrín and Lenin and others she didn't recognise – and light-shaded rectangles where the walls had been protected by posters now removed. Two men tried to manoeuvre a desk through a doorway and a moustachioed man held a candlestick telephone, listening and nodding. Another man dictated to a typist woman in a dress; there were papers everywhere.

When the telephone call finished, the guards saluted to the moustachioed man (something else she had never seen in Spain) and spoke too fast for Elsie to follow. The moustachioed man nodded but ignored her. He crossed papers from one pile to another, opened and slammed a drawer. He leant back, typed a rhythm on the desk. At last he asked, Who are you?

«Me llamo Elsie Stewart.»

«Quién es tú?» he asked again.

«...»

«Quién es tú?»

Elsie said she was a refugee.

The man asked whether she was American.

She said she was Northern Irish.

«Irlandesa?»

«Si.»

He asked why she was here.

«Refugiada,» she said.

He meant why was she in Spain.

«...»

«¿Por qué vino tú a España?»

She said she had a Spanish sweetheart. There was some laughter.

«¿El nombre?»

«Elsie Stewart.»

«¡No! ¿Tu novio?»

«Ramón Buenacasa Mavilla.»

«Ramón... Buenacasa... Mavilla.» He wrote the name and showed her the page to check his spelling. He asked to which union or political organisation Ramón belonged; Elsie didn't at first understand. «¿UGT? ¿PCE? ¿PSUC?»

«Ah,» she said, «CNT; Confederación Nacional del Trabajo.»

«CNT,» said the man. He typed a beat on the desk and watched her. «Mujeres Liebre ¿no? ¿Es usted una puta?»

«...»

«¿Una mujerzuela?»

«...»

The man chuckled, leant back in his chair. He took a packet of Lucky Strikes from his desk drawer and struck a match. «¿Es usted una fascista?»

She said she wasn't a fascist. She said fascists were sons of whores.

He asked whether she was an anarchist.

She said she was a domestic servant.

«¿Qué?»

«Criada.»

«¿Criada?»

She mimed cleaning and curtseying.

The man became angry and said that in Ireland she was a domestic servant but in Republican Spain she was a free woman and she hadn't answered whether she was an anarchist or explained why she was in Spain and he talked about the connections between fascism and anarchism, perhaps for the benefit of the still-waiting guards, for it must have been obvious that Elsie didn't understand any of this.

He asked where she had been living.

Elsie didn't understand; she was thirsty and near crying.

He pointed at a map of Spain but she couldn't find anywhere she recognised and the man grew impatient. He asked the whereabouts of her sweetheart but she didn't understand. «¿Dónde está tu novio, Ramón?» he said, pointing at the map and gesturing towards the town outside.

«Rusia Soviética,» she said, «Rusia Soviética.» The man pulled at his loose neck skin, thinking. He turned to a wooden drawer file on the cabinet to his right, his cigarette resting in the ash tray, whispering a spiral of grey smoke. On the adjacent desks typewriters clacked, faster and faster, trying to keep pace with the world's new speed. «Bien,» he said, laying a grey form on his desk. Elsie watched his precise writing and listened to the scratch of his pen. «Nom... Elsie Stewart, si? Irlandesa?» He copied Ramón's full name from the other page, and wrote on, sometimes pausing, drawing on his cigarette, reading back his sentences, as Elsie stood exhausted and dizzy in the heat.

12

While I was studying for my MA, Lempi was completing the second year of a BA in English Literature and Creative Writing. Lempi was– Lempi is– a poet; Lempi has salon-messy hair and mascara-long lashes; Lempi reads Levinas; Lempi wears flip flops in the summer (she has the only attractive feet I've ever seen); Lempi speaks a dozen languages (a dozen!); Lempi's parents are millionaires: her father, a Swiss-French businessman, worked in the 1980s as the chief executive of a Helsinki-based elevator and escalator manufacturer, and while there he married a cross country skier, two decades his junior, who, according to Lempi, was then a minor celebrity in Finland, as much because of her model looks as because of her athletic achievements. When Lempi was aged eleven, her father retired and moved the family to Dorset, from where he has managed his property portfolio, and watched his daughter mature, one imagines, with great pride and only occasional alarm (Lempi was suspended from boarding school after protesting the invasion of Iraq). When she reads poetry, Lempi mouths the words to herself, melting the sounds as they cross her lips.

I know what you're thinking, examiners: how does someone like me meet someone like Lempi? For some years now, almost long enough to call it a tradition, Creative Writing students have organised readings at a bar in the centre of Cheltenham. At the first reading I attended, there were funny poems and slam poems, prose poems, short stories, longer stories (one novella that near emptied the room), ballads and sonnets, and the sort of poems where the word *cunt* gets its own line; there were student poems and famous poems – it becomes, truth told, a little difficult to tell one piece of art from the next. And so I sat, frowning my most concentrating face, clapping when everyone else clapped. I don't remember what poems Lempi read (I didn't read; I had brought the 'Unbearable shiteness' and the opening page of my new magnum opus – 'Metaphysical reflections on the loneliness of freedom' – but every time I felt the folded papers in my pocket, my pulse quickened and my leg trembled), but I do remember her voice. She was sitting about half-a-dozen seats to my left, so her recital was a rare chance to legitimately stare (Lempi is pick-me-up petite but with such disproportionately large breasts that one can't help wondering whether they're real), as she read in a soft could-be-from-anywhere accent, ending each line with a slight inflection, a sound like she was looking up for approval. The poems she read were not, I think, her own poems; they may have had something to do with sex, but, recalling this scene years later, it's difficult to know if that interpretation was in the text.

Later, standing alone at the bar, I watched Lempi cross the room, smiling left and right, sipping her drink through a straw. She stopped in front of me so that I edged further into the corner, sensing I was in her way. Then, to my surprise, she spoke. 'Hi,' she said.

'Hello,' I said.

She looked into her drink and sipped.

I don't recall everything we talked about – I remember her explaining (apropos of what?) that most people don't get enough varieties of wheat in their diet; I know she asked me at least three times whether I snowboarded, apparently amazed that a person might not – but we stood there for a drink and a half, until she was snagged by a group of friends, and I watched as she paused, toggling herself at the door, waved – to me no more or less than to anyone else – and turned, cheeks pinking in the cold.

13

The room they shut Elsie in wasn't exactly a cell; it might have been an empty storage room, a cleaner's cupboard from the building's hotel days. Its door locked from the outside but stopped three inches above the stone floor, so that she could watch the clutter of feet when she lay down. She slept for some minutes but soon woke wet with sweat and fear; it seemed this thing she was caught in had a logic and momentum beyond anyone's control. The open window was wide enough that she thought she might be able to squeeze through it, but of course she didn't try this. She wanted to shout for water but was too afraid; she wished for a cigarette.

As it turned dark, a man in soldier's uniform brought her water and potatoes. When he opened the door, the sight of the empty office frightened her. But the man smiled and served the food in the style of a waiter from the old days, bowing and calling her señora. Elsie didn't know if he had been told to bring her food or if he was doing it for his own reasons. He stood in the door for a long time, like he wanted to watch her eat, and Elsie worried that he planned to have sex with her. Still, when he returned for the plate, she found the courage to ask if perhaps he had tobacco. The man closed the door and sat next to Elsie on the floor and they smoked together and listened to the shriek and chatter of swallows.

Later still, she heard a street fight: men shouting and brawling, breaking glass, calling each other fascist sons of whores and Stalinist horsefuckers, their voices breaking, too, with emotion you couldn't express in violence. Then she heard gunshots and running feet and angry scattered laughter, and a man, not much older than she was, lurched to the window, blood from a head wound drying across his cheek. He staggered in and out of view, calling her to come closer, cajoling and threatening until an unseen friend pulled him away, and the street fell quiet, and a dog howled with a wolfish noise that brought to mind five-hundred years of nightmares.

14

'Metaphysical reflections' evolved into my MA thesis: a novella-length existentialist story about a lone man known only as Thoof. Thoof finds himself in a non-descript room in an unidentified location, but at no point does he question where he is or why. In chapter one, Thoof peels an orange. In chapter two, he considers masturbating (but in the end does not). In chapter three, he washes his feet. In chapter four, he tries to sleep but discovers he is restless. And then, in the story's stark conclusion, Thoof repeatedly stamps his feet. The meaning of this denouement is left unclear: Thoof's stamping could be an act of frustration, or it could be some rudimentary attempt at dance.

Now, examiners, there is one reason why the above story is relevant to the current project: Thoof has no defined sense of self and other. He is conscious of how two hands interact with an orange, but he does not recognise the hands as part of himself or the orange as part of something else. He has words for hand and penis, but he does not have a single word for himself. The entire narrative is told in Thoof's stream of consciousness, but at no point does Thoof use the word 'I'.

15

When they released Elsie, she didn't have the courage to ask the meaning of the papers she had signed or to request back Ramón's bicycle; she walked north with the papers softening in the clamminess of her fist, and at the edge of town, where a goat was tethered to a broken crucifix, she sat on a boulder in the half-shade of a young ash tree. With great effort – for even English she read slowly – she understood that one paper was a letter to the British consul in Barcelona; what the letter *said*, however, she did not know, and the other paper forever remained a mystery. After a moment she stood up and looked at the scale of the land, shielding her eyes from the sun: it was half-past nine and already the horizon was shaking and the air was thick with insects.

Travelling north from Fraga, the road bent from behind the charred ruins of a tiny church, then ascended a short slope to where Elsie stood. Each time a vehicle passed – a water tanker, two cars that sprayed jet trails of dust – Elsie smiled and tousled her hair or wiped the sweat from her chest. As a CNT-FAI troop truck shuddered round the corner and heaved up the slope, a soldier shouted «¡Pare! ¡Pare!», waving his red and black handkerchief. The truck lumbered on a few metres then braked in a storm of sand. Before it was still, the soldier had jumped into the settling dust: «¡Salud compañera!» His trousers were held up with braces and his hair was combed back.

«Salud,» she said. «Yendo a Barcelona.»

«¿Barcelona? ¡Ya ya!» He clanged the back bumper, encouraging her to get in, but the other soldiers started shouting and the man with the braces gestured his innocence and shouted back – she couldn't hear what anyone was saying. Then an older man jumped down and pointed and said she should get the train from Lérida, at which point the man with braces said no, no, no she should get the train from Barbastro. And then Elise said she didn't have any money for the train, but nobody could hear her because they were all shouting again. Then the soldier with braces made bomb noises, throwing his arms out to indicate an explosion, and the driver climbed out to see what was happening – there was no cabin door – and the older man was laughing, saying no, no, no, and the driver spat into the dust. Then another man climbed out and surveyed Elsie and said, «si, si, si: Barbastro» and everybody was laughing. She saw then that they had dirty faces and that most of them had not shaved.

For a moment, Elsie was unsure whether she should get aboard. The truck was almost a flatbed – it had low wooden sides and a metal cage but no roof to shade the sun – and there were fourteen men inside, some shirtless. They were squeezed knees to chest, sheened with sweat, and scratchy with lice. One man had a yellow-orange eye that slouched to the side as he watched her. Seeing her pause at the back of the truck, the man with the braces made a footstep from his clasped palms, but Elsie ignored him, preferring to sit on the bumper and swing her legs round, using one hand to hold down her dress. The engine started before she had found a way to sit but the soldiers shouted and punched the back of the cabin because one of the men, Elise now noticed, had taken advantage of the stop to scuttle a few metres from the roadside, where he was crapping behind a shrub.

16

In late-summer 2008, as I was finishing 'Metaphysical reflections,' I learned that a doctoral studentship was being advertised by the English Department. The studentship was attached to Professor Thrub (whom I'd never met – a fact I considered to be in my favour), best known for his 1986 *Back to the Future: Metanarrative, Reflexive Epistemology, and the case for Historiographic Metafiction* (which I'd never read), and his 1989 engagement to a second-year student, whom he managed to date, marry and divorce, all before she'd completed her PhD. By 1998 he was re-united with his first wife, a turn of events that over the years appears to have embittered him. All this took place while he was a reader at University College London. Although his reputation had waned from its high-point in the late 1980s, Thrub continued to publish prolifically throughout the nineties. As the century turned, however, his output declined, and in 2002 he published a disastrous article on land reclamation as a theme in three 1980s novels. Today, it is hard to find anybody who has actually read this article, but for a while the controversy polarised the humanities. Thrub and a handful of defenders clung to one pole, while the rest of the world accused them of charlatanism and sexism.

I first encountered Thrub in September 2007. At the end of the English corridor, up the ramp, past the bare notice board (the notice board has been bare since management decreed that every notice must carry an official stamp), one arrives at a gothic doorway that leads into a dark corridor. The corridor gives access only to Thrub's office and so nobody has ever reported the broken light bulbs. A branched yucca plant, placed here by some previous occupier, has long ago died, and its bare branches reach up from the earth like the rising claw of some undead thing.

Thrub's office door was open and he was blasting Fauré's Requiem at antisocial volume. He had taken off his shoes and was resting his feet on his desk. He may or may not have been asleep.

'Professor?' I said, knocking the door. 'Professor Thrub, Sir?'

At this point, Thrub looked over his shoulder at me. He lowered his feet and creaked to a standing position, rubbing his eyes. He seemed utterly amazed to see me. 'Yes?' he said, turning off the music.

'I'm very sorry to have disturbed you, Professor.'

'What do you want?' Thrub was looking at me as if my presence was not wholly credible. 'Who are you?'

'I'm a postgraduate student. I'm interested in applying for your studentship.'

'My studentship?'

'Yes.'

'They're advertising that?'

'Yes.'

'What happened to the other chap?'

'I don't know, Professor.'

'Duncan? David? Donald? Something like that.' Thrub crossed to the window and peered outside, shrugging and shaking his head in a manner that suggested this question would weigh on him no longer.

I waited a long time for Thrub to speak again but he seemed to have forgotten I was there. Eventually I broke the silence. 'I thought, maybe, we could discuss my application. I mean, I wouldn't want any favours as an internal candidate – obviously – but I thought maybe you could have a look at my work and we could talk about the sort of project you're interested in supervising.'

'...'

'I've brought a draft of my MA thesis. It's the sort of stuff that I'd potentially be interested in developing in a PhD. It's about a lone man known only as Thoof. He's in this, kind of, non-descript room in an unidentified location, but at no point does he question where he is or–'

Thrub silenced me by banging his head against the glass. After a second head-butt, he turned with an elongated sigh and snatched my thesis. He opened it at a random page and read in a sonorous voice: '"So outside sadcoloured. Three of the clock. Hand. Hand. Hand to pleasure pole. Maybe. Pleasure pole ready, hard, could do, but– Noise. Hark! Shut thon obstropolos."' He closed the cover and dropped my work on a pile behind his desk. 'Thank you,' he said. 'It seems like quite a page turner.' Then, with surprising swiftness, Thrub reached past me and opened the door. 'Good luck with the application,' he said.

When he tried to close the door, I blocked it with my foot. 'It has... existentialist themes,' I said.

'Splendid,' said Thrub, gently pressing the door closed.

'Shouldn't we– Can't we, you know, discuss it?'

'Discuss what?' asked Thrub. He and I were now locked in an ungainly struggle over the door. Thrub was shouldering it closed, forcing me into the corridor inch by inch.

'You know,' I called round the half-shut door. 'The studentship. My writing. Your take on existentialism.'

The pressure on the door relented. 'Existentialism?' Thrub searched his bookshelves. When he found the volume he wanted, he grabbed it, made a weird whooping noise, and hurled the book at my head. 'There you go,' he said, picking up another book. This one he threw towards my groin. 'There you go.' The third book hit me on the shoulder. The fourth caught my backside. When Thrub was finished, he closed and locked his office door. 'Best of luck,' he called through the wood. 'Let me know if you need anything else.'

Examiners, I picked up the spine-dented books and strugled to read their titles in the half-light: *The Will to Power; Beyond Good and Evil; The Gay Science; On the Genealogy of Morals.* I decided this was Thrub's way of issuing a reading list. Holding the books with my elbows, I cupped my hands and shouted through the door: 'Thank you very much for your time, Professor. I'm sorry to have disturbed you.'

The music resumed.

17

Elsie and the soldiers drove north into the mad afternoon, through beet-fields and olive trees, across the bridge at Balloba, where a peasant clenched his fist in an anti-fascist salute, and a rabbit dangled dead from his hand. Near Barbastro, she heard the cannons firing outside Huesca, and she looked west where wheat fields buttered out to the horizon and cherry trees melted in the sun. She was hungry now and it was impossible to sit with modesty or comfort; still, the soldiers gave her cigarettes and water from goatskin flasks, and they held her and cursed the driver as the heat-warped truck bed threw them like something being sautéed.

When they dropped her on the outskirts of Barbastro, Francisco, the man with the braces, kissed the back of her hand, and held it, and with the other hand pointed to her wrist watch. Elsie showed him the time but she had not understood: Francisco released her hand and patted his empty shirt pocket and showed his bare wrists with exaggerated sadness. The older man nodded and turned out his watch pocket and tried to explain the shortage of such things at the front. Then, since Elsie was still confused, several soldiers enacted the disastrous consequences of an unsynchronised military operation: two whistled 'A Las Barricadas' while another two advanced with imaginary rifles; the two with rifles fell, clutching their chests in dramatic death poses; then the two whistlers nodded at each other and advanced towards the same contorted fate. When the play ended, Elsie, of course, was even more confused; she knew that anarchists executed their enemies and she wondered if perhaps this was some weird threat? The man with the beer-coloured eye reached for her arm and said «Que puc? Que puc?» He unclipped the watch clasp (which Ramón had made from the wire-net decoration on a wine bottle, when he and Elsie had been together in Toulouse), and he asked again «Que puc?» Elsie, who understood little Catalan, looked to Francisco; he took the watch from the other man, held it against his heart, and promised that he would look after it with his life and return it to her when they met in peace and victory. He said that whenever he was afraid, whenever he was cold and hungry and unable to sleep, he would feel this watch and think of her, and he would be as free as the eagles on the highest mountain peaks. But he spoke too fast and Elsie understood nothing.

18

I knew several things about Friedrich Nietzsche (1844-1900). He was a German-speaking philosopher with a hard to spell name. He *wasn't* anti-Semitic. In 1889 he suffered a mental breakdown and was 'of unsound mind' for the last eleven years of his life. This breakdown may or may not have been caused by syphilis. It may or may not have been preceded by Nietzsche's – most un-Nietzschean – emotional intervention on behalf of a horse. Most images of Nietzsche show him with a distinctive walrus moustache, but this was a style favoured by his sister and only forced upon Nietzsche post-breakdown. His sister was a baddie.

These facts, whether true or false, had enabled me to blag my way through the three or four Nietzsche-based conversations I'd encountered in my life up to this point. I had never actually read any of his books. Before my interview, however, I read the books suggested by Thrub – i.e., the books he had thrown at me. I sometimes think this thesis had two starting points: the first was when I saw Elsie's photograph; the second was when I opened the *Genealogy of Morals*.

You see, for Nietzsche, the idea of agency designated by the 'I' of Indo-European languages is merely a means of postulating a false freedom; when one part of our being dominates over another, identifying the 'I' with the side that dominates allows us to interpret this process as 'our' 'choosing' (1968 [1883-

1888], § 87). Nietzsche wrote that 'There is no 'being' behind doing, effecting, becoming; 'the doer' is merely a fiction added to the deed – the deed is everything' (2000b [1887], I, §13). So, a standard grammatical structure such as 'I think,' becomes, for Nietzsche, problematic:

> a thought comes when "it" wishes, and not when "I" wish, so that it is a falsification of the facts of the case to say that the subject "I" is the condition of the predicate "think." It thinks; but that this "it" is precisely the famous old "ego" is, to put it mildly, only a supposition (…) one has even gone too far with this "it thinks" – even the "it" contains an interpretation of the process, and does not belong to the process itself. One infers here according to the grammatical habit: "Thinking is an activity; every activity requires an agent; consequently–" (2000a [1886], I, §17)

19

In Barbastro, militiamen in broken boots swaggered through crowds of starch-shirted Popular Army soldiers, who parted before them, watching with narrow eyes. Mosquitoes buzzed everywhere and the whole town stank of faeces. A man with a half-paralysed face and cartridge sling leant against a time-bleached bull-fighting poster. Elsie now noticed that her forearms were pink and warm, and the back of her neck had been toasted by the sun.

She found the station in chaos. Its one platform was full of wounded soldiers and peasants slumped by baskets of maize. Men stood across the line, smoking beneath wide-brimmed hats, sharing a bottle of wine as a boy chased a hen up the track; the whole scene was honey-coloured in the evening sun.

The seriously wounded were grouped under the wrought iron shelter of the short station platform, or had remained in the concourse of the station building, crawling with flies. There was one man whose face had been shattered, by a bomb she supposed, and was encaged in a net of muslin, upon which flies crawled in such a way that she was reminded of a beekeeper. A kid-soldier rang the station bell and laughed as people looked left and right, for there was no train.

She crossed the tracks, walked into the sun. On the far side of a little stone bridge, she found a small market square and listened as a stall keeper told a militiaman that he had tobacco but no matches, beef tongues but no peppers, olive oil and garlic but no bread: «se terminó el pan. Mañana. Mañana.» She saw some caparrones had fallen to lie in the grooves between pavers, but she couldn't pick them up in front of all these people, and so she walked on, dizzy from the heat. When alone on a side street, she gathered three cigarette butts, and then realised she had no way to light them.

How did she meet Andriy? It was like this. After collecting the cigarette butts, Elsie sat at the roadside to read Ramon's letter. The writing seemed to dissolve and swirl and she couldn't read the words even though she knew by heart everything they said. She folded the letter back into her brassiere, and then she kicked her shoes off to inspect her feet: dirt and calluses, pink open blisters, purple-black dried blood.

When she opened her eyes, a young woman stood in front of her. Elsie didn't understand where she had come from and as she tried to stand up, the cliff turned like a carousel and she felt dizzy and the world went in and out of black. She heard the young woman scream and felt hands under her armpits and there were black shapes turning and turning and the ground was hard under her knees. The woman was saying «¡un momento! ¡un momento!» and walking backwards, and when she turned and ran Elsie vomited a dribble of yellow water into the long track-side grass.

When the young woman returned (how many minutes later Elsie couldn't say), she was flanked by two older women, who ran to Elsie at walking pace, taking short steps as they held the skirts of their black dresses. Behind them, wearing a soldier's forage cap, there followed a boy of about fourteen, who was kicking a stone and leading a mule. Neither boy nor mule at first showed much enthusiasm, but on seeing Elsie the boy quickened his pace and shouted at the slouchy mule in the style of a cavalry officer preparing a charge. The young woman tipped a flask of water to Elsie's lips, spilling the first drops down her front, and one of the older women jostled a bowl forward, demonstrating deep breaths as Elsie inhaled the scent of rosemary, lavender, and olive oil. Then the other old woman dipped her hand in the bowl and wiped the cool paste on Elsie's neck, forehead, and collar bones, as the mule lurched for the vomit-wetted road side grass.

When lifted onto the mule, Elsie sat side-saddle, but nearly fell as soon as the beast moved; so she straddled the mule, but in doing so pushed her dress towards her waist. One of the older women, seeing her struggling to return to a more modest way of sitting, touched her exposed thighs, whispering «no importa, no importa», and the young woman threw a stick at the boy when he looked back at Elsie too often.

The sun stroke passed in minutes but exhaustion and malnourishment had weakened her, and for two days the words she heard most were «no es molestia, no es molestia». On the first night the women cooked potatoes and borage by the light of olive oil burners, and they ate alfresco, beneath a timber-supported sheet of corrugated iron, with fowls pecking their feet and swifts circling higher and higher in the darkening purple sky. Afterwards, dizzy from wine now, Elsie asked «¿Tienes fuego?» holding forward one of the dog ends she had earlier found behind the market, and the boy, who had been recounting his heroic adventures with the Durruti Column, snatched the butt from her hand and threw it down with an exaggerated '*pah!*' Then he fetched a rust-edged cigarette case and ordered she take five pre-rolls, which, of course, she refused, and they haggled for some time before she eventually accepted two. The boy's generosity, she later realised, was not devoid of self-interest: the following day, when she was under instruction to rest – she had been struck with diarrhoea and had spent the morning conspicuously running out to the toilet – the boy came inside for his siesta, lying so close to her that she could feel him panting on the back of her neck. She lay with her eyes closed, affecting the deep breath of sleep, listening to the accelerating rhythm of his masturbation.

Still, it was the boy who introduced her to Andriy. Andriy had been fighting in the 153rd Brigade, formerly the Tierra y Libertad column, but he claimed to be on leave – he spoke even less Spanish than Elsie did, but repeatedly pointed to himself and said «de permís, de permís» until Elsie became convinced he was a deserter – and said he was going to France to visit a baby orphan, whom he had long ago rescued and named after his father. This story, which Elsie always doubted, grew weaker each time Andriy dragged her away from the road at the sight of a military vehicle, and conclusively fell apart when he managed to communicate that he hadn't seen said orphan baby for eighteen years, and then it had been in Eastern Ukraine.

Andriy Tykhenko's teeth were awful black things, charred like the church ruins of Aragón, and, in addition to his cleft lip, he had a frightening facial scar – a curved white crevasse that cut through his left eyebrow and ran to his jaw. To Elsie, he looked so old that he would be a burden on the journey; his hair was grey and scattered, and his creased face, brown with sun and dirt, resembled a chaotically ploughed field. He had on a ragged blue cotton shirt and a Sam Browne belt, in which he carried a hunting knife. And he was mad – he talked to himself and laughed at strange moments. For example, at some point he had managed to explain, with aid of gestures, that his first wife, or maybe his first lover, had been unusually short. 'A midget?' Elsie had asked. Andriy found this English word very funny, and often repeated it as though it was a shared joke. For instance, when they left the road at Aínsa, as they hiked into miles and miles of chalk and boxwood, Andriy lifted his arms to block the limestone cliff glare, and apropos of nothing he shouted 'Mijat!' and laughed with such intensity that Elsie worried he was choking. He was not the escort she would have chosen, but where in any of this did she have a choice?

20

But then, what is choice? In everyday understanding, historical change is possible because however restrictive their circumstances, however manipulative their influences, people can, at least potentially, 'choose' to do things differently. But choice in the fullest sense of the word assumes a transcendental 'chooser': a force that can stand beyond social and material laws of causation. If, on the other hand, choice refers only to determinate effects beyond a person's control, then standard descriptions of 'doing', expressed in our pronoun system, are grammatical rather than ontological truths.

It was not my intention to arrive so early at the crux of my thesis, but you will have noticed, examiners, that we have strayed into the territory of my research, into the question of free will and determinism, into my hypothesis, such as it is, that if we cannot locate a transcendental subject, then the 'common sense' worldview, reflected and reinforced by the novel as an art form, in which individuals are regarded as the initiators of action and the agents of historical change, though consistent with our practical experience, represents a particular interpretation of the world that has no *a priori* superiority, but assumes its self-evident nature within a historically-complex discursive moment.

Now, let us not create false suspense: the further I got with my project, examiners, the more I failed to account for human agency, the more I sought a new writing that effaced the subject as originator of action, the more I found myself obsessing over the human drives of emotion, desire, corporeal experience, until the confusing paradox of my endeavour began to depress me. My conclusion − I shall state it now lest it disappoint you at a later moment − is that a writer can neither give nor revoke a character's freedom, but must write always about the tension between agency and structure, recognising this antagonism itself as a primary truth of human being.

21

Ramón, Elsie's lover, had volunteered as a translator at an aviation school in the Soviet Union, and when she met Andriy, she had tried to explain this, but had got no further than aeroplane and Soviet Union, so that Andriy imagined Ramón to be a Republican fighter pilot, who at any moment might pass overhead. «¡Está Ramón!» he said again. «¡Viva los valientes! Allez-y doucement Ramón! Ton amour t'embrasse dans la nuit.» He crouched beside her, his laughter sloping away, and then he turned and saw she was crying. «Elsie,» he said, «un moment».

When Elsie opened her eyes he had gone, slipped into the gorge. She could hear irregular cascades of scree and when she crawled to the precipice, he waved at her, already metres below. He was edging down, his feet horizontal, like a cautious skier. Then he grabbed one of the mountain pines and swung out of view. *Waaaaoohwaaoooh!* 'Andriy? Andriy!'

He returned after five minutes – clothes white from the limestone, dust in his hair – and he beckoned with both arms: «¡Vamos! ¡Ven!» Elsie looked into the gorge and felt again the feeling of being too long on a carousel. «Yce dobre,» he said, «is okay.» When Elsie still didn't move, he shouted «¡date prisa! blyadt!»; the speed of his temper was amazing; before he shouted, she always saw the rage in his eyes, the way that lightning precedes thunder. So she slid onto the loose scree, stretching her hands out for balance, looking at him now and again as he nodded and beckoned and told her «tomárselo con calma; tomárselo con calma.» She paused to wipe the sweat from her hairline, looked down and saw the thread of the river, slipped, lost her footing and fell onto her hip, grabbing at the grass and the flowers as the panic flowed through her ears in spate.

Andriy stopped her, two metres short of the cliff face, and for a long time the only noise, growing quieter and quieter, was the rattle of dislodged rocks far below. He was on one knee: his thigh pressed against her buttocks, his hands on her waist. «¡Despacio!» he said, and then he laughed and kissed her head. Elsie tried to stand up but she was crying again and trembling from the terror of having lost control. When she saw the drop, her legs slackened. Andriy, paying no attention, grabbed the trunk of the mountain pine and swung to the far side of a moss-lined chimney. «¡Vamos!» he said, offering his hand. He told her, in Russian, not to look down; then he pointed where she should put her feet and said in English, 'One, doo, tree. Si? One, doo, tree.'

Nineteen years later, in Budapest, she recalled still how she had stepped across the chimney, one hand on the pine trunk, one hand stretching for Andriy, and how her foot had not quite reached, so that for a minute she was stretched, pegged out between Andriy's tug and her grasp on the tree. It was the sort of memory one adds to and reinvents long after the context has been forgotten. She remembered the shadow of the chimney, the thread of the river, the griffon vultures overhead. Then she let go of the tree and forever would recall feeling something beyond fear: a weightless nothingness, perhaps. Imagining this moment, she often saw herself as the damsel in a silent picture. As the years passed, it became impossible to visualise Andriy, and film stars, or even Ramón, would take his place on the far side of the gap. Sometimes she imagined herself swinging like a trapeze artist, at other times she seemed more like the pendulum of a clock. It was strange how the moment endured. On the far side of the chimney, a ledge cut diagonally downwards across the cliff; it was an ingenious route, but by the end of the War, Elsie remembered being by the water, and swinging across the chimney, but nothing in between.

22

Thrub never told me his opinion of 'Metaphysical reflections on the loneliness of freedom' and nor did he ever return the manuscript. I took his silence as ambivalence – lukewarm appreciation at best – and so, in the days before the studentship application deadline, I deleted all references to Thoof and searched for a new subject. The theory side was covered –

needless to say, my application referenced Nietzsche (specifically those books Thrub had thrown at me) in every second sentence – but I still planned this to be a Creative Writing thesis, and I now had no plan for the creative element whatsoever.

The day before the application date, I searched my bookshelves for inspiration. I made a pile of the sort of books that I thought might potentially trigger the sort of idea that might potentially appeal to the panel (*Ulverton* by Adam Thorpe, *The Mezzanine* by Nicholson Baker, *Austerlitz* by W.G. Sebald, *Everything is Illuminated* by Jonathon Safran Foer, *A Heartbreaking Work of Staggering Genius* by Dave Eggers, *Lanark* by Alasdair Gray, *Pale Fire* by Nabokov, *Philadelphia Fire* by John Edgar Wideman, *G* by John Berger, *Q* by Luther Blisset, *Goldberg Variations* by Gabriel Josipovici, *The Gold Bug Variations* by Richard Powers, and – of course – the complete works of David Foster Wallace, who, tragically, would die a fortnight later). In the other pile I stacked all the books that seemed unlikely to help with my predicament. Without thinking, I placed François Barrot's *La Revolution Libertaire D'Espagne* in the second pile. However, as I was shoving this pile out of the way, Barrot's book fell open at the picture of Elsie. Examiners, it was my eureka moment.

Today, the serendipity seems scarcely credible. I could not have known that I was stumbling into the fin-de-noughties zeitgeist, but within a year David Vann would publish *Legend of a Suicide,* David Shields would publish *Reality Hunger: A Manifesto,* Miguel Syjuco would publish *Illustrado,* Laurent Binet would publish *HHhH* – reality was where it was at, and I had a real subject. My application boasted that I would write a Nietzsche-inspired creative biography of an unknown woman from Belfast. I submitted it to the research office by hand. To my delight, I was invited for an interview.

23

When they reached the river they drank like horses, dunking their heads in the pool. They were in a basin, where time had scooped the rock into the shape of a cupped hand. The thumb of the basin, a submerged peninsula of rock, emerged near the middle forming a small stone island. Elsie could tell, from the sides of the pool, smoothed out and today stuffed with dry heat, that in the winter, the waterfall, which even now was a white shell burst of noise and spray, must have been a frightening thing. But the pool was still and clear, the water settled, sluicing over the far side and scattering across the rocks. She took her shoes off and sunk her feet in the water. Her legs, she now saw, were scratched white and pink from the fall, and her flayed palms stung with grit. Then she dozed, lying back on the warm rock, feet still in the water.

She woke to a great splash and white thrashing. Andriy was naked. He was laughing and laughing, shouting in Russian, calling her to join him. His clothes were piled where she had been sleeping and he was treading water, his pale torso visible, his silver chest hair like coils of barbed wire. Then he turned and paddled to the rock island, revealing, as he crawled onto it, first the serrated ridge of his spine, then his buttocks, and, dangling between his legs, swinging around like an old snuff pouch, his hairless-looking scrotum. As he pirouetted on the rock, Elsie laughed and turned away. '*Hoowawaaaa!*' He splashed into the water, thrashing his arms and laughing.

24

The interview was my second encounter with Professor Thrub, and this time the impression he made was of a man as learned as he was bored. His collar was open and he gazed towards the window, fidgeting with a loose button on the sleeve of his corduroy jacket. To his right sat Nick Andrews (our youthful Head of English, appearing typically suave in a metallic-grey suit and a steel-blue cashmere scarf) and Dr Johanson-Van der Heyder (the University's fiercely nice Post-Graduate Research Officer, who always sounds like she's just caught you masturbating but is determined to understand).

With breathless zeal, I explained the many ways my writing a fictionalised biography of Elsie Stewart would enhance the world intellectually. The interview – in truth, up to this point, an incoherent monologue – seemed to be going rather well, until Johanson-Van der Heyder interrupted me with a raised hand. 'Vat exactly do you mean by a "transcendental subject?"'

Half an hour earlier, transcendental subjectivity had seemed a straightforward concept; now, I looked lapwards, my hand scrunching the folded funeral programme that had burrowed in my trouser pocket since the suit's last outing. I began to think, through what connection I cannot fathom, of a fragment preserved in Kafka's diaries, in which an unnamed job applicant is subjected to a physical examination. You're tall enough, says the company director, but what can you do? Our attendants must be able to do more than lick stamps. Speak up a little! Your whispering makes me nervous! We had lapsed into silence, I realised. I had lapsed into silence. Johanson-Van der Heyder was regarding me with embarrassed urgency, eyes lunging from behind her glasses. If I refused to speak, if I just sat, for how long, I wondered, would the silence last? Gamely, I began to ramble: Buddha said that Actions exist and also their consequences, but the person that acts does not; in *Nicomachean Ethics*, Aristotle defined a voluntary act as one originating inside an agent, and an involuntary act as one where the moving principle is outside; in the work of Thomas Aquinas and other Christian theologians, the soul is necessary to account for free will; the self doesn't emerge as a term in English philosophy until Locke's *Essay Concerning Human Understanding*; the concept of the self is soon met with criticism – for example, in Hume's *Treatise of Human Nature* –'

With force enough to stop me talking, Thrub placed his palms flat on the table. It was the first time he had spoken since I'd entered the room, and I have never forgotten what he said. 'I am something of a bibliophile. Did you know that there were recovered at Nineveh, the site of the library of the kings of Assyria, some 22,000 clay tablets, dating from the seventh century BC? An amazing effort expended on writing, for each of these tablets had to be inscribed with a calamus, fired, carried, and stored, but still this great civilisation produced in four hundred years less writing than we may find, for example, on these busy bookshelves of our erudite colleague Dr Johanson-Van der Heyder. For all the splendour of the Ancient Library of Alexandria, it contained perhaps a few tens of thousands of individual works, and most of these, alas, have been lost to posterity.'

'Professor–'

'In the late middle ages, the papal library at Avignon, and the library of the Sorbonne, each contained maybe two thousand volumes.'

'Professor–'

'But in the age of the printing press, we see an explosion of publishing. Today, some one-and-a-half million new titles are published every year; indeed, even Dr Andrews has contributed a monograph.'

'Two.'

'Professor Thrub, may we–'

'The Library of Congress stores its collection on 745 miles of bookshelf. A Google search for the word *book* returns 923,000,000 results in around one tenth of a second.'

'Is there a point to this?' asked Nick Andrews.

'My concern is that if our young candidate is to continue his fascinating history of writing, and if he is to amend his pace through the centuries to reflect the volume of writing produced in the last three hundred years, then I may have to alter my plans; I had rather intended to take lunch at some point, and, perhaps, given today's fine weather, to enjoy a stroll through this town's bountiful green spaces. May I request, therefore, that our candidate now makes some effort to answer the question, if, at this late hour, any of us can remember what it was?'

Examiners, I left the interview convinced of my failure and was dumfounded when Johanson-Van der Heyder telephoned to notify me of my success.

25

Ramón had friends in Barcelona who were naturists. It was hilarious: they drove into the countryside and stripped bare. When he broached the topic with Elsie, he suggested – after explaining that it would be rude for him not to join them – that she might be more comfortable waiting in the house of Luis and Mercedes. For some reason, his tone made her angry, or jealous, and she insisted on participating. Five men and three women squeezed into a borrowed Tipo (which repeatedly needed push starting), drove north through Terrassa, walked three miles from the road, paused, conferred, nodded, and stripped in silence. And no chance was Elsie going to be the last one wearing clothes: as soon as she was certain that this was, definitely, what they were doing, she stripped with as much determination as anyone else.

Oh, they were crazy people. Luis and Mercedes refused to eat any animal – no chicken or pig or even fish – and Ramón said that Lora went with women rather than men; he said she had been with Mercedes, which he joked was because Luis had a small penis. It was winter, then, and they were cold as soon as they undressed, so they played tig, hopping on the sharpness of the ground. Luis *did* have a small penis, compared to Ramón at least, but all the willies looked silly, flapping about as the men ran. This thought made her think about her own body: the flatness of her chest was not yet unfashionable, but she was shamed by the pubic hair that grew on the inside of her thighs, between her buttocks, and, via a thin line, even to her belly button. Her hairiness had embarrassed her as a schoolgirl, and now she saw that even among Mediterranean women she had a lot of hair. She watched the game from a distance until Manuel approached her, moving from side to side, arms outstretched in case she tried to dodge. He stopped when she didn't try to run and his arms dropped. Eventually he turned to follow her gaze and they both watched Ramón seize Mercedes, hoisting her as she screamed.

She had thought, then, how incredible for her to be involved with a scene so mad. In England she had not let Ramón touch her between the legs. In Calais she accepted his fingers. In Paris she took his penis and tongue. In Lyon she let him ejaculate in her mouth. It was crazy. They travelled south and she wanted more and more of him. She would lift her legs up, wanting him deeper and deeper. In Toulouse *he* said no – he said she might get pregnant. In Perpignan she let him sodomise her. It was crazy. She stopped caring. Afterwards she would be left trembling from the terror of losing control – she felt ashamed; she needed to wash – but at the time she wanted more and more of him, wanted to give herself unconditionally. In Barcelona he took her to the compañero doctor and she let them put a silver gadget inside her so that she wouldn't get pregnant. In Valderrobres she asked what else he wanted her to do. Anything, she said. There must be something, she said.

26

I officially began my studies in January 2009. For reasons unclear to me, my office is in the Theology Department. When I first knocked the door I was invited to enter by a bearded white man who was dressed in slacks and a bulk purchase sky-blue packet shirt. With his hand still on his mouse, he had turned forty-five degrees and was waiting for me to state my business. Straight ahead, a smaller, bespectacled man in a waistcoat had spun 180 and bounced out of his chair. The walls were bare except for a tea-coloured chart of the Hebrew alphabet. A seven-foot bookcase dissected the room, hiding the fourth quadrant from view.

'I think I've got a desk here,' I said. 'I've just started my PhD.'

'Well, I reckon that one there oughta be free.' The white guy's accent was American (Tampa Bay, he soon told me).

'Yes. Thank you,' I said to them both. We were all smiling very hard. The other desks were piled with small family photographs in cushioned frames, photocopied articles in British Library cellophane, and theological texts arranged in Manhattan piles (*The New Brown-Driver-Briggs-Gesenius Hebrew-English Lexicon: Coded with Strong's Concordance Numbers; Postexilic Prophets; Civilizations of the Ancient East,* Vols I-IV; *Biblical Protology; Die Religion in Geschichte und Gregenwart* (Vols I-VII); etc.).

'I shall make some tea.'

'Man, Obi, I am sick of your Goddamn tea. Goddamn tea and mouldy damn biscuits.'

Obi laughed and clicked the kettle. 'Tea?' he asked, peering into the hidden quadrant.

There was no answer. The cups, I noticed, were upturned on a coffee-ring-dirty yellow tray, and there was nothing in the room to suggest any attempt at hygiene. I sat, waiting for the computer to warm up, sensing Obi watching me. 'Pictures of family are good,' he said.

'Sorry?'

'Family, it is a blessing.'

'Damn it, Obi – the guy's been here two minutes. Leave off that shit.'

'Are you blessed with a wife?'

'A wife? No.'

'Unfortunate. A picture of one's wife is good for a man at work.'

'Right,' I said, entering my password.

'You got yourself a girl down here?'

'No,' I said.

'Mm-mm,' said Obi, nodding as he dunked one tea bag in and out of four cups.

'You ain't gonna meet nobody round here. Man, I don't reckon there's been an unmarried woman up here since the Reagan years. You know any single girls, Samuel?' He shouted this through the bookshelves but there was no reply from the Hidden Man.

'Your tea, Jeremy,' said Obi, lowering the cup.

'Goddamn it, man; what did I say about this damned tea?'

Obi laughed and placed a cup on my desk. Then, in what I thought was an over-familiar gesture, he grasped my shoulder and said 'The union of a man and woman in holy matrimony is a very special thing.'

'What kinda girls d'you like? You do like girls, don't you? I don't wanna come in here one day and find you giving Obi a shoulder rub. You like American girls? Samuel, you like American girls, don't you? You ever watch that TV show, *Heroes*? That's a fun show. You know the cheerleader from that show, Hayden Panetierre? Man, I found the best pics of her. You remember those pictures of the cheerleader, Samuel? You wanna get yourself a good American girl.'

'We shall find you a wife,' said Obi.

It's still unclear why the office adopted this as a mission.

27

Now, remembering how it felt to be with Ramón, Elsie realised something that perhaps she had known from when she left the village: she was going to Russia – she was going to the Soviet Union to find Ramón – and Andriy, she decided, would take her there. She lifted her dress over her head and for a second the world was only light and sound. Andriy was floating with a gentle backstroke, eyes closed, ears below the water. She watched him for a moment and then she removed Ramón's letter from her brassiere and folded it under a quartz ovoid. While marking the spot with a small cairn, she was startled by a tiny movement – a fire salamander – and straightened, looking around her, surprised to feel wildly exposed now the world was so still. The far valley wall was shaded grey but looking this way the hot white hurt Elsie's eyes and she squinted up at the sky, imagining the silhouettes of Red Indians at the top of the canyon.

Wearing her underwear, still watching the horizon, and feeling, with every tentative step, at the centre of some unknown gaze, Elsie edged into the water, stumbling into the sudden depth and gasping as the mountain cool climbed her thighs. She was surprised by the force of the undertow. The water grabbed at her calves and took her legs from under her when the depth reached her waist. She shrieked and gasped and laughed and splashed and panicked. It seemed she might be sucked under the waterfall. Then the force changed and she let herself float in the other direction. But now she saw the rocks at the bottom of the pool and doggy-paddled against the current – Elsie was not a strong swimmer. Then her feet were grounded on the pebble pool floor and she was in the calm lagoon, next to Andriy, who was watching her, now, his laughter fusing with the sound of the waterfall.

Her teeth were rattling and she was out of breath as she climbed onto the rock in the centre of the pool. Andriy returned to his backstroke, humming a tune she did not recognise, seeming to make a point of ignoring her, as though consciously allowing her privacy. But as Elsie let the sun dry her, she felt again that feeling of being watched. So here I am, she thought, just sat here in the sun, not caring, and there, on the horizon, the Red Indians, wee black figurines– And she realised that the water had turned her underwear transparent. All that hair. She couldn't explain why she felt so sick at herself.

She waded through the calm lagoon, walked round the side of the pool, and crossed at the bottom, where the water overflowed and the rocks worked as stepping stones. Then she sat near her clothes, pulled her knees to her chin, and watched as inch by inch her wet footprints were reclaimed by the sun.

28

After starting my PhD, I didn't see or hear from Lempi until a chance meeting at the entrance to the library. There, in the second week of April, I saw her with Professor Thrub.

'Oh,' said Lempi. 'Hi.'

'Christ,' said Thrub.

I looked up-down-left-right, like a panicked Catholic crossing himself. I saw, in a ricochet of images, four strip lights, a cardboard-coloured corrugated carpet, a woman shaking an umbrella in a doorway, and a psychology student distributing a questionnaire ('Would you describe yourself as happy: almost always/ very often/ frequently/ sometimes/ rarely/ never. Which of the following best describes your attitude to vegetarian food...'). Examiners, you must remember that I hadn't seen Lempi in almost a year. Now, having run into her unexpectedly, I started thinking very fast in many directions at once. Imagine, if you'll forgive the conceit, a multi-lingual gathering of psychoanalysts, on a team-bonding away day, attempting to build a raft:

Subjectivity I smell honey library what are you up to coconut Cardboard Coloured Corrugated Carpet how are you breasts okay island been a while hurry up historical fiction Elsie nice Christmas now what. 'What?'

'Do you know Miss Bridgette?' said Thrub.

'Yes,' I said, nodding at her as though my recollection was uncertain. 'We've met.'

'She's helping us with... what are you here for?'

'The Summer School Open Day,' said Lempi, throwing her head back in lovely laughter.

'Christ,' said Thrub. 'What the fuck is that to do with me?' At this point he spotted Nick Andrews, our ambitious head of English, striding towards us followed by a line of suitably pliable undergraduates. 'What's this about a summer school?' said Thrub. 'Is this your bullshit, Andrews?'

'You've seen the directive, Professor.'

'A fucking *summer school?*'

'It's a transitional step towards a three semester academic year.'

'You *can't have* three semesters in a year.'

'In such a competitive sector, we can't afford not to.'

'Semester, from *semestris*, meaning–'

'This isn't about semantics, Professor; it's about maximising estate efficiency and innovating flexible responses to an uncertain future.'

As Thrub and Andrews continued this argument, Lempi raised her eyebrows and smiled at me in conspiratorial faux-awkwardness.

I smiled. Looked at her chest. Flinched. (I apologise to her and to you for this tedious behaviour.)

'So... well done on getting the scholarship,' she said, cuffing me on the arm.

I laughed but continued to stare at the carpet. Silence. Say something. 'Did you have a nice Christmas?'

'A nice *Christmas*?' she said.

'I haven't seen you in ages.'

'It was okay, I guess.'

'Cool,' I said.

Examiners, at this point, during a short silence, I purposely winched my gaze upwards. I am not a misogynist, and it is not my intention to fetishise Lempi's breasts, but the truth is that when one looks Lempi in the eye, she blinks, pointing those mascara-long lashes down the line of her nose and chin. 'We must go for a drink sometime,' she said. She was wearing a grey top (I'd call it a cardigan but that wouldn't capture the spirit of the garment) buttoned into a focalising V, and a bar pendant that pointed down the line of her cleavage. 'I've wanted to contact you for ages,' she said. 'But I lost my phone when I was surfing in Cornwall.' It was like trying to ignore the central vanishing point in a Renaissance painting with a checkerboard floor. It was like trying not to notice Niccolò Mauruzi's red hat in Uccello's *Battle of San Romano*. I looked at the library door, read a poster over her shoulder ('Your Communications Champions: promoting effective two-way communication across the University'), and eventually settled my gaze, staring hard at Professor Thrub's bum.

'Are you okay?' asked Lempi.

'Yes yes,' I said, still staring at Thrub's bum.

At this point, Thrub turned, looked at me, down at his arse, and then back at me. 'Jesus fucking Christ,' he said. As all departed, I stayed in the corridor, feeling a little dizzy, planning to return the book in the morning.

29

For how long had they walked when Elsie realised she'd forgotten Ramón's letter? Two hours, perhaps. The gorge, dark now, had narrowed to a mountain gully, and the slope had steepened to the extent that they would have had to retrace their steps, had not the crack of the river, here at the edge of the tree line, been bridged by a mountain pine that had fallen across the void. Andriy tested the strength of the wood, nodded, and began to cross with the assured calm of a tightrope walker. He waited at the other side, his hand extended to Elsie. When he saw that she was crying, he cursed her. But Elsie wasn't crying because she feared the crossing; she was crying because the bridge had reminded her of the swimming, and the swimming had reminded her of what she had forgotten in her exhaustion. She was crying because she already knew that she would return for the letter, that she could do no other. She would follow the thread of the river, on her hands and knees in the dark. She would find, by the pool, under the cairn, the paper – almost transparent-thin where it had been folded – and because she was right-handed, she would place it next to her heart.

JOURNAL OF THEORETICAL SOCIOLOGY   XXXIV, 2

vehemently opposed to any theory that conceives structure as a determining force separable from the activity of knowledgeable agents.

Despite his focus on human action, Giddens argues that action theories (ethnomethodology etc.) are "Strong on actions, weak on institutions" (1982, p-29). Giddens, of course, intends to be strong on actions; strong on the causes of actions, and to this end he introduces a theory of structure. But for Giddens, this is a 'virtual structure': "Social systems only exist in so far as they are continually created and recreated in every encounter, as the active accomplishments of human subjects" (1977, p-118). This is what Giddens terms the 'duality of structure', where "the structural properties of social systems are both medium and outcome of the practices they recursively organize" (1984, p-25). To this perspective, "structure is not 'external' to individuals," but exists as memory traces and in social practices (ibid); structure, he argues (rather like Foucault), is "always both enabling and constraining" (ibid).

Of course, this position is hardly new – the same idea is found in Marx's early writings,[2] and it is, at one level at least, a truism – *the world as a meaningful entity* only exists as the active accomplishment of human subjects.

What is unique about Giddens' theory (and sometimes rather obscure), is the extreme voluntarism that he develops from this position. As Derek Layder notes, Giddens' "social analysis involves a radical humanist element in which all social phenomena must be understood as inherently and indissolubly tied to human reasons and motivations" (p-154/5). He achieves this 'humanist element' by developing a

---

[2] E.g., "it is above all necessary to avoid postulating society once again as an abstraction confronting the individual. The individual is the social being" (1963, p-158).

187

theory of agency that avoids (or at least attempts to avoid) the traditional philosophical problematic of free will and determinism.

While I was working on this paper, my dome-bellied wife was on maternity leave. I would hear her pass our study door (during vacations I like to work at home), breathing in this odd way she had developed during her pregnancy – a purposeful blowing that reminded me of a weightlifter preparing for a serious lift. During those weeks I watched and tried to be supportive and felt, I remember, both detached from and impressed by her almost political determination to maintain her regular activity.

When she entered labour prematurely I was not prepared. I was in the study, holding a copy of Giddens' *Central Problems in Social Theory*, worrying about his attempt to avoid the traditional philosophical problematic of free will and determinism. It's easy, of course, to say that I *should* have been reading one of the birthing books I'd thus far neglected. My wife had bought these hard-backed folio books – they had cover photographs of giggling babies and smiling women in maternity clothes, but this is all I can tell you about these volumes since I never looked inside any of them. It wasn't that I didn't care or didn't want to be part of this amazing, miraculous experience; I just thought the Giddens article was the more imperative deadline. You see, we weren't even at the stage where you think, Oh heck, what if it happens early? – it was *too* early. It was an ambush. And anyway, I could have been a fully trained gynaecologist and it would have made no difference. I understand this and so does my wife.

I heard my wife calling my name and the name of a god she didn't believe in and the name of his son. I ran – of course – and put my hand on her back, and suggested she sit down, and offered to get her a glass of water, and did and said all sorts of stupid things that were totally wrong in the situation. I have always had the attitude that whatever happens the most

188

BRITISH JOURNAL OF THEORETICAL SOCIOLOGY   XXXIV, 2

important thing is never to over-react, as though no situation justifies risking unnecessary alarm. So I initially responded as though her panic was the problem; I didn't believe her distress was an appropriate response to the biological disaster inside her. I know she knows this. I also know she knows that my reaction was connected to a wider patriarchal discourse about women's bodies and hysteria. She could tell you all about this. My wife is a much better and more respected academic than I am. Indeed, it seems to me that I should have been carrying the child and she should have been writing a paper on structuration theory. My wife could tell you exactly why I failed her in those moments, but she won't – my wife is reasonable and she knows that those moments (three minutes? Ninety seconds?) made no difference.

And yet, there is something awful about the delay. I don't remember everything we said in that time – I don't know, for example, if she directly commanded me to phone an ambulance and I ignored her. I do remember that I kept saying it would be okay and telling her to calm down. I had my hands outstretched, fingers spread, pushing the air downwards: *just calm down, okay?* I told her to breathe. And of course it was I who was panicking; it was I who was shaking so badly that I spilled the tumbler of water all over the sheepskin rug. And then I was determined she should sit down! I was almost wrestling her onto the settee while holding a cushion, which for some reason I felt I had to prop behind her back. I was holding this big sequined cushion – a cushion purchased years earlier by my wife, who had claimed it would 'soften' the room – and trying to put it behind her back! Can you imagine how funny this would be if the baby hadn't died? This incompetent man pratting about in the midst of this emergency! Oh, my wife would remember and tease me and bring up the story at our daughter's birthday: we would laugh and laugh then blow out candles and present our girl with a pink bicycle – pictures of daisies on the stabilisers!

189

STRUCTURATION THEORY AND IMMACULATE CONCEPTION

Sparkling streamers tied to the handlebars! – and years later she would bring a boyfriend to dinner and as we ate lasagne my wife would put the young man at ease by telling him how I goofed around in the minutes before his girlfriend's birth, and the young man would laugh politely and he would have a nice smile and I would feel okay about him probably Xing my daughter. But the baby died so the story is unspeakable and the memory triggers painful feelings of shame.

Our baby girl spent five days in an incubator before she died. I remember thinking she looked like a burn victim. I would look at her and think – I have no idea why – of that naked Vietnamese girl who is forever running from American napalm. We never named our daughter.

At home, of course, we had to cleanse the house of baby stuff. There was the wallpaper we had bought for the nursery and the self-assembly crib I had yet to get round to building. There were birthing books and baby clothes and a bouncer we had received from my wife's mother. I loaded all these things into the car and drove to the dump. Then I hurled them, still boxed and packaged, into an almost empty skip. People watched from their cars.

But the things I really wanted to get rid of were the objects I had reached for in the moments when I denied that my wife understood her own body. For example, I noticed – or thought I noticed – that we both avoided the settee. And one time, as we were watching a documentary about the French Revolution, I realised that I was sitting half-on that stupid cushion. By the end of the documentary the posture it forced on me had become painful. But to have lifted the cushion from underneath me would have drawn attention to it. My wife would have said nothing, and I would have said nothing, but we would both have known what the other was thinking, and why we couldn't speak. And the tumblers, which are the sort of tumblers from which you would expect to drink in a family home – I don't mean they are children's cups; they are

BRITISH JOURNAL OF THEORETICAL SOCIOLOGY   XXXIV, 2

the sort of glasses out of which you'd expect to drink squash; they are the sort of tumblers we would not have bought five years earlier, when our glasses were designed for beer or wine or breakfast juice – are another continual reminder, I feel, of what neither of us can ignore, or speak about.

I have tried to talk to my wife. We are mature and we trust each other and we know it is important to discuss our feelings. I told her I felt ashamed about... She understood. She put her hand on my wrist and smiled. She said it was a frightening situation for both of us. She reminded me that the delay made no difference. The baby was born in hospital. She just came into the world too soon, she said. Then we both cried – which we know is good – and my wife tried hard to hug me. She reminded me what the counsellor had said about irrational feelings of guilt. My wife is reasonable. She knows it is important to think rationally, even at such a difficult time. Sometimes I turn suddenly and catch her looking at me and her eyes are like razors.

Time passed, summer ended, we both returned to work. My colleagues were – obviously – sympathetic. They said it was a terrible thing to go through. They said that we were both in their thoughts. And yet I could see that most of them were secretly wishing us better luck with the next try and hoping it would be okay in the end. They thought it was a loss similar to when you fail to back up your files and suffer an especially disastrous computer crash – all that effort and you have to start again! I'm so sorry. My colleagues are rational people. They know that one new born baby is the same as the next. They know that a new born baby has neither a soul nor a personality. If I wanted to explain it to them then I would say something like: the thing we were in love with was the empty space, the absent referent brought into being by the signifier 'our baby.' And this space is just as empty and just as big and just as deep as the empty space in which you love your husband.

191

STRUCTURATION THEORY AND IMMACULATE CONCEPTION

Anyway, the RAE was approaching and I had been under pressure to produce at least one article (unlike my wife, I have a very poor publication record). Our head of Social Science is a structural anthropologist, a gentleman who never forgets the name of anyone's partner or neglects to ask the secretary about her holiday. I am very fond of him. We talked about the RAE and my barren publication record. He knew, of course, that this was a difficult time for me. If you feel you can do some research just now, great, he said. But it's not a priority. Your well-being is much more important than an article or two. I thanked him and left the office feeling an intense pressure to publish.

So I returned to the Giddens paper and read and reread what I'd written. I realised that I don't care about the intricacies of Giddens' theory. I suppose it is clever enough in so far as it goes. I recognise that Giddens is a more committed and talented and knowledgeable Scholar than I am, but I dislike the man, and I dislike his theory for reasons that largely defy logic. I think he is an obsequious Blairite careerist. I think the wild voluntarism expressed in his analysis is a false solution produced by a self-promoting establishment man. I get angry when I discuss his work. Perhaps I am jealous of his success? But there is also something in his emphasis on human agency that seems intuitively incompatible with my experience of the world.

I sat without writing for days. I thought about practical consciousness and a stratified view of human actors. I remembered that in our discipline nobody – not even peer reviewers – reads academic articles all the way through. I decided to write a beginning and an end and to fill the middle with whatever came into my head. I apologise to the editors, to my colleagues, and to my wife.

Giddens' theory of agency focuses on action as the ability to change (or not change) a given situation. He is not interested in our ability to *choose* as much as our ability to

BRITISH JOURNAL OF THEORETICAL SOCIOLOGY   XXXIV, 2

'make a difference', even if that difference depends on unacknowledged conditions and leads to unintended consequences. Of course, a dog, or a thunderstorm, can 'make a difference' with unintended consequences, but Giddens' theory has two responses to such a criticism. Firstly, he insists that unlike a dog we are 'knowledgeable' actors. This doesn't necessarily mean we are conscious of why we act or what the effects of our actions will be, but should be understood in terms of Giddens' stratified view of human actors as possessing, in addition to reflexive consciousness and unconscious motivations, a 'practical consciousness'; a kind of implicit knowledge of how the world works. Secondly, Giddens insists that, unlike a thunderstorm, at any point, in any situation, an agent could have acted differently.[3] He argues, for instance, that "self-destruction is a (virtually) always-open option" (1979, p-149). So according to his concept of agency, a person ordered at gun point exercises agency in obeying, since being shot is an available alternative. As J.B. Thompson argues, in Giddens' theory:

> An individual who has only one feasible option is an agent, for the option is limited to one only in the sense that, given the individual's wants and desires, there is only one option that the individual would regard as reasonable to pursue. This response does not resolve the problem however; it merely bypasses the problem by

---

[3] If we *do* consider this in terms of free will and determinism, then his position seems to follow G.E. Moore's classic argument in *Ethics*, where a free action is any action where the actor could have done otherwise, had they so chosen. In other words, Giddens appears to be offering a (highly sophisticated) compatibilist theory of freedom.

193

STRUCTURATION THEORY AND IMMACULATE CONCEPTION

reaffirming a concept of agency which is, for all practical purposes, irrelevant' (p-74).

But I'm unclear *how* an agent in any given situation, could have acted differently: the 'act' of the person threatened at gunpoint is probably a series of (socially influenced) biological reactions. This is a very clear act of agency in the sense that underpinning the reactions is an impulse to stay alive. Equally, however, we could argue that it is *not* an act of agency, since faced with that situation, that body would only ever act one way.[4]

The same possibilities of analysis could be extended to any happening because, as Ira Cohen observes, beyond the attempt to achieve ontological security, Giddens never offers us an adequate "account of how subjective wants and desires are formed" (p-226).[5] If they are not produced by the individual, then we are faced with a familiar chicken and egg situation.

---

[4] Think of when your behaviour has been regrettable. Imagine time rewinds and you are back in the same situation – the same pattern of raindrops on the window; the same orbit of a housefly near the lamp – *exactly* the same situation. You have no knowledge of the future, no awareness of your subsequent regret, and in terms of your biology and life experience you are exactly as you were the first time you faced this moment. Viewing this fantasy from the future, surely you are forced to watch yourself make all the same mistakes again?

[5] Indeed, it is a curious feature of Giddens' theory that while it is probably the most voluntaristic of contemporary models, it is also one of the most sociological. As Lash & Urry argue, Giddens' actors are characterised by "an almost cybernetic-like 'monitoring' of conduct" (p-44), and his "notion of the self is grounded in a very strong positivistic ego psychology" (ibid, p-38; see also: Craib, pp-166-177).

BRITISH JOURNAL OF THEORETICAL SOCIOLOGY   XXXIV, 2

Giddens chooses to start with the egg but we might just as accurately start with the chicken; where Giddens describes society as the result of human activity; we could describe human activity as the result of society. To an extent, this is what structuration theory does when it describes how, through social practices, actors constitute, and are constituted by society. But as Derek Layder notes, "assertions of the kind that "we create society at the same time as we are created by it" (...) are rather vague and lacking in substance" (p-235).

The substance of Giddens' theory focuses on the egg, as far as I can discern, for two main reasons. Firstly, he considers that the alternative – a structural explanation – is simply not useful to social science (1984, p-214); secondly, he argues that structures do not exist in time and space, except in the practices of human agents (ibid, p-17). The first point, which we don't have time to discuss here, may perhaps tell us something about social science. To the second point we might add that 'acts', 'selves', and 'agents' do not exist in space and time either; like structure, these are concepts used to explain why things happen in the world, and to posit transcendental beings as the centres and origins of these happenings. If we say that structure doesn't exist, don't we have to abandon the idea of agency as well?

Azerbaijan Soviet Socialist Republic, 1937

30

Now, examiners, I confess that up to this point I have withheld a key piece of information. The first act of my research was to Google 'Elsie Angelenetta Stewart.' All the results of my search, except one, found the component parts of her name scattered through thousands of words of text: The Solar Person Biographical Database; the Green England Petition for a 10p Charge for Plastic Bags; the North Wiltshire Online Census Project. The exception was a website, built for no discernible purpose, by a man named George Stewart Steel. Mr Steel had built his site with black text on a lime green background, underlined blue links, and no graphics; it was the sort of basic HTML site one encountered more frequently in the 1990s. It had six pages: 'birding', 'rambling', 'botany', 'archaeology', 'blog', and – the page I first accessed – 'about me'. Examiners, Mr Steel was born in 1947 to George and Elsie Angelenetta (née Stewart); his mother died when he was nine.

I went on to read that Mr Steel, a keen angler and lobster fisherman, resided on the Isle of Skye, where he monitored golden eagle eyries. He was responsible for a complete list of Skye's burial cairns, forts, brochs, and 'ancient structures of mysterious or disputed function'. The botany page reported on the fauna Mr Steel had identified within a metre-wide square-frame (the purpose of this struck me as especially obscure) and much of the blog concerned the bounty, or lack thereof, harvested from his ill-fated vegetable patch.

I emailed to request a telephone interview, and after a short electronic rally, a back and forth of questions and answers, George proposed that I visit him on the Isle of Skye. In July 2009, I took the coach to Portree, the Island's capital, and there hired a taxi to drive me to Glen Spàirn; when the driver stopped at the end of the road, I feared I was the victim of some scam or robbery, for the only sign of human habitation was a Land Rover, rooted in the roadside mud, its windscreen and bonnet patterned with pollen and dirt. Then I saw two cottages, burrowed in the hillside: across a rope bridge, over a stile, two brush strokes of white in a watercolour landscape. George had warned me to bring books in case of rain, but I had thought he would live near *something:* a caravan park, a youth hostel, an aquatic centre – anything.

31

Where was Elsie's beau garcon on the last day of August 1937, as she was led into the Pyrenees? On the Eastern edge of Kirovabad (today Ganja), the second city of Azerbaijan, as one travelled in the direction of Baku, there was a large marshy lake, around which, in deference to the floods of the rainy season, no permanent structures had ever been erected. So this area, near Lenin-Körpü, was a de facto recreation park that resembled contemporary nature reserves more than it did the structured green spaces of Stalinist urban planning. It was here, at the end of August 1937, that a Moscow circus erected its tents on the firm ground that overlooked the lake. At dusk, Ramón Buenacasa Mavilla stood, one hundred metres from the big top, watching the lake over the shoulder of a young woman.

32

The books I took to Skye included the *Selected Philosophical Writings* of René Descartes. I knew even less about Descartes than I had known about Nietzsche. The only thing I knew about Descartes was that he had fathered a daughter with a servant called Helene. (His daughter, Francine, was born in 1635, and during her short life, Descartes referred to her as his niece. She died of scarlet fever at the age of five.) I also knew, of course, that Descartes was responsible for propagating something called 'dualism', and according to intellectual fashion, he was thereby responsible for most of the world's ills.

I studied the *Philosophical Writings* on the train from Cheltenham to Glasgow, but soon after the coach passed Dumbarton, as we twisted around the coast of Loch Lomond, I felt the first lurch of nausea and decided to rest my reading, letting my mind wander as raindrops blurred and distorted the grey-green landscape. Examiners, you will recall that for Descartes the only secure foundation of knowledge is the knowledge of self-existence, which is irrefutably evident in the experience of thought. In his *Meditations on First Philosophy* (1968b [1641]), he observes that our senses may deceive us (as when a stick appears to bend beneath water), and that even when sensory information appears overwhelmingly 'true', there is no certainty that we aren't dreaming. There is no certainty, either, that our whole experience of the world is not the effect of some malicious and powerful demon determined to trick us (or, to give a more modern example, there's no certainty that we're not plugged into some Matrix-like virtual reality). At the end of Descartes' radical doubting, his only certainty is that even if all his thoughts are the effects of demonic deception, the fact that he is thinking them is nevertheless proof that he exists.

Thus, in his *Discourse on the Method*, he concluded *je pense, donc je suis* (the more famous Latin equivalent, *cogito ergo sum*, appeared seven years later in *The Principles of Philosophy*); I think, therefore I am (1968a [1637], p-32).

The Cartesian world view, then, begins with a thinking subject 'separated out of worldly systems in order to found them' (Ermarth, 1992, p-106). In Descartes' theory of dualism, the mind, *res cogitans* (thinking thing), is ontologically distinct from all material substances, *res extensa* (extended thing), including the body. Today, this idea has fallen out of fashion: dualism seems rather odd to our physical monist worldview, and much fun is made of Descartes' conviction that the immaterial soul and the physical body somehow interact in the pineal gland.

Indeed, a story is told of a horse that became famous in North America during the late nineteenth-century. Whether through supernatural ability or, more likely, some legerdemain on the part of its owner, the horse was able to score highly in multiple choice examinations. At a public performance in Dallas, the horse stamped its foot to indicate correct answers to questions from various university exam papers; the only paper it consistently flunked was philosophy. 'Just goes to show,' said the beast's owner. 'You can't put Descartes before the horse.'

This joke is only one of several Descartes puns that I encountered as an undergraduate: you may, perhaps, recall the one about Descartes' swimming lessons? After three weeks of nearly drowning, Descartes completes a length of perfect breast stroke. 'How did you do that?' asks his bemused father. 'Simple,' says young René. 'I sink, therefore I swam.' These jokes aren't funny, of course, but they seem illustrative of how Descartes' work has been judged by a generation: Cartesian dualism is treated humorously.

33

Now, examiners, it's true that as Elsie was searching for Ramón's letter, Ramón was thousands of miles away, escorting another woman to the circus. And yes, in modern parlance, this was more or less 'a date'. But before we castigate Ramón for gallivanting, we should note that at work here were forces greater than our characters.

The Spanish contingent at the aviation school had been invited to the circus as honoured guests of the Raikom Secretary, who had recently been appointed to this region of the Azerbaijan Soviet Socialist Republic (his predecessor had been recalled to Moscow and sent from there to who knows where), because the Politburo – no less – had recognised the value of the Spanish cadets. The school had been purpose built at a cost of 3,462,600 rubles (paid for, of course, with Spanish gold), and by the time the Raikom Secretary arrived in Azerbaijan it was equipped with eighty-four aircraft (the older PO-2, UTE-1, and PT-6 models, but also at least a few of the I-15 and I-16 fighters that were then deployed in Spain); fifty ground vehicles; hundreds of staff (in addition to military personnel the school employed technicians, caterers, cleaners, medical staff, and administrators); and a head instructor, E.G. Shakht, who had already been decorated a Hero of the Soviet Union for the bravery he had shown over the skies of Madrid (see Kowalsky, 2004, chapter 14). It seemed to the Raikom Secretary that the school had everything necessary for its military purpose; indeed, during his feud with the military commander of the academy, Polkovnik Yashin, he puzzled at what idiocies must have been necessary, in these exemplary conditions, to lose in fatal accidents ten Soviet instructors and nine Spanish cadets. The Raikom Secretary considered his own role to be far more challenging; he was responsible for ensuring that the surrounding area appeared orderly and prosperous; that, whatever the rigours of their training, time was made for the Spaniards to enjoy the best of Soviet hospitality; and, just as importantly, that the people of the Soviet Union, Spain, and the rest of the world, had plentiful opportunities to see the Spanish cadets enjoy the best of Soviet hospitality. In attempting to discharge his duty he was (or at least this was how it seemed to him) hindered at every step by the Polkovnik. The Polkovnik and his underlings objected, for example, when the Raikom Secretary placed Kirovabad's most celebrated restaurateur in charge of the academy catering; during a heated telephone conversation, the Polkovnik claimed that neither he nor his Russian staff could stomach the Azeri cuisine, which argument the Raikom Secretary would have accepted, had he not two days later encountered the Polkovnik dining happily on plov at the said-restaurateur's premises in Central Kirovabad. When the Raikom Secretary helped organise a cadets' tour of Moscow – Voroshilov had directly ordered that the Spaniards should see the museums and theatres, the Aviation Factory no. 22, the Stalin Automobile Factory, and the Volga-Moscow Canal – the Polkovnik, backed by the war hero Shakht, complained that such 'sightseeing holidays' were disrupting the pilots' military preparations. Similarly, when the Raikom Secretary arranged for the Spaniards to address a youth rally in Baku, their military commanders refused them time to learn their lines, so that – with the exception of that one fellow (whose title the Raikom Secretary could never recall) – the speeches were an incomprehensible embarrassment.

34

George's house is a five-minute walk from the road and to reach it one must cross a rope bridge, wade through grass that in places grows to waist-height, clamber over a stile, and hike through a field. By the time I had reached the garden gate, my trousers, shoes, and socks were heavy with water, and George, presumably having seen me trudging through the field, had exited his cottage with a wave. 'Hello!'

'Mr Steel,' I said, extending my hand across the fence.

'George.' He grasped my hand like a castaway greeting his rescuer. 'Low cloud,' he said, nodding upwards. '*Pheeeeeeeuuuuuw.* It's really clagged in. It's been like this for days.'

'Really?'

'Look,' he said, pinching the top inch off a straggly purple weed. 'Ragged Robin.'

'Aha,' I said.

'See how each petal divides into four long fingers? They look like claws, do they not?'

'Yes, they do.'

'All its flowers are hermaphrodite. That's unusual in Campions.'

'I didn't know that.'

'*Pheeeeeeeuuuuuw,* come in.' We walked in silent single file on the path made where the long grass had been stamped flat between George's front door and gate. 'Wait,' said George, seizing just as he crossed a crumbling plank that bridged a drainage ditch. He tilted his ear towards the foot of the garden, perched mid-pace like a strange wading bird, and then he walked on. 'A meadow pipit, I think.' All I could see were two rectangles of clumpy earth dug out of the moorland (one plot was empty except for short bamboo canes; in the other, I recognised the yellowing hole-punched leaves of a dozen doomed potato plants).

In the porch, amid the paddles, tools, boots, and fishing rods, I followed George's lead in kicking off my shoes. George set his boots side by side and then we entered the long silence of the hall and stood there for a moment. The cottage smelled like clothes one has left too long in storage. '*Pheeeeeeeuuuuuw*,' said George, rubbing his hands together. 'I've started a fire in the living room. Please, go through and I'll bring some tea.'

I could feel the heat as soon as I pushed open the door: flames leapt and crackled and bent the air. Above the mantelpiece, there was a map of the world – the globe stretched flat so that Greenland looked bigger than Russia – and opposite the window, two bookcases stood shoulder to shoulder, their shelves sagging under the weight of books.

When George returned with the tea, I showed him the picture of Elsie. He held the book a long time and didn't say anything. I realised that more than half a century after her death, George was still deeply affected by the loss of his mother. Decency demanded that I donate the book to his collection of memories, but as he studied the picture I realised that I could not bear to part with it, and when at last he folded the book and returned it to me, I accepted it without a word. George said that he had never seen the picture before and then he concentrated on the tray he had brought from the kitchen. He passed some peanuts and a plate of oatcakes and a bowl full of sugar that had clumped into rocks. We stirred our tea, round and round, chiming the china where decades of teaspoons had scratched grey rings on the walls of the cups; I couldn't for the life of me think of anything to say. Sensing this, perhaps, George dropped onto his knees and busied himself with the fire. He placed another log on the blaze and the fire subsided and a thick damp smoke hushed across the room; then he poked the charred logs and blew on the embers until the flames returned with a noise like distant fireworks. 'Look,' said George, replacing the fireguard, 'these are some minerals I found while rambling.' He crossed to the window ledge and showed me several small stones. 'This is calcite, from Talisker Bay. Prehnite and quartz from Sgurr Nan Cearcall. Phillipsite, analcime, and calcite from Moonen Bay.'

'Wow,' I said.

'That's calcite as well... can't remember where it came from. Stilbite from Oisgill Bay. I think that's erionite.'

'They're beautiful, Mr Steel.'

'Help yourself to sugar. *Pheeeeeeeuuuuuw.*' (This noise, examiners, which sounded like an incoming missile, appeared to bring George comfort or pleasure. It seemed variably to be an expression of delight – especially delight in the natural world – or a nervous response to a sensitive or unfamiliar subject. Indoors it was usually the latter; outdoors, it tended to be louder and seemed in most instances to be an interjection of joy.) We listened to the fire for a moment and then, under his breath, George asked me to explain my interest in his mother.

'Well, Mr Steel–'

'George.'

'George. Well, I don't know. I– I'm interested in historical change, you see. My thesis is really about free will and determinism–'

'I see, yes.'

'And how one writes about these things. And your mother, Elsie, was born at the end of the first world war; she lived through the Russian Civil War; she witnessed the rise of fascism and the achievement of female suffrage; she saw the Spanish revolution and World War Two; she was alive at the time of the Holocaust and Stalin's purges; she saw the establishment of the welfare state and the end of colonial rule in India; she was there at the start of the cold war and she witnessed the Hungarian uprising. It's an amazing time to have been alive, Mr Steel – George. I'm just fascinated.'

'I see, yes.'

'What it is– It seems to me that if one wants to understand the contemporary world then– I think we're prisoners of– no, products of our historical moment. You see?'

'Yes, yes, absolutely.'

'And those years that your mother lived through, even more than other decades, seem to be full of opportunities – junctions at which humanity could have gone one way or another. We went via the Holocaust and Stalinism, but could it have been different? How was the Spanish Revolution possible? How was the Hungarian Uprising possible?'

George nodded and scooped a handful of nuts. 'I see, yes, *Pheeeeeeeuuuuuw.*'

I sat, frustrated, aware that I wasn't explaining myself well.

'These are pressed flowers,' said George, pointing at the shrivelled heads under the glass of the coffee table. 'That one's alpine bistort.'

35

Four-and-a-half minutes of the youth rally in Baku (or a similar event) are today viewable in the Filmoteca Española Madrid. The Spaniards' speeches do indeed look embarrassing. During The Great Research Trip, Lempi and I visited the Spanish Film Archive in Madrid, and there were able to watch 'Españoles en Rusia' (as this fragment is labelled in the comprehensive *Catálogo General del Cine de la Guerra Civil* (Amo García & Ibañez Ferradas, 1997, pp-429-30).

Even to a viewer who speaks no Russian, it is obvious that most of the Spaniards are unable to complete a coherent sentence. They hold their papers centimetres from their faces (one presumes the words had been written for them phonetically in the Latin alphabet) and pause and stumble and squint, and after making various apologetic noises, they bounce with relief into the closing salutations to Stalin (whose name they can at least pronounce).

But there is one young Spaniard who 'tosses off his appearance with verve and aplomb' (Kowalsky, 2004). When he says (this is Lempi's translation) that the strength of the Soviet people shall cause Franco to run under the skirts of Hitler, he mimics Franco's girlish panic, scuttling from the podium, flinching at imaginary danger, and is rewarded with a camera-shaking chorus of laughter. Now, having never seen him identified in a photograph, I cannot be sure that this man is Ramón; nevertheless, I would like to describe this speaker in detail. But here we encounter a second frustration: at no point is it possible to clearly see the man's face. He is filmed for forty-six seconds and his face is obscured by glare throughout. One can see that his hair is combed back in the fashion of the time. His shirt is unbuttoned at the collar and his sleeves are rolled to above his elbows. He is taller than most of his comrades; I would estimate, if forced, that he stands at 5'7 to 5'10. The end of his speech is not preserved on film so one cannot know whether he, too, closes by praising and thanking Stalin.

36

I waited two hours before George began to discuss his mother, but once started he talked for an hour without pause. Then, like a Hebridean Scheherazade, he stopped mid-story, citing the lateness of the hour. George's maternal grandmother, I learned, was born in Casalattico, in Southern Italy. For economic reasons, her family migrated to Belfast when she was still a child. There, she converted to Protestantism (or so George presumes) and married George's maternal grandfather. In 1918, she gave birth to George's mother, Elsie. Elsie was the eldest of the four children who survived infancy. In 1934 or 1935 – around that time – she sailed to England and there entered domestic service at a house in Richmond. George has a memory, from when he was four or five, of his mother holding a foul-mouthed argument with three serving girls outside a Didsbury mansion. He doesn't remember the context, or what caused the argument; he recalls only the fierceness of the language. George associates this memory with an image of his mother crying in front of the BBC test card, but he knows that they didn't have a television until years later. Still, it is a powerful memory, George says. His mother was drunk, he remembers, slumped in that arm chair, on the bare foam cushions.

37

The Raikom Secretary understood politics. He knew that the Polkovnik – one of those young Tsarist officers who had backed the winner in the Civil War – had spent the last quarter-century acquiring party influence, and he knew that Shakht had been personally decorated by Voroshilov; thus he had no desire to take a too-combative stance in his struggle with the academy's military command. The arrival of the circus, therefore, afforded the Raikom Secretary the perfect opportunity to film the Spaniards enjoying the best of Soviet entertainment, while simultaneously making an overture to the Polkovnik and his allies; hence, he booked an entire performance – 'in honour of Republican Spain' – and he sent gracious invitations to military commanders, senior NKVD officers, party officials whom he suspected of harbouring loyalties to his predecessor, the local Komsomol leaders, influential local Azeris, the cousin of Mir Jafar Baghirov, the film star Abbas Mirza Sharifzadeh (this was an error that the Raikom Secretary was forced to explain to the NKVD when, three months later, Sharifzadeh was charged with espionage), his actress wife, two Stakhanovite oil workers, and anybody else of interest or influence who was then in the locality.

There is, the Raikom Secretary thought, something staid about a social gathering devoid of young women; with this in mind, he extended two invitations to every Spaniard. He worried, initially, that the cadets might have problems finding suitable company (he didn't want them exposed to superstitious Azeri adolescents, illiterate former prostitutes, unclean peasant girls); in fact, the problem was the other way round: there was such excitement among the daughters of party members that several comrades contacted the Raikom Secretary to complain that their girls had been ignored. One can understand the girls' excitement: at this time aviators commanded a public fascination that would soon be the preserve of pop stars. More than that, these were *Spanish* aviators: foreigners who brought with them all the promise and excitement of *zagranitze* – the outside world. And these were military aviators: there is something no girl can resist, the Raikom Secretary thought, in the resolute features of a young man who is prepared to risk his life for a cause; these were young men who would enjoy the night with a carefree wildness, for they knew that in– Now the Raikom Secretary began to envisage romances and pregnancies, desertions and defections; too late it occurred to the Raikom Secretary that all the venereal diseases in all the exiled former prostitutes in all the Soviet Union would together not have posed half the risk that was hidden behind the lovely features of each Komsomol beauty. Ah, he thought, young love in a time of war!

38

I must tell you now, said George, that I don't know with any certainty why my mother was in Spain. Years after her death, my father told me that she had volunteered as a nurse. This may be

true, said George, *pheeeeeeeuuuuuw*. My father left a great number
of letters and personal files, most of which relate to his time in
the Communist Party. Amid them I found a letter to my mother,
dated June 1937, which had been sent from the Soviet Union to
an address in Spain. It is evident, George said, from the tone of
the letter, that there had been an intimate relationship between
my mother and the sender. The letter addresses my mother 'Mi
querida', my darling. After my father's death, *pheeeeeeeuuuuuw*, I
deposited all his papers at the Working Class Movement Library
in Salford. I advise you to read the letter for yourself.

My mother and father, George continued, met in February
1938 at a London Communist Party rally in support of the
Spanish Republic; to the best of my knowledge, however, my
parents were not in a romantic relationship until after the Second
World War. No correspondence between them survives from
this period and it's not clear whether they maintained contact
or later met again by chance. My father was twelve years my
mother's senior. He worked as a librarian.

At this point, George excused himself, and I paused the
voice recorder and sat alone in the living room, feeling like an
intruder. I could hear George moving around upstairs, and, to
assuage my sense of loitering, I decided to stoke the fire. By the
time he returned, I had, of course, extinguished it. I was on my
knees, ripping and lighting, ripping and lighting, shred after shred
of newspaper. The room was opaque with smoke. 'The flames
died,' I lied. George passed me his parents' wedding portrait and
while I studied the photograph he set about resuscitating the fire.
Elsie, at thirty, on her wedding day, looks more than a decade
older than the girl in the Barrot photograph. She is squinting
into the sun and one can see rings around her eyes. She has the
same inscrutable expression, however: a closed-mouth smile that
could be pride, or sarcasm, or resignation, or satisfaction, and

seemed to me, after much study, to express some wry detachment from the moment, as though she was already watching the scene from afar. Her coat is elegant but simple, knee-length, cut edge to edge, in accordance with utility clothing rules, and she wears a saucer-shaped tilt hat at a forty-five degree angle. One might not immediately recognise her as a newlywed were it not for the spray of chrysanthemums she holds in her left hand. Her right arm is linked to the left arm of the groom. The groom is dressed in a mix-matched suit: his trousers are pin-striped, his jacket is black, his waistcoat is mauve, and his tie is spotted. His hair is side-parted, cut to a severe grade at the back and sides. He wears a moustache and his expression is rather curious: he has the chest-puffed stern posture one sometimes sees exhibited in turn of the century photographs of association football teams. He looks younger than his forty-two years. As I was studying the picture, I saw reflected in the card the triumphant flames of George's fire.

39

Yulia Andreyevna Berkova worked as a telephonist and typist at the 20th Military School for Pilots. She had often seen Ramón and had smiled at him and had laughed at the polite flatteries he made in his slow, formal Russian. And yet, when Ramón said that he would be honoured to escort her – *her*, before anyone else – to the circus evening organised by his hosts, her first reaction, before she had even considered a positive response, was that something obscene was being forced upon her. Ramón must have seen her expression, for before she had replied he had assured her that his intentions were honourable: he merely sought to comply with the Raikom Secretary's wish that all his guests should have company. Comrade, since I have the privilege of working with you, Ramón continued, I hoped you might honour me with your company; I meant nothing more by this invitation and I withdraw it immediately if it has been misunderstood or has caused offence. And then, paradoxically, Yulia felt a pang of anger and disappointment. She slid back and forth the quarter-ruble beads on her abacus and couldn't meet his gaze.

Later, looking across the lake, she couldn't think exactly what Ramón looked like. The sun was setting behind them and from his shadow, laid in silken ripples across the water, she could see that he was broader and taller than she was, but she couldn't think what his face looked like, as though she had avoided his gaze in all their conversations. They were watching three flamingos. The flamingos waded in the shallow water near a small island and above the balalaika music and the splashes of laughter and the shouts of the kufta vendor she could hear the water lapping in the breeze and the shriek of gulls; it seemed to her that in the distance the flamingos were completely silent.

On the bus from the academy, Ramón had talked incessantly in his strange Russian. He had told an anecdote – to what end she could not fathom – about witnessing, on the train from Baku, the drunken phantasy of a mad man. The man, according to Ramón, had been convinced that unseen 'agents' were executing his fellow passengers. Ramón had tried his best to convince the poor fellow that besides they two there was nobody in the compartment except an innocent-looking Azeri family, but the man had carried on – apparently genuinely terrified – until the comrade guard had to be called. The man, however, mistook the guard for one of the agents, and ultimately had to be taken away for psychiatric evaluation. Yulia did not know whether Ramón had intended his story to be humorous.

She turned, at this point, to look back at the circus: the outline of the big top was illumined by electric bulbs and the rope of lights had been stretched zigging across the pines and junipers. The air was warping around the heat of the food stand and the smell of meatballs mixed with the nearby scent of pistachio trees. She caught the eye of a Spaniard and spun back to the flamingos. They were ankle-deep, back-bending their legs out of the water, stilting around the island. Their shadows, too, were laid across the lake: black replicas of pink beauty in the orange light. Then, as though obeying some secret signal, all three revved and flapped, skidded jet-trails across the water, and rose at an angle of ten degrees. When they were fifteen metres above the surface, they slowed, beat their wings, climbed steeper in an arcing curve, and passed overhead. They flew with their legs stretched behind them, bodies straight as arrows. She was reminded of the fighters she saw every day at work; already, a few months after the bombing of Guernica, one looked at birds and one saw warplanes.

40

My first home was in Wythenshawe, said George, on the outskirts of Manchester, as one drives in the direction of Stockport and Manchester Airport. Today, Wythenshawe is an area of socio-economic deprivation. (I remember it from my time at university, examiners: since 2007, it has been the outdoor filming location for the television series *Shameless*.) It was built immediately after the war, continued George, with little thought to the needs of its residents, in order, my mother believed, to clear the poor from the more desirable locations in the centre of the city. I don't remember being unhappy in Wythenshawe, but I think my mother was adversely affected by the lack of amenities. There were no shops – the town-planners simply hadn't thought that the residents might need to eat – and so my mother, with me in tow, had to walk great distances to acquire groceries.

In 1953, when I was five, our family moved to the more affluent neighbourhood of Withington. (At this point I mentioned that in my undergraduate days I had lived in the adjacent district of Fallowfield, but George did not seem interested by this coincidence. Instead, he began to discuss his father's work.) George Steel Sr., my father, was a curator at Manchester Central Library. He was responsible for the Gaskell collection. Built in the 1930s, the Central Library is a neo-classical building with Corinthian columns and a portico entrance; it is loosely modelled on the Pantheon in Rome. I recall my father approaching his work with the gravitas and sanctification of one devoted to worshiping a deity. As a child I was made to read the work of Mary Gaskell, and I have never returned to the texts since. I recall *North and South* as being the least awful, but I must confess to having a general aversion to fiction, which I suspect may be related to my early enslavement to Victorian novels. (After this, we lapsed into an uncomfortable silence, though George had not in the least offended me.)

41

The Raikom Secretary had invited more guests than there were seats for in the big top. In the hours before the performance, additional chairs had been commandeered from a nearby restaurant, but these seats, placed in an improvised inner circle, were so close to the performers that some of the female comrades were likely to be alarmed if there seated. The next row (the first row proper) was equally undesirable as the lack of tiering meant one's view would be obscured if one were seated behind a tall fellow or a comrade who declined to remove her hat. The best seats, the Raikom Secretary decided, were in the third or fourth row back, and at this level, near to the main entrance, he congregated his most important guests. Seated here were Spanish officers and their wives, the Polkovnik and Shakht, Abbas Mirza and his actress wife, the Partkom Secretary of the oil works, the beautiful and (the Raikom Secretary thought) scheming Raikom Ideology Secretary, and the Kapitan Gozbezopasnosti of the NKVD. The two Stakhanovite workers, when they arrived (mercifully alone), turned out to be lumpen sorts, whom the Raikom Secretary met in person, and easily convinced were privileged to be seated at the very front. He also kept near him that translator fellow (he made it a point, now, to learn the man's title at the next opportunity) and the Moscow paedologist who had arrived here, via Kharkov, through some misfortune of which the Raikom Secretary was ignorant. The doctor paedologist was evidently a man of no political value, but in this region he was one of few acquaintances whose company the Raikom Secretary genuinely enjoyed; the translator fellow needed to be on hand because the Raikom Secretary did not want to rely on the military people if circumstances necessitated he speak to the Spaniards.

Thus, Yulia was seated between Ramón and the wife of a senior NKVD officer, four seats to the right of Abbas Mirza, directly in front of the Raikom Secretary. She was embarrassed to admit, even to herself, that at this moment she felt an almost aristocratic pride. The performance area was in shadow but by the light of the auditorium bulbs she could see black figures moving in and out of the back of the tent. A few feet from her, the filmmaker lifted his camera from its tripod and held it at his hip, pointing the many eyes of the thing at the audience. Yulia could hear the camera's machine-gun whir and click above the chirr of conversation. She combed her bangs with her fingers and tried to relax.

Then, with a *thunk*, the main spotlight turned on the ring, shooting down from the top of the tent like a search beam. The audience cheered and a clown in a hideous mask hissed and snarled and threatened the audience until he tripped over his own feet. Be quiet! Don't you know who he is? said another clown. The first clown climbed to his feet, brushing himself down with mock dignity. I am Nestor Makhno, king of the bandits! At this point the crowd booed and both clowns stomped around the ring shaking their fists at the audience. The audience laughed louder the second time that the Nestor Makhno clown tripped over his feet. Now, the other clown, whose appearance seemed to have been inspired by First World War anti-Kaiser cartoons, extended his hands to help up the Nestor Makhno clown; however, the Makhno clown was too heavy and he pulled the Germanic clown on top of him to the sound of a loud gong. To punish the Germanic clown for his incompetence, the Makhno clown grabbed from the floor a great bullwhip (at this point Yulia heard Ramón light a cigarette). There was, at the back of their set, a paper-covered hoop, such as a performing animal might jump through. The Makhno clown cracked the whip twice on the ground, and then, in a rapid-fire of six fearsome swishes, he cut a swastika into the paper. This divided the audience: half the spectators applauded the clown's extraordinary skill; half the spectators remembered to boo the symbol he had created. The poor Germanic clown, meanwhile, was on his knees begging for mercy as the Makhno clown prepared to lash him. The whip was so close to Yulia, the noise of the thing so awful, that she had to remind herself that these were professional performers and that nobody was going to get hurt. As the Makhno clown swung the whip, he slipped, missed the Germanic clown's buttocks, and tangled the whip around his own ankles. For a moment, the Germanic clown continued to tremble in fear; then, hesitantly, he turned, saw the Makhno clown's predicament, and made a grovelling attempt to help. The Makhno clown, however, began to thrash his sidekick with an open palm (it looked to Yulia as though he was really hitting the poor clown in the face; indeed, once again the audience was divided, this time between those who laughed and those who gasped and winced in empathy); but since the whip was still wrapped around his ankles, the Makhno clown lost his balance, and as he fell he also lost his trousers. Before the laughter had subsided there was a great crash of cymbals, music, and firecrackers, and through the main entrance there galloped a white horse, ridden by a moustachioed man in a Civil War-era Red Army uniform. At this sight, the two clowns scurried on hands and knees – the Makhno clown still showing his enormous woman's bloomers – and exited at the rear of the tent. It was now, as the audience applauded, that Yulia became aware of Ramón's silence.

The horseman stopped in a cloud of smoke and the horse reared on its hind legs and held this position until the music ceased. Comrades, said the moustachioed man, have you seen any bandits? The question was too rhetorical for an exclusively adult audience and the spectators, with the exception of one Stakhanovite, fell awkwardly silent. The Stakhanovite, whom the Raikom Secretary thought to be quite drunk, stood up, aimed an imaginary rifle towards where the clowns had exited, and produced a series of childish gunshot noises. Comrades, continued the moustachioed man, welcome to this special performance in honour of Republican Spain. I have been a circus worker since I was a boy: my father was a strongman; my mother was an aerial acrobat. I have performed in many places, to many people. I have performed in Omsk, Siberia, when the temperature was fifty below. I have performed in Ashgabad, Turkmenistan, when the temperature was forty-five above. On

Tsvetnoi Boulevard, I performed, alongside Karandash, to men as great as Comrade Molotov. I tell you these things, not to boast, but so you know the depth of my feeling when I say that I have never been prouder, and never more honoured by an audience, than I am tonight. Comrades, during the next two hours you will see feats of daring and bravery – at this moment Yulia was distracted by the camera, which had turned from the ringmaster to film the audience's reaction – such as will make you gasp; you shall laugh one moment and cover your eyes the next. I hope, sincerely, that our show pleases you. But, comrades, what we do in entertainment, our guests tonight will do – with no less skill but a thousand times more bravery – in the great struggle against fascism. We welcome them tonight, as our great leaders have welcomed their courageous struggle; for, if the successes of the working class of our country, if its fight and victory, can aid the working class in Republican Spain and the capitalist countries, then our Party may say that its work has not been in vain. (At this point there began a loud and prolonged standing ovation.) Long live our victorious working class! Long live our victorious collective farm peasantry! Long live our Socialist intelligentsia! Long live the Azerbaijan Soviet Socialist Republic! Long live the great friendship of the nations of our country! Long live the Yezhovshchinist repression of the enemies of the people! Down with the Trotskyist-Bukharinite-fascist conspiracy! Down with the kulak-bourgeoisie-rightist saboteurs! Long live the Communist Party of the Soviet Union! Long live Comrade Stalin! (The Spaniards, confused by the Russian speech, clapped with the rest of the audience, as around them people clenched fists and shouted: Hurrah for Comrade Stalin! Hurrah for our great Stalin! Hurrah for our beloved Stalin!) Hurrah! shouted Yulia. Hurrah! Hurrah! Hurrah!

42

After George bid me goodnight, I read for three hours, and then, when I finally retired, I lay awake, disturbed by the moonlight. But when at last I did sleep, the night passed without interruption, and in the morning, I awoke from one of my recurring Lempi fantasies in a fever of sexual excitement. Examiners, I am embarrassed to admit that on my first morning in George's cottage, I stealthed to his bathroom and there, imagining Lempi so vividly I could smell her, I brought myself to orgasm with a silence I hadn't practised since adolescence. My caution was unnecessary, it transpired, for George was not home; in the queer silence of the glen, I had slept until eleven, and my host had kindly declined to wake me. He had left me a bowl of bran flakes, which I ate with my own soya milk, as raindrops meandered across the kitchen window, and water fell in ceaseless bars from the corrugated iron roof. Lambs sheltered under their mothers and the River Spàirn sped streaked with white water, but whatever else existed of the island remained for now in cloud. Reluctant to venture out in such weather, I turned my attention back to Descartes.

Then, sometime after noon, the low cloud moved east, the sun broke through, and the coy island revealed itself. The view from George's kitchen window is cut into sections; the wet beach sand is caramel-brown, the flat land in the valley is a yellow green, then there rises a hillock, purple with heather, and above that the slopes are russet orange. Rivers waterfall down the hillside in undulating silver lines. The peaks of the Cuillin Mountains emerge at the top like black fangs, snagging clouds and breaking free, and in the evening bursting the sun's red across the sea. It was genuinely the most beautiful view I had ever seen.

Not long after the weather lifted, as the sun came out and blades of glass drooped and sparkled with damp, I saw George clambering over the sea-darkened rocks on the far side of the bay. He pulled himself from the crags and stood on the moorland, like a vastly accelerated demonstration of evolution, and then he walked away from the sea, where the land rises at the foot of the Cuillin and the lazy beds are cut into the hillside.

At George's suggestion, we set out after lunch for a tour of the archaeological sites on the far headland. 'There's an abandoned crofting village, a burial cairn, a medieval dun, and an unusual example of a broch,' said George. As he spoke, he was clambering over a stile, at the foot of his garden, where the river loops a langurous S. 'Fine afternoon, isn't it?' he said from the other side of the fence, hand resting between barbs. The sun was warm and the air was sweet with gorse nectar.

'Yes, it's nice.'

'Yes,' he said, gazing for confirmation as I waddled over the fence. He was wearing walking boots with wasp-coloured laces and red plastic gaiters to protect his trousers from the wet grass. '*Pheeeeeeeuuuuuw*, yeah. Just enough breeze to keep the midges at bay.' He looked at his boots and rubbed his hands together as a helicopter peeled over the mountains and hung above the coire. 'Mountain rescue,' said George, watching this unexpected reminder of civilisation.

We paused on the rope bridge, watched fish swim through coins of light, listened to the tac-tac-tac of a wren in the undergrowth; then we set out across the meadow, through buttercups and clover and sheaves of grass, and on to lay footsteps across the beach. At the far side of the bay, beside clumps of hazel, around which were scattered rectangles of moss-green rocks, we stopped at an abandoned crofting village. The ruined cottages were full of frayed orange ropes and white plastic cartons, washed there by some rare tide, and where once was a doorway there grew a rowan tree, stooped in acquiescence to the prevailing wind. The earlier rainwater was running off the hillside, rushing to the sea, and wading birds shrieked and squawked far out on the low-tide caramel sand. Each gust of breeze brought in the smell of seaweed and then receded, like the waves on the beach, leaving the still warm air full of the sour lemon smell of fast-drying ferns.

For want of something to do, I picked from the ground a metre-length of orange rope, a piece of flotsam, and observed how it was, in fact, two ropes entwined together, and how each of these was, in fact, two smaller ropes entwined together, and how each of these was, in fact, two threads entwined together. After this silent moment, a pause that felt like remembrance, George continued towards the headland, and as I fell in step with him, throwing the rope back to where the sea had deposited it, he recommenced his account of his mother's life.

I remember, said George, that my mother once told me that she was a witch. It is one of my earliest memories and dates, almost certainly, from the time when we lived in Wythenshawe. Do you hear that? *Spek spek*? I wonder whether that might be a tree pipit, said George. He looked through his binoculars, back across the meadow, towards the far side of the bay where the Sitka spruces were planted in dark green rectangles. My mother was in the bathroom, said George, walking again, and I needed to use the facilities, rather urgently, and so I knocked and knocked and when at last the door opened my mother exited without a word and slammed it shut behind me. I performed the toilet as best I could but when I exited the bathroom my mother was sitting on the steps. Mamma, I said – I called her Mamma as she had called her own mother – and she said that she wasn't my mamma; she was a witch who looked like my mamma. She said my mamma was in a faraway place, living with a different family. I remember that we then began the long walk to the shop, which excursion at that time punctuated and structured our days, and I worried that there was now no way I could ever be sure whether she was my mother or a witch who had taken on my mother's appearance. I have no idea why she said such a thing – she was a kind and loving mother – but it must have affected me for the memory to have endured these decades.

My father was little involved in my upbringing before my mother's death, said George. At all times that my father was in the house, I was under great pressure to be silent. While my– Look, a ringed plover, I think. If a predator threatens a ringed plover's nest then the mother moves away from her babies, feigning a broken wing. *Pheeeeeeeuuuuuw.* While my father was at work I could play indoors or outdoors as boisterously as I liked, but when he was at home, reading in front of the fire, I was encouraged to sit on the floor beside him and was often expected to tackle books that were far above my reading age. Before I entered grammar school, I had read the *Communist Manifesto, On the Origin of Species,* Lenin's *"Left Wing" Communism: An Infantile Disorder, War and Peace, Les Miserables,* the first volume of Gibbon's *Decline and Fall of the Roman Empire, The Complete Shakespeare,* and other books to which no child should be subjected. If I disturbed my father on one of these reading evenings, he would not speak to me directly, but would, instead, complain to my mother. My mother would then discipline me, said George, for playing some innocuous game that she had encouraged, even participated in, a few hours earlier. The discipline had to be silent, too, so she would take me out of the room, often applying to my wrist a fierce grip (somewhat like the school torture we called a Chinese burn). Then she would shout at me, silently, straining her features to enunciate imagined words. There was never any need for her to discipline me while my father was at work.

At this point, examiners, I stopped to drink scoopfuls of water, hugging a tree with one arm, and reaching into the burn with the other. Behind me, I could hear George naming flowers. Alpine lady's mantle, he said. You can tell the difference from lady's mantle because the leaves are divided more than halfway towards the centre. Ah, I said. The path was steep at this point, twisting in hairpin bends, and as we climbed higher the river followed us, clattering through boulders at the foot of a gorge. Then the ground levelled and the path shrank to a peaty sheep track, and after a moment we emerged at a small loch. Slabs of rock surrounded the turquoise water, round and smooth like great whales basking in the sunlight. *Pheeeeeeeuuuuuw*, said George. He turned back to the mountains, rubbing his hands together. You were talking about parental discipline? I said, trying to steer George back to his family story.

Yes, said George. Although my father never rowed me, it was he alone who hit me. His beatings were rare, said George, but they invariably made me cry. My father abstained from alcohol and never lashed out in rage; rather, he would administer his thrashings, retrospectively, with the procedural disinterest of one who is carrying out the verdict of an impartial court. Sometimes the beatings came so long after the infringement that I struggled to connect the two events. This proved an effective disciplinary technique, for the fear of pain is always worse than pain itself. Hours, even days, *pheeeeeeeuuuuuw*, after some infringement, I would flinch if my bedroom door opened. On several occasions, said George, I was beaten for crimes I thought had gone unnoticed. This meant that I long feared the consequences of even my most private transgressions. The beatings had a routine: I would be summoned by my mother and taken, without explanation, to my parents' room. This was the only time I ever entered my parents' room. There, said George, I would be left alone, sometimes for as long as an hour. Eventually, *pheeeeeeeuuuuuw,* my father would enter and slowly, wordlessly, select a belt – by this time my crying would already be uncontrollable – then he would pull my shorts down, lay me face down on his bed, and thrash me with all his force. I never knew how many swipes to expect and on some occasions he would pause only to resume after a few seconds' delay. As I say, these beatings were rare, and they were all the more awful because of it.

What may seem strange, George continued, is that I never doubted that my mother was my ally. Even though she was complicit with the rule I thought unfair – even though she was, in fact, its principal enforcer – I never doubted that she was fundamentally on my– ah, kestrel. Do you see? Do say if you want a shot of the binoculars. Had I been blessed with a sibling then perhaps I would have found him or her to be a more consistent ally, but as it was I turned again and again to my mother. Somewhat paradoxically, my mother both arranged my beatings and then comforted me afterwards. When I was able to walk back to my room, said George, I would close the door and burrow under the covers. At some point my mother would come into my room, finger to her lips, *pheeeeeeeuuuuuw,* whispering that everything was okay.

43

Ramón had a private room in which there was a neatly made single bed and a wardrobe. On the bedside table sat a bookmarked copy of Lenin's *"Left Wing" Communism: An Infantile Disorder.*

Ramón offered Yulia a glass of vodka, which he diluted with water from the corner sink. He had only one glass. Apropos of nothing, for Yulia had not indicated any need, he mentioned that the lavatory was at the end of the corridor. It occurred to Yulia that perhaps Ramón intended them to have sex and she was expected to perform some unknown preparation in the bathroom. Was it, perhaps, a Spanish thing? Did Spaniards cleanse before intercourse? Or was there in the zagranitze some contraceptive trick of which she was ignorant? Yulia was very clear that she would not be having intercourse with Ramón, and even if she were going to she had no idea what preparation he expected. It was therefore a surprise to her that after a demure pause she excused herself and visited the toilet.

She tried to pee but couldn't. Squatting over the hole, she touched the wetness between her legs, anticipating how her obvious arousal would demean her before Ramón. For this reason, or because she suspected he wanted her to cleanse, she splashed water around her vagina and anus and then looked for something with which to dry herself. Someone had kindly left in the basket torn pages of a medical journal. As she dried herself, it occurred to her that this cleansing was another bizarre action: there was no possibility she would allow Ramón to touch her, so why did it matter how lubricated she was?

44

George stopped on a two-plank-wide wooden bridge and said to me, above the shriek of water, A sea eagle nested up there last year. He was pointing upwards, where the gorge cracked the hillside, and the water appeared twined like white rope. My father, he continued, walking again, was a man of contradictions.

He was a member of the Independent Labour Party, then the Communist Party, and then, in the years immediately after the war, he briefly served as a Labour Party councillor. In 1952 he re-joined the Communist Party. By the time he left the Communist Party, in 1965, many of his views belonged to the political right; and yet, if quizzed, I believe he would still have voiced support for the dictatorship of the proletariat. Now, what is difficult to understand is that this man, who espoused extreme left politics all his life, held all the typical prejudices of the British middle class. He reviled sloppy speech, regularly corrected my mother's accent, and would complain to her if he overheard me dropping consonants. My father's father, you see, a docker, had been a notorious drinker and ne'er-do-well, and had left the upbringing of his six children to my grandmother. As a child my father had earned a free-place scholarship at a Central School, attended sixth form at a grammar school, and eventually went up to the University of Manchester. There was a huge discrepancy, said George, between his educational attainment and my mother's. I think she was somewhat in awe of him. With his education, however, he acquired contempt for those who had failed to improve themselves. He hated sloth, ignorance, untidiness, and alcoholism. He abhorred promiscuity, idleness, and the habit of rising late. He reviled hippies. I recall, said George, when I was twenty, I returned from university with uncut hair. My father told me to visit the barber or leave his house. *Pheeeeeeeuuuuuw,* I visited the barber.

My father re-joined the Communist Party when it adopted *The British Road to Socialism.* It was a reformist document and it committed the party to working within democratic structures. My mother also joined the party at this time. By this stage, my father was in demand as an orator – I remember seeing him speak at the King's Hall, Manchester, on the same platform as Rajani Palme Dutt and Len Johnson, the great black boxer of the 1920s – and I was used to him going away on Party business. Usually, he was called to London, and I would look forward to spending time alone with my mother. But in 1956 they went away together. My father had written a number of articles, mainly literary criticism, in the *Daily Worker* and other Marxist publications (these, said George, were cut out by my mother and glued into a scrapbook, which again you will find in the Working Class Movement Library), and in 1956 he was invited to deliver a paper at a literature conference in Budapest. My mother went too – for a holiday, I suppose.

I stayed with my father's sister, said George, whose children I despised and feared. The first I knew that something was wrong was when Cousin Simon, whom I remember as always having a wet rash between his mouth and nostrils, told me with delight that his parents had heard on the wireless that there was a war in Russia and everyone was going to starve. One cannot underestimate the fascination children find in the similarity between the proper noun *Hungary* and the adjective *hungry*. For two weeks all discussion of my parents' fate revolved around the question of food. I don't remember being unduly concerned, and when they failed to return on the planned day, *pheeeeeeeuuuuuw*, my major emotion was anger at having to spend yet longer with my cousins. Earlier that week, we had played a war game, in which I was forced to siege the local children's stronghold. They had built their fortress in the wasteland that bordered the allotments. Six or seven children repulsed my unwilling assaults with canes, buckets of water, and earth clods. The earth clods, collected from newly dug allotment plots, had the advantage of breaking into pieces on impact. This gave the impression of multiple explosions, said George, as though I was enduring a massive artillery bombardment. During one such bombardment, I was hit on the head by an earth-coated stone. I was knocked unconscious and needed five stitches. One reads about mothers who claim to have some intuitive awareness that harm has befallen their children. I wondered for years, said George, if on the day she died, my mother felt a sudden worry for her little boy back home.

45

When Yulia returned from the bathroom, she and Ramón sat on his bed, drank vodka, and talked in whispers. After half an hour, she began to worry that Ramón was bored and waiting for her to leave. It was therefore a great relief when he finally kissed her. He set the glass down and held eye contact – she could not have explained why he had chosen that moment over any other – and then, as they kissed, he clutched her buttock hard, the tips of his fingers pushing into the crevice of her bum. His breath tasted of vodka and kufta and when he forced his tongue into her mouth she meant to pull away. She also decided – very definitely – to move his hand from her bum, but instead she went limp in his clutch. Encouraged, his other hand moved to her breast, squeezing it painfully. Ramón appeared to read her pain as arousal, for as she gasped he forced himself on her with even greater urgency.

And then she realised that she wasn't going to resist him. The erotic rush of this realisation felt to her like an orgasm, and later, when she relived the moment in private pursuit of an actual orgasm, it seemed to her comparable to only one experience. When she had first worked at the military school, she had accepted an invitation to ride upon a glider. The young captain who had invited her, a handsome and connected Muscovite, had driven a jeep north to Lake Mingachevir and there had heaved the contraption to the top of a hundred-metre cliff. At the summit, Yulia stood in her leather harness, unable to even approach the edge. She would have screamed and resisted had she not very consciously calculated the acceptability of death. Abandoning her claim on life, she felt the wind lift the rattling craft and the two of them soared, pressed together above the purple water. The rush of helpless excitement she experienced then was not unlike the feeling she experienced in the act of submitting to Ramón.

When he unbuttoned his trousers, his penis was erect at a forty-five degree angle, and his frenulum was stretched taut by the force of his arousal. He seemed so urgently hard that Yulia was reminded of balsam pods in the late summer. As a child, she had loved to burst them with a stroke of her finger, or even with just the breath from her lips.

46

When we reached the end of the headland, George pointed to the medieval dun and we scrambled over grass and heather to sit on the few surviving slabs of the castle walls. Built on a rocky plateau, surrounded on three sides by vertical cliff faces, the dun must have once seemed impregnable. Now, the walls are waist-high at their grandest, the other stones spread over the headland in dykes and pens.

Even after Khrushchev's speech at the 20th Congress, continued George, even after the Poznan riots, nobody could have predicted the Hungarian Uprising. As far as I know, said George, on 23rd October, as the revolution began, the literature conference continued as planned. I imagine my father and his comrades leaving their lecture hall for a world that was totally different from the one they had strolled through hours before. When my father returned to the hotel, *pheeeeeeeuuuuuw*, my mother was missing. What happened after that, my father discussed only once. In the early 1970s, he was in hospital with kidney stones, said George, and after surgery, under influence of morphine, he told me that in the morning martial law had been declared and my mother still had not returned. My father thought that perhaps she had been detained as a security precaution. On the morning of October 24th, after the curfew was lifted, he walked to the university, hoping to pressure his hosts to pursue the matter with the AVO. He passed Soviet tanks on the Danube bridges and found armed men and women at the university. As he tried to return to the hotel, he heard shooting and artillery fire. He saw children carrying Molotov cocktails. He saw AVO men hung from lampposts. It occurred to my father, said George, that my mother may have sought refuge at the British legation. To get to the British legation, he had to again cross the Danube. He didn't know whom to be more afraid of: the Soviet troops, who might think him a British spy; or the counter revolutionaries (as he thought of them), who might kill him for being a Communist. My father says that he strolled across a bridge on which the drivers of two Soviet tanks were holding fraternal dialogues with armed Hungarian freedom fighters.

The entrance to the British Legation, my father told me, was hidden in an old shop, and one then had to climb several flights of stairs. The entrance was so inconspicuous, said George, that it took my father almost an hour to find it. Once inside, however, the building was unexpectedly large. My father recalled that they had in the legation a stock of food as well as whisky and Hungarian champagne. They drank champagne, he said, and they slept on the floor. Nobody was allowed to leave the legation for a week. Even the consular staff, whose families were scattered over the city's suburbs, dared not venture out. While staying there, my father met Edith Bone, who had helped found the PSUC in Catalonia during the Spanish Civil War, and who in 1949 had been arrested in Budapest, accused of spying, while working as a correspondent for the *Daily Worker*. After seven years in solitary confinement, Bone had been released by the freedom fighters. My father admitted to me that he was then unsure whose side he was on, and yet he did not leave the Party for a decade. He seemed to cling onto a sense of irritation at the uprising, and I suspect that he always blamed the resistance fighters for my mother's death. On November 2nd, as Soviet tanks gathered on the edge of the city, *pheeeeeeeuuuuuw*, the legation ordered the evacuation of the British community and the families of the consular staff. My father recalled that one of the diplomats drove at the front of their convoy, with a union flag draped on the bonnet of his car. The roads were still held by revolutionaries, the border was open, and the convoy reached Vienna that evening. My father returned home alone. Thanks to the efforts of the British legation, *pheeeeeeeuuuuuw*, he received confirmation of my mother's death shortly before Christmas. She was killed on October 24th. The cause of death was a fractured skull. She had been killed, *pheeeeeeeuuuuuw*, according to the official explanation, when she was struck on the head by an object thrown from on high by criminals. That is all I know. I'm sorry.

For a long time, we listened to the screech of seagulls and looked down a hundred feet to where the waves broke white against the cliff. Eventually, George pointed at a tiny white flower. Fairy flax, he said. There were loads of them rooted in the moss and soil that crawled around the ruined castle walls. Each flower was no bigger than a punctuation mark. George lifted his head and used his hand as a visor against the reflected sunlight. Look, he said, you can see the Isle of Rum. But I was watching a dot in the ocean: a motorboat, too distant for its movement to register, trailing a white thread through miles and miles of grey-blue sea.

Heritage: Newsletter of the Historical society of North West Scotland and the Hebridean Islands

Background to a restoration: Skye-based archaeologist George Steel tells Heritage why he dreams of restoring a nineteenth-century crofting village in Glen Spàirn

An ornithologist friend who visited me once compared me to a red shank. Red shanks are solitary birds and that morning we had observed one on its own on the beach. I live in Glen Spàirn where there are only two cottages, one of which, a holiday home, is often empty. I think my friend meant that my existence seemed isolated. In fact I feel connected to the island, the land, the birds, the botany, and the history of the people who have lived here over the centuries. I am not a Skye-man by birth but I have learned to feel connected here.

There are many sites of historical interest within walking distance of my home. On just one headland there is a burial cairn (part excavated), an unusual example of a broch (sadly dilapidated by centuries of dry stone walling), and a medieval dun on the promontory. Less than ten minutes from my cottage are the ruins of a nineteenth century crofting village. I am trying to get support for a project to restore the village as a monument and museum. I believe the story of Skye's crofters is very important to global as well as local history. I think it would be of great interest to those curious about historical epochs and to travellers from the new world who want to get a better understanding of their history.

After the suppression of the Jacobite Rising at Culloden, the Highland chiefs were forbidden from commanding armed men. Since their dominance had traditionally been based on military strength they now had to find another basis for their power. Money became more important to these chiefs and their crofter clansmen could not compete with the rents offered by sheep farmers and gentlemen hunters. This was the start of the clearances and the end of the feudal system. On the other side of the world, these changes sped the disentitlement of the Maori and Native Americans.

During the Napoleonic wars it was difficult to import Spanish barilla, which at that time was used to manufacture soap and glass. One viable alternative was kelp. As the value of kelp inflated the Highland lairds lobbied for legislation to increase the price of transatlantic freight beyond the means of the peasantry. The clearances continued but instead of being forced to emigrate, the crofters were relocated to smallholdings of infertile coastal land, where they had to supplement their incomes by collecting seaweed. Lord MacDonald made £14,000 a year selling kelp for £20 a ton but he only paid 30s a ton for its production. When the Napoleonic Wars ended the kelp industry collapsed. The crofters were left to support themselves from their diminished plots.

In 1846 the Hebridean potato crop failed. The crofters were too poor to afford any other food. They were eating roots and seaweed and whole families were dying of scurvy, typhus, and cholera. The fourth Lord MacDonald bought a cargo of meal in Liverpool to alleviate the suffering of his starving tenants, but meal prices were rising every day that winter, and so he sold the cargo in London at a substantial profit.

In 1882 the Braes crofters initiated a rent strike. Lord MacDonald's deputy factor applied for eviction orders and since he was also the Sheriff Officer he duly granted his own application. When Sheriff Office Martin delivered the order a jeering crowd surrounded him and 'Threatened violence on his person.' The crowd ceremonially burned his documents.

The police arrested five of those deemed responsible for the assault but crofters armed themselves with pikes and stones and liberated the prisoners. Soon the crofters raised an army of over a thousand and marched on the Dunvegan police headquarters. They were armed with graips, hayforks and scythes. Over the next two years the rebellion spread across the Hebrides. Rents went unpaid. Fences were cut in the night. Land was illegally occupied. Telegraph poles were cut down. Roads were blocked with boulders. On the 10th November 1884 William Gladstone dispatched gunboats HMS Forrester and HMS Banterrer to the Isle of Skye. The troopship HMS Assistance supported the invasion with 350 marines.

When the marines came ashore they were met by a village empty except for what [continued on page 7]

Belfast, 1932

47

I returned to Cheltenham in September. I had been studying for eight months and had yet to write a word of the thesis. I had written notes – copious, voluminous notes – on Elsie's life and Descartes' philosophy. But I had written nothing permanent, and I had submitted nothing to my supervisor.

It seemed to me that Professor Thrub trusted me and respected my creative process. He had not once contacted me to check my productivity. In fact, the occasional emails that I sent to assure him of my scholarly engagement had all gone unanswered. More worryingly, my requests for assistance with the university's labyrinth bureaucracy had also gone unanswered. I received daily emails demanding Thrub's signature on something called a Progress Report Form, and I was aware that sooner or later I'd have to risk going to see the Professor in person. When I did, I wanted to present him with my opening statement. And so, in September 2009, I began to write Elsie's biography.

48

Elsie Angelenetta Stewart was born in Belfast in 1918. Her mother had been born in Casalattico, in Southern Italy, and below her Ulster accent an Italian lilt always remained detectable. Elsie's mother was a big-breasted woman with long dark hair, who had converted to Protestantism before marrying Elsie's father. Elsie's father was a stern working man, who was involved little with the upbringing of Elsie or her siblings.

Elsie's abiding memory of her Belfast childhood was of the greyness. It rained so often that the damp never seemed to lift, and a sulphurous smog hung over the city from the heavy industry that thrived before the depression. Every day, at five o'clock, the factory horns sounded and Elsie knew her father would be on his way home for tea. At this time, she would go to help her mother in the kitchen. The kitchen was the warmest room in the house and the steam would rise from Elsie's damp clothes, merging with the smoke from the kitchen range. Although born in Italy, Elsie's mother cooked traditional dishes such as champ (mashed potatoes with spring onions), the Ulster version of Colcannon. There was always a pot of soup stewing on the range.

When her father came home, the sound of his work boots resounded on the paved floor. He would drop a few coins – farthings and ha'pennies – into the money tin, test its weight, and shake it. Though coins always seemed to go into this tin, the tin seemed always to be near empty. When Elsie's father had managed to save a bit more – a few shillings, maybe half a crown – he would put the money for safe storage in the wooden wind-up clock. Then they would sit to eat.

Before eating, the family always said grace. Then Elsie and her siblings would describe what they'd done during the day. After dinner, Elsie's father would smoke his pipe and read the paper in front of the fire. At this time, Elsie and her siblings were free to play out on the street. They'd play hopscotch or skipping or fives, dodging the delivery horses' manure until dusk fell and the lamplighter passed with his long pole. Then Elsie knew it was time for bed.

On Monday, she was made to bathe in the copper pot, and if her turn was last then the water would be black. Then she would run out to the outside toilet, braving the dark and spiders. She would listen as her pee splashed into the pit far below. When she returned inside, her mother would lead her to bed by paraffin lamp. She shared a bed with her two sisters and they would huddle together for warmth. It seemed that at any one time, one of them would smell of goose grease, which their mother rubbed on their chests as a cure for the common cold. One by one, they would fall asleep, listening to the hacking cough of their next door neighbour, the tinkle of their brother using the chamber pot, and drunken rows from the street. In the morning, they would wake to the clatter of the early trams, the clip-clop of the milkman's horse, and the melodic chink of bottles.

49

After eight months in the office, I was yet to see Samuel. On one occasion, when the room seemed empty, I had dared to peek behind the bookcase, but dusty tomes and undrunk cups of tea were the only signs that Samuel had ever been there. Meanwhile, Jez and I continued to struggle for common ground. He was disappointed to learn that he was sharing an office with an atheist, even more disappointed to learn that this atheist was pro-gay, and most disappointed of all to learn that this pro-gay atheist didn't follow sports and had no interest in the Tampa Bay Buccaneers. Mainly he talked to me about women. Near the yellowed Hebrew alphabet, he had affixed a wall chart, which every week he updated to reflect how long it had been since I had last made love. Obi went even further: on one occasion, he tried to arrange a meeting between me and a girl from his church. You will understand, examiners, how lonely a researcher's life can be, when I tell you that I seriously considered his offer.

'I just saw the prettiest girl of all time,' I said, turning on my computer.

'Woah-ho!' said Jez, standing up to high-five me.

'Just now, as I was going to the library.'

'What's she look like?'

'She's lovely.'

'She Blonde? Brunette? Curvy? Petite?'

'She's called Lempi.'

'You know her, huh?'

'I shall make some tea,' said Obi.

'You listening to this, Samuel? You wanna get your ass downstairs and try to land this English honey. She's English, right?'

'Finnish.'

'Oh, so she's a blonde Scandinavian babe?'

'Finland's not in Scandinavia.'

'Man, I gotta tell you, me and Samuel, we were starting to think you were gay.'

'She's half-Finnish, half-French. She speaks a dozen languages.'

'I am very happy for you,' said Obi. 'Are you not happy for our friend, Samuel?'

'Thank you,' I said, logging in.

'Is your suit welcome?'

'I'm sorry?'

'Are your feelings requited?'

'Obi, shut up, damnit. This is England, man.'

'Of course not,' I said.

'In England, you don't have to give a girl's father six goats before you can touch her toosh.'

'This is difficult.'

'She knocked you back, huh?'

'No.'

'You're too scared to ask her out?'

'I'm sorry,' I said, beginning to type. 'I'm kind of in flow just now.'

'Samuel, tell this pecker-dick to grow a pair.'

'When you meet the girl you are meant to marry, you shall feel it here.' Obi reached around me and pressed a point between my heart and stomach. 'There is one that God intends for you and you shall know when you find her.'

'Amen,' said Jez. 'When I met my babe in July ninety-eight, I knew I'd met the girl God intended me to sleep with; two months later, when I met her little sister, I knew I'd met the girl He intended me to think about while we were doing it.'

'He works in mysterious ways.'

'Ain't that a fact.'

'Your tea, Jeremy.'

'Goddamn it, Obi.'

50

In 1932, Elsie discovered boys. More particularly, she discovered William Logan, a young man five years her senior. Elsie was only thirteen, and, as is the case for many girls of her age, her attitude towards boys was ambivalent. It certainly wasn't dispassionate, for the mere thought of Billy Logan was enough to make her blush and giggle and tingle inside; rather, it was conflicted. She might well have blushed and giggled, but she also felt painfully anxious whenever she thought of him. She desired to get closer to him but felt that to do so would involve sacrificing some unrecoverable part of herself. And so when Billy wooed her, she responded with indifference, which, of course, made Billy woo her all the more.

In October 1932, he escalated his courtship. He bought her a bag of chips and persuaded the fryer to chuck in some loose bits of batter. This was during the depression, when long queues of bare-footed, bow-legged children stood in the cold, dangling pillowcases, hoping to purchase three-pence worth of stale buns; when younger siblings scavenged for cinders at the railway yard or waited in lines outside the gasworks; when Belfast's poor bought flour bags from Rank's or Andrews' and stitched them together to make sheets and even bridal underwear (see Munck & Rolston, 1987, p-76). This was a time when a bag of chips could easily turn a girl's head. While Elsie was still munching, her hands tingling and pink from the warmth, Billy asked her whether she fancied accompanying him to the cinema; needless to say, she said yes. Who knows, she might well have married him and never left Belfast, but on the day of their cinema date, Wednesday 5th October, history intervened.

On that day, Elsie walked towards the cinema alone. Billy had offered to call in for her, but she had made an excuse, worried that relatives and neighbours would see her older suitor. Soon after leaving home, she encountered a strange sight. A crowd of men, all wearing shabby suits, bonnets, and ties, hurried through central Belfast, clenching their fists and singing a popular novelty song from 1922: 'Yes We have No Bananas.'

This was the time of the Outdoor Relief agitation, when Protestant and Catholic workers united to protest the conditions of the unemployed. Heavy industry had collapsed and among shipbuilders (to give just one example), the unemployment rate was over 73% (Bell, 1994). The day before, the *Belfast News-Letter*, a leading Unionist daily, had published figures revealing the suffering of Belfast's poor relative even to that experienced in other industrial cities: in Manchester an unemployed man with a wife and one child received 21s per week, in Liverpool a similar family received 23s per week, and in Glasgow the rate was 25s, 3d; but in Belfast the Outdoor Relief grant for such a family was just 12s (Devlin, 1981, p-121). Six days later, the protests would culminate in resistance to armed police and a day of cross-community rioting that would see two protesters – John Keenan and Samuel Baxter – shot dead.

The protesters that Elsie saw on October 5th carried banners saying 'down with the baby starvers' and 'struggle don't starve' (Ó Catháin, 2003, p-55). And they sang an oddly-cheery novelty song because, as Paul Bew explains in the preface to Paddy Devlin's *Yes We have No Bananas*, 'the musical heritage of both sides reflected the traditional Orange and Green divisions (…) so it was that 'Yes We Have No Bananas' – the only neutral tune available – became Belfast's anthem of progress' (1981, p-VII). Elsie listened to their singing and to her surprise she joined in. She watched the men pass and then – for reasons she couldn't easily have explained – she abandoned her cinema trip and turned to follow their procession. In other words, she stood Billy up. In that moment, one possible version of her life disappeared from history.

51

My opening chapter continued in this vein, but I won't force you to read any more. Excepting the tasters above, I was dissuaded from using any of this early prose by my supervisor. However, when I'd completed the first 5000 words, I felt delighted with my output. I emailed it to Professor Thrub with pride.

TO: Thrub, F.K. 11/09/2009   15:13

Subject: A sample of work and musings on questions philosophical and administra…

Attachments: Elsie1.doc; RPF.docx

Dear Professor,

I hope this email finds you well and I hope the pressures of preparing for the new academic year are not too onerous. I know how very busy you are – especially at this time – and I'm very sorry to add to your workload.

Since we last spoke, I have made – I hope! – good progress on the thesis. That said, there are – of course – many areas in which I need your expert guidance. As you will see, I have attached the beginnings of my thesis. I have tracked down and interviewed George Steel, the son of Elsie Stewart (the subject of this creative biography). I visited him at his home on the Isle of Skye and from him I have gleaned much important information. Thanks to these insights I have begun writing about Elsie's childhood and adolescence in Belfast. Next week I am again going away again but – don't worry! – my trip is for research purposes: I have realised that I will be better able to complete this chapter after a research visit to Elsie's hometown.

I will be fascinated to hear your thoughts on the attached material – though there is of course no rush; I know you have a very hectic schedule. In particular, I wonder if you could advise me your thoughts regarding how best I can incorporate my critique of the Cartesian subject into the creative work? This is the other area in which I've been working: I have been studying Descartes in light of my earlier reading of Nietzsche, and I want to interrogate the possibility of an autonomous – transcendent – chooser capable of 'deciding'. Forgive me if that is a little unclear – as I say, my thinking is a bit muddled and I could benefit from

your expert guidance! Needless to say, I am
free and keen to meet whenever there is an
opening in your busy schedule.

Finally, I'm afraid I have another rather
prosaic request: I'm being pressured
somewhat by the university bureaucracy
to produce a signed copy of a 'Research
Progress Form' and other paperwork. I hope
what I've attached reassures you that my
progress is satisfactory and if so I'd be
exceedingly grateful if you could append
your electronic signature and return the
form to me – I'm very sorry to be an
inconvenience.

Apologies for rambling and thank you so
much for your help. I look forward to our
discussions.

Sincerest best wishes, etc..

Examiners, I sent this email and waited. And waited. And then,
four days later, the day before I was due to leave for Belfast,
I logged on in the office and saw that my inbox contained a
response from Thrub. It was one of half-a-dozen emails and
such was my nervousness that I purposefully left Thrub's
message to the end.

Highchair, Sue   14/09/2009   14:58

Smethwick's House

Cc: SH users all

Dear Colleagues

I have been advised by the Estates
Department that as from now (today) and
henceforth, I am to enforce the removal of
all individual electric fans as they are not
permitted in University rooms/offices. This

was upheld at the health and safety review over seen by TCOM. Further, I have also been asked to effect the removal of all electric kettles etc. from offices/rooms. From now on colleagues are to utilise the kitchen facilities on the Ground Floor for the provision of hot drinks.

Best,

Sue

Unthung, Hannah   14/09/2009 16:37

RE: RD712

Cc: Thrub, F.K.

Hello again,

The original form could not be passed at the Research Council advisory team sub-group meeting in July as it did not carry your supervisor's signature. A new copy of the form needs to be submitted since in the previous version your signature is dated July and is hence out of date. We need to receive a hard copy accompanied by a new RD45/C which must carry the signature of your HOD or DOS (the signatures on the original RD45/C are also out of date and forms must be presented simultaneously to the next advisory team sub-group meeting if the documents are to be put forward for consideration by the Research Council).

Hannah

Hannah Unthung

Assistant to the Administration Officer (Research)

7G Navet Building, Krap Campus, Cheltenham University

Godturn, Ben   14/09/2009   16:52

RE: Smethwick's House

Cc: SH users all

Dear Sue,

Thank you for your email and your efforts in keeping us updated on this trying situation. I have a concern however, particularly with regard to staff on the higher floors of Smethwick's House in terms of access to tea/coffee making facilities. Exclusive reliance on the Ground Floor kitchen seems to entail an inherent health and safety risk what with the transference of hot beverages via several flights of stairs, while at the same time 'traffic' on the stairs will be increased as a result of these measures. Might it be worthwhile considering some form of shared arrangement for staff on higher floors? This would not only reduce the prospect of stair-related incident but would also be time-economical and conducive to increased productivity. Any assistance you can offer with this situation would be very much appreciated.

Kind regards

Ben Godturn

Gumthorpe, A. 15/09/2009   09:13

Enterprise focus announcement

Cc: Users all

We are pleased to announce the launch of the university's new enterprise strategy as approved by the Future Visions Entrepreneurial Initiative working group, in association with the University's Think Change Project strategy committee. The following 5 key mission points have been agreed.

To recognise and celebrate the entrepreneurial spirit and innovative enterprise of our staff and students.

To promote entrepreneurialism and fresh thinking as a keystone of university strategy.

To innovate new approaches to learning to ensure that local businesses and other stakeholders get the most out of their university.

To enhance the student experience by recognising enterprise initiative as key to our core project of promoting student employability.

Through promoting and rewarding income-generating industry partnerships, to foster an entrepreneurial culture of enterprise and innovation as a keystone of creating a dynamic and sustainable university.

I'm sure you will all join me in congratulating the committee on its work.

Regards,

A. Gumthorpe

Highchair, Sue 15/09/2009 11:15

RE: Smethwick's House

Cc: SH users all

Dear Richard/All

I have asked H & S Manager's advice on this. It may be that we will have to close the kitchen and all staff go to the Refectory for their drinks.

Sue

I closed the above email and returned to my inbox. **1 unread message. Thrub, F.K.**. I paused, stood up, strolled around the office. The theologians were at some bible conference and the only noise was the hum of the strip-lights. I retook my seat, spun two circles, bent a paper clip near straight. 'How bad can it be?' I said aloud.

Thrub, F.K. 11/09/2008 15:13

RE: A sample of work and musings on
questions philosophical and administra…

Cc:

What is this? Angela's fucking Ashes? This
is the most platitudinous boring crap I
have ever tried to read.

What the fuck's an electronic signature?

Regarding the Cartesian subject, etc.,
read all major works of Kant, Hegel,
Marx, Nietzsche, Heidegger, Sartre, Lacan,
Merleau-Ponty, Foucault, Derrida, and
Baudrillard. Until then, sod off.

In the meantime, desist from using personal
pronouns or any other descriptions that
imply originative action.

Thrub

Professor F.K. Thrub BA Ph.D. FRSA FRSE FBA

Professor of English and Cultural Studies,
Cheltenham University

52

...?

53

You can imagine, examiners, that I flew to Belfast a troubled man. En route I pondered Thrub's response. Even allowing for Thrub's polemical style, I had to accept that he hadn't enthused. And what did he mean that I should desist from using personal pronouns or any other descriptions that imply originative action? Was that even possible?

And then, somewhere over the Irish Sea, I realised what I had to do. The flight attendants were blocking the aisle with the trolley – some currency or change problem had developed between them and a passenger who had already bitten into his tuna baguette – and a blockage of two would-be toilet goers had formed to the trolley's rear. The man in the aisle seat, two seats to my left, was suffering some sort of aviation-related health problem. He was sweating and clenching his facial muscles and occasionally grunting. The whole scene made me think of constipation. I stood up. 'Excuse me,' I said. I needed them all to move. Suddenly, urgently, I needed to get into the overhead lockers. I needed my notepad. I needed to write. I needed to write something defiantly new, something ground-breaking, something–

54

Belfast, October 1932. Noise. A discrete empirical reality. Longitudinal waves, sinusoidal waves:

Some of these waves (not necessarily the ones above) are of frequencies between 20 Hz and 20,000 Hz, and these waves are about to enter history. Amplified changes of pressure are transduced into electrical impulses when they affect the fluid in the inner ear so that the membranes are, kind of, squeezed, which causes the little hair cell things to produce electrical impulses, which affect the ganglion cells in the basilar membrane, disturbing things called 'axons', which are long protrusions from these ganglion cell things that form the auditory nerve. In other words, these waves are on their way to becoming sound, are on their way to the brain, where, perhaps, they will enter consciousness, earn their own sign(s), and become part of history. It is an act of agency to turn these waves into a sign and yet there's no choice here. No more choice here than in the flow of a domino rally. These electrical impulses are thrown, crashing this way and that, jangling synapses and neurones, like a storm hitting the clangy parts of a wind chime.

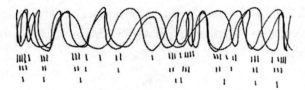

Maybe somewhat like that, perhaps.

55

On my first afternoon in Belfast, I visited the Linen Hall Library. It is a warm, hushed place, where, in addition to the Northern Ireland Political Collection and the Irish and Local Studies library, visitors can access the Genealogy and Heraldry resources. Patrons pad between aisles, whispering if speaking at all, so that the loudest noises are street-level shouts and horns. My target was the birth records, stored in a card index on the fourth floor. Elsie Angelenetta Stewart, I discovered, was born to Samuel Charles and Giacinta Carlina Stewart, on 16th October 1918. When I saw Elsie's name I hammered the air and shouted 'Yes! Splendid!' and stood there, long after I had recorded the card's meagre details, reluctant to slide closed the drawer.

Then I rode the 15, through Botanic, past conifer driveways and detached houses, and alighted, at the top of Malone, near Balmoral Avenue. The Public Records Office of Northern Ireland is guarded by a security hut and a barbed-wire-topped fence and concrete road blocks. It was often a site of frustration during my research – records were unavailable or unhelpful, or I couldn't find them, or they were closed to the public until 2032 – but my first visit was marked by another simple success. As I was waiting for RUC Special Branch records (T/2805), I noticed that back issues of the Belfast and Ulster Street Directory were on open access, stacked on shelves in the centre of the room: in 1932, Samuel Charles Stewart was resident at 155 Sandy Row. His occupation – frustratingly vague this – was recorded as 'machinist'.

56

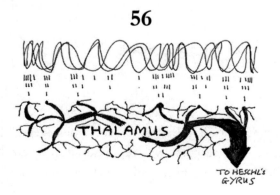

57

The next morning, I woke on Barry's couch. Barry, my old friend from undergrad days, lives in Andytown (where he keeps his background to himself), so once I'd showered and dressed, I caught the bus onto the Falls Road. I rode past the big Bobby Sands and the H block commemorations, the starry ploughs, the Basque and Palestinian murals, the tricolours, the Virgin Marys, the fresh graffiti near Castle Street – 'Six million Jews & they should have been Protestants' – and then, hangover kicking in, I walked past Europa and turned right towards Sandy Row. At the entrance to Sandy Row, right in the centre of Belfast, in an inverted reflection of the Republican mural in Derry, a man in a balaclava wields a Kalashnikov beside the slogan: 'YOU ARE NOW ENTERING LOYALIST SANDY ROW HEARTLAND OF SOUTH BELFAST ULSTER FREEDOM FIGHTERS.' I stopped where the kerbstones were coloured red, white, and blue, for a moment too scared to continue. The rain threw rings onto puddles and the only noise was the traffic shooshing surface water on Great Victoria Street. Then, from an unseen construction site, there came a clash of steel, and a scatter of seagulls shrieked towards the bus station. I was aware how conspicuous I looked, standing in the rain, and so I began to walk, shivering in the autumnal damp, onto Sandy Row.

Elsie's old house, when I found it, had a blue door and double-glazed windows, from which stretched across the street faded bunting left over from the twelfth of July. Across the street, a man was lashing a mould-patterned refrigerator onto a metal flatbed with tangled lengths of clothes rope. For a moment, I didn't know whether to keep walking or to turn back the way I had come, and then, almost as if a hallucination, Elsie appeared in my mind as a child. My vision blurred and the years dissolved and I felt as though I could see her. She was not quite fourteen, all cheek and collarbones and restless hunger, in a greying blouse and a home-hemmed dress.

Examiners, as I stood there, I imagined her walking to meet William Logan. I imagined her passing the Sandro Cinema because, according to the 1932 Belfast and Ulster Street Directory, the Sandro Cinema was located at 69 Sandy Row, between Elsie's house and the centre of town. I first heard of it in Munck and Rolston's excellent oral history of 1930s Belfast. Geordie Loughrey remembered the unemployed demonstration clattering past the 'old Sandro picture house' on Wednesday the 5th October 1932 (Munck & Rolston, 1987, p-28). Had Elsie encountered this demonstration, how would she have reacted? The depression of the 1930s produced a global socio-economic conflict that was resolved by World War Two, but what dictates how one life intersects with a macro-historical conflict?

58

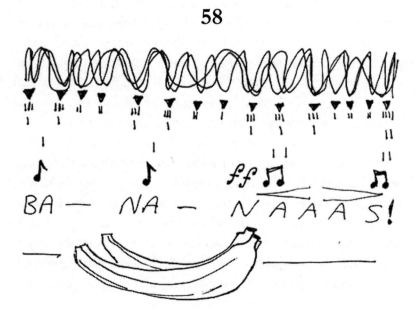

BA — NA — NAAAS!

59

I spent the afternoon in the Newspaper Library, which is on a side street, behind the offices of *The Belfast Telegraph*. One enters the Newspaper Library via an intercom-operated door, which doesn't suggest public access, so for several minutes I paced the alley, searching for a non-existent main entrance. Once inside, I found what I wanted on microfilm and then requested to see the original papers. An attendant wheeled a pair of metre-tall books from the archive and thumped them down on the angled reading desk, displacing cartoonish blasts of dusty air. I took a silly pleasure in lifting my feet up, perching on the stool, and imagining I was living in a giant world, or that I was some Disney character, struggling to open a normal-sized book, in a whole-hearted way that viewers found endearing. Then, as I turned the pages, the pink-brown articles cracked and crumbled, their corners breaking off and forming a sawdust pile in the ridge at the bottom of the sloping desk. At first this worried me – I thought I was doing something wrong – but as I looked around, I saw that these sawdust piles were gathering on every desk. The other surprise was that some articles and pictures had been cut out. For instance, when I turned to pages seven and eight of the Tuesday 11th October 1932 edition of *The Belfast Telegraph*, I found, right in the middle of page seven, a rough rectangle of white background – a gaping hole – where some unknown piece of news had been removed. These missing bits occur frequently enough that there must be some systemic explanation (I don't think it can be only that members of the public are stealing the past), and yet the rough-edged cuts hint at a violence that doesn't seem like the work of a professional archivist. They reminded me, somehow, of the holes hacked into Hungarian flags when rebel workers removed the hammer and sickle insignias.

60

Outside the Sandro Picture House, Wednesday 5th October 1932, a stomach contracts on nothing. This has happened a thousand times but only now, perhaps because the contracting muscles are exhausted, perhaps because the concentration of sugar in the blood is low, perhaps because the intestine is empty, or perhaps just because of the magic socio-historical appropriateness of the moment, does the contraction produce an effect, not confined to the hypothalamus or thalamus, but logged somehow, thrown into history, so that this contraction enters the symbolic universe, being, in short, a pang of hunger.

In twentieth century Europe there is hunger and there is hunger and the hunger here is not the protracted pain of starvation, not yet the collapsed and swollen bodies, the villages distractingly quiet because all the dogs have been eaten, the trees stripped of bark, the self-digestion or cannibalism; no, this is the hunger of bread and tea, of long bare-footed, bow-legged queues dangling pillowcases for three pence worth of stale buns, while younger siblings scavenge for cinders at the railway yard or wait in lines outside the gasworks; it is a commonplace everyday billion many times felt pang of hunger, but it is advancing into history, from subject to object, in a fraction of a second: hungry and food and Jacob's and White's; Taig and Silver, men, Billy, police and Jesus; Jekyll and Hyde, Classic, stalls; gargle and gaggle and glup. But the word that emerges, the word that is thrust into history, is 'bananas'. Bananas. In the perisylvian association cortex, in Wernicke's area and Heschl's gyrus, it is this word – bananas – that bounces into history: bananas! Bananas! In great fist-clenching surges of noise: Yes! We have no bananas We have no bananas today.

An advertising board – I *insist* on Jacob's Cream Crackers – crashes through a shop window and hands and arms cover ears and face, eyes blink shut, heads duck, and all this happens before the thought of it; then the reflex finally enters history.

A reflex is pure action only objectivised after it has happened, as opposed to conscious actions that are logged, transcribed, in advance. Consciousness, to this perspective, is a sort of dialectical process whereby certain actions and experiences generate the idea of themselves. For example, why does one stomach contraction generate a commentary – i.e., become an object of consciousness (a pang of hunger, say) – when other contractions do not? Why is it that just then the movement of my right index finger, picking at a hinge of dead skin near the nail of my thumb, should generate a second level analysis – should become, in its own very small way, an object of history – when I suspect my finger had been picking away for some seconds, as pure action, lost to reflection like a heartbeat in sleep?

Instead of banners the crowd waves signs ripped from the tram stops in Shaftesbury Square: White's Table Jellies – Try these jellies for tea; Tennent's 6d (not a light ale but a high strength stimulating and nourishing drink for winter or summer); Henry Blossom Boot Polish – Makes black or brown shoes brilliant. Four pence for the front stalls at the Classic and that picture they say is a dirty picture about this fellow that takes a potion and turns into some sort of devil but how else are you to see a picture at a time like this but with a fellow though Jesus ma would– The crowd is pulling out pillows and blankets, long curtains and embroidered double sheets, dragging them onto Sandy Row, holding them flapping in the wind. And those wee knees (still pink with the memory of childhood) bend towards the crowd, and a small voice cries Yes! We have no bananas/

No bananas today, soaring with the applause of shattering glass, as the sheets and blankets spread themselves in the breeze, and the reckless armada moves north.

61

'See, that's what I'm talkin about, right there,' said Barry. 'Is that not the biggest pile of pseudo-intellectual, obscurantist, bourgeois shite ye ever heard?' We were in the Duke of York, discussing Thrub's prohibition on personal pronouns. 'So hold the fuck up a minute, let me get this straight. This professor cunt, right, wants ye tae write a biography—'

'A fictionalised biography.'

'Wi no personal pronouns?'

'I think so.'

'And personal pronouns are like I, you, she, he, right?'

'That's my understanding.'

'I'd tell him tae suck my fuckin balls, so I would.'

'He said that I should desist from using personal pronouns or implying originative action until I'd read various theorists.'

'Who does he want ye tae read, like?'

'Kant—'

'Kant? Listen, Kant can suck my balls. Kant's fuckin... Here's yer problem wi Kant, right: the Gesinnung. The Kantian Gesinnung, right, is the— Ye've read Sartre, right?'

'I've read a bit.'

'Well, Sartre can suck my balls as well. The world is contingent, right, it just is. Of course it fuckin is. Human existence is de trop, superfluous, without character or reason, right?'

'Okay.'

'So there's no essential meaning and all meaning is a human projection, aye? And this gives humanity great power – freedom,

Sartre would say – to create our own meaning. The least shite bit in Sartre is about our distance from ourselves as we're described, right? Man is free cause he's not a self but a presence-to-self. Ye know all the famous examples of how we can always escape our roles – the fuckin waiter and all that there? See, self-consciousness implies a reflexive negation, a condition of always being other than how we're described. Fair enough, aye? Except that it's just Hegel with lipstick and a short skirt on. Anyway, so, Sartre differentiates between Being in itself – etre en-soi – and Being for itself – etre pour-soi. Etre pour-soi refers to all those aspects of human life that involve consciousness; etre en-soi refers to all the physical stuff distinct from consciousness. Now but listen cause here's the bit that melts yer head: for Sartre, consciousness is always free cause it must be the product of self-consciousness, cause if it wasn't it would be an unconscious consciousness, which is a contradiction. Right, that's not even worth tryin tae get yer head round cause even if that's true, right, even if self-consciousness is constitutive of consciousness, what the fuck constitutes self-consciousness? Sartre's theory would fall on its arse if consciousness was something externally derived, but–'

'What's this got to do with Kant?'

'Sartre's ontology is fucked cause he's fuckin adamant consciousness doesn't emerge from the unconscious or the physiological, right so, and Kant, right– Kant… Listen, the most fucked up bit of Sartre is the "original choice" made in forming the "fundamental project," which structures a person's subsequent goals and aspirations, right? Sartre calls this the "fundamental act of freedom" and here's where Kant comes in, right. This is the same shite as the Kantian Gesinnung, right? The Gesinnung was Kant's description of a person's underlying beliefs and motivations and all what have ye. There's no point goin intae the fuckin details or whatever cause, basically, the point is that somehow ye choose yer own fuckin character, right? And the problem wi this, right, is that the cunt only introduces the Gesinnung to provide the beliefs and motivations necessary for any choice to be made, aye? So it seems a wee bit fuckin illogical, d'ye not think, that those motivations can themselves be chosen? Yer man's got the same problem as Sartre. Also, even if we do accept the original choice can be called a choice, then if all subsequent choices depend on this choice, are we not choosing our whole destiny in one choice? A choice which isnae even a choice? It's like voting in bourgeois democracy: ye vote some cunts in an ye're stuck wi the bastards and there's fuck all ye can do when they invade Iraq or whatever. Right, that's Kant fucked. Who else did he tell ye tae read?'

62

In an article written to commemorate the fiftieth anniversary of the Outdoor Relief Agitation, the *Irish Times* described a catalysing incident of unrest at the Lisburn Road Workhouse, where today stands the City Hospital:

> On Wednesday October 5th, about 200 single men applied for "indoor relief" in the workhouse to dramatise their claim for assistance, which would cost less than it would to keep them in the workhouse (…). They caused chaos in the grim old building with its 19th-century regulations, refusing to go to bed at 8 p.m. and holding a sing song in the dormitories until the R.U.C. were called. They were ejected the next morning when they demanded eggs for breakfast. (Farrell, 1982, p-14)

But maybe this is only part of the story, the progeny of a bowdlerised Communist Party version of history, because exactly fifty years before the *Irish Times* article, *The Northern Whig and Belfast Post* presented the testimony of the master of the workhouse:

> [He] was sorry to say that not withstanding that the accommodation was both comfortable and sufficient a section of these inmates took advantage of the situation and destroyed quite a large quantity of clothing and hardware provided for their use as well as cracking and breaking panes of glass. (October 12th, 1932, p-3)

Which story should we accept? Examiners, if you write to the Head of Access at the Public Records Office, and present your scholarly credentials, and complete an undertaking regarding the Official Secrets Act, and earn access to BG/7/G/182 – Belfast Board of Guardians: Indoor Register for the year of 1932 – then you will find, beneath the date October 5th, an unusually large list of names, including, hard to read in that calligraphic hand, one William Logan. Why was he there? Why were any of them there?

63

'Hegel–'

'Hegel? Oh, fuck right off. Hegel can suck my balls as soon as Kant's finished.'

'You've read Hegel?'

'Of course I've not read Hegel. Listen, I took this wee girl out the other week, right, and she's a middle class type from fuckin Holywood or somewhere, so I've taken her out for dinner, ye know? And I says to her, what sort of cuisines are ye intae? And she says she'd quite like to go for Chinese. Grand, I say, Chinese it is. So we go to this posh place on the Lisburn Road and we get sat down and they bring the menus and all this here. And I'm lookin for the fuckin half-and-half sweet and sour like but I have to make do with, I don't know, fuckin prawns or something it was. Right so, they bring out all this here food and I'm set to start eatin when I notice there's no fuckin cutlery. I'm about to pull yer man over and say here what's wi this when the wee girl opens this packet and starts clickety clicketing with her fuckin chopsticks, right? Right, so that's the deal, okay. And I don't want to be scunnered as some lumpen cunt, right, so I open my packet and I try tae do the same thing she's doin. And after a minute or two there's food on the table cloth, food on the floor, food on my fuckin face, and fuck all's goin anywhere near my mouth, right? So the wee girl says to me, do ye not know how tae use yer chopsticks there? She's half-finished her plate by this point. I don't normally eat Chinese, I say. I just fancied it cause you did, right? And she starts tae laugh a wee bit and she says tae me, have ye never learned? And I get a wee bit pissed off now cause sure as I fancy her I don't like being looked down on cause I'm workin class, right? So I says tae her, no, as it happens, I haven't. And d'ye know why? Cause as a laddie I was taught tae use more sophisticated utensils: ye might have encountered them, love, they're called a knife and fork. What I'm sayin, right, is that there's no need tae go backwards if ye've already mastered a more sophisticated version. I can ride a mountain bike, right, but I'd be shite on a penny farthing. I've read Marx, right, and I'm no more likely to read Hegel than I am to eat my dinner wi a pair of fuckin knittin needles. Who else?'

'Marx.'

'...Who else?'

'Nietzsche.'

'*Nietzsche*? Listen, all ye need tae know about Nietzsche, right, is that he had fuckin biscuits for bones and cause he couldnae get a rocket he over-compensated wi all that *übermensch* shite. I'll see his will to power when he's suckin my balls. What's that mate? Ye've gone off Wagner, have ye? Very good. Suck my balls.'

'Come on, Barry: genealogies, affirmation, the critique of metaphysics, the–'

'I'll tell ye somethin else about Nietzsche: it was an anarchist, Max Stirner, who wrote "God is dead" and most of the other decent bits in Nietzsche. Read Stirner's *The Ego and His Own,* then go back to Nietzsche, then suck my balls. That's how it works, see: all interesting ideas come from radical thinkers who don't hold university positions. It's a fact. Then some over-privileged fuckwit comes along and takes the credit just cause he knows the right people and sucks the right cocks. It's like the Situationists and Baudrillard. Don't even get me started on Baudrillard. Vaneigem and Debord shite on Baudrillard from the fuckin moon. The Gulf War didn't happen? Suck the charcoaled bollocks of a severely burned Iraqi corpse.'

'Heidegger.'

'Heidegger? He was a fuckin Nazi. I wouldn't even let Heidegger suck my balls.'

'Lacan?'

'Lacan thinks my balls symbolise the acquisition of language. Lacan has a dream in which he bites my balls off and inducts me into the Symbolic Order. For that reason, Lacan can't suck my balls.'

'Foucault?'

'Foucault actually would suck my balls. Foucault would take a fuckin ticket to suck my balls. Late Foucault especially pisses me off. Create ourselves as a work of art? Suck my balls. Techniques of self, le souci de soi? It fucks up for the same reason as all theories of self-formation fuck up: there has tae be an agent that does the forming, and this agent has tae be formed, and the agent that has tae form it has tae be formed, and, somehow, if the theories are to crawl out from up their own arseholes, they have tae account for an original choice, a self that creates itself and all that there. Ye know yer woman Butler? The other day I was reading that fuckin Gender Trouble, ye know? And she's giving it tight tae Simone de Beauvoir, right, and she's like, aye, good one, but who does the becoming? Ye're still supposing some agent or cogito or what have you who could, according tae some mysterious power, in principle take on some other character or whatever. Simone de Beauvoir: I'd fuckin love her tae suck my balls, by the way.'

'Derrida?'

'*Derrida?* Fuck off. *Spectres of Marx* can suck my balls.'

'So what is the answer?'

'I don't even know what the question is.'

'Well, if you dismiss all these theories, isn't there an argument for examining a grammatical system that implies originative action?'

'...No.'

'No?'

'No.'

'Why not?'

'... Look, see, the problem ye've got, right... I went out for a drink wi Danny's workmates, ye know all they ones from the railway, right? And there was this wee girl out with them. I think she works in the ticket office or something like this. And I was buying a round and so I says tae her what'll ye have and straight up she says can ye get me a pina colada, right? So I come back wi a tray of drinks and hers is this big mad thing wi a straw and an umbrella and all this here, and she takes all the crap out her glass and she gets the ice out wi her fingers and she downs the whole thing. And after a wee bit it seems tae me we're getting along grand, right? She comes and sits next tae me on the leather benches they have in Robinson's and all this here. And then, totally out the fuckin blue, she asks do I like aubergines. I says what? She says d'ye like aubergines? I says what the fuck are ye on about– I don't say it like that, sure, cause I'm tryin tae be nice, ye know? I say, fuckin, I'm sorry, I don't follow ye? She says, it's just a question. Either ye do or ye don't.'

'What's this got to do with–'

'I says I don't know. I've never fuckin thought about it. If I've ever ate an aubergine, then I can't remember givin a shite one way or the other, ye know? And I'm fucked if I know why ye're askin me now. Again, I don't say it like that, ye know? Now, suppose I'm goin tae this wee girl's house for dinner, right? And she's in the kitchen gettin the tea ready and all that. And I'm in her livin room, makin small talk wi her flatmates and what have ye, and the wee girl shouts through tae me: here, Barry, d'ye like aubergines? Then I'll have a wee think about it and say I don't know. I'm not sure I've ever had an aubergine, but I'll give them a go, ye know? And then after we've eaten our fuckin aubergine salad or whatever it is, I'll say, fuckin, thank you very much, love, that was delicious so it was. I'll say that even if the aubergine made me boke, ye know? But the point is–'

'There's a point?'

'The point is that when she just came out and asked me if I liked aubergines – for no reason, like – I thought she was a fuckin eejit. The point is that without a concrete basis the question's stupid, is it not? The point is that without praxis, theory dissolves into methane and disappears up its own arse. The point is the fuckin Eleventh Thesis, is it not? It's basic fuckin Marxism.'

'That's why I'm trying to use theory to look at concrete historical situations.'

'And that's the thing, right? Do I know what yer wee girl, Elsie, was doing or thinking or fuckin sayin on this or that day? Of course I don't. But I can tell you some things she definitely wasn't thinkin. She may have been thinkin Oh fuck the peelers are bastards, are they not? She may have been thinkin Oh fuck the rioters are in wi Fenians, so they are. She may have been thinkin I'm fuckin hungry. But she definitely wasn't thinkin Oh fuck what exactly am I referring to when I use the pronoun I. Are ye hungry, Elsie? Would ye like one of these sixpenny ham bones we've looted here, Elsie? I don't know, I can't make a decision because I'm suffering a fuckin ontological crisis. That's just stupid. There's no more point tae it than askin me if I like fuckin aubergines.'

64

Outside the Classic Cinema. Muscle movement. Palmar interossei Lumbricales Dorsal interossei. Just movement: fingers jiggling coins in a hip-pocket, producing a noise, pure noise. Then, as quiet slides through Castle Lane, the noise generates a commentary – it becomes a jingling kind of noise – and the fingers slow until their movements feel like something intended. They begin to feel the tiny serrations, the differing circumferences, the slightly rougher contours on the tail side, and the objects become three and ha'penny – raised through collecting metal, helping to paint a fence on the Malone Road – not enough for one cinema ticket, let alone two. Toes curl. Feet arch, shifting weight, sparing raw patches of heel and little toe. Eyes push left then right, up at the big clock then down at those boots, laced with braided string, exuding the nervy engine smell of dubbin.

Right so when she if she gets here then– much later and we'll have missed the programme and that would be bloody handy but say she comes now which would be typical for a wee girl and but then you say, say you met one of the lads from work, at the shipyard, no that's daft, at a big factory with those machines that crack and steam and stamp on boot soles, and he's just out the matinee and it was wick like and not worth worrying with and why not go and get some cha at that place, not a bad sort of place though tea and toast– The assembled sensation of the Macleod Tea House with its smell of tobacco and the damp overcoats draped on the curved shoulders of wooden chairs, the toll of crockery and that stern-faced biddy pouring the tea out as all those lips pretend to sip, peering at the browned inside of empty cups.

Carts, seagulls, stomach pain, shivering, and a thousand other perceptions slide by without analysis, but now and then a tram passes, lashing sparks, belling and clattering across points, loud enough that a cursory investigation begins, and at some point during the decoding process there is a kind of *hang on a minute, guys; here, you might want to have a look at this,* almost every time a young woman passes. Words here are all metaphor because any connected linguistic interpretation comes after the motor process (the head following, the eyes siding) – this is a very biological reaction (not pheromones or facial symmetry or anything so fanciful; the triggers here are beige stockings or marcelled hair; the latest, perhaps the most transient historical fad).

Twenty feet along the pavement stands a news-vendor, bonnet low, jacket criss-crossed against the wind, calling the headline of *The Northern Whig and Belfast Post*. For most of the wait, the possibility of this message, like the seagull squawks and horses' hooves, has been brushed aside or left alone, but now, in this moment of rare coincidence, the cry is decoded and tangled up in a series of reactions: Workhouse to be invaded in force; outdoor relief workers' demonstration: yesterday's scenes: today's programme. And this, just as the thought of Macleod's gives on to the present moment and the shiver and the pang of hunger, as the wee girl in that fine coat looks not this way but across the street at a group of— well, men, but sort of shabby and carrying a red flag, so they must be the Bolshies, sure enough, and the hand jiggles those inadequate coins. Already the moment has passed, the decision to follow the flag has been made, and only now are the words asserting themselves, trying to make sense of it all, to impose some order, some sense of control, on the chemical process of time.

X T/1755/

1932
Workhouse (Lisburn Rd).

T/2805   RUC Special.

T/3667   Possible explanations for the recurring significance
          of holes, cracks, & chasms:

* There are inevitable gaps in history
* There is a hole in the Big Other
* Try to use the word 'Lacunae'
* Void constitutive of subjectivity.
* Nostalgia for the soul (i.e. the hole in the
  machine where the ghost used to be)
    * The Existential horror vacui
      * The empty attic of attained desire
        * That which cannot be sublated
          * Vagina / Cave
            * Impossibility of narrative
              closure
                * &c.

Ukraine, 1919

65

Despite Barry's admonishment, I persevered with this experimental prose style and by Christmas 2009 I had written 6000 words. Then, early in 2010, everything went wrong.

66

Examiners, I hope you'll recall Andriy Yaroslavovich Tykhenko, who in 1937 escorted Elsie towards the French border? You may recall, too, that he talked of an orphan he had rescued in 1919, and a woman with dwarfism whom he had loved at about the same time. But what I didn't mention, in the interests of maintaining a consistent point of view, and because I wanted Andriy to be a somewhat sympathetic character, was that in October 1919, Andriy decapitated a fifteen-year-old German boy. The boy had been raised in a community of pacifist Christians, and he was, as we would put it, intellectually disabled (his employers called him an imbecile, '*schwachsinnige*'; his Russo-Ukrainian co-workers called him 'The Idiot').

67

It started on Valentine's Day. I hadn't spoken to Lempi since before Christmas and for some reason – surely I could have found a more judicious excuse to contact her – I decided to send her a Valentine's text. It wasn't meant as a romantic gesture – I simply wished her a happy Valentine's Day (exclamation mark, smiley face, kiss kiss, lol) – but as soon as I'd sent the text I was racked with regret. I sat my phone on the desk and waited for it to beep. As the minutes passed, as I listened to Obi and Jez debate Deuteronomy, I became more and more appalled at myself. What had I hoped for? Had I thought she would reply to say she had no date, was at a loose end, and thought perhaps she and I could go bowling? I imagined her sitting with a group of female friends (or, worse, a boyfriend), holding her phone up with an expression of distaste, and briefly discussing my creepiness.

When I finally did receive a new message, it was an email rather than a text. It wasn't from Lempi. No, it was from Johansson-Van der Heyder. The Postgraduate Research Board, I read, were threatening to terminate my funding. Their repeated requests for timely completion of paperwork had been ignored, and they had grave concerns about the progress of my research and my suitability for a scholarship. Professor Thrub and I were required to attend an extraordinary meeting to discuss my academic engagement. Examiners, I felt sick.

68

The beheading of the German boy is hard to explain. The incident occurred at an isolated estate, near the Mennonite community of Chortitza, in early October 1919. To the north of the house, on the uncultivated road-side steppe-land, a layered ridge of limestone emerged from the shrubbery. Had you examiners somehow been standing on this vantage point – or lying on your stomachs, perhaps, watching through binoculars – then the estate would have seemed at first glance calm. The stables, from which puffed small clouds of steam, had capacity for a dozen horses, and from two wooden barns, one could hear the stomp and cluck and snort of unseen cows and hens and hogs. Firewood and straw lay piled and baled beneath log roofs peaked like inverted Vs. From the main chimney of a grand stone house, smoke angled upwards, dissipating in the reddening sky. And on the cold east breeze – a harbinger of the winter winds that bring the snowstorms from the Asiatic Steppe – there blew the evening smell of wood smoke and dying sunflowers. Yes, had you been perched on that limestone ridge, the scene might have appeared almost pastoral. And yet, something would have put you on edge. Something was not right. A stone arch bridged a small ravine and at either abutment the hawthorn bushes had once been sculpted into topiary horses; but now, untended, the horses' heads grew wild and diffuse, as if rotten or diseased. And behind them, a newly-ploughed winter wheat field lay unplanted, ribbed like the chest of some hungry thing.

The noise at first was like an earthquake. As it grew louder, grit scattered down the limestone rock face. Windows rattled and log barns creaked. A girl emerged from the stables, squinting into the setting sun. Following her gaze, you examiners would have seen a storm of dust, just visible through the sanguinary glaze of the freezing fog. From then, you would have watched only the arriving army: two-dozen riders, with black flags silhouetted against the setting sun. The army stopped before the bridge, guns and sabres raised. In the midst of their formation was a four-wheeled horse drawn cart, on the back of which was mounted a machine gun. Their flags hung from the ends of long uneven branches. As the cavalry encircled the estate, the horses that towed the cart shuffled in a semi-circle, so that the machine gun pointed at the farmhouse. Some of the men were shaking. All were scratching their collars and groins and thighs. One had blood dried like snakeskin on his shirt. For a minute, the only sounds were neighing from the stable and snorting and nickering from the riders' horses. On the far side of the house, a man screamed and laughed – at what, one could not say.

Then the door opened and a woman stepped from the porch. She looked old enough to be the mother of the now-disappeared adolescent. Even if one spoke fluent Russian, it would, from the rocky vantage point hitherto imagined, have been hard to understand the conversation that followed. But it was apparent that the soldier with the ripped trousers was interrogating the woman, who in answering took care not to offend. Above this conversation, there were other shouts: jokes, insults, threats, or accusations. Unable to follow the conversation, you would have noticed the awakening of nocturnal life. Silhouettes of birds arrowed overhead. Cirrus clouds reflected pink sunlight, scarring the darkening sky.

Then something strange occurred. The soldier with the ripped trousers dismounted his horse and lurched towards the machine gun cart. From the cart he removed a baby. Wrapped in a black flag, the baby cried noiselessly. The soldier gave the baby to the woman, who looked amazed, as though this had not happened in any of the thousand scenarios she had considered. Three other soldiers now entered the house, sabres drawn. Meanwhile, in the courtyard, the soldiers, relaxing now, chatted in pairs, lit cigarettes, or began to tether their horses. Two stood pissing in the ravine. The scream was therefore totally unexpected. From the limestone vantage point, you would not have noticed the boy until he was struck. His scream was chorused by the neighs of horses and the shrieks of the woman and the gasps and orders of the men. The noise of metal – of sabres drawn and guns cocked – was orchestral in its volume and synchronicity. For a fraction of a second, through the melee, you might have seen the boy clutching his shoulder,

and then, as he turned with the intention of escape, the sabre—
the noise was like a sharp axe striking the branch of a tree.
The boy fell face-first and lay twitching on the ground. By this
time the soldiers were in combat positions and the woman had
reached the executioner – she was still holding the baby because
what else could she do with it? And the soldier with the ripped
trousers – he who had hacked the boy – now threw the woman
onto the ground. He was shouting at her and the woman was
screaming and crying and praying in Russian and Low German
and any other words she knew and she was still holding the baby
and the soldier was shouting at her and cursing her. And then,
as the argument calmed, each of the other soldiers began to
stand up or dismount, depending on the combat position he had
assumed. One sprung to his feet, laughing and pointing at his
wet groin; then he turned his back, shaking his head, restarting
his piss. Meanwhile, the soldier who'd hacked the boy tried to
pull the wailing woman to her feet. Then he walked to the boy,
who was still twitching on the mud. He stood for a moment and
looked around him and looked at the woman. There were lights
moving inside the house and they made the night seem much
darker. Then the soldier lifted his sabre and swung two-handed
with a grunt.

69

I read the email three or four times and then I left the office to
visit Robin. Robin is a lecturer in the English department with
whom I had become friendly over the preceding year. Given
the tumultuous events about to unfold, there is little time for a
character bio, but for what it's worth, Robin is a scholar of post-
9/11 American literature, the fiction of Martin Amis, literary
responses to the Holocaust, and suicide as an implicit theme in late

1980s North American sports novels. He is a white wine drinker. Here are some of his favourite directors: Ingmar Bergman, Luis Buñuel, Federico Fellini, Michael Haneke, David Lynch, Andrei Tarkovsky, and Lars Von Trier. He wears spectacles.

On that particular afternoon, I found Robin in the midst of a crisis. His office floor was covered with books and papers. The books had been thrown open, face down, their peaked covers looking like suburban roofs seen from a low-flying aeroplane. 'How's it going?' he said as I shuffled into his doorway. 'I've lost one of the MA student's NOB12 forms. I don't know what the fuck I've done with it.'

'Is it important?'

'It's not that important,' said Robin, tipping a drawer onto the floor. 'It just means I'll get another bollocking off Gumthorpe.' Gumthorpe was employed by the University in some punitive capacity that resisted clear definition. 'Hey, I saw your girl today. I'm sure I've used it as a bookmark or something.'

'Lempi? Did she say anything?'

'She wasn't mute.'

'I mean– I did something a bit–'

'You're not still chasing her, are you?'

'I wouldn't say I've ever *chased* her.'

'I don't mean *chased*, sorry. I mean you've been pursuing– I don't mean pursuing. You've been wooing her, making advances – except you've not really been making advances, is kind of my point. Twelve months and no advance: it's like the Battle of the Somme or something.'

'It's not that bad.'

The phone rang from under a dictionary of philosophy. 'Fucksake,' he said, pressing it onto silent. Robin stood on one leg and stretched the other one. It was impossible for him to move without stepping on the strewn books; I imagined him as a giant trampling through suburbia. 'What brings you over here anyway?'

'I've a bit of a problem.'

'Paperwork?'

'Kind of.'

Robin fanned through his *Norton Anthology of Criticism*, hoping something would fall out.

'They're threatening to take away my funding.'

On hearing this, Robin stopped his search and stood wearing an expression of exaggerated shock. 'No way.'

'Yeah. We haven't–' I dropped my voice to a whisper '–*Thrub* hasn't done any of the forms. We've got to attend some sort of emergency meeting, and I know what he's going to say: he'll say my progress isn't satisfactory. The last thing I handed in to him he described as the most platitudinous crap he'd ever read.'

'You'll need to speak to him,' said Robin.

This was a hard blow to take; I'd secretly hoped Robin would volunteer to approach Thrub on my behalf.

'But I wouldn't do it today,' continued Robin, whose many functions in the department included providing colleagues and students with forecasts of Thrub's mood (it swung from indifference to hostility). Robin's door was always open (not because he desired shared experience, he claimed, but because, as he put it, there is nothing worse than being at work and your boss not knowing it), which meant that he had usually been able to hear whether Thrub had thrown anything that morning.

'Really?' I asked.

Robin squeezed past me and looked left and right down the corridor. 'Thing is,' he whispered, 'you know Debs, MA lit student? Well, this morning Thrub threw a book at her.'

'He does that.'

'Yeah, but this was serious. Wittgenstein.'

'Really?'

'*Tractatus Logico-Philosophicus.*'

'Wow.'

'Hardcover.'

'Shit.'

'Well, Debs was understandably upset. She told Andrews and he told Gumthorpe. Gumthorpe was knocking on Thrub's door all morning. Jenny, one of the cleaners, said that earlier today she saw Thrub trying to climb out of his window.'

'Where is he now?'

Robin shrugged. 'Might still be in there for all I know.'

'But I think you're right; I should leave it for another day.'

'Yeah, I would.' Behind me, an undergraduate had appeared in the doorway, and Robin made a resigned gesture of apology. 'We'll go for a drink soon?' he said.

'That would be excellent. Hope you find the NOB12,' I said, stepping into the corridor.

70

The Mennonite boy that Andriy beheaded was named Gerhard Dyck. Dyck was the eldest son of a landless peasant – an anwohner, as the Mennonites called their poorest people – and he was, like many of his brethren, intellectually disabled as a consequence of his parents' consanguinity. He was employed on the Loewen estate as an agricultural labourer, which the Loewen boys considered to be a very Christian act: they paid Dyck 100 rubles per annum (it would have been bad form to have paid a Mennonite any less), even though they could have employed a more productive Russian worker for seventy rubles. All contractual matters were resolved by the farm manager, Mr Wiens, for the Loewen boys had inherited the estate, unexpectedly, at an age when they were preoccupied with courtship and hunting and attempting to drive their late-father's automobile.

Thus, Dyck had been on the estate when the bandits first arrived to loot the Loewens' property. They had spoken to him kindly and asked whether he would like land of his own. Dyck had answered that if God were ever to grant him such happiness he would like it very much. To this, the bandits laughed, and one of them, pointing with his pistol, instructed him to take his turn. Dyck had watched the Russians select their share of machinery and livestock and it was his way of coping in the world to do as others did around him. So, trying to do the correct thing, he found his favourite animals – an old sheepdog that walked with a limp and a piglet who'd been the sole survivor of a litter he'd disastrously midwifed – and he walked them from the barn on leashes. Dyck knew he'd done the wrong thing the moment the bandits asked Mr Wien and the Loewen gentlemen to take *their* turns. Master Loewen said he would not legitimise (the word was unfamiliar to Dyck) this banditry, and that not for one second did he or his brother relinquish their claim to all they had rightfully inherited. This started an argument and the bandits shoved the Loewen brothers, and then Victor, the farmhand who chewed tobacco, spat at Mr Wiens and said he would lash honest toilers no more. But he was wrong, that man Victor, because when the bandits had ridden away, Master Loewen thumped Dyck on the ear and later Mr Wiens flogged him with the knout, for he had tried to take animals that were not his and that was theft and theft was a sin and the sin of a believer was an affront to our Lord.

So, one can understand Dyck's trepidation when the German army arrived in Grübenfeld. His instincts told him to join his neighbours, cheering and clapping and singing 'Deutschlandlied', but recent experience reminded him to be circumspect. It was not until he had chance to speak with Mr Wiens that he knew the correct thing to do. Jesus Christ taught us to avoid the sword, said Mr Wiens, but he was talking about the Kingdom of God. The word of God cannot be spread or defended by force – no, boy – and in this regard we are non-resistant followers of Christ. But when the Devil rises from Hell and walks in the bodies of men, it is our duty to defend law and order, would you not say? Dyck was silent. The German soldiers are our friends, said Mr Wiens. This was an enormous relief.

At first, Dyck was never allowed a rifle, but he paraded with the other young men and practised drills armed with a stick he'd snapped from a tree – these were possibly the happiest days of his life. Then, one day, for reasons Dyck didn't understand, Mr Wiens taught him how to use a real German army rifle. The last thing Wiens ever said to him was to keep the rifle always, to use it to catch rabbits, and if things got bad to use it against other vermin too. The next day was the Sabbath and the day after that, when Dyck rode to work, he learned that Mr Wiens and the Loewen brothers had left the estate for a vacation in Crimea. When the bandits returned, they recognised Dyck and asked about the health of his animals. Dyck said that they weren't his animals – they were the Loewens' animals – and he admitted that he'd been lashed for the sin of trying to steal them. This made the bandits curse Wiens as a brute and a coward and swear that if they ever found him or the Loewens they would put a bullet in each of their brains.

Dyck enjoyed the six months of the Loewens' holiday. It was then just he who worked with the animals (there were many fewer, but the bandits had left his favourites), and he took his orders from Frau Loewen, who was kinder than her gentleman sons and Mr Wiens. Best of all, perhaps, during these months he sometimes worked alongside Frau Loewen's daughter, Fräulein Magdalena. Dyck could not have articulated what he felt when in the presence of Fräulein Magdalena, but he knew it was something to do with love and marriage, and he knew that marriage was a Holy Union. There was also another thing, which he felt very strongly, and which he'd heard discussed by the Russians. This thing had something to do with his penis. The penis thing and the love thing were connected somehow, but also separate, and Dyck could not have explained where one ended and the other began. Still, every day, after finishing work, he pretended to ride home, but instead tethered his horse in the copse and crept back to the estate; it did not occur to Dyck to wonder why Fräulein Magdalena was so often naked or toileting in the estate's out-buildings. Suffice to say that despite his military pretensions, Dyck was not a subtle spy.

Magdalena had first noticed Dyck watching her, one evening in March, when she was in the stables de-saddling the horse. Her first reaction had been to ignore him – he was, after all, an idiot – and why, after a week or so, she had started to undress for him, she could not have begun to explain. She would have screamed – honestly screamed and bit and fought – had the brute ever touched her or even dared address her directly. It was, perhaps, this unbridgeable distance between them that enabled Magdalena to unburden herself of adolescence's newly-imposed restraints. The liberating euphoria of exposing her shame was as intense and addictive as it was inexplicable. At first she undressed to her undergarments. Then she stripped naked. She straddled a horse unclothed or crawled on all fours across the stable floor. Sometimes she squatted to piss or defecate. She toileted in the straw like the animals and turned her bum towards the watching idiot.

Six months deeper into adulthood, these incidents seemed to Magdalena like a story she had heard second hand. Dyck continued to watch, but she had ceased to perform; in fact, she intended to confront his perverted behaviour as soon as her own sordid crimes were a little more distant, a little more safely historical. It was with great guilt that Magdalena admitted to herself the relief she felt at Dyck's death; she could not now be judged in this worldly kingdom. On the night the bandits attacked, she gave little thought to Dyck's safety. She scurried inside and hid in the attic as her mother had advised. Dyck, meanwhile, picked up the rifle and bounded first one way then the other. At the last second, he ran into the cold house. The cold house was a storage cellar, which in the winter he had helped fill with ice from the pond. The ice was then covered with straw and used to preserve food. By October it had almost entirely melted and the straw and remaining icebergs floated on the black water. It was, however, too late for Dyck to close the cellar door. With the door open, his head was visible even if he crouched on the lowest step, and so he splashed into the icy water. The cold of it robbed his breath. As Mrs Loewen met the bandits, Dyck held his rifle above the water and waited. But the cold was awful. He started to shake and his teeth were rattling so loudly he feared detection. The cold was a pain that rose in pitch, and when he could endure it no longer, when the bandits had begun to relax, he slapped up the cellar steps, stumbling and trembling in the dark. Cold was so much like fear. In his final moments, he reminded himself there was a God who saved. Against this he weighed God's likely dim view of his recent sins: his lusting after Fräulein Magdalena, not to mention his trying to steal the Loewens' animals. The pink night seemed bright and warm after the dark horrors of the cellar. Dyck climbed out to say hello, bearing his gun in proud and soldierly fashion.

71

I procrastinated. Every day I found a new excuse why I couldn't speak to Thrub. On the eve of the extraordinary meeting, I could put the task off no longer.

'Have you... heard anything?' I asked Robin.

'From Thrub? It's been pretty quiet so far. He was playing music earlier.'

'Not Mahler again?'

'No, Schubert, I think.'

I thanked Robin and edged towards Thrub's corridor. To my surprise, I could see that his door was open. I stood in the gloom, beside the dead yucca plant, while I gathered my courage, and then I stepped into Thrub's doorway. The Professor was seated at his desk, whistling the principal theme from *Peter and the Wolf*. His computer was on the floor and his entire desk was covered with a half-assembled jigsaw. Thrub was oblivious to my presence. As he whistled a trill, which may have signalled the entrance of the birds, I knocked the open door. 'Forgive me intruding, Professor.'

Thrub stopped whistling and turned to inspect me. His expression suggested no recognition. 'Yes?' he said.

I hesitated, unsure whether, a year into our supervisory relationship, I needed to introduce myself. 'I... well....'

Thrub checked his watch.

'I wanted to speak to you about tomorrow's meeting, Professor.'

Thrub returned to his jigsaw. Piece by piece he was constructing a pirate ship. 'Wait,' he said, turning back to face me, 'what meeting?'

'The meeting to discuss my research progress? My funding?'

Thrub shook his head.

'At two fifteen?'

'And where is that?' said Thrub, searching for a pen.

'Johansson-Van der Heyder's office.'

'Well, thank you for letting me know. Now, if you'll excuse me– Hang on: I know you.'

'Yes, Professor, I'm–'

'You're friends with Lempi Bridgette, aren't you?'

'Kind of.'

'Amazing tits,' said Professor Thrub. 'Truly remarkable.'

72

Examiners, without wishing to presume, I'm going to gamble that – despite your intellectual eminence – you're not experts on the Ukrainian Civil War. And therefore, if you're to make sense of Gerhard Dyck's death, it seems necessary I provide a crude (and very optional on your part – please feel free to skip this section) outline of the warring factions. If you do read this section, you'll probably find it impossibly chaotic and confusing, and in that case, you'll have acquired a fair impression of Ukraine in 1919.

Following the October Revolution in Russia, the newly formed Ukrainian People's Republic declared independence from Russia and the newly-formed West Ukrainian People's Republic declared independence from Austro-Hungary and Poland. By mid-1919, Poland had occupied the whole West Ukrainian People's Republic, but we shan't focus on the horror germinating in Western Ukraine as it was on the opposite side of the country from Gerhard Dyck and the man who killed him, Andriy Tykhenko. Similarly, we shall ignore the Komancza Republic, which wanted to join with the West Ukrainian People's Republic, and the Russophile Lempko Republic, which wanted to join with the autonomous province of Carpathian Ruthenia. (All these territories appear to have existed for the sole purpose of exciting future generations of stamp collectors.) The Bolsheviks, meanwhile, initially forced out of Kiev, established the north-eastern border town of Kharkov as the administrative capital of their Socialist Soviet Republic. But soon they were marching on the capital, pushing the Ukrainian Nationalist forces south. Unable to stall the Bolshevik advance, the Ukrainian Nationalists concluded a treaty with the Central Powers (i.e., Germany, Bulgaria, and the Ottoman and Austro-Hungarian empires), which sent troops into the Ukraine and forced the Bolsheviks across the Russian border. The Austro-Germans et al. installed a puppet government led by Hetman Pavlo Skoropadsky, whose regime restored feudal property rights and whipped, shot, or hung peasants suspected of rebellion. After the Allied victory in WWI, Skoropadsky's Austro-German-backed regime collapsed and was replaced by a new version of the Ukrainian People's Republic, soon led by the Ukrainian Nationalist Symon Petliura (hence 'Petliurists'). The new regime faced an aggressive Romania and an invading Poland, while the French seized Odessa and General Mai-Maievsky's Don Cossack and Chechen White Army pushed north from the Crimea. At the same time, Petliura's disillusioned peasant soldiers were deserting to independent militias or wandering homewards. Then, in December 1918, the Bolsheviks reinvaded from Kursk, while General Denikin's force consolidated its base in the Kuban, preparing to march on Kiev and Moscow. In addition to the White Army, the Red Army, and Petliura's nationalists, there were various independents: isolated peasant insurgents, mobs of bandits and deserters, paramilitary bands of Cossacks, and the armies of independent war lords, including that of notorious anti-Semite Nikifor Grigoriev. Significantly for our story, there were also pro-white militias, including the Selbstschutz, an army established by avowedly-pacifist Mennonite colonists in the summer of 1918. Initially the Selbstschutz operated alongside the armies of the Central Powers, but after the allied victory in WW1, they briefly made an independent stand against the peasant uprising.

However, of all the independent armies, the biggest and most famous was that led by Nestor Makhno. Makhno was born in 1888 and started work at the age of seven. In 1910 he was sentenced to death for his involvement with the local anarchist group's programme of political assassinations and armed robberies; however, the sentence was commuted to life imprisonment with hard labour. When Makhno was released during the February 1917 revolution, he returned to his hometown, Gulyai-Polye in Eastern Ukraine, where he organised the collectivisation of land and property. In response to the Austro-German occupation and the violent restoration of property rights, he and his comrades took to the Steppe on horseback, and for the next three years, they fought a guerrilla war against anyone who tried to govern Eastern Ukraine. Makhno's story is an extraordinary one – he survived more than 200 attacks and battles, during which time bullets went through his hat, his hand, his ankle, his thigh and appendix, his nape and right cheek – but it's not the story I wish to tell here. For our purposes, it's enough to make a few notes about Makhno's army: you see, it was while serving in Makhno's army that Andriy decapitated Gerhard Dyck.

Three things distinguished the Makhnovists from the other independent armies then operating in the Ukraine (do feel free to skip this section, examiners). First, unlike the other armies, they received widespread support among the civilian poor: while the Makhnovists' enemies publicly denounced them as bandits, they privately bemoaned their enormous popular support. The

Bolsheviks conceded that 'Attacks on Makhno infuriate the local population' (see Butt et al., 1996, p-88) and complained that while the peasantry refused to help the Bolsheviks, and often actively misled them, they aided the Makhnovists in whatever way they could (see Palij, 1976, pp-236/7).

Second, while Makhnovist units sometimes participated in the arbitrary and excessive violence then endemic throughout Eastern Ukraine, they were unique among the independent armies in that they had some vision of a positive political agenda. Within their anarchist-communist 'free territory', previously-landless peasants worked large estates as communes, and some factories were collectivised. The Makhnovists organised classes to increase literacy, developing a libertarian education system based on the ideas of Francisco Ferrer. They tried to make decisions democratically; for instance, their Second Regional Congress was attended by 2245 delegates from 350 districts, soviets, unions, and front-line units (Skirda, p-362). The congress expressed its opposition to 'plunder, violence, and anti-Jewish pogroms' (as Arno Mayer observed, 'Makhno stands out for having stood against the torment and victimization of Jews' (p-525)). A draft declaration of their Military Revolutionary Soviet, adopted on 20th October 1919, insisted on democracy from below and demanded the total freedom and independence of all peasant and worker soviets. On the issue of civil liberties, the document advocated 'freedom of speech, of the press, of conscience, of worship, of assembly, of union, of organization, etc.' (quoted in Skirda, 2004, pp-368-380).

Finally, they were by far the biggest and most influential of all the independent armies. In autumn 1919, Makhno commanded forty thousand soldiers, who defended a region the size of England in which lived more than seven million people. As we shall see, their 1919 counter-offensive changed the course of the Russian Civil War. Examiners, for better or worse, Andriy's actions helped shape the twentieth century.

73

When I arrived at Van der Heyder's office, Nick Andrews was already seated, legs crossed, stabbing at his Blackberry. 'Ve are vaiting,' said Dr Johanson-Van der Heyder, 'for Professor Thrub.' We sat for some minutes, listening to the insect-like buzz of the fan and the easy laughter of students crossing the quadrant lawn.

'It is cold today,' said Van der Heyder, pretending to shiver.

'There's snow forecast, apparently,' said Andrews.

Twice Van der Heyder's computer pinged, alerting her to new emails. 'Very vell,' she said, perhaps sensing that we had already run out of small talk, 'maybe ve should start vithout Professor Thrub?' The problem, she explained, concerned a total absence of paperwork: according to the research faculty office, we had failed to submit an RD1, an RD12, an RD45/C, or even a Training Needs Assessment Form. It was therefore necessary to assess the research progress to date.

At this moment, examiners, I made a disastrous tactical error. I removed from my bag multiple copies of the notes I had written since my trip to Belfast. I passed a copy to Johansson-Van der Heyder, passed another copy to Nick Andrews, and laid a third copy in front of Thrub's empty chair. It was then that the Professor entered, with a bottle of water in one hand and *The Guardian TV Guide* in the other, and sat down with a great release of air. He is one of those older men whose big frame now seems like something leftover, like some by-gone youthful fashion he has recently rediscovered in an attic trunk.

'Ve are discussing your student's progress.'

Thrub yawned and picked up his copy of my work, puzzling at it in the angle of the sunlight. While the academics studied the print outs, Johansson-Van der Heyder's fan heater filled the silence, whispering warm breeze across the desk and undulating the scattered papers. Eventually, Nick Andrews asked if I could possibly explain this:

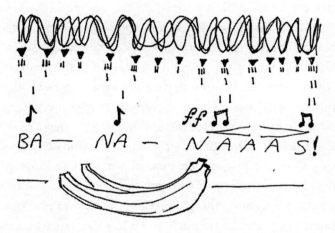

'I'm trying to avoid using personal pronouns or other grammatical structures that imply originative action.'

The academics were regarding me as nineteenth century anthropologists might have watched a Polynesian tribesman whose ceremonial doodah involved having his penis on show. Johansson-Van der Heyder removed her glasses. 'I thought ve might talk a little bit about you, about how you are finding the research experience, because for many people it can be very difficult and stressful to be so much vorking on your own, yah?'

'Absolutely,' said Andrews. 'I did my PhD at Cambridge and it wasn't easy settling into a new town.'

'Are you avare of the support structures ve have in place?'

'We're thinking maybe you should get in touch with the Student Help Zone.'

'Ve are vondering if you have any medical problems?'

'We have to decide if your progress is satisfactory – if we can continue to fund this project – and, frankly, without medical evidence....'

In the distance, a car engine banged, zoomed, faded. We sat for a moment, listening to the sleepy drone of the heater, the fluttery breaths of my loose thesis, the kick-start revs of a motorbike. Thrub yawned again – he has a way of yawning, examiners, that is truly enormous – and then he stood up and shuffled towards the window. I have noticed that Thrub spends a lot of his working life gazing through windows, as though the campus is a sort of cage, as though even now he imagines a more fulfilling life on the outside. Sometimes, when I'm feeling generous, I like to imagine that Thrub occasionally glances at a time-yellowed hand-written manuscript, an autobiographical novel he laboured over as a young man, which is now stored in a box of dusty forgotten things, next to honeymoon photographs and pictures of women with whom he has long since lost touch.

'Vell then, the other thing ve must consider is the supervisory relationship.'

'Yes,' said Andrews, 'I'm curious how that's working out.'

'It's excellent,' said Thrub, 'tickety-boo.'

'Yah, I see. You are having regular meetings?'

'Very regular,' said Thrub. 'Bloody clockwork.'

'And I presume you've been completing RDX3s?'

'Absolutely. I've got a whole stack of them filed chronologically in the office.'

'I think it would be very useful to see those forms,' said Andrews.

'Yah!'

'Now?' asked Thrub, snapping the leaves of Van der Heyder's spider plant. 'I can't get them now, Nick.'

Andrews reclined in his chair, arms folded. 'Why on earth not?'

'Because,' said Thrub, looking at the ceiling, 'I'm locked out of my office.'

'*Locked out?*' asked Van der Heyder.

At this point, Thrub turned from the window, picked up Johanson-Van der Heyder's African man statuette, and set it down before Andrews. Thrub's expression was that of a chess player who has just played a slightly desperate gambit and is waiting to see how his opponent will respond. 'Yes,' he said. 'I lost my key at a zumba class.'

'Vell, ve can help you out vith the skeleton key, yah?'

Examiners, we sat there so long I tracked the progress of the winter sun across Van der Heyder's desk. Eventually, Thrub reached for the African man statuette and solemnly laid it on its side. 'There are no forms in my office. There have been no meetings. I have not read one word of this lunatic nonsense.'

'Professor?'

'You heard me. I wish to relinquish my chair. Tell them to give me voluntary redundancy. Tell them to give me early retirement. I will be gone before you can find the appropriate form. I will have emptied my office before you can evaluate my commitment to sustainable bloody enterprise. Enough!'

74

To understand why Andriy, Gerhard Dyck's killer and years later Elsie's mountain guide, was in Nestor Makhno's peasant army, we have to go back to the First World War, when Andriy, who was born at the turn of the century – at the stroke of midnight, let's say – was seventeen and drafted in the Imperial Army. Andriy had been born with a mild cleft lip, and during his brief stint in the army, he was relentlessly mocked for his speech defect: the sub-ensign, for instance, amused his fellow officers by standing Andriy on a barrel and forcing him to try to sing 'Along the Petersburg Road'. When these same officers ordered him to advance on German lines as part of the Kerensky Offensive, Andriy honestly couldn't think of any reason in the world why doing so would be in his interests. So, on July 12th, he began walking east, soon followed by the rest of the Russian Army, soon followed by their former enemies, and upon returning to their villages, these armed mutineers began to settle scores with the landowners. But in Andriy's village, Andriy's father persuaded his neighbours that they should collectivise the pomeshchiki estate and appropriate, rather than burn, the squire's property. So the squire's collection of faux-medieval oil paintings was shared between the artistic-minded brothers Mikháylov, while Anatole Shovkovskiy, who was desperate to burn something, was allowed to torch some especially ugly religious icons. Unfortunately, when the briefly-victorious Austro-Germans installed Hetman Skoropadsky, there were reprisals in the name of restored order, and Andriy's father was hung from an oak tree in the village square.

If this isn't sufficient reason for a young man to join an insurgent group, then it's worth mentioning that Andriy had entered the Imperial War late and when told to fight had flatly refused, which meant he had no wounds or tales of heroism and wasn't quite considered a man yet, he felt, and thus was further compromised in his pursuit of women. Andriy was at this time a virgin, and when he did approach women they tended to either laugh or scream. During his time with the army, he had been introduced to a prostitute (again, this was probably for the amusement of other soldiers), and when he tried to kiss her she yelled and swore and threw a chamber pot at him.

So, late in 1918, he joined the insurgency, and did indeed succeed in impressing – though not copulating with – one or two women, largely through his acquaintance with Fedor Schuss. Schuss, a sailor turned anarchist insurgent, was already much talked about by the younger women. They would ask Andriy what sort of a man was Schuss, and Andriy, keen to emphasise the intimacy of their acquaintance, would explain that Schuss was a man of few words, a man who was naturally suspicious of others, but a man who loved his close comrades like brothers. But Andriy – who shared none of Schuss's swashbuckling charisma – grew irritated by all the Schuss this and Schuss that and one day told a group of schoolgirls that Schuss had bitten off the head of an Austrian soldier. Schuss found this so hilarious that he started repeating the story, pretending – for comic effect – to be enraged by anyone who doubted his word. He would issue draconian threats and even draw his sabre, which was very funny, but somewhat alarming for those who didn't know him. Andriy often felt that with Schuss one never knew whether a joke was a joke or a vehicle for something more sinister.

75

When I returned to my office, Obi was up on Jez's desk hacking away at the corner of the window frame with a rolled up religious journal. Either he was tackling the cobwebs or he was trying to kill something. Jez was on his knees by the printer, rattling the paper tray, pulling bits out and shaking them and cursing the stupid damned thing and cursing Obi and telling him to sit the hell down. Then he slammed the printer shut and stood up, dusting his hands. 'Goddamned stupid thing. How was your meeting?'

'Good,' I said, turning on my computer.

'Did they kick your ass?'

'No. It was all very constructive, very positive.'

'Jesus Christ, Obi, sit your ass down.' He pulled him off the desk, wrestled the journal from his clutch, and flung it on the floor. 'Make some tea or something. Jesus.'

I typed in my password while Obi – this was something I continued to find infuriating – placed his hand on my shoulder. 'Do you want tea?' he asked.

'No, thank you.'

'Jeremy and I are having tea.'

'No thanks.'

'They didn't kick your ass?'

'No.'

'Tea gives you spirit in difficult times.'

I spun round, shrugging and bucking and doing everything I could to throw off Obi's hand. 'Listen,' I said, 'I don't want tea. The meeting was great. Everyone's... *enthused* with my progress.'

'Huh. Then how come they called you in?'

'I don't know. They're doing everyone.'

'Man, we were gonna clear your desk while you were in there. Ain't that right, Samuel? Say, we were going to clear his desk, save him the trouble, right Obi?'

Obi, taking this somewhat too seriously, returned from the kettle, placed his hand on my shoulder – *again* – and informed me that a faithful friend is a sturdy shelter (or some such). For a moment I thought I was going to do a Thrub.

'*Now* he's a faithful friend,' said Jez. 'Ten minutes ago he was all about the girlie he thought would be taking your place, ain't that right, Samuel? He was talking about some honeyz coming in here.'

Obi explained for the hundredth time that he loved and respected his wife.

'Speaking of the *laydeeeez*,' said Jez, 'How's your hunt for a honey going?' When I didn't say anything, Jez marked another week on the giant tally chart he'd stuck next to the Hebrew alphabet; it had been 142 weeks since I had last made love. However, before we could fully explore my sexual failure, the door – which was already open as wide as it can go – crashed against the bookshelves with such force that it dislodged volume two of *Die Religion in Geschichte und Gregenwart*, smashing the book spine-first into the tea cups. And there was Thrub, like a fucking mad man, trembling in the doorway. Examiners, I don't mind admitting that I was scared. We all shrank towards the corners of the room and the world went awful quiet. Thrub pointed at me and said '*You*!' and it was like some dark creature had come to collect its due.

'I want you to know,' he said, 'that I've been in academia for nearly four decades. I want you to know that I survived a department full of senile Leavisites. I survived a department full of radical feminists. I've survived Thatcherism and Blairism. I've watched the debasement of the academy and the mercantilisation of education. I even stuck it out when I had the *humiliation* of marrying and being divorced by one of my students. And I want you to know that it's only now – now that I have to work with *you* – that I cannot face another day. Because working with you – working with your lunatic PhD – is like... It's like...' Thrub seemed totally exhausted by his speech and also somewhat calmed by it. '...It's awful. It's just awful. And that's all I wanted to say.' But as he prepared to leave, he paused on the threshold, and turned back to me with an aftershock of anger. 'Do you know why I can't stand you?' He seemed to be genuinely awaiting an answer.

Examiners, I thought of Thrub flicking though the manuscript of his one-time novel. I thought of the passionate young intellectual who had penned *Back to the Future: Metanarrative,*

Reflexive Epistemology, and the case for Historiographic Metafiction. And I thought, yes, maybe I do know why he finds working with me difficult. Quietly, almost to myself, I answered him. 'Yes. I imagine that I remind you of yourself when you were younger.'

Thrub looked just completely amazed. 'No,' he said. 'It's because you're a cunt.'

76

The first time Andriy experienced what he considered to be a proper battle was in a settlement called Schönfeld, where lived some very wealthy Germans. Schuss and Makhno's troops had galloped into this settlement— And then, quite unexpectedly, the horses were rearing and screaming and the noise of gunfire seemed so loud and sustained that later Andriy couldn't believe there were any of them left alive. For what seemed a very long time, but may have been less than a second, he was immobilised by fear, flinching from the noise, hugging his horse's neck; then, of its own volition, the horse galloped back the way it had come, and Andriy held on as the earth streaked and blurred beneath him.

They gathered in a ditch on the edge of the settlement, catching their breath out of range. Schuss was shouting that he would bite the bastards' heads off and piss down their necks and fuck their daughters and dig up their mothers' corpses. There were loose horses trotting across the steppe-land because their riders had been shot or unsaddled.

Meanwhile, Makhno remained calm. Andriy watched as he assembled the artillery piece, checking each bolt and lock. Soon after he started to shell the village, the militia rode out, emboldened by their earlier success. There were at least a hundred of them. Makhno ordered twenty men to wait with the tachanka gunner, while he and his comrades rode up the ditch to the left. Schuss's troops, including Andriy, took the opposite flank.

Before the charge, Andriy committed to firing his gun. He had not yet shot at anybody and it mattered to him that he contributed, that he discharged his weapon, even if he didn't hit the enemy. But when they reared out from the ditch, Schuss and others were in front of him, and the scene was so blurred and noisy that Andriy couldn't think which way to aim.

At any rate, the militia, outnumbered and outflanked, turned and fled, and would have been routed had not Makhno feared a trap. He halted the charge and the Makhnovists rode cautiously into the settlement. When they found it empty but for workers, they climbed on the rooftops and waved their flags. They drank imported wines and cognac and played guitars and sang. Then they dressed up in fur coats and monocles and velvet breeches. Wearing jewels and ball gowns, they fenced with walking canes. In master bedrooms, they threw themselves on mattresses. Outside, they built huge bonfires of furniture and leapt through the flames. They draped their horses with necklaces, walked them into the dining halls, and enacted banquets with ironic toasts and formalities and elaborate blessings. Then they ripped hunting trophies from walls, tied deer antlers to their heads, and charged each other on all fours. Later, when they'd mastered the ignition, they drove automobiles in wobbling circles until they crashed or ran out of fuel. Then they lay in the grass, dressed in silk and fur, swigging from bottles of vodka until the starscape was a dance of fireflies.

77

Yes, examiners, I hit the drink. By nine o'clock I was walking in S-shapes and tildes. My shoelaces were undone, but when I stooped to tie them, the blood rushed to my head and the cobblestones spun and reeled. Before leaving the last bar, I had dribbled urine down my inside leg, and I was now walking – staggering – with one hand held ape-like across my crotch. Robin – who by the time we'd met had already heard three versions of what was now being called 'Thrub-gate' – was escorting me with a hand on my back, asking me every minute or two whether I was alright.

The open readings at this time were held at a late license bar at the far end of Cheltenham High Street. Robin and I arrived noisily-late, mid-poem. On the stage, a woman in leggings read a poem that, I sensed, had been going on for long enough that people were beginning to wonder whether there was any prospect of it ever ending: 'Leaf of heart/ Wind of music/ Lost time/ And you. And you. And you.' This was delivered in such a conclusive manner that the audience stopped whispering and raised hands in uncertain preparation for applause. 'You cunt-thief/ You circumciser of dreams/'

'Drink?' I said, miming.

'You are rowing and the ripples like nipples dilate from your oars/'

'Yeah,' mouthed Robin, nodding emphatically.

'Incurably ill this insanity laugh of realism/'

As I ordered our drinks, a guy in specs and combat trousers angrily hushed me.

'Begging on the bathroom floor, blue the shriek of nothing/'

I spotted Lempi, half-visible in a crowd of her peers.

'Your camouflaged mandolin face, paper boy!/'

It was extraordinary how just the sight of her could revive me.

'Incurably ill this— sorry I've done that bit, hang on... Shotgun train angel fuck/'

A girl in a corduroy bonnet made a big show of tip-toeing as she broke for the exit.

'Falcon spiral golden slaughter protest/ Cock fear. Cunt fear. Woman fear. Man fear/ This breast that is ripped and laid bare/ Shoulder deep in genital froth/'

'Eight-eighty, please,' said the barman.

'Emotional crevasse of shattered dreams/ I look into your eyes and see fear of my inscrutableness/ Fear of my cunt. My cunt. Your fear/'

'Have you met Stan?' whispered Robin, introducing a guy in a Black Sabbath T-shirt.

As I reached to shake Stan's hand, the poet said, again, 'Your fear/ *Your* fear.'

The guy in the combats looked irate by now, so it was helpful that the poem finally ended – 'I rub your face in my shit' – with a great outpouring of relieved applause.

78

Makhno's army grew fast. By April 1919, 20,000 soldiers defended a 550km front around their autonomous zone. At this time, Andriy was stationed in Gulyai-Polye – the capital of the free territory – where his role was to collect contributions from kulaks and merchants. It was easy work: around Gulyai-Polye most members of the bourgeoisie were friendly, ingratiating even, and certainly none of them dared mock Andriy's speech. At first, they would always plead poverty: I've given everything, they would say. I wouldn't dare withhold money from Batko

Makhno. I cannot afford to feed my family. Andriy and his comrades would let this go on for a few minutes – it was a ritual that seemed necessary – and then, when the time was right, they would draw their sabres and issue baroque threats of violence. Stage three of the ritual – and again it seemed necessary that this stage was performed – involved each bourgeois accepting the hopelessness of his situation and wailing about his imminent death. Of course, the bourgeois knew not to drag out this stage, and after a minute or two he would, invariably, plead for one hour – just one hour – to try to come up with some of the amount demanded (the proportion offered was always 40-60% of the original demand). So, remembering to issue a few more threats, Andriy and his comrades would go to the next estate, or wait outside drinking vodka, while the bourgeois collected money or jewels from his secret stash. The final stage involved affecting a friendly parting: Andriy would thank the bourgeois for his contribution and explain how his money would be used to pay soldiers' wages, buy medical supplies, or support the new schools. Of course, in a few weeks they'd go back to demand more. Andriy didn't know what they'd do when the rich really did run out of money.

Only once did Andriy embezzle expropriated wealth for himself (a practice for which he'd heard a soldier could be executed), and he did so to pay for sex. The woman he paid was a proportionate dwarf named Natasha, whom he first encountered at the Makhnovist cultural centre. The cultural centre was situated in a former bank, across the road from the insurgent army headquarters. From the outside, the building was unchanged except for a giant black banner bearing the slogan 'War on the palaces, peace to the cottages,' but inside, the vaults housed printing presses and the main foyer had been converted into a theatre. The theatre group had built a stage by nailing planks to tables, and to accommodate the audience, from all over town they had collected more than a hundred mismatched rickety chairs. Andriy went to the cultural centre for literacy classes and would sit at a desk in what had been the manager's office, moving his finger slowly across a page of *The Road to Freedom,* but his reading was regularly interrupted by the commotion produced by theatre rehearsals.

One day, his head hurting from concentrating on newsprint, Andriy stood at the back of the foyer and watched the actors work. The first thing he noticed about Natasha, of course, was her height: had they stood together, she would not have reached far above his navel. He might have taken her for a child, had not her dress been so obviously womanly – she wore a wide brimmed hat and a straggly feather boa – and had not she been so obviously in control: as he entered the room, she was screaming at a bearded man that *of course* her opinion was more important than his: had *he*, she demanded to know, ever performed at the Moscow Art Theatre? The man said that he had not, but that neither had she nor any other dwarf. Natasha then stomped forward, pulled his beard, and shouted that if he'd ever left this shitty town he would know that dwarfs were the most coveted actors in all of Russia. This was too much for the man, who raised his hand to hit her, and then, when restrained by the other actors, jumped from the stage, kicked a chair over, and walked from the theatre shouting that he refused to take orders from a bourgeois midget whore. It was then that Natasha spotted Andriy.

You, shouted Natasha, as Andriy turned to escape the room. Wait there. She sat on the edge of the stage and lowered herself to the floor; then she walked through the chairs, her gait somewhere between a strut and a waddle. Halfway to Andriy, she tossed the boa over her shoulder, lit a cigarette, and threw the match away as though she had an inexhaustible supply. Nobody spoke and Andriy couldn't decide whether he found her impressive or ridiculous.

You have come to join us, she said. It was neither a question nor a statement. When Andriy explained that he was a soldier in the insurgent Makhnovist army, who had been practising reading and had no intention of playing childish games, Natasha smiled and said, You're perfect. You will be our evil Hauptmann. Andriy, of course, protested that he would sooner die than have anything to do with the bourgeois German army, at which point Natasha turned to the other actors and said, He has come to spy! He refuses to help the revolution! So Andriy reached into his coat and fumbled for his army card, and while he held the card up for all to see, he protested that he'd fought with Schuss and Makhno from the start, and he would not tolerate the taunts of a decadent midget.

Sit down, said Natasha, and Andriy sat. She hopped onto the adjacent chair, her legs swinging above the floorboards, and she passed him her cigarette. As Andriy smoked, she rested her tiny hand on his thigh. Her head was normal-sized, Andriy thought, and her lips were painted red. Andriy felt an urge to kiss her. Do you have any idea, she said, speaking in a whisper now, what this play will mean for the revolution? When people see this play, they will leave with the spirit of freedom beating in their hearts. After we have performed here, we will take the play on tour all over Russia. It will do more for the revolution than all the guns in the world. You will be a hero.

Andriy looked at the stage and tried to imagine how this might work.

79

At some point, when the stage had waited empty for several minutes, Lempi stood to read. There was a light to help the bar staff and a red bulb on the stage, but the only other electric illumination came from fairy lights splashed in constellations across the ceiling. In the extended break between readings, friends rearranged their chairs to accommodate new arrivals; a girl wearing a knitted pommel hat stretched, big and reaching, like a wave to a figure in the distance; a boy wearing a trilby hat passed her a drink over several obligingly ducking heads. Lempi emerged from this tangle of body parts, *excuse-me*-ing between tables, holding a folded page and smiling a thousand ways at once.

'Yay, Lempi!'

'Go Lempi!'

The front tables clapped and I clapped and Robin clapped and Brian, whose poems always concerned the taste of semen or the pleasure of rimming, stood up and loudly wolf-whistled. Lempi slowed as she reached the stage, laying her heels flat in careful sideways steps. 'Nice shoes!' shouted Brian.

'Yay, shoes!' said Lempi, extending one foot in a kind of battement tendu. She struggled to loosen the bolt on the microphone stand, gave up, stood on her tiptoes, giggled at herself, and swanned her neck. As Lempi unfolded her paper, a guy in a waistcoat scuttled forward to adjust the microphone stand, stooping with the surreptitious movements of a stage hand or sound technician. He lowered the microphone too far, and Lempi made a big show of hunching and said 'I'm not *that* small.' This brought him scurrying back as the audience laughed and Lempi pretended to flounce, stomping her foot in ironic cutesy tantrum.

'Is that okay?' he asked, looking up at the stage.

Lempi said, 'Thank you,' laughing at nothing in particular, and the tables at the front gave the waistcoat guy a humorous pitter-patter of applause.

As Lempi read, examiners, I found myself concentrating on just one part of her. She was wearing a grey University of Colorado T-shirt that had been cut, possibly by her, into an off-the-shoulder shirt, with sky-blue ribbon tie straps fixed over her shoulders. It was not her cleavage that I stared at; it was her collar bone. Lempi is noticeably thin. I don't mean unattractively so, but I remember, for example, that when she wore a halter neck top to the Literature Society Christmas drinks, her shoulder blades seemed to me like tiny wings. And so I found myself watching the triangle of her neck, shoulder and collar bone, the way that when she tensed, her bones and tendons surrounded a deep concave, and when she pushed her shoulders back the bones slid inside her. I watched this triangle throughout her reading, as though the whole of her was something infinitely elusive.

80

In Natasha's vision, the play was to open with men in German army uniforms (she insisted the Makhnovists would supply these uniforms) extolling the greatness of Kaiser Wilhelm. The audience would be enraged by what they'd been duped into watching, and the anger would grow when the orchestral section (during the rehearsals this was represented only by a broken piano, which nobody could play) would accompany a chorus of Deutschlandlied. The jeering and booing would be led by Natasha herself, who at this time would be seated amid the audience. Just before a riot started, she would clamber onto the stage and halt the music at gunpoint. At this point, the audience wouldn't know that she was part of the play. To cheers and applause, she would sing a song lampooning the German soldiers; the lyrics, which she'd written herself, were all about the disarmed weapons between the German soldiers' legs (Andriy found the lyrics hilarious). Then Natasha would escape stage left, leaving the fuming Germans to demand her execution. The German general was to be played by the only German speaker – an elderly and impoverished Mennonite anwohner who had joined the Makhnovist cause – and only after his speech would the audience realise that they'd been tricked: what they'd seen in the opening minutes was a play within a play. It was a staged re-enactment of the German army celebrating the capture of Kiev. The star of the *real* play was Natasha, the impish heroine who had disrupted the Germans' obnoxious triumphalism, and the rest of the play would follow her perilous journey across Ukraine, back to her home village in the Dnieper valley. At every stage, of course, she would be pursued and hunted by evil Germans and treacherous kulaks, and, with the aid of various immiserated but heroic peasants, at every stage she would find a new way to outwit her pursuers.

To Andriy's distress, Natasha had scripted a tragic ending. When she finally reached her home village, she would find several members of the cast sprawled dead on the stage. Their blood was to be symbolised with scraps of red cloth. Natasha, believing her whole village murdered, would then commit suicide in a very slow, very melodramatic, goodbye-cruel-world sort of way. Her final act would be to grab a sword discarded amid the bodies, and, standing side on to the audience, stab herself under the armpit. She would stagger, drop onto her knees, throw her sword to the stage, clutch her chest, and fall. For thirty seconds she would lie there in silence – the audience would wonder whether the play was over. Then, off stage, several cast members would knock wood on wood to produce the sound of horses' hooves. The noise would get louder and louder until, throwing handfuls of chalk to create clouds of dust, the peasants' army would appear on broomstick horses. One of the soldiers would recognise his sister Natasha and grieve her passing. Finally, to close the show, a leading organiser would address the audience directly (it was thought Peter Arshinov might fulfil this role, or maybe even Makhno himself); he would acclaim the achievements of the anarchist revolution and remind everyone of the work still to be done. He would shout, The land to the peasants, the factories to the workers! Liberty or death! The audience would stand and clap and cheer and clench their fists. Yes, *as a vision,* the play was a thing of beauty.

As a reality, however, there were problems. For a start, Natasha could almost never assemble the whole cast for rehearsals. People had to work, or they got drunk, or, like Andriy, they had military duties that could hardly be put on hold. Natasha herself was often drunk, and sometimes she lay on the stage, kicking her legs in tantrum at the incompetence of her troupe. She was the only one with any theatrical experience, and the others struggled with the very idea of acting. For instance, Andriy's main scene involved searching for Natasha in an abandoned bourgeois house. The idea was that Natasha would conceal herself amid a pile of dolls. She would be so tiny and so still that Andriy's character would be unable to find her. Natasha had decided that Andriy's speech invariably sounded comical, but that with his ugly appearance, he could make a frightening baddy if he only snorted and grunted and cackled. He was supposed to hurl the dolls against the back wall (the dolls had yet to be constructed, which made rehearsing difficult), one by one, until he was standing in front of Natasha. This was supposed to be terrifying.

This was supposed to put the audience in fear for Natasha's life. The idea was that when he grabbed Natasha, she would perform a slow arabesque twirl, as if she were a music box doll, and Andriy's character would be so in awe of this beautiful doll that he would carry Natasha offstage, intending her as a present for his evil wife. But during early rehearsals, Andriy's character had epiphanies mid-scene: Wait, he said, in his ridiculous slurred speech, why am I helping the bourgeois oppressors? I shall join the just cause of the peasant rebellion! No, no, no! Natasha shouted. You're supposed to be evil! You're supposed to be frightening! When she did coax him to the end of the scene, he used picking her up as an excuse to grope her bum and feel between her legs. Each time he carried her, Natasha kicked and slapped him, while yelling that he needed to face the auditorium.

81

What happened once the readings finished? In my mind I have often tried to reconstruct that disastrous night. Two hours passed before the violence was set in motion, but I can remember little of how I filled that time. I do recall that sometime after midnight, I marched towards Lempi, my countenance that of a man who has decided, against the counsel of his comrades, upon some fatalistic act of heroism. I was much drunker than I'd realised when propped at the bar. I was lurching through a collage of disjointed objects – a melting ice cube sliding across a table; a drink straw twisted into a bow – thunderbirding through the melt of colours. Halfway to Lempi, I crashed into a table.

This was not in itself a major incident. I knocked over an almost-empty pint glass and extinguished the table top candle. However, by the time I looked up, two men stood over me, arms outstretched, shouting that I was a fucking cunt and what the fuck was I doing.

Now, examiners, I do not remember exactly what happened in this unexpectedly consequential incident. I know that I offered to buy each of them a drink and I know that for some reason this caused further aggravation: I remember one man poking my chest and calling me a fucking faggot homosexual. And I can only assume that in my drunkenness I could not foresee the gravity of the situation, for at that point I advised the speaker that he had probably meant to pronounce the first syllable of 'homosexual' like the ho in 'holiday', rather than like the hō in 'home,' and I added that his mistake had been to confuse the Latin homo (human), as used in Homo sapiens, with the Greek homos (same), as used in homosexual. I don't know how coherently I expressed this, but I remember continuing my journey with something approaching a swagger.

Lempi was waving to me, patting the space to her side. 'You've not talked to me all night!' she said. Lempi's glory depends in part on her generous pretence that it is she who is desperate to talk with you. 'Hey, what did those guys at that table want?'

'Those guys?' I said, sitting beside her. 'They're just a pair of dicks.'

'They so are! Oh my God, before, when I was dancing, they were like coming up to me and I was just like no way, you know? And the guy in the red T-shirt was gyrating against me, so I took a step back and I was like, okay, personal space, yeah? It means that, like, I stand here, yeah? You stand there, yeah? There's, like, a space between us, get it?'

'Lempi,' I said, emboldened by my earlier triumph. 'I wanted to tell you something.'

'Oh-oh, when guys say that I get kinda nervous.'

'No, it's nothing bad. I wanted to say that… There was a sociology conference in North America, sometime in the seventies.'

THE DECONSTRUCTION OF PROFESSOR THRUB

'Woah-kay.'

'And they defined love as "a cognitive affective state characterised by obsessive and compulsive fantasising regarding the reciprocity of amorous feelings by the object of the amorance.'"

'Isn't that kind of a narrow definition of love? I mean, *please.*'

'I'm trying to say that–'

'How many of those have you *had?*'

'Listen, do you know how Umberto Eco defined the postmodern attitude?'

'Tell me.'

'He said he thought of it as the attitude of "a man who loves a very cultivated woman and knows that he cannot say to her, I love you madly, because he knows that she knows (and that she knows that he knows) that these words have already been written by Barbara Cartland. Still, there is a solution. He can say, As Barbara Cartland would put it, I love you madly. At this point, having avoided false innocence, having said clearly that it is no longer possible to speak innocently, he will nevertheless have said what he wanted to say to the woman: that he loves her, but he loves her in an age of lost innocence.'"

'Listen, I should go speak to Brian cause I've not said hi all night.'

'What I'm saying, Lempi–'

'Like, I get it, yeah?'

'I'm sorry.'

'You're just a bit drunk.'

'Sorry.'

'Will you excuse me?' She kissed me on the cheek.

'Wait,' I said. 'Lempi?'

'What?'

'You know the poem you read tonight? Have you still got the sheet?'

185

'You want to read it?'

'I'd love to.'

'But the sheet has been inside my bra.'

'I don't mind.'

'I'll bet you don't.' Lempi smiled and pushed back her hair. Then she reached into her top and slid the paper from beside her heart. She held it out to me, between her index and middle finger. Examiners, I kept it with me all the time I was in hospital. I'm sorry about the blood.

82

One afternoon, Andriy and his comrades called to expropriate contributions from a wealthy Jewish merchant, and Andriy was surprised to find Natasha in the Jew's house. While the Jew began the ritual plea of poverty, Natasha was languorously fixing her hair, acting as if Andriy was a stranger.

Is he your father? asked Andriy.

Yes, said the Jew.

Don't be ridiculous, said Natasha.

Then what are you doing here?

What do you think? She collected her boa from the back of the Jew's armchair, tossed it round her neck and strutted from the house.

The Jew began to protest his innocence – how could he, he who had given all his money to Makhno, afford to pay even a dwarf? – but Andriy wasn't listening. He ran after Natasha and grabbed her arm.

What do you want? she asked.

Andriy didn't know.

The world has made me a whore, said Natasha, just as it has made you a soldier.

As Natasha started to walk, Andriy called her every name he could think of: a bourgeois-fucking, labour-shirking, filthy midget pig whore.

Natasha stopped, turned, and repeated all his insults in a mocking impersonation of his speech. If it wasn't for whores, she said, how would retards like you get sex? Then, perhaps fearing the consequences of his temper, she softened her voice and started to explain her story (or at least a version of it). Standing in the merchant's orchard, amid the bare apple trees, she told Andriy that she was a poor Jew who had lost her family, a midget whom nobody would employ or marry, a woman who'd made a living as a burlesque performer, a performer who'd learned that it paid to satisfy male curiosity. And she had come to Gulyai-Polye, she said, to escape the pogroms, because she'd heard that Makhno tried to defend the Jews (which was true) and that he was a dwarf (which was an exaggeration – he was about 5ft 4). And on that journey, she asked Andriy, with what but sex could she use to pay a train guard or bribe a soldier?

But you're here now, said Andriy. He could hear his comrades shouting threats inside the house, while their tethered horses stomped and snorted in the spring sunshine. Why do you still do it? he asked.

Natasha shrugged and lit a cigarette.

How much do you charge?

500 roubles.

500? For a dwarf?

In Moscow, people pay more for a dwarf. Men are curious. A dwarf is special.

Andriy said he didn't believe anyone would pay 500 roubles for a dwarf.

Do you want to have me? asked Natasha.

I won't pay.

No, but you should give me a present. If you like a girl, you should give her a present.

Like what?

A ring. A necklace. Cigarettes. Vodka. Whatever you have.

Andriy had started to tremble. He felt driven by some powerful unseen force. From his coat pocket, he withdrew a pair of ruby earrings; that morning, he'd expropriated them from the widow of a high-ranking Russian officer.

Natasha closed her hand around the earrings and walked deeper into the trees. Her step was so light she barely flattened the grass. Beyond the apple trees, the merchant had a walled area, which perhaps had once been a herb garden, but where now the ground was bare. In the shade of the walls, the earth was still striped with shreds of snow. They forced the gate open, dragging it through the mulch of fallen leaves, and then they stood in the afternoon quiet, sharing the cigarette.

When the flame was burning their lips, Natasha threw the butt onto the frozen mulch of leaves, and then she pressed her hands against Andriy's crotch. He flinched and jolted, for his erection was too sensitive to be touched, but Natasha untied the cord of his trousers. She barely had to stoop to bring his penis to her lips. As soon as she put it in her mouth, Andriy thought he was going to ejaculate. No, he said, pushing her head away, I want the normal.

Natasha shook her head. I don't do that.

I paid for the normal.

No, you gave me a present.

Then I want it back.

Not while I'm bleeding.

Andriy had heard conflicting stories about bleeding women. He'd heard it was the best time to fuck an unmarried girl because bleeding women can't get pregnant; he'd also heard that fucking a bleeding woman could make your penis rot. Right then, the risk seemed worth it.

Anyway, said Natasha, that's how you get syphilis. Soldiers have more diseases than whores.

I don't. I've never been with a woman before.

Never? Natasha thought about this and then reflected aloud that probably no woman would choose to kiss a deformed mouth. She turned away from him, and Andriy thought she was going to leave. Instead, she spat three times into the cup of her hand, lifted her dress and rubbed the saliva between her legs. Then she put her hands against the stone wall and waited. You'll need to go on your knees, she said, when Andriy didn't move.

No, said Andriy, the normal way – lying down. Anticipating Natasha's objection, he took off his overcoat and spread it on the wet ground.

You'll need to be quick, said Natasha, as she lay down on his coat.

Andriy kneeled before her, hoisted her dress to her waist. She showed no reaction to what he was doing; her head was at an angle, staring at the branches that overhung the wall: on the nearest apple tree, amid the spring buds, a trio of sparrows had begun their evening song. Andriy pulled down her bloody shorts. There was blood dried purple and black on her thighs. He climbed on top of her so that they lay belly to belly, his head far above hers, and he pushed forward trying to get his penis inside her. He couldn't find where her hole was. At one point he thought he'd got it, and he started thrusting, but then he realised his penis was just between her thighs.

What are you doing? she said, her tone irritated. You need to go down a bit.

Andriy felt embarrassed, humiliated. By the time he had shuffled lower, he had lost his tumescence. He could see how it worked now – you had to point it upwards – but it wouldn't go in now it wasn't hard.

Natasha reached to put his penis inside her, but she stopped when she felt its softness. She laughed, still looking up at the trees. The eyes can see it, she said, but the teeth can't bite it.

Wait, said Andriy. He propped himself with one hand and squeezed her breast with the other. He concentrated on her lips – he was amazed to think that his penis had been in her mouth. He wished she would meet his gaze, but she remained impassive beneath him. Still, after a minute or so, he thought it worth trying again. He reached between her legs and tried to stuff himself inside her.

Stop, she said, swatting his hand away. She squeezed the shaft of his penis tight and poked the tip into her vagina. Andriy lay still, enjoying the sensation. You need to hurry up, said Natasha.

Andriy tried to move his penis in and out, but it wasn't hard enough. He saw that his hand was covered with her blood. After a few seconds, his flaccid penis slipped out. There was blood on his overcoat.

Are you done? asked Natasha.

Yes, he said. I'm done.

83

Deferral

When I can't decide what to wear
I call you up and say 'What should
I wear?'

At first there's a pause----------------------
----

and an understanding that this question
wears on you, but I know I'll ask it
of you until you say something

'wear something sexy', or 'wear something
desirable' or 'wear something

I can show you off in:
wear heels, your nipples wearing through '
or better.

'wear something I can fuck you through
or undress you out of
or tear or tie you up in.' But when you do

finally answer, it's more likely you'll
pause---
----
then say 'wear anything; we're going bowling'.

84

It was three days before Andriy went near the cultural centre, and then he did so only to beg for the earrings back; as much as he was ashamed of his sexual failure, he was more afraid that Natasha would tell his comrades about the looted earrings. But when she saw him, she seemed relieved and happy and insisted they rehearse his scene. Andriy protested, but the other actors were watching, and eventually he had no choice but to shuffle on stage in character. His heart was in it even less than it had been in previous rehearsals, and he apologetically slouched across the stage, searching for Natasha in meek silence.

No! said Natasha, breaking her statuesque pose. You're ruining the whole play! Do it again, but look frightening – look like you want to kill me!

Andriy tried again, but he felt pathetic. He couldn't look at Natasha, let alone threaten her.

Stop, she said. She turned to address the other actors. Do you want to know why he is so timid? His penis doesn't work.

Everyone laughed, except Andriy, who shouted at her to be quiet.

He's not a man, said Natasha. He told me that last summer he visited a prostitute – a toothless crone was all he could afford.

Andriy crossed the stage, blood pounding at his temples. He was almost dizzy with hurt and rage.

He gave her all his money and couldn't even–

Andriy shoved her to the floor, spat at her, yelled that she was a filthy lying whore.

To his surprise, Natasha smiled and clapped. *Now* you've got it! she said, standing up. *Now* you look like you want to kill me.

85

I walked out, heartbroken and elated, my head filled with a thousand thoughts of love and distance. As I turned the corner onto the High Street, I stopped below a street lamp, suddenly overburdened by the day's events. I saw two men walking towards me. I immediately knew they were the men with whom I'd argued in the pub. They were five or six metres away, smiling in a way that I haven't forgotten, but have only ever been able to describe as sadistic.

86

The play was never performed. One week before the opening night, General Denikin's White Army routed the Bolsheviks north of the Don River and crushed the Makhnovists near Gulyai-Polye (see Denikin, 1992 [1930], pp-233-235). Denikin commanded 55,500 well-armed troops (ibid., p-233) and was heavily backed by the British – Britain supplied Denikin with 250,000 rifles, twelve tanks, 1,685,522 shells, 160 million rounds of ammunition, and about 100 aeroplanes (Palij, 1976, p-184). Trotsky decided to abandon the Ukrainian front altogether, withdrawing the Bolshevik troops to Central Russia, while Makhno's army began a long retreat west. Meanwhile, Denikin's forces advanced through Ukraine and Russia, boasting that they would capture Moscow by Christmas.

In so far as the Denikinists had a political programme it was based on the restoration of landlords and the re-establishment of a single Russian state incorporating the Ukraine. This brought them into conflict with the local population, and even one of their own commanders, General Wrangel, described 'pillage and speculation (...) debauchery, gambling, orgies (...) looting, violence and arbitrary acts' (quoted in Skirda, 2004, pp-148/9).

He recalled that at this time the White Army hunted down anybody suspected of any contact with opposition groups, even if that contact had been involuntary – a policy that he denounced as 'insane and cruel' (Palij, 1976, p-188). Otherwise sympathetic chroniclers are scathing about the White's abuses in the Ukraine: Richard Luckett (1971) bemoans the 'casual brutalities of the Cossacks,' the regular pogroms (p-327), and other 'appalling acts of barbarism' (p-391). They issued proclamations encouraging uprisings against 'Jew-communists', and they were responsible for hundreds of pogroms and the deaths of tens of thousands of Jews (see Mayer, 2000, pp-519-526). 'Many of their victims were beaten, mutilated, raped, hanged, burned, dumped into wells or thrown from rooftops, and buried alive' (ibid., p-519).

For Andriy, the onset of this terror produced one consolation. Those who guessed what fate awaited them tried to flee with the Makhnovist army. The play may never have been performed, but Andriy was not yet separated from Natasha.

87

Next memory, I am about twenty metres further up the road, and I have blood coming from my nose and mouth. I'm trying to get onto my knees and someone in a high-visibility jacket is telling me to stay down. I'm trying to say that I'm okay, that I don't need to go to hospital. I can hear the screech of unwinding tape and a woman says 'Are we treating this as a crime scene?' and a man says 'We have to, don't we?' And then I must have lost consciousness again because the next thing I remember, I am strapped into a stretcher and I can't move my head. They are sliding me into an ambulance and I'm on my back, looking up past the streetlights, where the sky is purple, and the horizon is light blue with the promise of tomorrow.

88

Makhno's army travelled west on horseback, their machine guns mounted on carts. They crossed lands once controlled by rogue Petliurists and independent war lords. They passed three children hung naked from the bough of a tree. They dynamited bridges as soon as they'd crossed them. Some nights they dispersed into small groups, buried their guns, and disappeared among the villages and farms. They captured a group of Siberian Bolshevik deserters, gave them food and vodka, and told them to go home and fight for freedom. They armoured abandoned railway wagons and carried their wounded along the train tracks. When they could, they stopped in villages and townships and demanded to be billeted; in return, they paid the peasants with expropriated gold. They slept with the animals on beds of straw or dirt. They ran out of ammunition and launched daily counter attacks just to capture armaments. When a detachment was outnumbered, they created the impression of a huge cavalry, by asking the peasants to ride on the horizon holding sticks.

One day, near Krivol-rog, they encircled a stately home. Its windows were broken, its fountain was dry, and its lawn had grown to the height of Andriy's knees. Six undressed corpses lay in a line against the moss-patched garden balustrade. When the Makhnovists called out to the mansion's occupiers, they were answered with gunfire. Five minutes later, 100 men filed from the building with their hands raised in surrender. The men wore animal skins over their heads and shoulders, and they had smeared their faces with blood. Andriy didn't know who they were – a militia of bandits, or strays from Nikifor Grigoriev's army, perhaps – but after a discussion, they were allowed to join the Makhnovists.

Two days later, Andriy went looking for Natasha.

Since leaving Gulyai-Polye, she had been helping the army as a seamstress, trying to stitch and repair soldiers' clothes. By this stage, many of the men were dressed in rags or clothes that didn't fit. Their trousers would fall down or their jackets stopped at their elbows. Some of them fought barefoot. But Natasha had somewhere found and restrung an old kobza, which in the evening she strummed for the amusement of the soldiers. She'd pluck a rudimentary tune and sing one of her funny sexual songs; the soldiers would often request the one about the genitally-disarmed Germans. That night, however, when Andriy searched the mansion, nobody he spoke to had seen the midget.

Eventually he found her. She was alone in the dark, sitting in the mansion's partially-enclosed pagoda-style folly. Her face was swollen and there was blood coming from her mouth. Who did this? Andriy demanded. He stamped his foot through the rotten wooden bench, vowing that Makhno would avenge this outrage. Natasha stood up and limped towards the mansion; she held a dislodged tooth in her palm, like a child awaiting reward.

89

'Is there anyone we can contact for you?'

'Can you lift your arm up for me. There we go.'

'Do you feel sick at all?'

'I'm just going to shine this in your eyes.'

'Do you have any allergies?'

'This will hurt a bit. There we go.'

'Can you feel this?'

'And your other arm.'

'This?'

'It's best to look away.'

'Do you know where you are?'

'And... there we go.'

'Do you remember what happened?'

At no point have I ever recovered memory of the attack, and yet I had then, and still have now, vivid awareness of my attackers' rage and hatred. This knowledge is not substantiated by any sensory recollection, but does feel like a memory rather than a supposition. Of emotions, I most remember my shame.

Later – how much later I cannot say – I was wheeled to a CAT scan. I lay inside its tube and remembered when, as a child, I had been startled by a rat in a tunnel. I had resolved to follow a river from its source to where it entered the sea, but as I climbed uphill the river shrank and branched until I was following the sound of runnels that were hidden beneath the bracken. Soon my runnel was a trickle of water visible only where it briefly abseiled from the moss onto the peat. Even then I wasn't satisfied, examiners. I dropped onto my hands and knees and crawled through the bracken, looking for the start of this trickle. I wanted to find the very first drip. And then the morning sun broke through and I saw caught in its light a million droplets scattered on the hillside like rhinestones.

I must have thought about more than this in the CAT scan, for I was there so long I feared they had forgotten me. However, I now remember nothing else. After some minutes, I started to feel sick. I fidgeted my legs, hoping to attract attention. When I was returned to the ward, the lights were dimmed, and I was left alone. In fact, maybe it was at this point that I recalled the river. I followed it under a bridge, I remember. At first, I could scramble on the sloping concrete sideway, but after a few metres, the water entered a cylindrical tunnel. I was reluctant to abandon the waterside having followed it so far, so I waded into the river, uprooting water weed with every step. In the middle of the tunnel, where the water was thigh-deep, I could see little except the light at the far exit. As I paused, unsure whether I should continue, I gazed at the brickwork on the near wall. There appeared to be a large rock floating in the dark. When it moved, I screamed. When I screamed, the rat screamed, and as I flailed and stumbled – soaked now – back towards the entrance, the echoes of these screams bounced behind me, as though gaining ground.

I must have flinched, I think, for the nurse asked if I needed more painkillers. Then she asked if I knew my name and where I was. When I asked to go to the toilet, she brought me a plastic jug, but I couldn't conceive of a way to urinate in it without spilling, and I was embarrassed to ask for help.

I don't remember the order of events, but at some point I spoke to a police detective. 'I have to tell you,' he said, 'that we currently have two men in custody on suspicion of assault.' I tried to explain that it was entirely my fault, that I didn't wish to press charges, but he seemed unable to hear me. I don't know whether this was before or after I came out of shock. I think it was before because by the time I started shaking, the ward was quiet and gloomy, as it was in the hour or two before morning. I do remember that before the detective left, he put my jacket in a bag and asked for my blood-leathered shirt. One of the nurses, who called everyone on the ward 'lovely' (a kindness for which I'm still grateful), helped me unbutton it and disconnected the drips from my wrists. Then the policeman asked for my trousers. I didn't want to give him my trousers because I didn't want to walk home in my pants. The nurse gave me green hospital pyjamas and said I had to give the policeman my trousers. Okay, I said, I will put on the hospital clothes, but I want to keep my trousers. How will I get home without my trousers? You're being admitted to hospital, said the nurse. You have serious injuries. I asked again whether my nose was broken. Your trousers are evidence, said the policeman. When I asked the policeman whether I was legally required to give up my trousers, he said the trousers weren't that big a deal; the jacket and shirt would probably suffice. I kept my trousers in a grey hospital bag.

90

One night, when they were near Uman, Andriy's sotnia carried out an especially reckless raid on Denikin's supplies. The raid was an act of desperation from which they feared they might not return, but Denikin's guards had gone into the village, or got drunk, or fallen asleep, and Andriy's sotnia captured a cartload of ammunition without firing a shot. They also snatched some bottles of vodka, and when they got back to the barn where they were billeted, they sat on the straw and drank in celebration. When the vodka ran out, one of the soldiers opened a vial of anti-freeze.

Natasha had drunk with them and had sung a couple of songs. Her face was still bruised, but to Andriy she seemed to have recovered her spirits. Then, as they lay in the straw, joking and laughing above the snores, apropos of nothing, Natasha said, Look at this. She picked up someone's pistol and shot herself in the head.

91

When I arrived at Gloucestershire Royal Hospital, the porters wheeled me to a private room in the Maxillofacial Ward. A group of doctors soon entered in a great hurry and between occasional questions (does this hurt? Does that hurt? Do you remember what happened? Can you feel this? Do you know where you are?), they talked about me in the third person at such speed that I could catch only occasional words (multiple fractures, retrograde amnesia, internal bleeding, mandible, radiology). When they were ready to leave, a doctor with a beard and a French accent (the senior registrar, I later decided), asked me what the hell I'd been hit with. I was finding it harder to speak, and so I raised my hand and mimed a slow punch. 'No,' he said. 'A man would break his hands before he has done this. You have been used like a baseball, yes?' He laughed, wildly, and momentarily looked to me like an etching of a Victorian lunatic.

And then, examiners, I was taken in a wheelchair to the Radiology Department, where the porter parked me at the entrance to the waiting room. The room was full of outpatients – sprained wrists, sore ankles – and I began to feel self-conscious. First, hospital pyjamas are not dignified. My blood-stained top had a low V-neck with two popper buttons, and the pyjama bottoms were so thin as to be revealing. It occurred to me that this would be the worst time ever to become erect (in fact, I needn't have worried, for I was impotent for more than a month). Second, I realised that nobody could look at me or avoid looking at me. The receptionist, the other patients, even the vending machine repair man, would glance at me, flinch their gazes away, and then, a few seconds later, glance back. Worst of all, perhaps, I was now very worried about wetting myself.

And admittance to the radiology room did nothing to ease my discomfort. The radiologist took ten or twenty pictures and some of the poses were excruciating. For example, for one x-ray, I had to look upwards and push my chin against the screen. Throughout the day, I had found it increasingly hard to swallow and had used tissues to catch the watery blood that drooled over my chin. But in this position, the saliva couldn't leave my mouth. The radiologist arranged me as she desired, and there was then a pause while she walked behind the screen to shoot the pictures.

During this time, the saliva ran down my throat and I choked. When I was finally allowed to move, I dribbled strings of pink saliva onto the floor. I looked, I imagine, like some hideous magnification of a feeding insect.

Still, upon being returned to my room, I learned that because twelve hours had elapsed since the attack, I was now allowed to use the en-suite. There was, of course, a mirror in the en-suite. Later, the nurses would nickname me 'Shrek' because my head was so swollen and because the bruising spread over my shoulders and abdomen giving me an inhuman colour. Apart from the size of my head, the first thing I noticed was my nose. Flattened in the valley between my swollen cheeks, my nose had disappeared. Standing in front of the mirror, I was surprised that I could see myself, for through the swelling I could not see the eyes through which I saw. Then I saw my mouth; it wasn't the shape of a mouth at all. It seemed most of my teeth had been knocked out; there were three teeth here, then nothing, and then two teeth more. I would later learn that this was because both my mandible and maxillary arch were broken in several places, and so my jaw line was tiered across my face. All morning, I had been trying to smile, and now I understood why nobody reciprocated; with my jagged mouth and ballooned lips, what I thought was a smile appeared to others as a monstrous void.

92

By September 1919, the Makhnovists had been on the retreat for four months and they were near Uman, 600km from Gulyai-Polye. Exhausted, lacking arms, and burdened by eight-thousand sick and wounded, they found themselves surrounded by Denikinists and Petliurists.

At this point, Makhno counter-attacked. First, he agreed a truce with the Petliurists: whatever Petliura's opinion of peasant anarchists, the Makhnovists were all that stood between him and Denikin's marauding Cossacks. Thus, Makhno could persuade Petliura to shelter his eight-thousand invalids. With this sorted, Makhno turned his exhausted men and women to face the Denikinists. He convinced them that the entire retreat had been a tactic to over-extend Denikin's forces, and then, on September 26th, with a cry of 'Liberty or Death', he and his famished troops attacked the centre of Denikin's position (Arshinov provides a predictably heroic account of this battle, 2005 [1923], pp-144-148).

Contagious panic seized Denikin's forces, and in the ensuing rout hundreds were slaughtered on the banks of, the Sinyukha River – Voline and Arshinov describe corpses strewn for miles. While Makhno may have exaggerated in claiming 'complete annihilation' – Denikin's sources suggest they lost 637 men (Palij, 1976, p-195) – this was a decisive moment in the twentieth century. The Denikinist officer Sakovitch understood this: 'All of us ranking officers sensed that something tragic had just occurred though nobody could have had any inkling of the enormity of the disaster which had struck. None of us knew that at that precise moment nationalist Russia had lost the war' (Quoted in Skirda, 2004, pp-136/7).

The Makhnovists charged east covering 660km in eleven days (Denikin, 1992 [1930], p-281). In town after town they destroyed regiments that knew nothing of the White's defeat and were unprepared for battle. As Denikin himself recalled: 'Makhno's bands, sometimes numbering as many as thirty thousand men, roved far behind in the vast territory between the Dnieper and the Sea of Azov, disorganising our rear and on one occasion even threatening Taganrog, the seat of G.H.Q.' (ibid., p-254). Denikin had to withdraw troops from the northern front, effectively halting the march on Moscow; he later reflected that the Makhnovist revolt 'had the effect of disorganizing our rear and weakening our front at the most critical period of its existence' (ibid., p-282). It was on this basis that Max Nomad labelled Makhno 'the bandit who saved Moscow' (n.d. [1939]).

93

Robin later told me that when he approached my room, he peeked through the door and then – having seen my face – withdrew to compose himself before announcing his presence. He had brought me a newspaper article about Philip Roth, a first edition of *Libra*, and four bottles of crème de cassis. He held these items as if now unsure what to do with them, and then he walked towards the window. He was talking to me, I'm sure, but I remember only watching him cross the room. As I rolled my head with his progress, I saw myself as a child in a swimming pool. My ears are full of water and the other swimmers appear to be moving in slow motion. I am in the Victorian baths and the sunlight is amplified through the glass roof. Arches support the roof and architecturally the building is reminiscent of a cathedral. I do not remember swimming; I only recall the rubber bracelets in which one stored one's locker key. Do you examiners remember the pleasure of fitting the key into its rubber cocoon? Do you recall the slight ping of the rubber on the back of your wrist?

Robin stood near the clinical waste bin, swearing and shaking his head and smiling. He stood on the foot pedal, and I remember him saying, 'That's good, isn't it?' Given all the intelligent and compassionate things I have heard Robin say, it's strange that I remember his comments on environmental hygiene management.

Later, when Lempi arrived, she cried but tried to hide it. Of all the visits, this is the one of which I remember least; I don't even recall feeling the acute embarrassment that I experienced during subsequent visits. Maybe it was the painkillers, or maybe it was my exhaustion, but the conversation floated around me like the comforting chatter of strangers, and I now remember only the departure of my friends. They both searched for a gesture to replace a hug, for I must have looked too fragile to hold. Robin placed his hand, as light as a fern leaf, on my shoulder. I remember his words very clearly. He said, 'Be strong, my friend. I am thinking of you.' Lempi hesitated at the foot of my bed, and then, through the covers, she squeezed my toes.

94

What about Andriy? What did he do in the weeks following the battle of Peregonovka? Where did he get a baby from? How did he come to kill Gerhard Dyke?

On his triumphant journey east, Andriy smelled the village of Danylivka long before he reached it, and it was only morbid curiosity that dissuaded him from bypassing it at haste. On the outskirts of the ruined hamlet, the fetid stench of a shot-dead ox mixed with the after-fire smell – the deadly-nightshade aroma of burned hair and flesh – that for five days had hung across the steppe, impervious to the wind. At the next house, a goat strained against its tether, carving a collar of blood around its neck. Andriy did not at first notice the baby. When he did see it, neither he nor his men moved to help; instead, they remained astride their horses, covering their faces with strips of cloth. The baby wore only a dress-length embroidered grey tunic and it cried only silent gusts of breath. Behind it, a khata stood thatched and whitewashed (though others in the village had been burned), and behind that, the heads of sunflowers hung brown in the cold. For a second, the child rose on its knees, but then it wallowed on its belly, swimming across the dirt. Meanwhile, the ox, grotesquely yawning, lay stiff with cold and death, its eyes gone and its insides slumped and melting.

And then the child changed direction. It flapped its right side, steering its trunk forty-five degrees as though making a calculated readjustment. Then it continued forward, moving in uneven jerks, extending its hands to paw the dirt. It was moving only inches but its course had definitively changed: it was crawling directly towards Andriy. Examiners, it seemed to Andriy that the infant had somehow chosen him, that the infant had elected him in some primitive way, and at this point he dismounted his horse and walked towards the baby. As he stood over it, the loudest noise was the drone of the flies that crawled around the ox's boundaries – its open belly, the bullet wound through its head, its mouth and genitals. The flies were emerald green and humming. There were maggots, too, wriggling around these boundaries. There were maggots inside the ox and the smell of cadaverine and putrescine attracted more flies. The ox's legs stuck out at an absurd angle and the smell made Andriy choke. He felt dizzy and faint and feverishly hot. He looked back at the baby. No one spoke, except Vasily, who shouted orthodox prayers and laughed and cackled and saluted the goat. After a second, Andriy lifted the child. Batko Makhno would have helped the child, he thought.

Inside the khata, he found the corpse of a young woman – the baby's mother, he presumed. A mezuzah had been hacked from the doorpost and smashed underfoot, so Andriy understood that this had been a Jewish home. The Jewess's face was so bruised that her husband, wherever he was, would not have recognised her. She was naked, blue-white, and it seemed wrong for him to look at her. Andriy wanted to do something respectful, but her eyes were too swollen to close, and he knew none of their rituals or sacrifices or whatever they did with their dead. He thought about Natasha, and he remembered, with discomfort, how they had left her where she'd fallen. Her eyes, he remembered, were glassy and still. In death, she had looked like a broken doll, her tiny legs splayed out in a V.

The baby was a Jew baby, he realised, but that made no difference: Batko Makhno said the Jews were comrade toilers like any other comrade toilers. He spoke to the woman aloud and was startled and self-conscious at the sound of his voice. Batko Makhno would avenge her death, he said, and then he walked outside, where the ground was ragged with the melting frost.

95

After visiting hours, the French doctor returned with his entourage. 'Okay,' he said, flapping my x-rays. 'Good.' He looked through the pages. 'Okay. This eye socket is fractured up here and also down here. The cheekbone, here, is cracked. Good.' He looked back at his papers. 'Around the right eye we have a fracture across the brow, yes? Here, under the eye, complex fractures. We will have to check his eyes tomorrow. Has that been booked? Book that, yes? Here, across the cheek. We will have to rebuild his nose. Good. There is a fracture of the skull, up, you see, here, yes? Then the mandible, the jaw, is broken here, here, and here; here… and here. Good. And there. This is the main work, I think. We will have to cut here, along your brow; here and here under your eyes. Good. And we will drill into each side of your jaw, here. The rest I think we can do from inside. Has he signed consent forms? We will need you to sign consent forms.

There are risks, of course. When you operate on the eye there is always the chance that you are losing your sight, yes? But do not worry. It is something that exists in the literature, this is all. And do not worry about the cuts. We will not leave you looking too much like Frankenstein!' A curious feature of the French doctor's bedside manner was that he laughed wildly at his own jokes. When he stopped laughing, I said, 'Don't worry; I've long-considered wearing a beard.'

'A beard! Yes! Like mine!' The French doctor grabbed his chin. 'I am wearing a beard! A beard!' he said again as he strode to the door. 'Oh,' he said, turning. 'Do not sneeze. Did I mention this? Your nose is blocked, yes? And there is very much pressure from the bleeding. And you have this little skull fracture, here. If you sneeze... how do I say? If you sneeze – *bang*! Like a bag of crisps, yes?' And once again the French doctor laughed, like one adversely affected by the phases of the moon.

96

Andriy picked up the child because it seemed to him that the baby had entrusted its safety to his care. Only afterwards, once he was holding the thing, did he rationalise this act of mercy as doing what Batko would have wanted. So is it ridiculous to suggest that the baby's life (and thus in a small way the history of the Soviet Union) would have been different had the child not at that moment changed its course to crawl towards Andriy?

Why did the baby turn? As its hands scratched the dirt, a small stone rolled an inch. Flies perched along the spears of feather grass. The baby's hands pushed up and its knees dug in. Flakes of stone had embedded into the heel of the baby's left hand, and a pebble the size of a grain of rice had impaled its left knee. There was a cry of air but the baby's vocal folds had been damaged by days of screaming and the air passed though as a breeze. The crow cawed and flapped and flew towards the child, all claws and beak, like it wanted its eyes. The flies around the ox's vacant eyes crowded together, shimmering with oily reflections of light. The baby's left leg wouldn't press because of the stone in its knee. Its right side flapped and the child began to turn, driven off-straight, like a boat being rowed with only one oar. Its breath was softer than the drone of flies. Then the stone dropped out and the left knee dug into the dirt, and the child's direction straightened, and it crawled directly towards Andriy.

97

I received dozens of injections: saline drip, intravenous-painkillers, antibiotics, anti-inflammatories, anticoagulants. The first bruises were on my inner elbows, but as the nurses searched for new veins, my wrists, forearms, and upper arms patterned red, blue, brown, and yellow. At 6:15 every morning, after injections, I would shuffle my drip stand to the en suite, and there I would try to wash in preparation for the doctors' round. I would scrub my scalp and armpits with anti-bacterial hand wash, and I'd dry myself with paper towels, for it hadn't occurred to me to ask for shampoo, soap, or a towel. I would pour Corsodyl into my mouth and drool it into the sink. Some days, I would slurp a breakfast of porridge, swallowing only a percentage of each spoonful, resigned that the remainder would dribble down my chin and back into the bowl to await the next expedition. Porridge was the only thing I ate, examiners, except on two occasions when minestrone soup was on the lunch menu. I am a vegan, you see, and I was on a liquid diet. I cannot now explain why I never mentioned that I was starving, but by the time of my discharge I weighed just fifty-three kilos.

Yes, it was exhausting. Four days after the attack, they

wheeled me to the Ophthalmology Department, and there I spent fifteen minutes, trying with one eye obscured to place the hoop of a pointer over a dot on a grid. Then, just after we'd returned to the ward, my nose began to bleed. A nurse brought me a cardboard receptacle shaped like a bowler hat. When this bowl was full, she brought me another one. Then, since nothing would stop this nosebleed, she called the Ear, Nose, and Throat Doctor. The Ear, Nose, and Throat Doctor, the least personable human being I have ever met, argued for some time that I wasn't her patient, and then, in a fit of pique, she rammed a Rhino-Rocket up each of my nostrils. Examiners, would anyone want anything called a Rhino-Rocket shoved anywhere near his nose? A Rhino-Rocket is essentially a tampon, some three inches in length, which is inserted till it prods your brain; then, in a seemingly needless malevolence, it is inflated. I cannot imagine this ever being less than excruciating, but if all one's nasal bones are broken then the pain is honestly fearsome.

Was I fearful, examiners? Yes. I panicked every time I heard footsteps in the corridor, and weeks later, after I had returned to my flat, I shouted at Lempi when she opened the curtains; though I live on the third floor, it seemed to me plausible that my attackers could glance up with periscopic vision and see me defenceless and weak. But was I vengeful, examiners? This is a harder question to answer. The questions of justice, responsibility, and free will never seemed more relevant. What else is theory for but moments such as these?

98

Soon after they left Danylivka, Andriy's sotnia stopped at a village and demanded to swap horses and eat. Andriy asked for some vodka, too, because even in the afternoon sunshine he had been shaking with cold. They ate rabbit soup with their cupped hands, plunging their arms deep into the vat in search of meat. Afterwards, Andriy remembered the Jew baby in the tachanka. When he went outside to fetch the creature, the light hurt his eyes so badly that he walked head bowed like a priest, and when he returned and presented it to the women, they said they already had too many mouths to feed and that, in any case, it wasn't right to have a Jew baby in a gentile home. Andriy stood up, head spinning, and said that Batko would execute them for such an attitude, but the women knew he was bluffing, and after they had fed the baby some milk, he wrapped it in one of the flags and placed it with Vyacheslav in the tachanka.

For some reason, when they left the village, he for once failed to arrange his outriders, and so it was undoubtedly his fault that they were ambushed. Under fire, Andriy still lost all composure. When he regained control, he had arrived at a rise in the road, beside the tachanka and two dozen cavalry. The rest of his sotnia – there had been ninety-eight of them that morning – had scattered into the forest. He could not estimate how many had been killed. It was now quiet except for the wheezing of wounded horses. When Vyacheslav shot one of the horses, a wounded mare harnessed to the tachanka, Andriy jumped at the noise and blood pounded his temples. He was so tired and thirsty.

When he finally spoke, he acknowledged his blame and proposed they elect a new officer, but Vyacheslav shouted that this was no time for debates. We need to act, he said. This intervention only further convinced Andriy that Vyacheslav would have made a better commander than he did. He needed to issue an order. Makhno and Schuss would have counter-attacked; he was sure of that. The ambushers – whoever they were – had at least one machine gun, but they would be set up to defend an attack from the forest. If he and his troops circled round and attacked from the rear– Or maybe they should pretend to retreat and then– Or dig in, hold this high ground. His head was spinning and his limbs felt like stockings filled with ice.

Once, as a child, Andriy had owned a clay marble. It was just before he started work so he must have been eight or nine. The way they played marbles, one child threw his marble up the road, and the second child aimed to hit this marble with his own. If he was successful, he kept both marbles. If he was unsuccessful, the first child would then have the chance to throw at the second child's marble. When Andriy played, he would hurl his marble at pace, knowing that if he missed – and the way he flung it he almost certainly would – then his marble would at least carry far up the road, leaving his opponent a long and difficult shot. In this way, Andriy neither won nor lost marbles but recorded a succession of no score draws. When playing the village champion, however, he threw his marble in the opposite direction. His opponent wandered off, appalled by Andriy's disregard for the spirit of the game, and Andriy ran to collect his marble. But he had thrown it so far into the roadside weeds that days of searching did not retrieve it. He worried sometimes that his life would be forfeited like his marble, thrown away for want of courage.

99

One week after the attack, I was ordered into a hospital gown, instructed to remove my compression stockings, and wheeled on a trolley to the operating theatre. The operating theatre was smaller and busier than I had imagined – seven or eight people and lights and gas cylinders and pipes. Looking up at the lights and the faces, hearing a hiss, hiss, hiss, like an old man's laboured breathing, hearing, too, the anaesthetist's questions – 'Do you support a football team?' (Yes, I said, though I do not.) 'Did you see the West Ham match?' – I started to count to ten.

100

Andriy did not regret killing the German boy. He had not meant to kill him, exactly, but it became a defining act in his self-narrative. He had felt so hot and tired and dizzy that he worried he might have been poisoned. The German woman, Anna, had said there was no one but her in the house. Either he– that bastard baby! He had just given her the baby or he was going to get the baby. If you tap the bottom of your kneecap, your leg extends, you know? If I throw dust in your eyes then you blink. It's not that you've chosen to blink, is it? You can do no other. This is what you are. You extend your leg. You blink. Andriy saw the bayonet and he didn't flinch. That was the thing. One year ago, maybe one hour ago, he would have jumped and panicked as he had jumped and panicked when Vyacheslav shot the horse. But that was not him anymore. If I throw dust in your eyes then you blink, yes? That's who you are.

He remembered telling the woman, Anna, that if she told him another lie he would cut her head off, and it felt good to say it because it was true. He had hit the boy, just like that. The way you blink. But the second blow, the one to the neck, he saw before it happened. The woman said the boy was an idiot, but how was he to know? Besides, one needn't be Prince Kropotkin to fire a gun. Batko would have done the same thing. Batko would have killed him. Andriy said to the woman, why didn't you tell me he was here you bastard whore? And she said she didn't know he was there! And Andriy said, same as you don't know where your husbands and sons are, I bet! And to Andriy's surprise, the woman said, I do know where they are: they are with the army, but as God is my witness I swear they are soldiers against my wishes and against the wishes of our Lord. Then, because she had said this, Andriy felt mercy towards the boy. Was it then or later that he gave the woman the baby? Sometimes recklessness makes one safe and ruthlessness makes one kind. The boy stank of shit and he was twitching like a caught fish. Andriy– He did it and it made him vomit but he did it. And then he said, you horse fucker you cry now but where was your kindness when he was alive? You horse fucking bastard crone, you cry now but where is your mercy when you have one of us by the throat? And then, because he wanted to behave in a way that would make Batko proud, he said to the woman, listen, if you answer me honestly now, I promise you will come to no harm. Who else is in the house? And the woman was quiet for a moment and then she said that her daughter, Magdalena, was hiding in the attic. Please, she said, she is only a child: leave my daughter her virtue, please. When Andriy gave his word that the girl's honour would not be harmed, he felt more powerful than the Dnieper in spate.

101

One of the surgeons had explained to me that part of the operation would involve fitting arch bars to my teeth. The arch bars were huge metal things and it's now impossible to understand how, in the recovery room, and for at least another twenty-four hours, I couldn't feel them in my mouth. Soon after waking, I asked the orderly in the recovery room whether the operation had been a success. 'Don't worry about that just now,' he said, which I took to be a sign of disaster. I checked that I still had both legs. (This took longer than you would think, examiners – for fifteen minutes or so, I couldn't be certain one way or the other). I think I'd been in and out of consciousness several times before I realised, or thought I realised, that the promised arch bars were missing. 'Will I need another operation?' I asked. 'Would you like more morphine?' he said.

The orderly supervising my recovery was trying to impress a girl, whose charms I never saw, who did not usually work on the recovery ward. I don't know if she worked in another part of the hospital, or if she was a trainee, or a kid doing work experience, but when her shift finished – it was now late: more than nine hours since I had left the Maxillofacial ward – the guy supposed to be looking after me asked her if she'd had fun and if she wanted to come back in the morning. He kept hitting me with morphine to keep me quiet, and when it was time for us to leave, he started wheeling me away while I was still intravenously attached to a wall-mounted machine.

The rest of the evening appears to me in strobes. I recall, for instance, that back in Max-fax, Lempi tried to kiss my head and gagged at the stench of anaesthetic. I remember waking up to shout at Lempi and Robin (and a nurse who was taking my blood pressure) that Jeanette Winterson was awful, sententious, pretentious, tedious – the adjectives went on and on. I do not remember, though I've subsequently been informed, that at around the same time, I turned my head towards Lempi and told her that I loved her and sincerely believed that we would one day be together. This must have been before I remembered what I had neglected to check in the recovery room: my penis. Had they left me my penis? As surreptitiously as possible, I wriggled my hand across my thigh and touched something tiny and shrivelled but indisputably genital. The relief was brief, for attached to my penis there was a tube; I mean, there was a tube going up my urethra. Now I began to worry; to what was it connected? Inch by inch, while Robin and Lempi talked among themselves, I followed the length of this tube. Soon my hand emerged from under the cover and found that the tube terminated in a bag of liquid hung on the side of the bed, right by Lempi's knees. Lempi, lovely Lempi, had spent the evening staring at a bag of my piss.

102

Of the next two weeks, Andriy remembered only fragments. These memories – an image, a smell, a minute or two of a life he thought was ending – remained forever lodged in him like shrapnel. He dreamt of lice the size of horses. He remembered the German woman, Anna, unbuttoning his shirt and pointing to his typhus rash. She had tied a rag over her face and Andriy, delirious, reaching for any sort of weapon, knocked over a jug of soup or water or milk. At some point new troops arrived: he heard soldiers hailing friends, singing, brawling, debating politics by candlelight. He woke one evening, when the room was dark and the only light was the glow of paraffin lamps in the hall, and he saw that men lay stretched on the floor around him – hawking blood and shaking and shouting the names of women – and from through the wall he heard guitar notes plucked to a melancholic rhythm, while a woman's voice sang German words he couldn't understand. He dreamt he was a decapitated head in a pile of decapitated heads and the bloody beard hair of another head was in his mouth and then a boy with whom he'd worked more than ten years earlier picked him up and cradled him, singing, The rooster is riding the horse: It is raising dust. Where are you? Where are you? The hen is asking. I am leaving, hen, goodbye, for a great war. Where are you? Where are you? The hens began to sob. He remembered someone pouring liquid in his mouth and he was choking and it was in his lungs. He pissed himself more than once. At one point, he shit his pants.

He slept through a thunderstorm and he thought the lightning was artillery fire. When he woke up, he felt lucid and clear, but when he tried to stand to organise defences, he found he was wearing no trousers. One morning, a man lay with his feet near Andriy's head. The man's leg wound was gangrenous and Andriy remembered screaming and trying to kick him away. There is no smell more awful than the smell of gangrene; it was to Andriy like the terror of suffocation. He spat where he lay because he'd coughed and vomited so much that his throat was ripped bare and it hurt too badly to swallow. At some stage, someone had placed candles around the room and in the night he thought his bedding was on fire; by the morning, he was shaking with cold and his teeth were loose and rattling like the storm-hit locked door of an abandoned building.

103

Over days, perhaps over weeks, I struggled to decide whether I wished to press charges. The police informed me that one of my attackers was to carry the burden of guilt alone. The other man, somebody Anderson, had accepted a caution for affray, but Daniel Thomson would later be charged with Grievous Bodily Harm: he had beaten my face repeatedly with a monkey wrench.

It seemed at that moment that there was no separation between the practical and the theoretical. Theorists, writers, and academics, we are told, must abandon their ivory towers and 'engage with the real world'. Where once this was a progressive demand – an appeal for thinkers to match their words with political engagement – today it is a demand for industry-focus, vocational education, business partnerships, income generation, employment-based learning; in short, examiners, it is a demand that education be subordinated to the needs of the economy.

But as I lay, mopping saliva from my chin, pondering the fate of Mr Thomson, rarely has the 'real-world' seemed so real; I repeat – at that moment there was no separation between the practical and the theoretical.

Why might one wish a man imprisoned? To rehabilitate him, perhaps. But Gloucester Prison has the second highest reconviction rate of any jail in the country – of male prisoners who serve less than twelve months in jail, 74.6 per cent are reconvicted (Ministry of Justice, 2010) – and it is hard to see how one can rehabilitate a violent man by incarcerating him in a cramped environment full of hard drugs and other violent men. Then what of incapacitation? People said to me, look what he did to you; he shouldn't be on the streets. But prison is temporary, and its effects are permanent, and violent crime occurs in prison too. Okay, then the rationale must be one of general deterrence: imprisonment may make individual prisoners more dangerous, but the existence of prisons nevertheless makes society safer. This hypothesis is currently untestable. However, if one's justification is deterrence, why not really go for it? Why not poke litterers' eyes out with bamboo sticks or castrate speeding motorists with rusty garden shears? Because, I suppose, that would seem unjust. And therefore, however one approaches the question, one encounters the problem of retributivism: the problem of what punishment is deserved.

Let me explain what most troubled me: if a man is to deserve punishment then we must assume he had some control over his actions. In 1998, the Metropolitan Police Commissioner, Paul Condon, said that black men were disproportionately likely to commit street robberies. Condon's statement caused a furore, not because it was untrue – even if one allows for racism within the criminal justice system, it seems apparent that blacks do commit some crimes more often than whites (see Lea & Young, 1984) – but because it confronted us with a dilemma: avoiding a racist explanation meant we had to qualify the micro-analysis that attributes criminal responsibility to individuals; which is to say, it meant acknowledging that criminality is associated with socio-economic and cultural circumstances, while quickly pointing out that most black men in socio-economically deprived situations do not commit street robberies. The logical progression of this argument, however, would require us to consider the differences in circumstances between those men in socio-economically deprived situations who do commit street robberies and those who do not. We're faced with a choice: either we posit a theory of human action partially *independent of circumstance*, or we accept that criminality is an imponderably complex consequence of social and biological forces.

Before we consider the first option, we should note that accepting the second option leads to another choice. One version of free will, 'compatibilism', advanced by Hume and others, contends that free will and determinism are potentially coexistent: a person is free and responsible for her actions so long as those actions are based on what she believes and desires. In fact, a compatibilist perspective would note that an act can only be considered to belong to an agent if it can be attributed to that agent's antecedent condition. To an *incompatibilist* perspective, however, free will necessitates not just that a person can act according to her beliefs and desires, but that those beliefs and desires are also in some way freely chosen.

104

One afternoon, when the rain was shaking the windowpanes and running from the gutters in bars, Andriy crawled upstairs and found the barracks abandoned. In the master bedroom, where the German women must have slept, he donned a pair of girl's riding breeches and a cardigan stitched with buttons made of cherry pips. His troops had moved on, how long ago he couldn't say, and it seemed only the sick and dying remained. In a room that had once been a library, he lay too tired to move. Some of the books had been ripped for kindling or toilet paper and there were rags and bottles strewn on the floor. There was a globe of the world on the central table but someone had smashed a hole where Russia should have been. He saw that notices had been nailed to the walls and stood to pull them down; outside, the rain was raking the earth like machine gun fire.

Andriy was proud of the reading he had learned in Gulyai-Polye in the months of peace between the German and White invasions. Sitting in this grand room, now convinced that he would survive the typhus, he felt the same sense of power and worth that he had felt when he guaranteed the safety of the girl. He had to know the latest developments. He had to read the news. Then, when he was well, he would say to his troops: here are the latest instructions from the shtarm; I read them while recovering in my temporary headquarters. Patiently, one word at a time, he began to read. To the entire working population of the city of Aleksandrovsk and environs. Comrades and citizens! Detachments of the Revolutionary Insurgent Army of the Ukraine (Makhnovist) are at present stationed in your city. That army has broken the back of the Denikinists, defeating them between Uman and Pomoshnaya, and is hotly pursing the remnants of the enemy as they flee eastwards. His eyes had closed when he had read barely a paragraph.

He woke when the German woman returned. Calling to her, he was surprised by the sound of his voice: it sounded much weaker than he felt. He heard her set down a churn or a chamber pot or some such and then he heard her footsteps on the stairs. You are awake, she said. She was wearing a great coat and her wet hair straggled over her shoulders like waterweed. The Jew baby, about whom Andriy had forgotten, was hung from her neck in a papoose. Yes, said Andriy, I have to report back for duty: Batko will be worried about me. I need to know the latest developments. I was reading the news, but I feel so dizzy that the words are blurring. The woman was silent. Andriy was suddenly conscious of his ridiculous clothes. The baby started crying and the woman soothed him with her thumb. What is your name? Andriy asked. My name is Anna, she said. She was searching the shelves and toppled books. Well, Anna, I cannot tell you my name: if your soldier friends knew the identity of Makhno's dear comrade, they would kill me and my brothers and my brothers' wives. You'd like that, wouldn't you? Will you at least tell me *the baby's* name? said Anna. Andriy had not expected this and he took a moment to reply. His name is Yaroslav, he said, for Yaroslav had been Andriy's father's name. Yaroslav, she said, nodding. Do you know this book? She held a thick leather-bound tome. It's by Lev Tolstoy. He was an anarchist and also a Christian. Andriy reached out for the book, unsure whether he should believe her. He flicked through it, enjoying the delicacy of its pages. Thank you for nursing me, he said. Do not thank me, said Anna; thank the Good Lord. God is merciful and he has saved you, for what purpose it is not my place to speculate.

105

The day after my operation (or was it the day after the day after?), a nurse arrived to remove my catheter. 'Don't worry,' she said, 'we try to maintain your dignity.'

'Will I wet the bed?' I asked.

The nurse's expression suggested that this was an especially odd question. 'Do you normally?' she said.

She pulled back the covers, lifted my gown, and searched for my penis. Then, trying not to look at the poor, bullied little thing, she ripped off the tape – Ow! Ow! – and slid out the latex tube. There, she said, glancing at my emaciated nakedness and shrunken sex. Examiners, it was at this moment that Thrub arrived.

At first, I saw only his shadow. The light dimmed and when I looked round I saw that Thrub had entered the room and was looming over me, while Robin stood behind him, shoulders hunched in apology Thrub wore a grey suit and a black tie and his white eyebrows peaked in the corners like jags of lightning. He was carrying a large old book of the sort one would expect to see in the hands of a medieval warlock. 'Good God,' he said. 'What on earth are you doing to him?' Thrub's tone was strong enough that the nurse felt she had something to apologise for; she bowed and gathered her things and apologised again. Meanwhile, I pulled the covers over my privates. 'What a fucking abominable sight,' said Thrub. It was unclear whether Thrub was referring to my face or my genitals.

He sat in the plastic chair normally reserved for Lempi, while Robin took up position in the arm chair on the far side of the bed. 'What the fuck have they done to you?' Robin started to list my injuries but Thrub interrupted him by dropping the warlock's tome on my bladder. 'Kant,' he said. 'Immanuel Kant. Yes, it appears we're stuck with one and other. No early retirement for me. So, you'll need to read that,' said Thrub. 'And, you know, get well, etcetera.'

106

Andriy heard the horses just as Anna had, at his request, begun to read from the book by the Christian who was also an anarchist. She was describing Anna Scherer's soirée, and Andriy was wondering why a supposed anarchist would write a book in which everyone was a prince or a countess or similar – to show the error of their ways, perhaps? – and that was when he heard the thud of hooves and the shouting in the courtyard. In the evening chill the rain had turned to sleet, and the bearers of gold epaulettes appeared from the white night, as though they had been summoned from the pages of the German woman's book. Without hesitation, he staggered downstairs, passing on the way the German daughter, who was carrying the Jew baby. The sick room was foul in a way he had not realised while he'd been part of it: it stank of faeces and gangrene and the men were covered in sweat and mud and one had blood dribbling from his mouth. The rubbish basket was filled with discarded bandages and rags and pages of books that had been used to wipe away the filth. Andriy tried to wake his comrades but none could move: one spat a tooth out and drooled blood on his chin. An older man murmured about mouldy bread and promised a sailor's mutiny that would end the Russo-Japanese War. Andriy could find no weapons.

He stumbled upstairs just as the door opened. Downstairs, the soldiers, on finding the sick partisans, whooped and yelled, and Andriy heard crashing and hacking and screaming. Tell them I'm a German, he whispered. Tell them I'm your son, you bastard German vipers, you filthy scheming whores. The baby was crying and the girl was soothing it, and the older woman was bent over, weeping into her skirt. Through the window, Andriy saw that in the courtyard the soldiers were dragging a naked partisan through the mud. When they released him, he lay sprawled on his back, and the sleet that landed on him did not melt; his hair and his beard turned white, and in a second his nudity was covered. Then one soldier tied him by the neck to a horse, and the other whipped the horse into a gallop, so that the man was dragged into the sleet until he could not be seen. Someone was climbing the stairs. Tell them I'm your son! Tell them I'm your son or I'll kill you! Do you understand? I'll kill you and your daughter. Batko will kill you. He will kill you and your sons and your soldiers and your God. Andriy sat on the table beside the German woman. The man who'd climbed the stairs did not seem to be moving. Then, after a pause, he stepped into the library. Is it my honour, he said, to now address the rightful owners of this estate? He wore a Great War visor cap and an Imperial Russian Cossack uniform with braided aiguillettes, and his mouth was half-obscured by a waxed moustache. It is no honour, said the German woman, but, yes, I am Frau Loewen. Then I am Lieutenant Dunyásha, at your service. Why do you weep, Frau Loewen? Your ordeal is over, n'est-ce pas? He removed his gloves and observed the girl with the baby. What crime has been done here? The baby is an orphan, said the German woman, and this is my child Magdalena. The soldier kissed her hand. War is dirty and uncouth, Miss Loewen; I am ashamed to present myself before such beauty. And I weep, continued the German woman, because the Lord has saved us and we are unworthy of His mercy and grace. Quite, said the Lieutenant. And who are you, young man? What business have you with these ladies, besides, it seems, modelling their clothes? Andriy thought his only chance would be to try to grab the soldier's sword. An apt choice, Frau Loewen, said the Lieutenant, toeing the book written by the Christian who was also an anarchist. Soldiers! he shouted. Andriy heard more men climbing the stairs. He knew he should say something defiant and thus die with honour, but he had lost control of his voice and could not order it into action. Andriy saw that the soldiers were mountain people, Tereks or Chechens or something like that. The lieutenant spun the vandalised globe. Shall we, perhaps, continue our business out with the presence of the ladies? Yes? No? Come on, dear boy, you were a fearsome anarchist bandit not ten minutes ago, and now you are as scared as a baby shrew! Andriy rose to his feet, trying to think what Batko would do.

He is not one of them, said the German woman. The Lieutenant removed his pocket watch and checked the time. I see, he said. He is just a loyal servant boy, she continued. A simpleton. An idiot who works with the animals.

107

In popular, judicial, and literary understandings, we maintain an Aristotelian conception of a voluntary act. When a person acts freely, examiners, it is quite different from the snooker ball that rolls as the effect of another ball; it is not even an infinitely more complicated version of such a movement, but is qualitatively different in that we originate action in a way that cannot be explained by the laws of cause and effect. The problem of transcendental freedom, then, is a problem of causal explanation: if all movement has a cause, how can we be in control of our actions?

Descartes resolved the problem of how the originary agent could avoid external 'moving principles' with his theory of dualism – because the free part of a person is ontologically distinct from the outside world, it could originate action without being subject to external forces. This, however, left the problem – formulated by Spinoza and others – of how the spiritual self could interact with a material world that included its 'host' body; how can a thought, 'I will raise my arm,' have a physical effect? Descartes suggested there was a site of interaction in the pineal grand, a solution which, unremarkably, was not deemed satisfactory. Kant's approach was to accept the laws of cause and effect as applicable to the knowable physical world, while maintaining the possibility of a separate, unknowable world inaccessible to scientific study.

This is the basis of Kant's distinction between the 'noumenal' and the 'phenomenal'. The phenomenal world is reality as it appears to us, while the noumenal pertains to the Thing in itself – the world as it exists beyond human perception. This is reminiscent of Platonic dualism – the assertion that there is a higher knowledge of 'form' to be discovered beyond the physical world of appearances – but for Kant the noumenal by definition will forever elude human perception. If we are to examine, say, a red wooden cube, then when we say it is red, we have no way of knowing whether we share the same experience of 'redness', because we have no way to experience the colour beyond our categories of perception. In other words, we can only know the block phenomenally as it appears to us; we make the phenomenal block in thinking of it, which, of course, is not to say that a noumenal block does not also exist.

Kant's solution to the problem of causal explanation was to accept that it applied to the phenomenal world, while maintaining that we have a noumenal transcendental freedom. In other words, there are two subjects – one which is 'empirical' (or 'sensible') and subject to causal explanation, and one which is 'intelligible' (or 'intellectual') and cannot be understood to be determined by antecedent conditions. According to Kant, a person:

> must suppose there to be something else which is its ground – namely his ego as this may be constituted in itself; and thus as regards mere perception and the capacity for receiving sensations he must count himself as belonging to the sensible world, but as regards whatever there may be in him of pure activity (whatever comes into consciousness, not through affection of the sense, but immediately) he must count himself as belonging to the intellectual world, of which, however, he knows nothing further. (Quoted in Lukes, 1985, p-283)

The obvious question is that if we have no sensory access to the noumenal world, how does Kant know we have an 'intelligible' freedom? His answer to this is found in the book Thrub dropped on my bladder: the *Critique of Pure Reason*. Specifically, it is found in his resolution of the Third Antinomy.

What is at stake in the Third Antinomy is whether we can still believe in an Aristotelian conception of voluntary action, defined by Kant as 'the power of beginning a state spontaneously' (1965 [1781], p-533). Against this he proposes the anti-thesis: that 'everything takes place in accordance with mere laws of nature' (ibid., p-444). Kant's argument is difficult to follow, especially when one has a fractured skull, but his attempt to prove the impossibility of the anti-thesis seems to rest on the claim that if by the laws of nature (*Gesetz der Natur*), everything happens because of a prior cause, then such an explanation cannot explain the first cause, therefore it cannot be the only type of causation, therefore the anti-thesis is untrue. Peter Strawson (1966, pp-207-210) is among those who, contrary to Kant, argue for the anti-thesis. But by rejecting the anti-thesis, Kant is able to posit the existence of an intelligible agency, unknowable to, and able to transcend, empirical laws. This is essential to Kant's theory of freedom since he claims:

> If we could exhaustively investigate all the appearances of men's wills, there would not be found a single human action which we could not predict with certainty, and recognize as proceeding necessarily from its antecedent conditions. So far, then, as regards this empirical character there is no freedom... (1965, p-550)

It is true, of course, that if we could exhaustively understand the antecedent causes of action then we could predict all actions, but we can't have such exhaustive knowledge and never will. Nevertheless, Kant claims it is essential that we regard ourselves as empirically free – as possessing something more than determined animal will (*arbitrum brutum*) – and that this necessitates an appeal to transcendental freedom.

This claim, however, gives rise to a problem not dissimilar to that generated by Cartesian dualism – if freedom is transcendental and beyond the phenomenal world, how can it be relevant to the practical freedom that will form the basis for Kant's theory of morality? H.E. Allison's solution to this problem is to claim that Kant is merely saying that 'it is necessary to appeal to the transcendental idea of freedom in order to conceive of ourselves as rational (practically free) agents, not that we must actually be free in this transcendental sense in order to be free in the practical sense' (1990, p-57). Are we to understand transcendental freedom as existing only as a necessary way of thinking, necessary because without such an idea we couldn't conceive ourselves as decision making creatures, a position from which Kant claims it would be impossible to act?

Kant may well be right here – that a conception of transcendental freedom is implied by our practical experience of the world – but, according to Professor Thrub, it need not necessarily be implied in what we write. Allison quotes Kant as stating:

> If I say I think, I act, etc., then either the word "I" is used falsely or I am free. Were I not free, I could not say: I do it, but must rather say: I feel in myself an impulse to do it, which someone has incited in me. If, however, I say: I do it, this signifies a spontaneity in the transcendental sense. (ibid., p-60)

Kant's perspective is that of an ethical and moral philosopher, and this leads him to defend and explain the transcendental spontaneity referred to with the word 'I', but Thrub seemed to uphold the opposite view – that the word 'I' is indeed repeatedly used falsely. As far as I can tell, examiners, this reading was fundamental to Thrub's prohibition on pronouns.

108

After Andriy had left, after the White Soldiers had left, Anna Loewen dug up one casket of valuables. She took out five hundred rubles, some jewellery, and a gold-plated carriage clock, and then she reburied the box and re-spread the snow and twigs. She carried the baby to the house of a Russian neighbour, a young widow who had once worked as a housemaid, and she explained that the baby was an orphan rescued by the Makhnovist army. They had left the valuables, she said, to pay for the baby's upbringing.

In 1923, her three children emigrated to Canada, but Anna Loewen withdrew from the journey at the last moment. She stayed, as she put it, to face the wages of sin. When Party officials came to inspect her ruined estate, they felt in the presence of the dead, for Frau Loewen had marked graves for all who had been killed on her land, and in the distance, through the snow, the crosspieces of the rough wooden markers appeared like arms outstretched. The party officials ordered the removal of the crosses, but they never suspected that three extra graves marked where Frau Loewen had buried the last of her wealth.

During the famine, she did not forget young Yaroslav and his adoptive mother, but kept them alive with food from the Mennonite international relief effort. She worked on a collective farm until the German liberation, and then, under pressure from the SS, she retreated to Berlin. When the war ended, she wished to emigrate to Canada, but instead the Allies extradited her to the

Soviet Union. Her last years were spent in exile in Kazakhstan, where she thought often of her children, and occasionally of the orphan child whom she had willed to survive.

109

But, examiners, have you tried debating Kant's Third Antinomy with a Detective Constable from the Gloucestershire Police Force? Let me truncate a long and rarely interesting story: I pressed charges.

My reasons were ignoble; in part, I believe I was affected by peer pressure; largely, I was seduced by the prospect of criminal injuries compensation. Lately, I have wondered whether my decision was ever really in doubt.

I'd like to claim that I did not know Thomson would be imprisoned. The police officer, presumably to encourage me to prosecute, had informed me that a custodial sentence was unlikely. In fact, as perhaps I secretly knew, it was inevitable. I know this because when the case appeared at Gloucester Crown Court, I submitted a plea of leniency and requested the court find an alternative to imprisonment. The Judge, William Hart, described this as an 'extraordinary act of forgiveness,' and then he sentenced the accused to thirteen months in jail. This was, he claimed, the most lenient possible sentence.

About one year later, I received £11,000 in compensation. Since the Victim Support Service notified me of Thomson's release, I have neither sought nor heard news of him. In this small town, doubtless we have passed shoulder to shoulder in the street, but I would not recognise him even in a line-up. Still, it is strange to think of us passing quietly, politely minding our private space. We will go on, must live as well as we can, our actions determined, for better or worse, by what the other has done. But then, are we not always sliding by strangers, never realising that their lives have determined our actions, or that our actions have determined their lives? Go well, Daniel Thomson. Go well.

Holiday poems, by Lempi Bridgette

Home Help

The space is white and male
and lacking in the usual unsightly
bulges of previous holidays and partners,
or the expels of sport, or art, or casual sex.

Of course there is the tell tale
weight of study: the freights of jotters
and dust covers, but even these are modest:
housed in the hearth, unobtrusive.

But when I wait between rooms for you
and contemplate the small instances
of change here: an abstract and painted
ornamental bowl, the hand soap and scented

sprigs of lavender sensationalising your décor,
it pleases me to think that any intruder
here would sense that you are loved,
or at least overseen by a woman.

Currency

This summer,
I have bought
a miniature replica
of the Berlin Wall
& spent
a sojourn in the east
at ex-Gulag camps
under Gulag conditions
for thirteen days
paid
annual leave.

Speaking at Night

Between our beds are valleys
mountains as long as populace

where roads were never etched
and telephone lines just erected.

From this steep side bed side
I ring you- strapped by the straps

of my night dress to a line
'connecting people' with 'minutes'

we both assumed were free.
And this is unusual for ranges:

the line between our sheets
is good. You talk a little

'What is the word, in Spanish,
for 'endearment'?'

I tell you. Until you get cold.
Until your questions are in-

comprehensible behind the chatter
of your teeth.

Rehabilitation

You expect there to be a bridge
step stone crossing of sorts
Slaughter
the path that's designated
that's signalled on surveys
the two places are connected

moat or cow grate, swing kissing
to continue our walk from Lower
into Upper the path you want to ramble,
for rambling, that's signed and posted,
because the ordinance alleges
joined and negotiable

(except they're not)

London, 1936

110

A fortnight after the attack, I was discharged from hospital. Whenever she was available – and only her lectures could not be rearranged – Lempi drove me to Gloucester for my outpatient appointments. Once, when I asked Lempi why she was being so nice to me, she shrugged and said, 'You would do the same for me, wouldn't you?' This was true: I would wish to devote myself to Lempi were she to suffer an injury; but then, I would wish to devote myself to Lempi were she to suffer poor TV reception. I adored her, examiners, but until my hospitalisation, she had treated me with cordiality no more intimate than that which a friendly neighbour might extend across a privet hedge.

The surgeons had fitted arch bars to my teeth, so that over months they could realign my jaws by tying my mouth shut with elastic bands. Initially the bands were thick little circles that offered no detectable give, but as my jaw strengthened, with great effort I could prise my teeth a millimetre apart, and as my recovery continued, the consultant fitted successively looser bands until I could open my mouth two or three centimetres. During the first weeks, however, my jaws were clamped together, and I had to sieve liquefied food through the gaps between my teeth (the best passage was around the incisors). Lempi bought me a blender and cooked big tubs of pureed vegetable soup; she assured me the soups smelled delicious, but since my nose was blocked with blood, my only appetizing cues were visual, and regardless of the vegetables Lempi selected, the soups, once blended, resembled bile.

At any rate, one's stomach quickly shrinks when under-deployed, and the combination of drugs (I was taking codeine and paracetamol and Diclofenac Sodium) and illness (my weakened immune system admitted a series of colds and stomach bugs), meant that I rarely felt hungry. Even had I wanted to eat, my throat was scarred from the operation (I suspect my larynx and oesophagus had been scraped and cut by the anaesthetist's tubing), and swallowing was intensely painful. But the biggest reason why I refused food was embarrassment. Every spoonful was smeared around my mouth so that when I finished eating I was crusted with snotty-coloured soup. Worst of all, my atrophied digestive system responded by expelling food as quickly as possible: within minutes of eating, I suffered roaring diarrhoea.

The first time, my desire to hide the problem, to nonchalantly wait for Lempi to finish describing a misunderstanding with her Vietnamese nail technician, meant that I locked the bathroom door and soiled myself before I could tug down my pyjama bottoms. When I splattered the pan, the noise was so loud that, even though two doors separate the bathroom from the living room, I had to try to disguise it. So I banged my feet and hummed as loudly as I could the only song that came into my head, which happened to be 'Onward Christian Soldiers'. This attracted Lempi's attention. After a minute or two, once I'd finally evacuated my bowels, she knocked the bathroom door. 'Are you alright?' she asked.

'I'm fine, thank you.'

'What are you doing in there?'

'...Give me a minute, please.'

'Okay, cool.'

And then the problems really started: I couldn't walk out of the bathroom wearing shitty clothes, so I stepped out of my soiled pyjamas and turned on the shower. There was another knock. 'Are you having a shower?' This time, I pretended not to hear Lempi, threw the pyjama bottoms into the shower cubicle, and watched as the draining water turned brown. When the excess had been washed from the bottoms, I began to scrub them, rubbing the material against itself, as I had seen clothes washed in historical dramas. I soaped the affected area with shower gel and shampoo and— Examiners, a problem became apparent. Even if I managed to clean the stain, how would I explain my sodden pyjamas?

My bathroom is at the rear of the building and it overlooks commercial rooftops. These are roofed with felt or asbestos or moss-lined corrugated metal, and beyond them one can see the giant oaks in the church yard and the peak of the church tower. Therefore, assuming no campanologist has chosen that moment to ascend the steeple, it is possible to raise the blind and open the bathroom window without exposing oneself to anything more sensitive than a seagull. I imagined the smell would fast dissipate with the breeze swirling around the bathroom. As insurance, I sprayed air-freshener and scrubbed the toilet with bleach. But when I'd finished these ablutions, I was no closer to solving the problem of the sodden pyjamas.

'Hey, are you okay?'

I stopped the shower.

'Are you okay in there?'

'Yes, thank you.'

'What you doing?'

Examiners, I cannot now explain why I thought it advisable to launch my pyjama bottoms from the window. But once I'd seized upon this course of action, I thought only about the execution of the deed. It was necessary to hurl them beyond the nearest rooftop, into the small storage yard at the rear of Krunchy

Fried Chicken. This seemed achievable provided I clenched them into a ball and took a short run up. Alas, examiners, I slipped as I approached the window, my muscles were weakened from underuse, the pyjamas unballed mid-flight and spread like a sail in the breeze – everything conspired against me. The soiled garment splattered on the rooftop below, sprawled in full view of my bathroom window.

'Hey, are you sure you're okay?'

Did I think of climbing down the drainpipe? Yes, I did. I had one naked leg out the window, one soft-soled foot testing the strength of the pipe. But could I, in my atrophied state, descend two metres to the roof? And, more seriously, would I be able to return to my flat once I had kicked the pyjama bottoms over the edge? I pictured myself stuck on this ledge, nakedly awaiting rescue, as a Turkish chicken fryer shouted at me from his courtyard, brandishing my shitty pyjama bottoms on the end of a stick.

No, examiners, I closed the window, pulled down the blind, and wrapped my bruised skeleton in every towel I owned. 'Will you excuse me,' I said when I finally opened the door. 'I'm going to change into something fresh.'

It was two days before Lempi noticed the pyjama bottoms (in the interim period I had made a serious but ultimately unsuccessful attempt to hook the garment with a long rod of wire coat hangers). 'Why are your pyjamas down there?' she asked. In all the time that had elapsed, the best I had come up with was that I had decided to clean the outside of the bathroom window and had dropped the pyjamas while using them as a rag. Lempi listened to this explanation and looked as though she was trying hard to believe it.

As a footnote to this incident, examiners, it's worth recording that the pyjama bottoms remain in place to this day; they have rotted somewhat, and encouraged by the spring sunshine, last April a sprig of rosebay willowherb took advantage of the amply fertilised material and burst through somewhere near the crotch. The weed flowered in the late summer, around the anniversary of my hospitalisation, and its flimsy tip bobbed in the breeze; it wasn't quite a poppy, but it was a moving symbol nevertheless.

111

On a Sunday, according to convention rather than contract, the master, Dr Menzies Flynn, required of the maid, Miss Elsie Stewart, no services but that she prepare and clear an adequate Sunday dinner. There were, of course, multiple interpretations of this arrangement. One prominent interpretation believed this to be a generous, even philanthropic, settlement that allowed the young maid some time to do whatever young maids liked to do; another prominent interpretation noted that the wages paid for Sunday duties didn't justify the long commute from the East End, with the consequence that Sunday's labour always generated special feelings of dismay. The former interpretation gained hegemony in the brain identified by the signifiers 'Dr Flynn' and 'Sir', while the latter interpretation gained hegemony in the brain identified with the signifiers 'Elsie' and 'maid'. The ascendance of different interpretations can be explained by the contextual knowledge, which is to say memory traces, inscribed in the respective brains: data relating to the maid's journey was either never inscribed within one brain (that brain identified with the signifiers 'Sir' and 'Dr Flynn'), or the neural connections that inscribed said data atrophied through disuse and were lost to consciousness. It is not difficult to imagine why such information should be disused in one brain while remain prominent in the other, for while one brain was in a body whose maintenance necessitated repeated recall of said information (i.e., it had to arrive at work at a certain time in order to take possession of monies and thus afford food), within the other subject position, such data served no direct function and, in fact, tended to clutter and contradict certain key narratives of self.

On this day in particular, 4th October 1936, the commotion in the East End of London had meant an especially arduous and lengthy journey, such that the maid was late, and the widower master, an ageing history professor, was experiencing frustrations to nutritional and sexual drives. The nutritional frustrations are self-explanatory (though, I should add, aggravated by a bout of diarrhoea), but the sexual frustrations require explanation. For very complex reasons, the maid's presence provoked sexual arousal including penile tumescence, and while the entire young-servant fetish was abhorrent to many manifestations of consciousness, the habitual bodily response was nevertheless to masturbate to orgasm in the bathroom. This motor activity resulted from a struggle between opposing forces (i.e., the aforementioned internalised societal arousal and the almost equally intense internalised societal reprobation), and since the arousal terminated suddenly (and messily), in the refractory period the opposing force filled this evacuated emotional space. Worst of all, the images and words that were invariably forced into consciousness during the masturbation concerned the feel of the girl's body, the smell of her hair, the warmth of her thighs, the way her mouth opened in shock at the sight of his penis, and other memories derived from an incident in the summer, during which the master, on pretext of nursing the maid's wasp sting, committed what you or I would term a sexual assault.

In other words, the arrival of the maid resulted in an orgasm that resulted in an experience of shame so intense that it triggered a depressive or 'melancholic' state. Since the dominant cognitive schema believed in the sovereign power of the ego to choose a rational course of action, and since masturbating while imagining violating the maid invariably resulted in negative consequences that outweighed any positive experiences associated with the masturbation, it was proposed that the masturbation was an involuntary act. But once this interpretation became hegemonic, it was necessary to identify the agent responsible for forcing this act upon the master, and since demons and such like were incommensurable with the interpretative paradigm of positivist epistemology, the obvious scapegoat was the maid herself. And so all sorts of hitherto disregarded details came to be written as wanton displays of coquettishness or harlotry, such that loose hair was suggestive of sex and pinned hair was tartish vanity and a button unpopped on the girl's blouse was a calculated attack on the master's decency. This account has been necessarily simplified, for Menzies Flynn will play no further part in our story, but we do need to understand the emotional maelstrom greeting the young maid on Sunday 4th October 1936.

Suffice to say that the appearance of the maid provoked feelings of arousal but also emotions of anger, frustration, and disgust. Had Elsie not eloped to Spain with Ramón then it's possible this volatile mixture of desire and contempt would have been responsible for a second sexual assault or even a rape. (This dangerous situation owed its strength not only to the patriarchal discourse of sirenic female sexuality, but also to the realities of class society in the 1930s, which is to say that then as now proletarians were forced to sell their labour power in order to access the wealth of society, but then more than now the threats of hunger and the workhouse loomed even larger than a sexually pernicious history professor, who suffered from seborrhoeic dermatitis.) As it happened, on this occasion, all these factors contributed to a far more mild attack; when the door knocker finally sounded, the above-described situation produced an unexpected punitive order: the maid, in addition to producing the usual Sunday dinner, was now required to clean the front windows with vinegar and newspaper.

112

During this period, Professor Thrub declined to communicate with me directly, but through Robin he issued books, seemingly as a kind of punishment. When I finished *The Critique of Pure Reason*, I sent Thrub a long appreciative email, filled with deferential disclaimers. Thrub did not reply; instead, he dispatched Robin with a copy of Hegel's *Phenomenology of Spirit*. When I'd finished that, he sent *The Science of Logic*. Of all Thrub's instruments of punishment, Hegel was the cruellest.

As Schopenhauer put it:

> [T]he greatest effrontery in serving up sheer nonsense, in scrabbling together senseless and maddening webs of words, such as had previously been heard only in madhouses, finally appeared in Hegel. It became the instrument of the most ponderous and general mystification that has ever existed, with a result that will seem incredible to posterity, and be a lasting monument of German stupidity. (Quoted in Houlgate, 1991, p-1)

Still, Hegel's dissolution of the subject-object opposition, when applied to the relationship between self and society (in Hegel's terms specifically the relationship between self and civil society mediated through the constitutional monarchy he terms the 'organic state') allows for the grandest theory of freedom ever constructed.

In our society, the question of freedom is largely explored from a liberal or negative perspective: a person's freedom is restricted if her wants and desires are frustrated by her circumstances. Hegel raises the more radical question (later taken up by Marx and Althusser) that if a person's wants and desires are themselves the products of the social system – of 'ideology' or 'socialisation', say – then how can they properly be called her wants and desires? Examiners, it is the formulation of this problem in Hegel (1991 [1821], §15) that provokes his attempt to reconcile total freedom with societal being in an elaborate social contract theory.

Crudely summarised, Hegel's twist on the social contract is that since the organic state (like everything else) is the realisation of Spirit, and since the historical development of Spirit is propelled by 'the progress of the consciousness of freedom,' at the point of absolute knowledge, when the self 'apprehends nothing but self and everything as self' (Hegel, 1977, p-296), it recognises the organic state as the necessary product of its own free will. Following the laws, norms and regulations of the state is therefore not an act of subordination, because if we are living an 'ethical life' (*Sittlichkeit*), we recognise those laws as the ultimate expression of our free essence.

Like Kant, examiners, Hegel observed the 'gap' between our knowledge of things and their pure nature; in self-reflection, for example, where we think 'I am', the 'I' is always already removed from the 'am'. In other words, the thought of being is never exactly coincident with being. But unlike his predecessors, Hegel didn't conceive this gap as a frustration to selfhood; rather, Hegel considered it to be selfhood's essential feature. For Hegel, the distance between the noumenal and the phenomenal is not an epistemological problem, but the basis of our capacity to become other than we are, to be 'self-moving'.

To understand this, we need to recall Hegel's vision of the dialectic. In his *Science of Logic* (1969 [1812-16]), Hegel attempted to lay the basis for a 'presuppositionless logic'. Starting with the thought of pure being, he argued that any attempt to think of bare existence would collapse into the nothingness of the concept. The first thesis, *being*, invokes its negative, nothing, and the contradiction gives rise to the idea of becoming. This is the basis of dialectical movement: ideas are not stable but rely on an interaction with their negative, and in Hegel's thought, through the untranslatable notion of *Aufhebung* – 'at once to 'raise up', 'to abolish' and 'to preserve' (Foshay, 2002, p-303) – they are sublated into a new concept.

At the risk of over-simplification, we can characterise the Hegelian self as precisely the effect of this negative displacement: the ability of thought to separate itself from what it took to be reality and out of the contradiction to become something new, to *move*. As Hegel explains in typically lucid style:

> The realised purpose, or the existent actuality, is movement and unfolded becoming; but it is just this unrest that is the self; and the self is like that immediacy and simplicity of the beginning because it is the result, that which has returned into itself, the latter being similarly just the self. And the self is the sameness and simplicity that relates itself to itself. (1977, p-12)

Perhaps one can now guess what Hegel means when he claims that the entire 'history of the world is none other than the progress of the consciousness of freedom' (quoted in Singer, 1983, p-11). For Hegel, true history begins with the Persian Empire, for this is when he sees the emergence of self-consciousness, and, for Hegel, the crucial factor for the progress of history is the objectification of self in reflection, a move that allows for the progressive reconciliation of the subject and object of thought. Hegel's idealism, of course, allows him to claim that this movement describes the whole development of what he calls Geist (mind/ Spirit), which at the end of The Phenomenology will reach a state of absolute knowledge, which will occur when it recognises that the things it once considered independent, actually appear as they do according to the constitution of Geist. Simple, right?

113

The maid was eighteen, but she had the rough-skinned hands of an older woman. When she arrived at her workplace that Sunday, the rap of the doorknocker shook two bullfinches, hop-flying from a rhododendron bush, and when the door opened the face that appeared was dry pink, flaky and razor-scraped. The mouth had white paste in the corners when it smiled.

The hallway smelled of lavender [2%], menthol [1%], tobacco (Player's Digger Tobacco, 8d per Oz: Smokers who want quality find pure satisfaction in this famous brand) [9%], coal (Barkley's: London's best and brightest) soot/ smoke [24%], mildew [5%], dust [6%], boiled Oats (White's Water Oats: The direct way to health) [3%], Brasso (The Brightener) [6%], body odour [4%], Faeces [12%], Henry Blossom Boot Polish (Makes Black or Brown shoes Brilliant) [2%], Bovril (Shackleton says it must be) [2%], onion [2%], laundry starch [5%], other [17%].

Most sensory information is mediated by the thalamus, but when chemicals stick to hairs in the olfactory epithelium (i.e., up one's nose) they generate electrical impulses that go direct to the olfactory cortex of the brain. Examiners, perhaps this is why smells often trigger Proustian moments (i.e., unexpectedly vivid memories of another time and place)?

Elsie washed her hair weekly and then only with soap. She used no deodorant. By the time she had travelled across London, aprocrine glands had produced sweat, which had been broken down by bacteria in her armpits, producing propionic acid.

The smell of this acid we would recognise as mild body odour. However, neither Elsie nor Menzies Flynn was aware of it.

This is because they were habituated to human smells – it was not a new smell so they didn't notice it. Habituation occurs in all sensory receptors (a sustained image doesn't fade but only because of saccades – the constant slight movements of the eyeball that ensure the image falls on different retinal cells [see Pritchard, 1961 for an experimental demonstration of visual habituation]). Our sense detectors habituate, examiners, because that which stays the same rarely requires action; we need to take notice when something changes.

If our sensory experience is discontinuous then we are surprisingly bad at noticing changes. For example, if you briefly interrupt a subject's experience of an image (a blink can be sufficient) then there's a good chance the subject won't recognise major changes that occurred during the interruption. In an experiment by Simons & Levin (1998), one experimenter would ask a pedestrian for directions and mid-answer two other experimenters would carry a door between them – 'excuse me, coming through' – and while the door obscured the pedestrian's view, the first experimenter would slip away, his place taken by someone else. So the pedestrians started to explain the route to one person (Simons, let's say) and when the door was out of the way, almost half the pedestrians continued their explanations to another person (Levin, perhaps), oblivious to the change.

The point, which is not as irrelevant as it seems, examiners, is that we are able to symbolise only a fraction of our sensory experience, and what we symbolise and store in memory depends on the unique motivations to which each of us is subjected. And so all the olfactory information Elsie encountered produced only some revulsion at the stench of diarrhoeic faeces and recognition of the smell of Brasso (recalling yesterday's labour, bringing into consciousness the glow of a Middle Eastern coffee pot and a previously silent muscular ache in the right elbow). Meanwhile, the smell of laundry starch on the white muslin apron invoked a sense of dismay. The apron was a sort of uniform that designated cleaning time, and in response to the master's order to clean the windows, it was bow-tied at the back of the daisy-patterned just-above-knee-length rayon dress, by hands that moved with habitual distraction. Even as the visual cortex constructed a shirted arm held up to show a wristwatch, which provoked the thought that a wrist watch was a strange thing to see on a man, there appeared the image of a composition doll that always flopped by the bathroom door. The doll's left arm was melted to a stump, its big wax face cracked open where its papier-mâché insides had expanded and burst out.

There was a telephone in the hall and it was such an object of fascination that sometimes there was a perception of the arm extending, involuntarily we would say, and touching the receiver, even picking it up. This image was so vivid (and again we might say involuntary) that it seemed almost real, as if the arm had at least started to reach towards the telephone of its own volition. Perhaps what sustained the fantasy was the incomprehensibility of what would come next – the cognitive apparatus lacked the experience to know which bit one should talk through and which bit one should hold to one's ear. It was a black candlestick telephone with a tulip mouthpiece and a wooden bell set with bulging metal ringers. The cord was actually two cords entwined.

Some unknown violence had broken the third balustrade so that it was just an ankle of jagged wood. The vinegar was most probably in the larder, which was a cupboard under the stairs, opposite the entrance to the kitchen. The larder door had a button knob and a painted metal latch that was to be kept closed for reasons that were obscure. The vinegar bottle was behind the clothes pegs and the blacklead, which was for blacking the kitchen range. The label on the bottle said– Because there is one part of the brain to recognise the letters and another part to imagine the sound, there existed here patterns of experience that knew to expect a delay when reading and so, without any conscious analysis, the hands uncorked the bottle and brought it up to the nose. The smell was recognisably vinegar. SARSONS VINEGAR said the bottle. The vinegar had dried brown around the rim and the smell was sharp. The word was vinegar but the smell was of late-summer evenings and games of conkers with boys. The smell was also of the incident in the bathroom after the wasp had–

Once again there arose the image of the doll with the big orange face and the papier-mâché brains leaking through its eye socket and the melted stump-arm. From the noises upstairs, it was evident that the master was on the landing, beside the doll, and any second– there, the click of the latch. The living room had an intricate cornice and white-painted wainscoting above the skirting boards. In the living room The African Man – a wooden statuette carrying a spear – wore a rough-wool shawl that was short and open to reveal his penis. Beside The African Man was The African Pot. The pot was made of thin wood and the master sometimes removed the lid and put the pot to Elsie's face and implored her to 'breathe The Smell of Africa.' The Smell of Africa was like the smell of brewing mixed with the damp smell inside an empty kitchen drawer. There was also a globe that could be turned (but ought not to be spun) to show all the countries of the world including Africa. There were some books on a bracket shelf but most had difficult titles (Gibbon's *A Vindication of Some Passages in the XVth and XVIth Chapters*, Scott's *Heart of Midlothian*).

Concomitant with all this linguistic commentary and peripheral analysis, however, there endured the memories triggered by the smell of vinegar: the trickle of the cistern, the doll outside with the big orange face and the papier-mâché brains leaking through its eye socket and the melted stump-arm, the lavender smell of the bathroom, the sun warm through the mottled glass, the shadow of the lace curtains patterning the floorboards like sunlight on water, the ascending footsteps, the wasp sting, Wheesht now. There was a whole room of books upstairs called The Library (with smile) and this was different from the Public Library, which was called The Library (with no smile). The pain of the wasp sting. The anger at this unexpected cleaning task. 'Wheesht now; get inside and I'll find some vinegar.' The smell of faeces noticeable in the hallway. The doll at the top of the stairs with one arm melted into a blistered stump. The clunk-creak of cupboard doors. The chink of bottles. The sting of vinegar on the wasp sting. The doll with the big wax head that was cracked across the face where the papier-mâché inside had swollen. The bathroom tiles patterned forget-me-not blue. The Library. Wiping a finger across the living room window would have left a clear trail across the glass and a fingerprint smudged dark so you could press it on paper like a library stamp. And then, before these daydreams could continue, movement perceived near the door elicited an alarm response and the hands folded across the chest as the body spun, right foot tracing a perfect semi-circle, too fast to ever be remembered.

114

It was around this time that I first suffered the nightmares. The plot varied little: I am once again leaving the bar, walking towards the High Street, when I see the men who attacked me.

I cannot see their faces but their identity is not in doubt. I know that I need to run, but, as is so common in nightmares, I cannot control my body: my legs flail and bend like plant stems. I don't feel their blows; in fact, I only know they have attacked me when I see they have snapped off a body part. Usually the first piece is a hand: I see my amputated hand lying bloody on the road. Then I see a toe or a foot or an ear. Then a whole leg. Sometimes my nose. Sometimes my head. These body parts do not die upon being separated from the whole; rather, they begin to advance on whatever non-corporeal part of me is left. By this stage the attackers have gone and 'I' watch as my amputated hands crawl forward and the mouth on my severed head bites at—

And of course I wake. Initially, this drama played out almost every time I slept. I remember, for example, waking in Lempi's bosom, as she stroked my head and said 'It's okay. *Shhhh* now, it's okay.' I have an open plan kitchen-living room-bedroom and I had fallen asleep while she was in the kitchen making soup. The shut curtains yellowed the afternoon sunshine and around my bed balled tissues congealed with blood and saliva and bile. My right arm, still attached, draped on Lempi's thigh, the skin scarred and bruised, as if I was metamorphosising into some non-human thing. It occurred to me, as I recovered my sense of place, what an extraordinary contrast there was between us, and for some reason, I felt the need to articulate this. Still half-asleep, I murmured that I was unworthy of her beauty. Examiners, I fear that as I said this I was staring directly at Lempi's cleavage, for she let go of me and stood up. 'They're just modified sweat glands surrounded by fat and collagen, you know.'

'I didn't mean—'

'I've got a lot of fat around mine,' said Lempi. 'And they're especially big just now cause I'm due to menstruate, so I've got a lot of water retention. And this is a push up bra.' She pulled her vest lower, exposing the bridge of her brassiere. 'You know how it works?'

'I wasn't talking about your—'

Lempi walked to the kitchen, speaking louder with every step. 'It's wired so that it, like, pushes my breasts upwards and inwards, and then I put in these— Hang on, I'll show you.' I could only speak through my teeth and it was impossible for me to communicate at such distance. So I sat up in bed and listened as Lempi slopped the soup. When she returned she brought with the soup a dishtowel that I could use as a bib. 'Look,' she said, settling the bowl on my lap, 'I put in these silicon inserts.'

'Lempi, I was—'

'Eat your soup, honey.' She reached into her vest and scooped one hand under her breast while holding her top up with the other. '*Dadah!*' She smacked my arm with the wobbly fillet she had removed from her bra. 'Abracadabra.' She turned her back to me as she replaced the insert.

'I meant your face, Lempi. You're incredibly beautiful.'

'My face? Well, that's different,' she said, sitting down on the bed. 'This,' she said, pointing at her face, 'is much harder work than these.' She searched the tissues for one that was clean and then wiped the soup from my chin. 'For a start, I've had microdermabrasion. D'you know what that is? It's like... What they do is they get this, like— It looks a bit like a hand-held blender, but I guess it's kind of like a sanding machine. And it's got, like, aluminium oxide crystals or something, and it scrapes the top layers off your face, you know? And you look like – keep eating. And, like, you *do not* want to meet anyone on the way home cause you're all scarred and red, but after a day your skin is like super smooth and radiant and all your spots and dead skin cells have been cleared and— Keep going; do a few more spoonfuls. But I only get that done a couple of times a year, you know? Most months I guess I'll probably go for a facial, which is completely lush.'

'Thank you,' I said, placing the bowl on the floor.

'Come on,' she said, returning it to my lap, 'two more spoons. A facial is, like, really relaxing. First off they do you like a skin assessment, to see if you've got, like, congested skin or dry skin or excess oil on the T-zone or whatever. And then they remove your makeup— Well done! And so and yeah they wipe off your makeup and they massage you with a cleansing lotion, which is so lush. You're like just lying there listening to some gentle music. And so, like, they— Do you want anything else to eat or drink? Okay, so, you just lie there – you're naked, wrapped in towels – and just, you know, totally chill out.'

'It sounds really nice.'

'Sshhh, rest your jaws. And so, yeah, then they do the exfoliation which is— It's, like, they wash your skin with like grit or pomace or sometimes peach kernels or microbeads or like oats, in a cream, you know?'

Already I could feel the soup racing through my intestine. I imagined it hurtling round corners, like a Boy Scout troop black-water cave-tubing after heavy rainfall.

115

Elsie journeyed home unusually late, because, for reasons she couldn't possibly understand, her employer had ordered her to clean the windows. Had she been returning at her usual hour then she would have encountered the crowd at a different moment and her life and my life and your life (or at least that bit of it you're spending reading this thesis) would presumably have been very different. That said, examiners, since the events that produced the order to clean the windows (only a fraction of which we've mentioned, incidentally: we haven't described, for instance, how Menzies Flynn's pregnant wife died in 1918 from a massive pulmonary haemorrhage, brought on by the deadlier second wave of the 1918 H1N1 influenza, the spread and virulence of which owed much to the First World War, the causes of which included, as we all know, colonial rivalries, the Baghdad Railway, and that Franz Ferdinand chap) were, in a sense, inevitable, there perhaps isn't any point pondering the *what ifs.*

When Elsie had left for work, a tram had already been abandoned at Gardener's Corner, and young men had begun to assemble on Royal Mint Street. The intention of the crowd, Elsie knew, was to obstruct the free passage of Oswald Mosley's British Union of Fascists, who intended to march through Stepney, which then had the largest Jewish population in Britain. In coordinating responses to the world, Elsie's brain, like everyone else's, drew upon a personal narrative, which at that time did not acknowledge a political stance. Nevertheless, the crowd triggered in her vague feelings of sympathy, which perhaps derived in part from it reawakening in her positive memories of the Outdoor Relief Agitation and maybe feelings of homesickness. The Outdoor Relief Agitation had made a lasting impression on Elsie and had especially defined her opinion of Catholics: she could not remember giving them much thought before 1932, but if in 1936 you had told her that you despised Fenians, Elsie would have agreed with you about all that hocus-pocus with the wafer and the wine and what have you, but she would have added, for the sake of her conscience, that since moving to London she'd lived two years with all those ones from Cork, and once you'd got the hang of the accent, they were as kind and helpful people as anyone could hope to meet. Anyway, she'd have added, when all's said and done, we all bleed the same colour, do we not? Or some such. In so far as she had one, her attitude to the Jews was essentially the same. However, the crowd she had seen in the morning definitely wasn't for her – it was exclusively male and there were some Communist types and Jews gabbling Yiddish and unemployed Irish men and unshaven dockers and she saw some tailors too. At any rate, she had to make Menzies Flynn's Sunday lunch.

When she returned, however, she alighted from the 164 tram at Tower Bridge and then walked towards the East End, past the now-assembled Blackshirts. We must recall that Elsie's experience at work meant that on the journey home her brain activity was unusual: there was decreased activation in the right posterior cingulate and right SII, increased activation in the dorsal pons and anterior pons, bilateral activity in the insula, and anterior and posterior activation in the cingulate cortex. If a word had entered consciousness to define this state (and none did), it would most probably have been 'sadness'. However, we should note that there remained something like revulsion, too, and that, for no apparent reason, there appeared a recollection of the gruesome smell she had suffered outside the barbers on Tarling Street, where the barber burned hair in an open fire.

The sight of the Blackshirts and the police – at a quick glance they were indistinguishable – resulted in the pituitary gland releasing glucocorticoids and adrenocorticotrophic hormone, which caused the adrenal gland to release adrenaline, which increased the heartbeat. This new emotion, which did not dissipate for some hours, would later generate the signifier 'fear'. 'The Yids, the Yids! We are going to get rid of the Yids!' The fear catalysed a motor reaction that walked Elsie down East Smithfield. 'M-O-S-L-E-Y! We want Mosley!' Soon it became apparent that the anti-fascist crowd, which had looked from Mint Street to have been cleared, had in fact swollen to enormous numbers, and was filling every street she could see. To join them, she had to pass through a police cordon, where the officers barred her until she proved she was en route to her legal abode. The crowd was chanting 'No Pasaran! No Pasaran!' with a noise so intense it made Elsie's insides shake and caused hypothalamic neurons to release beta-endorphins that produced in Elsie such a rush of awe and well-being that she unconsciously reciprocated the smiles that everywhere surrounded her. This feeling of elated solidarity was especially intense as it immediately followed an experience of fear. For the second time in her life, her right fist clenched, and the words produced by her throat were the words produced by the crowd: *no pasaran* – they shall not pass.

Perhaps then it was a misplaced confidence that pushed her through the crowds on Cannon Street, taking a more direct route home than might in the circumstances have been wise. For at the junction with Cable Street, the police, attempting to clear a path for the fascist march, had broken through the anti-fascist's barricade and were galloping into the crowd ('Batons are drawn and heads broken as the anti-fascist demonstrators resist efforts to disperse them,' the BBC newsreel applaudingly reported). There were marbles scattered on the road and bottles and stones in the air and of this panicked moment the only thing memory would later recall was seeing the sign of Gronovsky's Tailors and remembering that Flynn's breeches remained unpatched.

116

It seemed to me the world had changed irrevocably since I had last been on campus, yet right down to the books open on the desks of my peers, my office in the Theology Department was as familiar as if I had only been gone for coffee. 'Jesus be praised,' said Obi.

'They got you wearing a brace?' said Jez. 'Shit, Samuel, come see this. Man, that is some evil shit they've done to you.'

'God have mercy upon them.'

'Screw mercy. I hope He gets Old Testament on those dudes. An eye for an eye, man. Ain't that right, Samuel?'

'Come now, Jeremy. Jesus Christ taught us that if an evil doer strikes us on the right cheek, we should turn to him the other.'

'Can't you see he already tried that?'

'Love your enemies, Jeremy.'

'What's your limey justice system gonna do with them? Counselling? A course of acupuncture?'

Examiners, when I explained that I hoped to dissuade the court from imposing a custodial sentence, Jez slammed shut *Biblical Protology* and began to summon the rage of his God. 'I'd want Him to kill their children and their cattle and their cattle's children. And their children's cattle. *Especially* their children's cattle.'

'It comes back to the question of free will, I suppose.'

'Man, do not even start that bullshit.'

'I am reluctant to agree with Jeremy,' said Obi, 'but if moral evil is not the act of free agents, then from where does it come?'

'Look,' said Jez, 'don't give me this liberal crap. God gave men free will, *liberum voluntatis arbitrium*, okay? Because otherwise we'd all be automata, and He saw that such a world would be morally void, and therefore it was better to give us the gift of free will, even if it meant some asshole would take a monkey wrench to go get a beer.'

'Amen, Jeremy.'

'And He can't intervene to prevent a morally evil—'

'He could,' said Obi.

'Of course he could, Obi, but he doesn't want to, because then he'd be denying that asshole his free will.'

'But if you put him in prison then isn't that also denying him his free will?'

'You're not getting it,' said Jez.

'Yes,' said Obi. 'You are closing yourself to the Word of God.'

'It's like, say you're on the top of a hill, okay? And there's a track that goes round the circumference of this hill, yeah? Then you can see everybody who's hiking this track, even though they can't see each other. Likewise, all at once, God eternal can see past, present, and future. But just cause he can see your future doesn't mean you haven't freely chosen it.'

'What's new with you, Jez?' I asked to change the subject.

'Not much. I'm doing Obadiah now.'

'Weren't you doing Obadiah before?'

'Tell me,' said Obi, perhaps because Jez's metaphor had made no more sense to him than it had to me, 'are you suffering from Demons of the head?'

Unsure how to interpret his question, I began to describe my recurrent nightmare. 'I'm walking towards the High Street,' I said.

'You are on a road?' asked Obi.

'Goddamn it, Obi.'

'Do not scoff, Jeremy; the scriptures are clear that He shall make Himself known through dreams. Does it not say in Numbers—'

'There's a talking donkey in Numbers, Obi.'

'Did not He appear to Abraham in dreams? Did not He appear to Solomon in dreams?'

'Damnit, Obi, you know the Word of God must be spread in the language of the people.'

'What of Joseph and Daniel? There are 121 mentions of dreams in the Bible, Jeremy.'

'Samuel? Talk some sense into this homo.'

'The road is our journey in life, Jeremy, and a repeated dream occurs because the dreamer has yet to act on the message He has conveyed in the dream.'

'I'm on this road and two guys come up to me and though I can't see their faces—'

'You can't see their faces? Jeremy, Samuel, isn't this exciting? The Man whose face you cannot see is Jesus of Nazareth.'

'I don't think so.'

'Tell him, Jeremy.'

'He isn't Jesus,' I said.

'This is wondrous news, my friend. Does He speak to you?'

'No. He brutally attacks me and hacks me into pieces.'

Obi seemed deflated by this answer and sat down to think. In my own analysis, the dream was a Lacanian comment on how, from the start, the self is generated externally through a phantasmic adoption of an image of unified totality – I was fantasising about the pre-mirror stage fragmented body in 'bits and pieces'; the violent men probably represented the imposition of the nom du père, and my dismemberment was probably a kind of symbolic castration. However, I didn't share this analysis with Jez and Obi.

Eventually, Obi asked, 'Is there any bread in the dream?'

'No.'

'A snake?'

'No.'

'A golden calf?'

'Why the Hell would he dream of a golden calf? Jesus, Obi, shut up and make some tea or something.'

117

A crowd is a peculiar thing. When pushed and jostled in a crowd, we cannot determine our own direction but must wait for the flow of bodies to move us one way or another. The crowd has its own logic: it will stand its ground or flee, independent of the will of any individual. In the crowd, the individual cedes power to the mass. And yet, the crowd is nothing but the movements of individuals, and the importance of each individual's movement is magnified ten thousand times. It is, as Elias Canetti wrote in *Crowds and Power*, 'as though everything is happening in one and the same body' (1973, p-16). When an individual gives herself to the crowd, and ceases to struggle against it, she experiences this as freedom.

Elsie's experience of this crowd was short-lived and panicked, for as the police charged and the crowd stampeded, an Irish mother, eager not to miss the moment, dropped a cooking pot from a second floor window. The pot had been meant for the head of a police officer, but the mother must have been over-zealous, or perhaps her grip slipped, for instead the pot landed on Elsie. Elsie momentarily lost consciousness, and then stood up, legs wobbling, mouth filled with the earthy metal taste of old coins. She was carried to safety by two men, one of whom, Ramón Buenacasa Mavilla, was a visiting delegate from the Spanish CNT. Examiners, I believe that Elsie fell in love with Ramón when first he held her, and I believe she remained in love with him for the rest of her life; which is to say, examiners, that I believe Elsie was in love with Ramón for the next twenty years, nineteen days, four hours, and thirty-two minutes.

118

By the time I finally ventured out alone, the seasons had turned. On one of my first non-hospital-related outdoor excursions, I took Lacan's *Ecrits* to Pittville Park, and there I lay on the dry grass and listened, eyes closed, to the *thunk-rattle* of tennis balls served into the wire fence, and the giggles and splashes produced by the captains of row boats and pedalos as they crossed the lake in hesitant off-straight courses. A fortnight later, examiners, I travelled to Manchester, determined to find the box of papers relating to George Steel Sr., which his son had deposited at the Working Class Movement Library in Salford.

To reach the library from central Manchester, one must take a train to Salford Crescent, via Oxford Road. One rides on the elevated viaduct, looking down on pub rooftops, and seeing, now and again, the River Medlock appearing, Dickensian, in the chasm between moss-etched red brick walls. Then, after Oxford Road Station, one journeys alongside Little Ireland, the one-time island of squalor between the river and the railway line, where Frederick Engels and his factory-girl lover researched *The Condition of the Working Class in England.* And after Knot Mill Station, one rides into the forgotten heart of modernity. In bright sunshine, examiners, the water in the canal basin reflected the tangle of wrought iron bridges as it slid through the great arched mouths of converted wharfs and warehouses. From the Salford Branch Viaduct, one can see the 1761 Bridgewater Canal, the world's first industrial canal, which terminates in this brick-lake sump; and looking in the other direction, one can see the destination of the world's first passenger rail service, which in 1830 terminated at Liverpool Road Station. And then, in seconds, the train crosses the Rochdale Canal, ducks under the Great Northern Viaduct, bridges the River Irwell, and accelerates away from this forgotten centre.

The library's reading room has two long tables and seats sixteen people. At one table, two young men, who had the earnest, unfashionable appearance of Trotskyist students, worked in silence, barely distracted by my arrival. I sat at the other table, by a fireplace, on which was propped a framed announcement of an 1882 public meeting at the Stratford Dialectical and Radical Club. (On April 30th, the notice read, Prince Krapotkine and M. Nicholas Tchaikovsky would attend and address the meeting on the subject of Russian Exiles.) After a minute or two, a woman arrived with the box of papers that I had requested in advance. Examiners, I sat until closing time, and all the next day, only moving to visit the toilet.

What did the box contain? The treasure, of course, was the letter sent to Elsie while she was in Spain. This was in a file marked 'Papers relating to Elsie Steel, wife of George Steel.' The file also contained letters of commiseration sent to George in 1956. Often these referred to Elsie only as 'your wife', but they were sent on behalf of a range of by then declining organisations: the Manchester and District Federation of the Labour Party Leagues of Youth, the Warrington Branch of the National Union of Railwaymen, the Manchester and Salford Trades Council, the Collyhurst Branch of the British Labour Esperanto Association, the Manchester Union of the National Clarion Cycling Club. This last letter was written on headed paper, designed in the forties, with 194 typeset on the page, so that the sender had needed to score out the four before he could pen in the 56. There was a copy of a letter that George Steel had written in response to a request for information on his late wife (the addressee was illegible). It concluded 'You ask for my observations. Although I wish you every success, I feel it is twenty years too late. Only those of us who knew her will truly understand. Still I thank you for your efforts. Yours sincerely, George Steel.'

The other nine files held the political papers of George Steel. There was correspondence from his time as the Communist Party's Manchester recruitment officer for the International Brigades, including letters sent from soldiers, addressing him 'Dear Comrade'. The letters followed a template: after relating a detail or two about barrack life, or after describing, with amazement, the revolutionary mood of a Spanish factory, they commented with affected smugness on the fine weather, bemoaned the lack of real smokes, and signed off with an exclamatory 'Salud, Comrade!'.

There were articles he had published, mainly in the *Daily Worker,* on Marxism, on literature, on the Soviet Union. There was a flyer for a public lecture he gave on the Russian Revolution for the Communist Party North West District History Group, at the AUEW offices in 1972 (tickets 10p each). There were electoral campaign materials urging constituents to give their vote to George Steel, the Communist (sometimes) or Labour (at other times) Party candidate. There was a news article clipped from the *Manchester Guardian,* which described his arrest, with fifteen others, for alleged obstruction following the People's Congress, held in the Free Trade Hall, on 9th May 1931. There was the transcript of an interview conducted with him in his dotage, in which he urged the interviewer to 'Get our young people to read Marx, Engels and Lenin, and not bother with all the philosophers who are busy improving Marxism.' There was documentation about a Communist Party recruitment campaign, which was run as a competition, with the comrade who attracted the most new members being rewarded with a complete set of the selected works of Lenin.

From all this, examiners, I present just two documents. The first is an article on Marx and Lenin, published in the *Daily Worker* in 1948, which I was allowed to photocopy, and which

I present here as an example of Elsie's husband's political and philosophical thought. The second is the letter that Elsie received at an address in Valderrobres, Aragon, which neither George nor Elsie ever threw away, even though it was clearly sent by a former suitor of Elsie's: a man named Ramón Buenacasa Mavilla.

Basics of Marxism, 15: Marx and Hegel

WHAT did Engels mean when he wrote that in Marx's work, "The dialectic of Hegel was placed upon its head; or rather, turned off its head, on which it was standing, and placed upon its feet"? Let us look first of all at what Marx inherited from Hegel. Then we will better understand the necessary improvements he made to Hegel's thought.

PHENOMENOLOGY

What did Marx consider to be "The outstanding achievement of Hegel's *Phenomenology*"? Hegel "grasps the self-creation of man as a process". Hegel "conceives objective man (true, because real man) as the result of his *own labour*". Remember that the German word "Arbeit" has a wider meaning in German than "labour" has in English. Many ignorant interpretations of Marx develop from the mistranslation of this term (in Russian it is translated to "trud"). Marx was right to emphasise industrial labour. However, in both the early and late writings, he intends the concept of work to embrace any activity concerned with "the purposeful transformation of the objective conditions of human life". This includes intellectual labour. So the inspiration Marx took from Hegel was the understanding that humans are inherently world-historical creatures. Men's practical and meaningful human world develops dialectically through lived activity. Hegel called this meaningful human world "Spirit". Marx called it "species-life".

VOLUNTARISM

Marx was right to emphasise the essence of humanity as the totality of social relations founded on relations of production. He was right to oppose voluntarism such as is espoused today by ill-disciplined agitators and Trotskyist agent-provocateurs. However, he was also right to insist that "Men make their own history", albeit "under circumstances directly encountered, given and transmitted from the past". What did Marx say about history? "*History* does *nothing*... It is *man*, real living man... history is *nothing but* the activity of man pursuing his aims". What stops a man's aims being synonymous with his world-historical moment? Marx states that a man's aims emerge distinct from his world-historical moment through his practical engagement with the material world. His aims emerge through the progressive dialectical overcoming of contradictions inherent in social ideas and structures.

ALIENATION

What else did Marx inherit from Hegel? Marx was right to develop Hegel's concept of alienation (*Entfremdung*). In his version of the master and slave dialectic, Hegel examines how each self-consciousness requires the recognition of the other. This is frustrated because simultaneously their demands for independence result in a conflict out of which one emerges as master, and neither achieves adequate recognition. For Hegel, the slave can develop a sense of self through observing the material effects of his subordinate labour. Marx saw what was wrong with this. He radicalised the concept of alienation, observing that under capitalist relations of production, workers are denied the fruits of their labour. Therefore, they are unable to recognise themselves in the material effects of their work. What are the consequences of alienation? Marx believed that a creative engagement with the material world is the very thing that makes us species-beings. Therefore, to be unable to control the terms of one's labour is to be alienated from a properly human condition.

PROLETARIAT

Throughout his writings, Marx regularly associates alienation with being denied control over the means of production. How does this situation arise? This situation arises when the worker "does not produce for himself, but for capital", when "only that worker is now 'productive' who produces surplus value for the capitalist". We know that Marx is right because his theory of social change and the history of the twentieth-century concur in demonstrating how such alienation results in a conflict between wage labourers and the coercive forces of the capitalist state. At this moment the former emerges as a class for itself. We Marxists call this class the revolutionary proletariat.

In conclusion, Hegel thought that the "history of the world is none other than the progress of the consciousness of freedom". Marx and Engels understood that "The history of all hitherto existing society is the history of class struggle". This is the great advance of scientific Marxism. It is why working men should look to Marx, not to Hegel, for assistance in the great struggle to come.

George Steel

Ramón Buenacasa Morilla
Каминский проезд 13/33-28
Кировабад
АзССР
Советский Союз
Unión Sovietica

Mi Querida,

A ship will sail tomorrow with our first Russian trained pilots so I am writing you with my greetings to take the chance that my letter be carried with the care of the comrade mariners. When the comrade pilots arrive in Cartagena I hope it the turning point in the war and that the fascists will be chased out of Spain forever, and from it will emerge the people free from the fascist yoke progressing to freedom and socialism. In the meantime, mi querida, I hope only that this letter is arriving to you well and happy, free and proud, not broken in spirit, not changed in beauty.

I am missing you very much Effie. At night you are in my dreams and by day it is with you whom my thoughts converse. There is so much I hope one day to tell you of life in the Soviet Union. The people is very interesting. For me my work is very busy, and I make long days for it. In their is a mistake of communication and there have been too many, this can be disastrous or hilarious, can mean an air crash or a man toileting in the closet ... and but in time too for to see the great canals and factories of Moscu and I wish I could show you this surely in the picture I have stored in my head. Today is thunder and lightning but the men they remain enthusiasm and they are officious - one must be believing - that the glorious final battle is ending in victory to Spain.

Send my revolutionary greetings to all Valderrobres and especially to their papa Eloise mi querida. I can not write much in this letter for I still must finish before leaves the ship. I want that you know you are as precious to me as when first I carry you, as delicate as a little flower, unconscious through the vermilion gourd, and that time I not hold you in my arms, I have held you everyday in my heart Florecita. But we both must know that this is a time of war, and we must live free, and know that one can never betray the other for it is no other person that has made us separate but only our duties in the historical struggle for what is right and though our bodies may be a thousand miles apart, encircled by others,

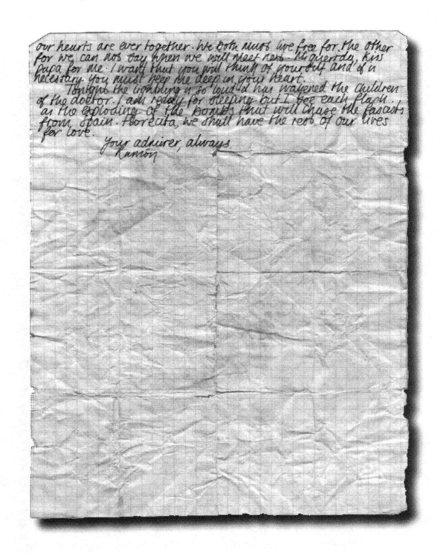

our hearts are ever together. We both must live free for the other
for we can not say when we will meet next. Mi querida, kiss
papa for me. I want that you will think of yourself and if is
necesstary you must keep me deep in your heart.
    Tonight the lightning is to loud it has wakened the children
of the doctor. I am ready for sleeping but I see each flash
as the exploding of the bombs that will chase the fascists
from Spain. Florecita, we shall have the rest of our lives
for love.
        Your admirer, always
            Ramón

Kazakhstan, 1947

119

I returned to Cheltenham preoccupied with questions about Ramón: why did he never return to Elsie? What course directed his life subsequent to writing that letter?

My first move, of course, was to Google Ramón's full name: Calvo Mavilla, Sergio Buenacasa, and Ramón Jimenez were among those selected to play for an Aragonese under-fourteen's football team – I had drawn a blank. Next, I found the Cyrillic symbols with which to write the address Ramón had printed on his letter: his postal address in 1937 was in Kirovabad, a town (today called Ganja) in the Azerbaijan Soviet Socialist Republic. Examiners, when I searched for 'Spaniards Kirovabad' I found a book on *Stalin and the Spanish Civil War* and an article in *Air and Space* magazine. I tried 'Spanish pilots USSR' and 'Pilotos españoles URSS'. I read and read but while I found testimonies from surviving pilots and lists of those killed in action, never once did I find Ramón's name. I began to wonder if perhaps he had never returned to Spain. I searched 'Spaniards settled in the USSR' and 'Los pilotos españoles se asentaron URSS. .The most promising lead I found came from an unlikely source: according to an online forum, which seemed to be run by neo-Falangists, a number of Spanish pilots were interned in the Gulag. I searched 'Spanish pilots in the Gulag' and 'pilotos españoles en el gulag'. I learned that a group of pilots were for a time in a concentration camp near Karaganda, Kazakhstan. I searched 'pilotos españoles Karaganda', 'Spanish anti-fascists Karaganda', and 'Karaganda españoles antifascistas'. With this last search, I found a possible lead: there was a book in the catalogue of the Fundación de estudios libertarios Anselmo Lorenzo, entitled *El Terror comunista en España: las chekas; ¡Karaganda!: la tragedia del antifascismo español*. I ordered a copy immediately.

When the book finally arrived, it did not disappoint. *Karaganda! La tragedia del antifascismo español* was originally disseminated by exiled Spanish anarchists in 1948 with the intention of publicising the plight of those Spaniards detained in the Soviet Gulag. At the back, examiners, there is a list of names (MLE-CNT, n.d. [1948], pp-134-136). The names are divided into three categories: 'pilotos de Aviación,' 'Marinos del «Cabo San Agustín»,' and 'civiles' (civilians). Two civilians are listed: Juan Bote García (a doctor) and Ramón Buenacasa.

My heart thumped and my blood rushed so fast I could hear it, as though I had put my ear to a shell. I knew that in 1948 Ramón was still alive, but what happened to him after that?

120

The only author named in association with the 'Karaganda' document was one José Ester Borrás. I googled his name, thinking, unrealistically, that he might still be alive. He is deceased, of course, but his papers are held in archives at the International Institute of Social History. Borrás fled Spain to escape Franco and was active in the French Resistance during the German occupation. He was arrested by the Gestapo in 1943 and survived Mauthausen concentration camp. After liberation, he established an organisation called the Federación Española de Deportados e Internados Politicos. This organisation's papers are also archived at the International Institute of Social History. 'Founded in Toulouse shortly after the Second World War,' the IISH website explained, the FEDIP 'aimed at the relief of Spanish political prisoners, former political prisoners in German concentration camps and refugees from Spain [and it] started a campaign in 1947 for the relief of a group of republican Spaniards, consisting of aviators in training and sailors, who were left in the Soviet Union in 1939.' If I was going to learn Ramón's fate from anywhere, it seemed likely I would find the truth in these files. There was just one problem: the International Institute of Social History is in Amsterdam.

Examiners, it was at this point that I set my heart on a grand European research trip.

From the start, Lempi was an essential part of my plan: first, because I genuinely needed a translator to make sense of all these Spanish documents; second, because if we were together for a fortnight in Europe then surely she would learn to love me. It was a slightly desperate strategy, I concede, but these were desperate times. Lempi had finished her studies – she graduated with an MA (distinction) – and in September she was moving to Tucson, Arizona, to study an MFA in poetry. It was now or never.

In exchange for her help, I paid her full expenses and agreed that our first stop should be Venice (where Lempi had never been). How did I afford all this? Well, examiners, you may remember that around this time I was awarded £11,000 in criminal injuries compensation – my pay off for prosecuting Daniel Thomson.

121

Examiners, I'm aware that I'm running out of time and words to tell these stories. This thesis is not what I meant to write, but it's too late to start again. Let me at least try to provide some endings. First, we should learn the fate of Yaroslav, the Jew baby, who never knew the identity of his biological parents, or what name they had chosen for him. Examiners, Yaroslav died in Siberia in 1953.

For Yaroslav, the worst thing about the Gulag was an administrative culture committed to interference. This was a conclusion he reached when labouring in Karlag in the late 1940s. During the winter he had survived in Vorkuta, he had most loathed the cold, but later, when he remembered this, he decided the cold was merely another kind of interference. Hunger, too, was an interference, but for Yaroslav, who had survived the Holodomor, who knew of people who had eaten their own children, Gulag hunger was a mild interference. In his last days, once again in Siberia, perhaps he considered death to be the final interference. But always the central problem to him remained one of interference. He thought of the intrusion, the noise, like the electromagnetic interference that had produced a whine in the Vorkuta camp radio speakers, on the dark mornings when the northern lights had appeared in ghostly swirls. Interference. The Russian word for radio interference, радиопомехи, when spoken by Northern Russians, always seemed to Yaroslav to possess an onomatopoeic quality.

It was, officially, for possession of a wireless receiver that Yaroslav had been incarcerated. He had been drafted to the Red Army as a young man, twenty years after the man who named him had been drafted to the Imperial Army (and about the same time that he was deserting from the Spanish Republican Army), and he had at first welcomed what seemed to him generous rations. But then he had been sent to support the war against Finnish fascists, who were, according to Yaroslav's commanding starshina, responsible for all the hunger of the last decade. Yaroslav worked on a railroad line North of Lake Ladoga, and during rare breaks from interference, he had delighted in this empty land, where the snow formed buttresses on their haphazard log barracks, and the pine trees, which they felled for timber, dropped silently on to the cushioned earth. Then, in the height of winter, he was sent with no training to the front, where he never saw a Finnish fascist, but where on one occasion he endured a sudden unseen attack, against which he blindly fired his rifle. He fired his rifle, he later thought, because it had just seemed the correct thing to do.

Apart from that incident, his platoon waited in the freezing dark, apparently forgotten by the world. Soon it was too cold for any other kind of interference and their rifles froze and jammed. One day, dug in, slowly freezing to death, Yaroslav saw an arctic fox padding patterns fine as lace in the snow. The fox came to inspect him, it seemed, with mild curiosity and condescending disdain. He could have shot it, perhaps, and eaten it, but it seemed so perfect, and the moment so silent, that he watched it unmoving as if in a dream.

By the time his platoon was relieved, he had developed frostbite in his feet and fingers. His right foot later became gangrenous, and in the summer of 1940 it was amputated by a military doctor in Leningrad. Yaroslav returned to his home in the Dnieper Valley, and as a result of his amputation was excluded from the conscription launched with the onset of the Great Patriotic War. Working in the fields, he re-learned to walk, and soon, when the fascists advanced, he learned to scuttle at a pace equivalent to a fast jog. During the Soviet retreat, the NKVD burned crops and villages, and executed civilians with an arbitrariness unseen since the Civil War. Yaroslav, as Andriy had done twenty-four years earlier, took refuge on the uncultivated Steppe. In the great purges of 1937 and 1938, the NKVD of the Dnipropetrovsk region had hunted down old Makhnovists and their sympathisers, but on the steppe, Yaroslav found a small group of unpurged rebels: escaped Jews, stranded Red Army soldiers, orphaned boys and girls who lived half-feral in the scrubland. For a time they survived by preying on the supply lines of armies – German, Croatian, Romanian, Hungarian, and Italian – which had been stretched to the east, just as Denikin's supply lines had once been stretched to the west. After the Battle of Stalingrad, when the Germans retreated to the Dnieper Line, all that could be burned was once again burned; on the steppe highland, the horizon darkened, the wind cast black lines of ash, and the world looked as if newly sketched.

Then, as the Red Army pushed west, the men and children resettled their villages, some crying with joy to see a picture of Stalin, and were, depending on their condition and age and the whims of the NKVD, sent into punitive battalions or shot as malingerers or praised as heroic peasant defenders of the motherland. Some of the children immediately denounced their former comrades for anti-Soviet agitation, because they hoped for favourable treatment, or because they had rowed over a girl, or because they knew no better. In any event, the front soon passed and some of the peasants, Yaroslav included, resumed their guerrilla activities, attacking and robbing the Red Army rearguard as they had attacked and robbed the Nazis.

As the war concluded, and this low-scale guerrilla activity continued, the NKVD came under pressure to produce a quota of offenders. Unable to tell a wrecker fascist from a rural Stakhanovite, they invented charges at random. In Yaroslav's Kolkhoz, most men were charged with some section of Article fifty-eight: a man found with a German-manufactured cigarette case received twenty-five years under section six – assisting a foreign state at war with the USSR; a woman who bemoaned the destruction of all the farm machinery received ten years under section ten – propaganda designed to subvert or weaken Soviet power; those found with shotguns, even knives, were sentenced under section eight – conducting or preparing to conduct acts of terror; an elderly man received ten years when he was found to have used as toilet paper a copy of *Trud* that bore a picture of Stalin. When the NKVD searched the ruined khata that Yaroslav had begun to repair, they found a wireless receiver he had stolen from a German patrol. Accepting his story – that he, a Red Army veteran, had captured it to aid the defence of the motherland – they gave him ten years for failing to hand it to Soviet authorities after the Germans withdrew.

You will understand from this selective biography that the hardship of the Gulag was to Yaroslav unexceptional; what he loathed most was the interference.

122

In July 2011, Lempi and I landed in Europe via a budget flight to Venice Treviso. We caught the coach to the outskirts of the city, and then spent two hours trying to find our hotel. Eventually, just after nine o'clock, we set out in search of dinner. We ate in a candlelit patio courtyard, where the walls hung with ivy, and geckos crawled across the decking. The house wine, I remember, was so layered and full-bodied, that every drop seemed to pause languorously in my throat, before ambling onwards at touristic pace. Afterwards, we strolled, with no clear objective, across bridges, along canals, through alleyways so close we walked in single file. When we reached Rialto, Lempi's wonder climaxed, and she pointed to the Grand Canal, whose black water was streaked with impressionistic reflections of light.

Later, we dangled our legs from a small bridge. We could hear the hum of vaporetti cutting through the Grand Canal, and in our backwater lagoon, the water lapped against doors so rotten their wood might crumble in one's hand like earth. Beyond that, the chinks and laughter from a nearby restaurant sounded from our range like the distant chatter of seabirds. It was easily the most romantic moment of my life.

If ever there was a time to kiss Lempi, or to tell her that I loved her, then surely this was it. My heart was thumping and I wished I'd had more to drink. I didn't know what to say or do. So, instead, as we sat in silence savouring the beauty, I started to shuffle closer to her, moving a millimetre at a time. I thought that maybe I could move the way a tree grows – so gradually that one never notices it's moving. At some point I entered her aura, felt the warmth of her body, smelled Gaultier perfume and hairspray and the almond smell of her skin cream. After another minute of painfully careful bum shuffling, our thighs touched, and the feeling – a holistic charge of energy – I can only explain as being like a cross between terror and orgasm. I have no idea what Lempi was thinking, or whether this moment – which was as sexually charged as any in my life – even registered with her. There was no sign she had noticed that our thighs were touching, that the heat of our bodies was connected through thin fabric.

'This is impossibly romantic,' I said.

'Yeah,' said Lempi, 'it's a beautiful spot.'

'I feel like....'

'Yeah,' said Lempi, 'me too.'

I doubt we were talking about the same thing. Before I could think what to do next, Lempi rolled to the side and clambered to her feet. She walked to the end of the bridge and peeled a strip of moss from near the high water mark. Then she leant on the rusted bridge rail, sprinkling the moss into the canal, where strips of reflected moonlight bent with the rhythm of the water. 'Wow,' she said, glancing up. 'Look at the moon.'

'Yeah,' I said.

'Who would you most like to be here with if you could be here with anyone ever?'

Examiners, how could I tell her that I wanted nobody but her? I thought for a moment, while Lempi sat back down, a foot or so further from me than where she had been sitting before. 'Elsie,' I said.

123

According to a popular western democratic analysis, the Soviet system sought to control its citizens' minds as well as their bodies. But this analysis assumes a rightful separation between the individual private sphere and the collective public world. A popular Soviet analysis might have thought such separation false, for the interests of the individual and the interests of the Soviet State were synonymous; and therefore one had to re-educate an individual who sought to harm the state, just as one had to re-educate an individual who sought to harm himself. Yaroslav rarely thought theoretically, but if pushed for long enough he might have rejected both positions. For him, the experience of contentment, задоволеність, could be individual or collective, and the disruptions to the experience of contentment could come from inside oneself or from the intervention of another. But either way, Yaroslav felt, whether the disruptions were internal or external, they derived from the Soviet system.

The contentment was merely the absence of interference. Back in the Ukraine, Andriy had made love to an orphan girl, and during the act, and in the moments afterwards, he had experienced the contentment. Years ago, he had experienced the contentment when playing targets with the German children. And in Finland, he had experienced the contentment when watching the arctic fox. You see, the contentment is nothing but a total immersion in activity. The activity could be ploughing a field, or hiking between villages, or eating soup, or singing in chorus, or sleeping, or smoking a cigarette, or making love, or watching a sunset, or just *waiting*. Even when put to labour in the Gulag, it is possible to experience the contentment. What makes life unpleasant is the interference.

Let us consider an activity such as eating vegetable soup. It is true that at times the vegetables (in Karlag these were usually carrots, potatoes, or cabbages) were so rotten that one could not eat the soup contently under any circumstances. But at other times, eating even this watery gruel should have been a moment of pure contentment. But in Yaroslav's camp, the division of food was part of an exhausting micro-economy, where ladlefuls of gruel and grams of bread were divided based on favouritism, nationality, the nature of one's crime (political or criminal), hierarchy, and – most of all – productive output. One was entitled to rations, kotel, on a grade from one to thirteen, and it was awful to see the rozdavshik, in response to some bribe or threat, serve a man kotel three when he should only have received kotel seven. These rations were then bartered and exchanged and squabbled over, with the result that meal times were as unpleasant as any other. This interference could be external to Yaroslav – as when a suka tried to tax his bread – but it was more likely to be internal – as when he thought about the food he might have enjoyed had he worked harder, or resented a fellow zek who had been served from the thicker gruel that settled at the bottom of the cauldron.

Or, consider those moments when they had light in which to play checkers. What chance for contentment! But in Yaroslav's camp, though the huts were made of mud (there is little timber on the Kazakhstan Steppe), and there was no lighting but from the paraffin lamps of the guards, there was a generator-powered wireless system, which would broadcast through speakers such shows as 'Letters to Stalin,' and of course Yaroslav risked punishment should he lose himself in the game and fail to cry 'hurrah for Stalin' at the appropriate moment. At other times, his eyes would be drawn to the sheets of *Putevka*, the official newspaper of the Karlag NKVD, which were affixed to the barrack walls; then all the slogans and distortions would fill his head as more and more internal interference.

Even at work, it should have been possible to find the contentment. Karlag was largely an agricultural farm, and its zeks faced the Sisyphean struggle of cultivating the desert-like Steppe of Hunger. The land was flat and dry, ravaged by wind, and under snow for four or five months a year. At this time, Yaroslav's work gang was supposed to be digging an irrigation channel, cutting a ravine into the steppe, to divert river water from its course towards Lake Balkhash. Even in this labour, hacking a cut in the earth with a rough-handled pick-axe, Yaroslav could have found the contentment. But any time he came close to losing himself in the task, he would hear a barked 'Dzhe-7225' and he would jolt to alertness, quoting his productivity. Notes on barrels filled and metres cleared were collated and contrasted, individually and collectively, they were graphed and charted, plotted against targets and previous performances. The brigade leaders' results were scrutinised by the foremen. The foremen's results were scrutinised by the supervisors. The supervisors' results were scrutinised by the work chiefs. The work chiefs' results were scrutinised by the camp commanders. The camp commanders' results were scrutinised by the NKVD regional officials. And on and on until every one of them was being watched by Stalin himself.

Most of the supervisors were themselves prisoners; in fact, in a way, every prisoner was a supervisor. A brigade's work was compared with the work of other brigades and used to determine the distribution of food, so that even if one felt like going slowly, one risked the wrath of one's colleagues; and worse, if one saw one's colleague going slowly, one looked upon him with wrath. This wrath, of course, was another internal interference. The wrath was strongest if the man working slowly was also a stoolie, who might ask mid-swing, 'Why are we doing this, Yaroslav?' To such a question, Yaroslav would have to gather himself and reply, 'We are doing this, citizen, because we are in the great proletarian country under the leadership of the party of Lenin with the genius leader of the world proletariat Citizen Stalin at its head. And we are here to see that none of this great land is neglected or wasted and to contribute to its economic flowering by applying socialist forms of organization to agricultural activity.' All this noise. Constant, constant *interference*.

124

On our first night in Venice, Lempi and I lay in our twin beds, separated by two feet of floor, and I experienced an awful yearning. The word 'yearning', which at the time I felt I'd always known but never used, seemed to have been kept in wait for this moment. In my dreams, the soft rhythms of Lempi's breathing merged with the sound of lapping canal water, and when I woke in the humidity of night, Lempi had thrown off her blanket and her legs straddled her sheet, as though she planned to use it to abseil from a window.

In the morning, I was awoken early by the noise of Lempi performing something she called a 'micro workout'. She was doing sit ups on the floor, wearing only boxer shorts and a vest. This might have been – for me – another sexually charged moment, had I not needed to use the bathroom. You see, examiners, in the morning it is my habit to move my bowels, and I was reluctant to perform such an act while Lempi was exercising directly by the bathroom door. When my morning arousal had subsided, I emerged from bed, with my back to Lempi, and pulled my jeans on over yesterday's boxers. Then I told Lempi that I was going out to purchase a phone card.

Once free, I power walked to a café and ordered an espresso; then, I evacuated my bowels in their WC and left before my crime was identified. In my haste, I had paid little attention to the route I'd walked, and for an hour I wandered, lost, increasingly panicked. Bridges and canals, sidewalks and water. Campos and corsos. A church I'd maybe seen before. When I finally found the hotel, Lempi was gone, but she had left a note on the bed: 'At breakfast!!! Where you been!? ☺ xxx'.

I washed, changed my underwear, and ran downstairs to join her. To my surprise, Lempi was not alone. Breakfast was served at white-painted wrought iron tables in a closed patio courtyard to the rear of the hotel. An elderly French couple were spreading jam on bread rolls at a table in the corner, while at a central table – set with a pot of coffee and baskets of bread and conserve – Lempi was in animated conversation with a young dark-haired man. 'Hey!' said Lempi, waving to me, 'come and meet Alfredo.'

'Hi,' I said, shaking his hand. The first thing I noticed about Alfredo was his right bicep. He was wearing a tight black T-shirt and his brown arms bulged with muscle.

'You won't believe this,' said Lempi. 'Alfredo's a poet!'

Of course he is, I thought. I sat down, studied the man. He wore steel-blue semi-rimless spectacles and a goatee beard. His hair was shiny with some sort of haircare product. It was messy at the sides and pushed into a careless fauxhawk at the top. He said how great it was to meet me, speaking in an educated North American accent, but he was – apparently – Venezuelan.

'You don't sound Venezuelan,' I said.

Alfredo explained that when he was six, his parents had fled Venezuela, fearing persecution for their part in a 1992 coup d'etat. He talked at some length about government corruption and IMF-structural readjustment programmes, but I wasn't really listening. Some relative of his – a third cousin or something; someone he'd probably never even met – had been killed during fighting at a TV station. Lempi listened, her big eyes fixed on him, nodding as though he was recounting how he'd survived Auschwitz.

'So what sort of stuff d'you write?' I asked when he was finally quiet.

'Hey, man, I don't even know. I just kind of scribble and hope for the best. What sort of stuff… I guess pretty shit. Is that a genre?'

'I'll bet it's wonderful,' said Lempi. 'I'd love to read some.'

'Trust me, you wouldn't. It's kind of a bit all over the place. Like, I suppose I'm trying to sort of develop a form that's never quite realised, you know? I kind of disrupt the order of some lines, so the reader has to collaborate in the articulation of the stanzaic space.'

'…'

'It sounds amazing,' said Lempi.

'You published much?' I asked.

'Nah, man. I'm kind of just starting out. My last collection won the Hayden Carruth Prize, which was pretty awesome.'

'Wow,' said Lempi.

'I reckon they just felt sorry for me.'

'Fuck,' I said. 'Italian breakfasts are fucking shit, aren't they? A cup of coffee and a fucking breadstick.'

'Dude,' said Alfredo, 'that's so true. Like, give me some pancakes, man.'

'Where abouts in the States are you based, Alfredo?' asked Lempi, sipping her cappuccino.

'Just now I'm– Would you guys forgive me if I smoke when you've finished eating?' He took out a pouch of tobacco and some papers.

'Of course not,' said Lempi.

'I'm supposed to have quit, but it just seems like what you should do in Europe. Where am I based? That's a funny one. I've just finished my MFA at Brown and next year I'm starting a teaching gig in San Bernardino. So I guess just now I'm kind of homeless.'

'Really? That's awesome. I'm moving to Tucson to do an MFA.'

'Well, we won't be so far from each other. You'll have to ride over the desert and come see me some time.'

'Fucksake,' I said, throwing down my bread roll in disgust. 'This shitty breakfast.'

'I know, dude.' Alfredo lit his cigarette, leant back and exhaled in pleasure as the sun broke over the neighbouring buildings.

I slurped the last of my coffee and crashed the cup onto the saucer. 'We should get going,' I said to Lempi.

'Oh yeah?' asked Alfredo. 'What you guys up to today?'

'I'm taking Lempi to see the Basilica and Piazza San Marco.'

'You know where it is? Man, you wouldn't believe– I'm like the classic American idiot abroad. Like, that stereotype is so true for me. I went looking for that place yesterday, and I, like, wandered in circles all day. It's a miracle I ever made it back here.'

'It's pretty hard to miss,' I said.

'I don't suppose– I mean, I don't want to impose, but you sure would be doing me a favour if you'd let me tag along for a bit?'

'That would be awesome,' said Lempi.

'I don't know,' I said. 'I mean, the thing is, we were pretty determined to get there early. The guidebook's very explicit about the need to arrive there early if you want to beat the queues.'

'Hey, no worries there. Let me just grab my camera, and I'll be good to go.'

'Shit,' said Lempi, 'I need to get ready!' And so, in unison, we stood up with affected haste, promising to rendezvous in the lobby ten minutes later.

125

In October, it snowed. When Yaroslav awoke, the world was white and dark like the negative of a photograph. All morning it seemed the sun did not rise. The snow landed on the prisoners' hats and duffel coats and when they lined for roll-call they looked like chess pieces preparing for battle.

Upon hearing his number, each prisoner had to say his full name, his date of birth, his father's name (Yaroslav gave the name of his adoptive mother's dead husband), and his date and place of sentence. Then they marched to work flanked by dogs and armed guards. When in the company of other guards, the guards cursed the prisoners and called them fascist Banderist bastards: Are you waiting for your fucking mother? You fucking fascist bastard. I will fuck you until eggs turn grey! But as soon as they were alone with the prisoners most of the newer guards chatted amiably, shared matches, reminisced about the war, or asked questions about distant parts of the Soviet Union.

Strangely, each new guard seemed to think he was unique in establishing friendships with the prisoners. For example, there were two Ukrainian men of Yaroslav's age, who had both recently entered the NKVD as inadvertently as Yaroslav had entered the Gulag. When unseen by other guards, each man would often sit where Yaroslav worked and reminisce about their homeland. But when these guards were together, they competed to find the vilest ways to insult the men with whom they had earlier made friends. Yaroslav imagined that in the evenings the guards drank vodka and bonded in their pretend hatred of the fascist enemies of the people. Was this true of other groups? When the children of free workers threw stones at the prisoners, did each child, perhaps, throw his stone because he thought that was what the other children expected him to do? The entire system, Yaroslav thought, was sustained by people who pretended to believe in it because they thought that others really did.

Mid-morning, the wind picked up and the snow arrowed horizontal – there was nothing to break the wind for a thousand miles. And then, as the day heated up, the snow turned to sleet, then rain, and the water trickled in the newly dug ditch, and the earth was heavy to lift. By lunch time, the snow survived only in tatters, and Yaroslav's boots congealed with mud.

As the sun set, the rain turned once again to sleet, washing the world white. They ate from metal tins that, according to camp legend, had once held US or German Army meat rations. By the time Yaroslav had carried his tin from the serving hatch to the shelter of the barracks, the broth was cold and sprinkled with snowflakes. Soon it would be so cold that tobacco would be worthless: in the winter, nobody removed his gloves unless he really had to. In the winter, the snow banked up on wind-exposed crests and rises, curling at the top like giant waves. The barracks would be barred with icicles. There were days when men hid in ditches, hands between their legs, terrified to move. The cold started in your extremities and worked its way in; but the cold that kills you, they said, starts inside you and works its way out. Around the forbidden zone, near the barbed wire, the snow spread flat like fresh bed linen. There were days last winter when Yaroslav wished to throw himself into it. When the sky cleared, the snow was miles and miles of bejewelled desert; the Steppe turned pink in the setting sun and the prisoners' shadows stretched a hundred metres tall.

During his time in Karlag, Yaroslav spoke with everybody he could. When he had spare makhorka tobacco, he shared it with anybody who might in the future prove useful. They spoke afterwards, but they always smoked in silence – in the Gulag, every prisoner wanted his contentment to be free of interference. Yaroslav met an underworld leader, a blatnoy who obeyed the criminal code and would not even carry barbed wire, who had gold teeth but only seven fingers, and whose throat was scarred in parody of a smile. He met a Russian who in exchange for tobacco offered Yaroslav the chance to fuck a plough pony – it was, said the Russian, better than any woman. He met a gypsy from Moldaviz who for some reason badly wanted siphoned petrol. He met a Polish doctor who had been an officer in the Home Army. He met an exiled Volga German who was suckling piglets through the fingers of a rubber glove filled with goat's milk. He met Japanese men who cleared snow from the railway track and between them could speak barely a sentence of Russian. And one day he spoke with the prisoners who were digging the irrigation trench from the opposite end. Every day, Yaroslav's group and this group moved a little closer together – in theory, they were competing to see which brigade would hit the mid-point first. Yaroslav was surprised to discover that the other brigade was comprised entirely of Spaniards.

126

During our first day in Venice, Alfredo managed to annoy me in almost every way. For a start, he insisted on stopping every ten minutes to take a photograph. I don't mean urging us to pull funny faces while he snapped holiday poses in front of famous sights; rather, he would be moved by how the light filtered through a Serliane window or wobbled on the water of a quiet río. He would then spend several minutes fiddling with the lenses on his fancy camera, crouching into strange positions, while checking all the time that the delay wasn't inconveniencing us – which invariably it was.

He turned out to have 'an amateur interest' in renaissance art, and though he claimed to have no idea where he was going, he would periodically seize midstep having recognised the name of a signposted church. 'Wait,' he'd say, 'do you guys know [such and such neglected renaissance painter]?' – which invariably we didn't. He'd then lead us to yet another picture of Jesus or Mary (or, occasionally, an ugly cherub cavorting around plump naked women), ponder it at agonising length, and then explain its supposed significance in the history of painting.

'Wow,' Lempi would say, 'how do you know all that?'

'Actually, I just read it somewhere. I just didn't want you to think I'm a dumb American, which, frankly, is exactly what I am. Truth is, I don't even know if we're looking at the right painting. They all look the same to me.'

'Then why must we keep visiting them?' I asked.

'Man, you're so right. Like, I'm just trying – hopelessly – to break the stereotype of American cultural ignorance. I'm not even sure I *like* renaissance art.'

This was one of the tactics Alfredo used to ingratiate himself: he pretended to agree with whatever I said. For instance, mid-afternoon, when I was tired of walking in the stifling heat, when I was sick of Alfredo's art lessons, I said I was going to sit in a shady pub and drink a carafe of wine. 'Dude,' said Alfredo, 'now *that* is a plan. I've had enough culture for one day; guys, let's just hang out and get hammered' – which we did.

By the time we got back to the hotel, I was totally pissed. I therefore wasn't ready when Alfredo said what an 'awesome' day it had been, how 'cool' he thought we were, and how much he'd like to say thanks by buying us dinner. I said I would accept no such charity, but, with Lempi crying her assent, I was unable to rebut the preposterous plan that the three of us should dine together. Once again we parted, promising to rendezvous in the hotel lobby.

'What a cool guy,' said Lempi, as we climbed the stairs alone.

'Don't you think he's a bit up himself?'

'I think he's really nice.'

'That's what he wants us to think,' I said, which even to me seemed like quite a weird comment.

Back in the hotel room, Lempi felt the urge to beautify herself before dinner, a task for which she was abundantly prepared. For nearly an hour, I waited, increasingly irritated, while she preened and painted herself. Still, Lempi's make-up regime was a ritual practised with such devotion that it deserves to be recounted as fully as memory allows. Before starting she cleansed and toned. While the toner was drying, she plucked her eyebrows with heart-shaped tweezers. She used an almond-essence body moisturiser and an oily-skin face moisturiser, which she applied on top of an anti-ageing serum, and then she rubbed her whole body with Rimmel medium matt sun shimmer. She applied the sun shimmer with a white glove of the sort one might once have used to declare a duel, and so this stage of her beautifying always seemed especially ceremonial. Next, she applied illuminator to her cheekbones and the crest of her nose, and then – remember that each layer must dry before the next layer is applied – she applied her foundation. She applied her foundation, not with a large sponge, but with a delicate paint brush of the sort wielded by a careful water-colourist. Next, with her gold-coloured YSL

Touche Eclat pen highlighter, she drew under her eyes and around blemishes too small for anyone but her to notice. Then she produced the mineralised skin finish powder – I don't know exactly what this did, but it required its own brush. And then she applied the bronzer – Maybelline cream blush – with something that looked a bit like an old-fashioned shaving brush (Lempi had the complete Bobbie Brown brush set, which she carried– which I carried around Europe in a massive toolbox). And then she turned her attention to her eyes. She produced a tray of shimmering little bricks, laid out like an artist's palate, and she swirled and tapped her brush, dabbing different shades into the creases and corners of her eye lids, before blending them with her finger. Then she closed her eyes and struck a crayon of kohl across her kissing lids. Lempi dyes her eyelashes black every thirty days and complements the effect with Lancôme Icone mascara. When applying mascara, Lempi's mouth forms that strange O only otherwise seen on the faces of choir singers and inflatable sex dolls. Finally, at last, she applied two layers of lip liner, and then stroked her mouth with lipstick. Then she pursed her lips and pouted, slumped, leant on the sink, and gazed at herself with the look of a painter who is dismayed that her canvas has once again failed to capture the natural beauty of the landscape.

During this long process, I was dispatched to the lobby to relay her apologies to Alfredo. I had grown increasingly angry throughout the day – first with Alfredo and then with Lempi. Sitting in the hotel room, watching Lempi paint herself, it had occurred to me for the first time just how superficial she was. Still, I was surprised by my own cattiness: 'Hi, Alfredo,' I said. 'I'm afraid Lempi's running a bit late.'

'That's cool,' said Alfredo.

'She's got terrible diarrhoea.'

127

To understand why a group of Spaniards was digging an irrigation trench in Kazakhstan – and let's not forget why Lempi and I were in Europe in the first place; let's not forget why I was paying for her travel and accommodation and food – we must return to the tragedy in Spain. Examiners, few historical episodes have been as extensively discussed as the Spanish Civil War, but there has been a conspicuous silence regarding the fate of those militants who survived Franco's victory. While tens of thousands were killed in the repression that immediately followed the war, and many more were forced into labour battalions, others evaded capture, continuing guerrilla resistance in Spain, escaping to South America, or, in the case of around 2000 Communists, emigrating to the Soviet Union. Most Republicans, however, ended up in France, either crossing the Catalan border or arriving via North African ports. As is well known, the French rewarded some 350,000 Spanish anti-fascists with internment in concentration camps, where sanitation was non-existent, Communist denunciations continued, and around 4,700 prisoners died (Thomas, 1965, p-922). Some of these internees would later join the French Foreign Legion, distinguishing themselves in units that included the 9th Company of Leclerc's Second Armoured Division, a force comprised almost entirely of CNT/FAI members who manned tanks named 'Durruti' and 'Ascaso', and fought in North Africa, before leading the liberation of Paris and continuing through Strasbourg to eventually capture Berchtesgaden (see Fernandez, 2004). Many Spaniards also fought in the French Resistance with 6000 participating in the liberation of Toulouse and 4000 taking part in the Maquis uprising in Paris. After the defeat of Germany, many of these partisans returned to the Franco-

Spanish border lands, waging guerrilla war against Francoism until the 1960s (see Tellez, 1994). Other refugees were captured by the Gestapo, handed over to Franco (as was the fate of Juan Peiró), or interned in concentration camps – more than 5000 Spanish Republicans died in Mauthausen alone. Given this mass displacement of Spanish Republicans and the large numbers missing, existing in underground organisations, killed in conflict or repression, disappeared in concentration camps, or lost to their comrades through distant exile, it is easy to understand how a small group stranded in Russia could be forgotten.

Despite the British inspired 'non-intervention pact', Hugh Thomas estimates the value of foreign military aid during the Spanish Civil War to have been between $1,425,000,000 and $1,900,000,000 (1965, p-977). While the Nationalists could rely on assistance from Italy and Germany (paid for on credit), and, to a much lesser extent, Portugal and Ireland, Republican forces were largely reliant on sub-standard arms from Mexico and over-priced shipments from the Soviet Union. Stalin's trade came at a heavy price – both in terms of Communist power and Spanish gold. At the start of the war, the Spanish gold reserve was the fourth largest in the world, worth an estimated $788,000,000 (ibid., p-974). In total $500,000,000 worth of gold was shipped to Russia (ibid., p-488), most of it carried to the Ukrainian port of Odessa by the Spanish Merchant Navy. The sailors of these boats, like the rest of the Spanish working class, were organised into trade unions, principally the CNT and UGT.

What did the Republic receive for the gold it exported? The Soviet Union provided T-26 tanks, anti-aircraft guns, machine guns, ammunition, lorries, and oil. They also sold the Republic around 1000 aircraft including I-15 and I-16 fighter planes, and SB-2, Natasha and Rasante bombers (ibid., pp-980/1). They provided some pilots to fly these crafts, while also offering to train Spaniards at the 20th Military School for Pilots, near Kirovabad in Azerbaijan.

128

'So the Soviets,' I said, 'trained Spanish pilots at this military school in Azerbaijan.'

'Okay,' said Alfredo, nodding his head in an affectation of interest. Earlier he'd explained that our research especially fascinated him, because his grandparents had moved to South America as refugees from Francoism. I pretended to believe him, though I suspected he was really descended from Castilian slave traders.

'And Ramón,' said Lempi, 'who was, like, Elsie's boyfriend, went over there to help as a translator.'

At this point the waiter brought our food outside. I'd insisted on returning to the restaurant where Lempi and I had dined the previous night (mainly because I sensed Alfredo wanted to lead us somewhere else), and I'd ordered exactly the same meal: pizza Siciliana, penne arrabiata, and another litre of house red wine.

'Wow, guys,' said Alfredo, 'this looks awesome.' He made appreciative noises as he cut into his crustacean-ridden spaghetti. 'So what happened to this Ramón guy?'

'If we knew that,' I said, 'we wouldn't need to traipse across Europe.'

'We know that he was put in the Gulag,' said Lempi.

'No way. Really?'

'Yes,' I said. 'Really. He was in a camp in Kazakhstan. That was in 1948. We don't know what happened to him after that.'

'But we're going to find out,' said Lempi. 'There's, like, archive stuff at this big institute in Amsterdam.'

'Is that where you're headed? I'm flying home from Amsterdam Schiphol.'

'No, we're not,' I said.

'We're going to Switzerland and Spain first,' said Lempi.

'Awesome,' said Alfredo. 'When I leave here, I'm planning to get the night train to somewhere Swiss.'

'That's what we're doing!' said Lempi.

'Fucksake,' I said, throwing down my knife and fork.

'What?' said Lempi. She, Alfredo, and several other diners were looking at me.

'Can't Italians build a fucking sewage system? I can't eat when the whole town smells of shit.'

'I know, dude. Like, didn't the Romans invent sanitation?'

'Woah-kay,' said Lempi. 'Anyway. We're getting the eight o'clock tomorrow night. We're going to... what d'you call it?''

'Lausanne. We're visiting the archives at the Centre International de Research sur l'Anarchisme. We'll be spending all day in the library reading out-of-print foreign-language books about a revolutionary experiment in a small Spanish town. There really is literally nothing else to do in the locale.'

'Awesome. I've heard it's like this amazing journey, you know? Northern Italy to Switzerland? Like, you fall asleep in dry scrub land, and you wake up in this northern landscape surrounded by green hills and snow-capped mountains.'

'You should totally come with us,' said Lempi.

'Hey, careful what you say – maybe I will. You guys will be sick of me, but I guess it's like... I've been travelling round on my own for weeks and I've met some real douchebags, you know? Like, if I meet another group of frat boy US backpackers, I'll fucking scream, man.'

'That must be awful,' I said.

'I know, dude. I came here to get away from those assholes.

But meeting you guys has been awesome. I think you're both really cool.' He raised his wine glass. 'Hey, to your health, and to the success of your mission.'

Examiners, what could I do except raise my glass and agree with Lempi that it was 'awesome' we'd met each other?

'What are you guys up to tomorrow?' asked Alfredo when the toasting was over.

'Probably the same as you,' I said.

Alfredo was incapable of accepting an insult. 'Yeah, dude. Like, what else can you do in Venice but see the sights? You fancy getting the vaporetti out to San Servolo? You know, the island they go to in "Julian and Maddalo"?'

'That would be awesome,' said Lempi.

'Maybe visit the Guggenheim in the afternoon?'

'Let me guess,' I said; 'you're an expert on Picasso.'

'I love Picasso,' said Lempi.

'Nah, man, but I saw that movie about Jackson Pollock.' Alfredo laughed and slapped me on the back.

'This is great,' I said, standing up to go to the toilet. 'The three of us hanging out together – isn't this just fucking awesome.'

129

At the end of the Civil War, the Spanish pilots were transferred to Moscow and accommodated in a rest home where they received the same good treatment they had experienced at the aviation school (MLE-CNT, op. cit., p-100). At this time there were also around 300 hundred Spanish mariners stranded in the Soviet Union. Approximately 30% of these sailors were repatriated between August 1939 and June 1941, while others joined the Spanish community in exile. However, a number of unfortunates were placed under arrest either in April 1940, June 27th 1941, or at later dates.

In 1941, the USSR entered the Second World War and simultaneously its attitude towards the Spanish antifascists became more sinister. The Pilots and mariners were interrogated and asked whether they wanted to stay in the Soviet Union. Many accepted Soviet citizenship, with the risk that they would never see loved ones again, and most, if not all, of these Spaniards were released to work freely. Many fought in the Soviet Army. Those who declined Soviet citizenship in most instances requested safe passage to Mexico; Ramón was one of these men. They waited, assured their journey was being arranged, but instead they were arrested during 1941.

Ramón was arrested with the pilots on the 22nd of July, 1941, and taken to the Transit Prison at Novosibirsk. They were held in temperatures that reached fifty degrees below zero, they were without winter clothing as all their personal effects had been confiscated, and they were regularly forced to strip for the amusement of the jailers (MLE-CNT, op. cit., p-101). After five months, Ramón and the pilots were sent to work at a sawmill in the region of Klasndiark. Many of them suffered serious injuries, including Vicente Montejano Moreno, a CNT member then aged twenty-two, who lost several fingers from his right hand.

The sailors were also put to work, constructing a railroad in the inhospitable and remote region of Yakutia, in the North East of Siberia. It was not unusual for prisoners to be transferred, often over vast distances, and in extreme conditions, according to no obvious logic, and this happened to the Spanish antifascists: both Ramón's group and the sailors were sent via Novosibirsk to Karaganda, Kazakhstan. At the end of 1942, including Ramón, there were sixty-seven Spanish anti-fascists in Karaganda. Those who survived remained there until the summer of 1948. It is therefore worth making a few notes about the Karaganda complex.

130

Examiners, you won't be surprised to hear that Alfredo pursued us to Switzerland. We shared a compartment with three Korean students, with whom we communicated only through smiling. On the journey, I could find only two consolations. First, I claimed the top two couchettes for myself and Lempi, so that Alfredo had to sleep underneath me, and during the night I found several excuses to clamber from my bunk and kick him. Second, Alfredo was right: it was a wondrous journey.

Leaving Venice, we rode through countryside scorched the colour of sand, and somewhere in northern Italy, where the line was flanked by vineyards, we turned the seats into beds and partially undressed in an awkward ballet full of smiles and nods and apologies. From time to time I woke in the night, when the rocking of the train ceased, and I pulled back the curtain and saw that we were idling in a deserted station where the platform lights exaggerated the emptiness. Once in a long while, a truck would hiss through this secret nocturnal world. And then the train would ease that inch of reverse, brace itself, pull forward. The soothing rhythm of progress would overtake me, and I would fall asleep once more as the train sped through the black countryside.

Later, I pulled back the curtain and saw that the sun had risen on another world. Alpine houses, cattle barns, triangular log stacks ledged on green hillsides. The light was a cool early morning blue-grey that refracted through thick valley fog. 'Lempi,' I whispered, reaching across the chasm between our bunks. I touched her shoulder and pulled back the curtain: 'look.' She looked outside, looked at me, and then looked back at the passing scenery. In shorts and vest she climbed barefoot down the ladder, located her toiletries, and clambered over the

Koreans' suitcases. Then – to the frustration of a German-speaking family, who for the next hour paced the corridor and rattled the door – she locked herself in the washroom.

During this time – while I was still half-awake – Alfredo pursued what he called a 'bro-down'. I was still in bed on the top bunk, my head level with Alfredo's. He was standing, wearing only shorts and a T-shirt, speaking in a whisper though the Koreans were by now awake. 'Listen, buddy,' he said, 'this is kind of a weird situation. Like, I don't really know how to say this. I mean, I feel like me and you are– Meeting you has been so cool and I love the work you're doing. And what it is…. See, I realise that I've kind of…. Oh, man, this sounds so fucking lame! I think I'm kind of falling for Lempi, you know?'

'No shit.'

'Is it that obvious? Oh, fuck, man. I wanted to, sort of, bro-down with you and check the deal man to man, you know? I mean, if you're cool with that?'

'…'

'Like, I realise I don't know what the deal is with you two. Like, if you're involved or what?'

'Me and Lempi?' I said, trying to sound amused. 'Ha, no. We're just friends.'

'Dude, are you sure? Cause I'd totally back off if you wanted me to.'

'She's sort of like a sister to me.'

'Fuck, man, that's a relief. All night I've been worrying that you'd turn out to be madly in love with her, and I'd be like this asshole American who shows up and just fucking ruins everything.'

At this point the train braked with a scream. Everyone and everything lurched forward and a second later slumped back into place. When Lempi re-entered the compartment, Alfredo and I acted as though this conversation hadn't taken place, but I could tell from the Koreans' expressions that they'd understood some of what had (and hadn't) been said. In a way, they'd understood more than Alfredo.

131

The town of Karaganda is the industrial centre of Kazakhstan and in 1939 its population was 156,000 (Shapovalov, 2001, p-164, n.4). From 1931, a large network of labour camps (often referred to as 'Karlag') developed in the arid region around the town, and by 1st January 1941 there were 33,747 prisoners in the complex (Khlevniuk, 2004, p-359). This group of camps remained operational until 1959, deploying prisoners in mines, factory work and timber logging, but primarily in agricultural labour. Karaganda and the surrounding area was also a common site of exile, where large numbers of Volga Germans (including Anna Loewen and many other Mennonites) and former Gulag inmates (including, briefly, Alexander Solzhenitsyn) were re-settled (see Solzhenitsyn, 1978, pp-372/3). Both prisoners and exiles usually lived in huts made of earth.

The Spanish anti-fascists were held in a camp situated between the towns of Karaganda and Spassk, known to the Soviet authorities by its number and postcode area – '99/22 Spassk'. They were held with about 900 other detainees in an area 300 metres long by 200 metres wide, surrounded by three lines of barbed wire, armed guards, and ferocious dogs (MLE-CNT, op. cit., p-105). There was no heating or electricity (ibid.) and during the war daily rations could be as little as 100 grams of bread and one bowl of watery gruel (usually made from rotten cabbage and carrot). After the war, this increased to 600g of bread, 10g of margarine, 17g of sugar, and two bowls of gruel (ibid., p-104). The prisoners' health suffered severely, with many afflicted by tuberculosis – for example, Jurado Manuel Vasquez was described as totally debilitated by this illness (José Bravo Basan, FEDIP 104). Between 1942 and 1948, eight of the group died.

132

I was glad that I had economised on our pre-booked accommodation in Lausanne, for Lempi and I were booked into a mixed dormitory at the local youth hostel – an arrangement that prohibited sexual encounters. Nevertheless, Lempi and Alfredo had taken to holding each other's hands, and chastely kissing each other goodnight. Worse than this unedifying spectacle, they had started to speak in Spanish. This was an obvious attempt to exclude me, and whatever they said to each other invariably descended into inane laughter.

During the day, we worked in the archives, 'assisted' by Alfredo, who without invitation had thrown himself into our research project. We did learn bits and pieces about life in Valderrobres, but I had lost much of my interest. It was now apparent to me that Elsie had been mistaken in ever leaving the UK, that Ramón had ditched her at the first opportunity, and that whatever happened to him after 1948, he'd given little thought to the woman who loved him. I started to turn against Ramón. When I thought of what we might find in Amsterdam, I began to hope that we'd discover he'd been executed in Siberia or had died of tuberculosis in Kazakhstan.

In the evenings, despite Alfredo and Lempi's protests, I insisted on leaving them alone. I would sit in the cathedral, where I listened to an organ recital, or I would ride the free trams to their terminus, disembark, wait half-an-hour in a graffiti-covered shelter, and then catch the same tram back into town. When I could kill no more time, I'd buy some pasta and sauce, cook it in the hostel's communal kitchen, and eat it slowly with a bottle of wine. On both nights I was the first in the dormitory to go to bed, and on both nights I was woken by Lempi and Alfredo whispering and giggling in the dark.

On our third day in Switzerland, we relocated to Geneva, preparing to catch the sleeper to Barcelona. That afternoon, the three of us strolled down to Lake Geneva, bought ice creams, and relaxed in the sun. When Alfredo wandered off in search of a toilet, Lempi and I were for once left alone.

'Are you okay?' she asked, rubbing my shoulder.

'What d'you mean?'

Lempi shrugged. 'You seem down.'

'Well, I'm not.'

We were sitting on the pier, watching the pleasure boats slide in silent courses, their engines as quiet as the swans. On the far bank, the jet d'Eau fountain shot 200 metres high, casting its spray on the breeze, refracting the sunlight into a rainbow of colours.

'Isn't it beautiful?' said Lempi.

'…'

'You can see every colour of the rainbow.' She started to sing. 'Red and yellow and pink and blue, purple and orange and green.'

I stood up, planning to walk to the end of the pier where I could sit alone.

'Sorry,' said Lempi. 'I've always loved rainbows. Like, when I was a kid I thought I could catch them, you know? I'd, like, run away from home and panic my parents. I must have got the idea from some fairy tale or something, but, like, even after the rainbows faded, I'd keep trying to find where they'd been, as though at a certain spot the earth would be scorched or golden.'

'How did that work out for you?'

'Usually I'd end up exhausted and crying. Once I was taken home by the police. But I think I grew out of chasing rainbows when I was eight.'

I'd no idea what this anecdote was supposed to mean, but it sounded like the sort of crap Alfredo would put in a poem.

133

The plight of Ramón and his comrades only became known in 1947 when other detainees were released. First there was the testimony of Fransisque Bornet, a sixty-year-old French national who had been repatriated in 1946 after spending five years in Karaganda (CNT-MLE, op. cit., p-120). In his book, *Je Reviens de Russie*, Bornet recalled meeting Spanish Republicans, and this was confirmed by a desperate message from an unnamed Republican pilot, hidden inside the shirt of an Austrian woman released from Karaganda. The case was investigated by the anarchist prisoner support group, FEDIP. In 1948 they published a list of sixty-one surviving Spanish anti-fascist detainees – twenty-five trainee pilots; thirty-four sailors; the doctor, Juan Bote García; and the translator, Ramón Buenacasa Mavilla. One of the sailors, Secondino Rodríguez de la Fuente, had died by the time the list was published.

The solidarity work of FEDIP was exhaustive, whole-hearted, and free of political dogmatism. In addition to sending numerous ignored letters to Moscow, they wrote to anybody who may have been able to help – the United Nations; the Red Cross; the Workers Defence League in New York; the World Jewish Congress; the British Soviet Society – and they contacted an array of celebrities to raise the profile of their campaign. One address book includes contact details for Eleanor Roosevelt, Pablo Picasso, and Charlie Chaplin. Many potentially sympathetic writers, artists, and intellectuals were invited to join a 'Comité d'Honneur et de Patronage,' whose illustrious membership included Albert Camus, Jean-Paul Sartre, François Mauriac, René Char, Ignacio Silone, Carlo Levi, and André Breton (Ester Borrás 15). Albert Einstein respectfully declined to join (against the wishes of his heart), explaining that he had learned from experience not to lend his name to committees over which he had no control (personal letter, Ester Borrás 15).

Needless to say, the PCE was furious that the reality of the regime it supported was being brought to popular attention. Felix Villanueva Flores, brother of the incarcerated pilot Julio, and himself a member of the PCE, sought to raise the matter with the party leadership at their congress in Paris. He spoke to none other than Enrique Lister, the Moscow-backed commander who had overseen the invasion of Valderrobres in 1937. Lister told Villanueva, 'It doesn't matter whose brother he is, they are traitors and they have to pay,' and this attitude was typical of the PCE leaders, who maintained that all the detainees were Falangist spies who should be grateful they weren't shot (CNT-MLE, op. cit., pp-122-125).

But despite the PCE reaction, ripples of the solidarity campaign reached Moscow, forcing them to respond to the adverse publicity. First, in June 1948, they moved the sixty one survivors (Secondino Rodríguez de la Fuente and José Pollán Ozaento had died earlier that year) to a camp on the outskirts of Odessa, which the prisoners were told represented the beginning of their repatriation to Spain. They also granted some improvements to the prisoners' conditions; for example, they were allowed to send mail via the Red Cross. Then, a special commission from Moscow told the prisoners that they would be released if they signed letters saying they wanted to adopt Soviet citizenship (FEDIP Report, 30/10/50, p-1, FEDIP 104). This was a propaganda exercise designed to prove that the Spaniards were in the USSR voluntarily and that the stories of imprisonment represented another Trotskyite-Bukharinite-Fascist plot. Needless to say, the prisoners were given considerable encouragement to sign and those who refused lost the right to write to their families (ibid., p-3).

The signatures were published in the Soviet newspaper *Trud* on the 19th August 1948. In total there were forty-nine signatures including nineteen from the group that had been held in Karaganda. Among the signatories, I saw the name Ramón Buenacasa Mavilla. Those who signed were released as free workers and most of them were settled in Kolkoses, in the region of the Black Sea. I am unsure how many of them ever returned from the USSR. The others stayed in camp 7159 near Odessa, 'persisting in their dignified and courageous attitude' (ibid., p-2). The stance of those who refused to sign certainly was courageous, but many of those who signed had compelling personal reasons to leave the Gulag immediately – Manuel Jurado was debilitated by tuberculosis, Luis Serrano had lost his wife and was separated from his daughter, and Ramón, as we shall see, had his own special reason to accept Soviet citizenship.

134

In Barcelona, Lempi and I were pre-booked into a twin room at a budget hotel near Diagonal, and – to my irritation – Alfredo found an empty single on the same floor. Predictably, on our only night in Barcelona, they used the privacy of his room to consecrate their relationship. The noise of their coupling was impossible to ignore. I heard the usual giggling and ticklish shrieks, then a period of pleasant silence, then the creaking of mattress springs, and soon the rhythmic thumping of a headboard against the wall. This noise, regular and slow and angry, sounded like a prisoner forlornly pounding the walls of his cell. And then I heard this awful noise from Lempi. It sounded more like she was giving birth than experiencing pleasure. And then the thumping stopped. Alfredo Laughed. I heard Lempi say 'Oh fuck fuck fuck,' and then 'oh no no no oh fuck oh no oh fuck.' And then a thrashing noise as if they were fighting. And then more of Lempi's awful screaming. For a minute, the only noise was Lempi's breathless panting, and then the mattress creaking restarted, grew faster and faster – cue more awful screaming – and eventually, after no audible climax from Alfredo, the rattling stopped and the only noise was their inaudible post-coital whispering.

I don't know how long they rested, whether they slept or talked through the night, but at some point I was woken by the headboard once again thumping the wall. My voyeuristic curiosity was exhausted and I now felt only revulsion. I wrapped my pillow around my ears and tried to shut out the noise of Lempi's orgasm, but at some point I heard her cry 'no, not that! Baby, no!' (What on earth were they doing?). Despite her protests, whatever they were doing caused her to produce a guttural howl of pleasure, and then to scream 'oh fuck oh no oh God oh fuck me Jesus.' At this point I sat up and thumped the wall.

In the morning, minutes after I'd clambered from bed to move my bowels, Lempi knocked the door and let herself in to our room. I have to say that I was revolted by how she smelled. She may not have realised it, but she stank of sex. She smelled of body odour and latex and the acidic smell of vaginal secretions. I was appalled she thought it appropriate to use our room to clean herself. She flopped onto her still-made bed, smiling stupidly, as though her coitus was some unspoken joke we could share.

'How did you sleep?' she asked.

I ignored her and shut myself in the toilet. Examiners, despite being revolted by Lempi's undisguised corporeality, I remained determined to conceal my bodily processes from her. While Switzerland was crammed with resplendent public toilets and blessed with gushing reservoirs of alpine water, in our Barcelona hotel room, the porcelain at the back of the toilet had, over decades, striped brown with a trickle of silty flush water, and one could flush the toilet only by pumping the handle as if drawing water from a well. Worse, the toilet door had no lock. To disguise what I was doing, I turned on the shower and padded the toilet with loo roll to cushion any splash. Then I sat on the pan with my legs extended and both feet kicked against the door. As soon as I began to move my bowels, the door strained against my feet. 'Hey,' said Lempi, 'there's something blocking the door. Hey, are you having a shower? Can I come in? I need to pee!' Lempi seemed to think that we had the sort of sibling friendship whereby modesty could be discarded. 'Hey,' she said again, 'can I come in?'

'Lempi!' I shouted. 'I'm sorry, but can you please just leave me alone?'

135

Examiners, given the length of time that the Spaniards spent in Stalinist camps – and given that they endured the harshest (in terms of death rates) years in the Gulag's history – it is surprising that so many of them survived.

I lack accurate figures for how many of the Spanish anti-fascists died in 1941 and 1942 (the year which had the highest prisoner mortality rate in the whole history of the Gulag), but during the next decade ten out of sixty-seven prisoners died.

Had their death rate matched the Gulag average then we would have expected fifteen (22.4%) to die in 1943 alone, and, although average death rates declined sharply as the war turned in Soviet favour, we would have expected twenty-five out of sixty-seven detainees to have died by the time some were released in 1948. In fact, only seven died during this period.

There are a number of factors that may explain this. First, the Spaniards were relatively new to the Gulag in the war years when a general shortage of food combined with typhus and dysentery epidemics meant an especially high death rate. In other words, they were likely to be physically stronger at the start of 1942 than prisoners who had been in the Gulag system since the thirties. Indeed, given their age range – in 1942 the youngest turned twenty-three and the oldest turned forty-nine – and the fact that they had been deemed fit for their respective duties, we can conclude they started as a healthier than average section of the Gulag population.

Perhaps the biggest factor in their favour was that through the worst years of food shortages they were detained in an agricultural camp. Many Gulag memoirs agree that there was always slightly more food at agricultural camps, and, despite the rigorous searches, it was sometimes possible for prisoners to conceal small quantities of what they harvested. However, while an agricultural camp was no doubt preferable to the Kolyma Gold Mines or other camps in the extreme north, it is not clear that they offered better than average chances of survival. A report from the Gulag sanitary department (reproduced in Khlevniuk, 2004, pp-209-212) records that in 1938, 7.17% of prisoners in agricultural camps died, slightly more than the average death rate of 6.69%, and that in 1939 the death rate in agricultural camps was 2.76%, just under the average of 2.91%.

We should therefore also consider the importance of solidarity between prisoners in the group, demonstrated in their ability to take collective action. The FEDIP records of the Spaniards' incarceration mention numerous short work stoppages, as well as hunger strikes that lasted five days at a time. In other words, the Spanish anti-fascists were better prepared to collectively resist and endure the totalitarian system than their Russian counterparts.

Finally, it seems likely that the FEDIP solidarity campaign was important, beginning as it did at a time when many of the detainees were seriously ill through prolonged malnutrition and tuberculosis. The knowledge that a sustained and high profile solidarity campaign was concerned with the Spanish detainees may have influenced their treatment – José Ester Borrás and the others involved in the campaign might not have been able to effect the prisoners' release, but their tireless work may have helped reduce the death toll.

136

By the time we reached Amsterdam, I only wanted to go home. The first day of our research at the International Institute of Social History was Alfredo's last day in Europe, and as we sat in the reading room sorting through the manila folders of documents, it was obvious that Lempi's mind was elsewhere. After only two hours, during which we'd learned little we hadn't already known, I called the whole project off. 'Let's stop this,' I said. 'I know you want to spend the day with Alfredo, so let's stop pissing about here.'

At first, Lempi pretended to protest. 'No way,' she said. 'Like, this is what we travelled here for. Come on, we've not looked at even a quarter of what's here.'

'Yeah, well, not every story has an ending worth learning.'

'Come on. Let's give it a few more hours at least.'

'Lempi, I've got a headache and I just want to go back to the hotel.'

'Are you sure?'

'...'

'Well, I suppose we'll have plenty of time to come back tomorrow.'

'Yeah, maybe.'

So we packed the papers back into the folders, stacked the folders in their boxes, and returned the collection to the surprised archivists. On the tram back to central Amsterdam, Lempi talked about her romance (she hoped it wasn't just a holiday fling), while I watched the raindrops scratch lines across the window. From her lack of sensitivity, I can only assume that she still had no idea how I felt about her – or, rather, how I had once felt about her. At one point she did ask whether her relationship with Alfredo upset me.

'Why would you say that?' I asked.

'I don't know. Like, it just seems you've been kind of off with me ever since I started seeing him.'

'Why would I care that you're seeing Alfredo?'

'I don't know. Like, maybe you don't like him or something.'

In fact, examiners, as I'd gradually resigned myself to Alfredo's triumph, I'd found him to be perfectly likeable and friendly. If anything, it was Lempi whom I'd grown to dislike.

Back in our twin room, which Lempi used as a kind of en suite dressing room, I went to bed, feigning illness. Lempi spent two hours preparing for her big romantic farewell, and my irritation grew by the minute. One of the most frightening sights of the whole research trip had been seeing Lempi remove her hair extension. I had no idea she wore a hair extension, so it seemed to me she had ripped out half her hair. Now, her beauty routine involved wrapping strands of her hair in tinfoil, giving her the appearance of an electronic medusa. For some reason, she seemed to think I was interested in what she was doing. 'It's, like, so much work,' she was saying. 'Like, every Sunday I treat it with henna before I go to bed. And I use L'Oréal Colour Protect because, like, I have platinum set half-head highlights with ash and strawberry blonde lowlights, yeah? And, like, you don't want to go to the salon every week, do you? I like the John Frieda thickening conditioner and the Tigi Bed Head shine spray is cool. I totally will not use Tresemmé. And it takes so long, you know? Like, while we're away, I just don't have time to dry and straighten it. That's why I wash it the night before, yeah? Like, you know how I put it in braids? Well, that's so that in the morning it's got some volume, yeah? It's, like, you just curl the ends around the straighteners and, presto, you've got that, sort of, come back to bed look, you know? And then you just put on the hairspray. Just now I'm using L'Oréal Ellnette because–'

'Lempi!' I cannot explain why at that moment I snapped. The tone of my voice must have been awful because Lempi was immediately silent.

'Don't shout at me,' she said.

'Sorry,' I said, 'I didn't mean to snap.'

'Like, what the Hell's wrong with you?'

I didn't answer and for a long time the only sound between us was the disgruntled hum of the hotel's zealous air-conditioning.

'Well?' she said. 'Are you jealous? Is that it? D'you feel like you've not got your money's worth from me?'

At this point I clambered from bed – I was still fully dressed – grabbed my wallet, and ran out of the hotel room. I wandered into the rain and spent one of the most desultory and miserable evenings of my whole life. What did I do? I walked to the Red

Light District, sat in Stone's Café Bar, drank tankards of Wicks Witte, and then I wandered, spaghetti legged, through side streets and across canals. There are few sites sadder than the Red Light District in the early evening. Tourists shuffled sideways, watching immigrant women pout and beckon in bras and pants, fishnet body stockings, vests and suspenders, thigh-high boots, mini kilts, school shirts tied across their stomachs. The city reeled and the neon-pink glow blurred off the canal water. Everything was fragmented, the totality of it elusive: luminescent aliens smoking plastic joints; Febo burgers in automats; LIVE FUCKING SHOW; red velvet curtains; bridges and canals; slices of pizza; 'Sir, sexy show – you want to see live anal? Most beautiful girls in Amsterdam. What's wrong, you are a faggot?'; smells of skunk and urine and canal water; bicycles chained to railings; seagulls; huge dildos; stilettos; blow-up dolls.

At some point, when I thought nobody was looking, I walked into a sex shop, shuffled into a video cubicle, and pulled the curtain behind me; the cubicle had the chlorine smell of semen. As I searched for Euros, I thought of Lempi, thought of my hypocrisy, thought how unkindly I'd treated her. Then, when I'd found some coins, I channel surfed: two skinheads copulating on a beach; a blonde woman masturbating a horse; a man in a leather mask being whipped by a woman dressed in red PVC; a woman dressed as a school girl fellating an older man; two females with breast implants squirting each other with cream; an Asian girl urinating through her underwear; a muscular bald man grabbing a young woman's pigtails as she squatted on his penis and clutched a teddy bear; a Brazilian transsexual fingering her anus; a woman defecating on another woman's chest; a skinny bespectacled man having sex with an obese older woman; a tattooed woman inserting an aubergine into another woman's anus; on and on.

137

Before I reveal what I know of Ramón's life after his release from Karaganda (and what I know of his reasons for accepting Soviet citizenship), let me conclude the story of those Spaniards who remained in the gulag for another six or eight years. In January 1954, the Spanish prisoners were concentrated at Krasnopol, in what today is Belarus. Also interned in this camp were over 200 Spanish prisoners of war. These were fascist volunteers from General Muñoz Grandes' Blue Division, who in 1942 had gone to fight with the Nazis on the Russian front. The Spaniards' sudden release was universally unexpected as negotiations appeared to have gone sterile. However, on the 27th March 1954, Radio Moscow confirmed that the previous day 291 Spanish prisoners had been sent to Odessa with representatives of the French Red Cross. In Odessa they boarded a Greek boat, the Semiramis, and sailed for Istanbul. The majority of this group had been fighting with the Blue Division but many anti-fascists also boarded the Semiramis. Others, including three prisoners sentenced to an additional twenty-five years in 1949, continued to be detained. The last survivors of the group emerged from Soviet detention in 1956.

From Istanbul, the prisoners carried on the Semiramis would sail direct to Barcelona. The French government had offered the anti-fascists asylum and there was some confusion over whether the boat would make a stop in Marseille en route. In the end it sailed directly – according to one story, some of the anti-fascists pretended they had fought in the Blue Division and were rewarded with desirable local government office jobs. As the boat arrived in Barcelona, the Falangists gathered on the deck shouting 'Long live Spain! Long Live Franco!' They had volunteered to fight on the side of Hitler and lost. But they had spent less time in the Gulag than their anti-fascist counterparts, and now they were returning in triumph to their fascist fatherland. They must have struggled to believe their luck.

Out of those Spaniards who at the end of the Civil War were stranded in the Soviet Union as a result of performing their duties in the anti-fascist war effort, at least thirteen died or disappeared. Some survived against improbable odds, including Vicente Montejano Moreno, who emerged from thirteen years of Soviet detention despite having lost several fingers in his first year of captivity. But all the detainees were deprived of their health and a large section of their adult lives. Writing to José Ester Borrás in 1956, Felix Villanueva, the brother of a detained pilot, who confronted Enrique Lister and subsequently left the Communist PCE in disgust, describes his brother as suffering from fatigue, struggling to find work, and unable to forget what he had seen: 'Of my brother Julio I can tell you nothing but the memories he possesses' (Ester Borrás 15).

138

Examiners, I shouldn't neglect to write my own ending. I should trace some character arc, hint at some moral journey. I'd like to describe how, stirred by what I'd seen in the Red Light District, I experienced an epiphanic realisation about my own hypocrisy, and returned to the hotel determined to make amends to Lempi. I'd come to realise, you see, that what I disliked about her was exactly what I'd objectivised and fetishised: her sexual unattainability; her sexual value within a complex commodified system. Something like that. Perhaps, when I returned to the hotel, the receptionist passed me a message for our room, and the message was from Alfredo, because in their excitement he and Lempi had neglected to exchange contact details, and, realising this, he had phoned the hotel and left his addresses and numbers with the receptionist. Now, I had power over their future happiness. I would consider destroying the note, but in the end, when I realised how much Lempi loved him, I would present her with his contact information, thus making their relationship possible, and in the process redeeming myself. Then Lempi would fall asleep in my arms, and I would feel no desire, only compassion and love and honourable intentions. But that would spirit the old lie that passion and desire are subordinate to reason; that the ego can be and should be king; that human selves are centralised, built in the image of modern nation states; that self-control is possible.

No, what really happened was that I fell asleep alone and woke with a hangover. I stayed in bed until the afternoon, and when Lempi returned from the airport – her mascara blurred, her eyes teary – I pretended to still be asleep. 'Hey,' she said, shaking my shoulder, 'are we going to the Institute or what?' It was our last full day in Amsterdam.

'No,' I said.

'Fine,' said Lempi. She sat on her still-made bed, and after a minute I heard her start to cry. I listened to her cry for a long time and then – this is as close as I get to redemption – I got out of bed, sat beside her, and put my arm around her. Lempi accepted the gesture, leant her head against my chest, cried quietly. Oh, examiners, there's no point starting to lie now: I was wearing only my underwear; her elbow was resting on my inner thigh; I felt the early stirrings of arousal.

'It's okay,' I said, perhaps out of guilt. 'You'll see him again soon.'

'No, I won't,' said Lempi. 'He's just saying that. Once he gets back to the States, he's not going to wait for me.'

'He'll wait,' I said. I paused, chose my next words carefully.

'If I was lucky enough to be in his position, I'd wait for you forever.'

'Do you like my nails?' asked Lempi, fanning her fingers with a sarcastic flourish. 'I got them done at the airport.'

'They're fake?'

'Of course they're fake. Feel.'

'They glue them on?'

'I've worn fake nails since high school. Lots of bulimics wear fake nails. The idea is that you can't make yourself sick. But in fact you do still make yourself sick; the only difference is that now you tear your oesophagus.'

'...'

'Like, that's what most bulimics die of.'

'Lempi, I want you to know that—'

'I got them done today to treat myself, cause I was sad and— I mean, what the fuck does it actually mean to treat yourself? Like, I understand it, I do it, but the other day I was thinking— Why are men never told to treat themselves, you know? They treat their wives or their wives treat them or but— I mean, how can I treat myself? How many of me are there? What the fuck does it mean?'

'I'm sorry, Lempi.'

'It's okay,' said Lempi, 'I'm sorry too.' And then she started to cry again, and then I started to cry. We were both crying and it was no longer clear who was supposed to be comforting whom. And after a while this was funny and we started to laugh and cry all at the same time. We were sobbing and laughing and making strange snorting noises. And the snorting was really funny, and soon we were giggling like idiots.

'Oh my God,' said Lempi, standing up. 'Look at us!'

'I know,' I said. 'What are we like?'

'This is, like, our last day in Europe, and we're just sitting here crying. We should do something to cheer ourselves up.'

'Anne Frank Museum?' This was funny – everything was funny now.

Lempi hit my arm. 'No! Like, we should… I don't know. We should go the Heineken Experience.'

'The Heineken Experience? Okay,' I said, 'let's do it!'

And so on our last day in Europe, we watched Heineken adverts from around the world, made a video in which we explained – speaking in comedy Dutch accents – how Heineken stops one from crying, paid to have our names engraved on a bottle of Heineken, and held hands on the boat trip to the gift shop. And after that we went to the Sex Museum, where we sat on seats shaped like giant erections, shrieked at the robotic flasher, giggled over the fetish equipment, feigned innocent confusion, laughed about ancient wood carvings of complex orgies, and gaped in faux shock at photos of enormous phalluses. Then we walked into the night, ate falafel sandwiches, smoked fierce skunk of Lempi's choosing, and drank a bottle of wine. Drunk and stoned, we toasted our fortnight together, drank to our friendship, and then, because we'd discovered the importance of endings, we resolved that in the morning, in the hours before our flight, we would return to the Institute of Social History, where we would try to find an ending for Ramón.

139

And our final trip to the IISH proved especially worthwhile. We worked without pause, scanning through the files, both desperate to find *something*. Lempi read and I scribbled notes, but as morning turned to afternoon, as we started to calculate how long it would take us to reach the airport, we still had no sense of Ramón's ending. And then, just as we were about to admit defeat, it happened.

We were on FEDIP file 102 (women and children of the interned Spaniards in Karaganda and other relatives), and it was Lempi who saw it first, of course. Her mouth gaped open and then she clenched her fist and kissed my cheek. 'What is it, what is it?' I said, pulling the papers before me. Lempi threw her head back and laughed so loud that every reader in the library looked towards us.

Let me explain. At the time of the Spaniards' arrival, Karaganda was a mixed camp, holding men, women, and juveniles. The juveniles included children of adult prisoners, some of whom were born in the camp. Between 1946 and 1948, men and women were separated throughout the Gulag system, but before 1946 it was not unusual for them to be held together. While some accounts of mixed camps describe endemic rape, others emphasise great love affairs, enduring relationships, and marriages. Indeed, one account describes how women in the Spaniards' camp declared a hunger strike after they were separated from their husbands. Several days later, they were reunited (L'Association D'Etudes et D'Information Politiques Internationales, 1954, p-7).

Interned with the Spanish anti-fascists were detainees of many nationalities but initially the majority were Austrian Jews (MLE-CNT, op. cit., p-105). These were presumably refugees who had left Austria as anti-Semitism escalated before and after the 1938 Anschluss. There may also have been Austrian Social Democrats – Schutzbündlers – who had fled to the Soviet Union in 1934 after defeat in the February Uprising. A number of Spanish anti-fascists had serious relationships with Austrian women in Karaganda and nine children were born within the camp. To my knowledge, all nine mothers were able to leave the camp with their children in good health. Indeed, in response to an article I subsequently published online, two of the children contacted me looking for more information: the first was Ramón Sánchez-Lövy, son of Vera Lövy and Ramón Sánchez Gómez; the second was Peter Sagal (formerly Pedro Sagalowitsch), son of Sonia Sagalowitsch and Pedro Armesto Saco. The other child-bearing couples were as follows: Helga Blumenfeld and Eusebio Pons López (a pilot who sadly died, shortly before the Spaniards were released, on 15th September 1953) had a daughter; Almer Picker and José Garcia Santamaria had a daughter; Emma Löff and Maximo Ramos Arribas had a son; Tania Losch and Arturo Fernandez Prieto had a daughter; Ita Rathsprecher and Tomás Rodríguez Tenedor had a son; Frieda Schneider and Juan Conesa Castillo had a daughter; and – wait for it – Terezia Meyer had a daughter with Ramón Buenacasa Mavilla.

Yes, examiners, Ramón had a daughter. In Karaganda, he fathered a child with an Austrian prisoner, and can you guess what they called her? They called her Elizabeth, a name whose many diminutives include 'Elsie'. And there's more. There's one more detail you need to know in order to understand our excitement. In the early 1950s, five of the mothers lived in Soviet Vienna; three others settled in another capital of the former Austro-Hungarian Empire (the whereabouts of Almer Picker were unknown). Examiners, can you guess where, according to FEDIP file 102, Terezia Meyer and young Elizabeth were resident in 1951? Can you guess where Ramón must have planned to move when he accepted Soviet citizenship? No wonder we punched the air. In the 1950s, Ramón's family lived in Budapest.

Paragraphia, 2012, Vol.25, no.4

Leave our Dicks Alone: the Spectre of the Real in the Market-Stalinist Post-Fordist Academy

F.K Thrub

ABSTRACT: *A deconstructive study of the mind-body dualism as it is symbolically represented by the sibling relationships in three novels:* Waterland *(Graham Swift),* Midnight's Children *(Salman Rushdie), and* A Maggot *(John Fowles). In this provocative essay, renowned cultural theorist Professor F.K. Thrub breaks a decade-long publishing silence. Using the metaphor of the revenant, he rediscovers the half-present and repressed, directing us always to the periphery and to the conditions in which knowledge is produced. In celebrating, rather than repudiating, desire, the id, the extrinsic, the tangential, and the corporeal, Thrub suggests a future for a radical phenomenological attack on the Cartesian subject.*

Recently, I've been haunted by a ghost. The creature has a name, a ridiculous name; it is called Gulliver Broom. It has a face, too, no less ridiculous. I have seen the apparition's face only in a headshot on our Student Records system, have seen its earphones, its misaligned knitted cap, its expression suggestive of total vacuity. It is a ghastly thing, no different to hundreds of other semi-literate students who through the years have sat drooling in my classes, except that this thing is a ghost, a spectre, a haunting. Not quite a visitation; no, I chance that the corporeal Gulliver Broom has never attended one of my classes, may not in fact be aware that he is registered to attend my classes, may not in fact be aware that he once upon a time undertook to attend this Higher Education institution. Gulliver Broom is a ghost, a misregistration, a technical glitch, a student who appears on the system but shouldn't. What opened the portal and allowed Gulliver's ghost to walk among the

Paragraphia, 2012, Vol.25, no.4

living was a simple clerical mistake: whilst I was entering the marks for my first year Shakespeare module, I entered Broom's mark as a oF. O, woe is me!

During the period of my haunting, whilst I was plagued by this spectre, I was working on what one might term a retirement chapter. The subject of this chapter concerned three dicks. Three Dicks. Or, to be precise, two Dicks and Shiva the Procreator. The three dicks are the virile but stupid 'almost' brothers of three impotent but clever characters in three novels. In Graham Swift's *Waterland*, we have the half-brothers, Tom and Dick Crick. Tom is bookish, the scholastic child whose 'little instrument (...) droops utterly,' despite the sight of Mary's deliciously pert 'baby breasts'.[1] In contrast we have Dick, half-witted, 'Strong, stupid Dick...', 'who has no mind of [his] own (...) but will perform on occasion quite remarkable feats of dexterity and strength'.[2] Dick represents the body. Tom represents the mind. The former's association with the bodily side of the dichotomy is further enforced by his dick, his giant cock, his 'tubular swelling of massive and assertive proportions', his phallus of 'sheer and astonishing dimension', 'That monstrous swelling, that trapped baton'.[3]

Far be it for me, in my dotage, to suggest that our finest fin de siècle novelists relied on phallic comedy, on knob jokes, on the sort of cock-based humour directed against me on students' Facespace pages, but in John Fowles's *A Maggot*, we find an uncannily similar pair of 'almost brothers': the Lordship is a Cambridge-educated scholar, a young philosopher worthy of Sir Isaac Newton's attention, who travels with a servant and companion (whose mother nursed the Lordship as a child), a man born deaf and mute and 'simple into the bargain', who is also called Dick, is described as being as 'lecherous as a Barbary ape', and is ordered by the Lordship to copulate with a woman who goes by the name of Fanny.[4] Fanny takes Dick and assumes the scholarly Lordship to be impotent. Now, before the feminists start posting me accusatory letters, may I opine that I'm not responsible for how John Fowles named his characters, and may I add that by the time you read this I will have left my office for sunnier climes, and will have been too busy grabbing my balls and wolf-whistling to have arranged a forwarding address.

Besides, if we return to the texts, we have a third such almost brotherly couplet, for in Salman Rushdie's *Midnight's Children*, Saleem and Shiva are brothers

---

[1] Graham Swift, *Waterland* (London: Pan Books, 1984) p. 160
[2] Ibid., pp. 295; 210; 32
[3] Ibid., pp. 161; 165
[4] John Fowles, *A Maggot* (London: Guild Publishing, 1985) pp. 193; 194; 36; 41

Paragraphia, 2012, Vol.25, no.4

in the sense that the people Saleem consider to be his mother and father are Shiva's biological parents. Saleem is bookish, boastful of his wide reading, but physically puny and impotent – he is 'unmanned', which is to say that 'Despite Padma's many varied gifts and ministrations, [he] can't leak into her'.[5] Shiva, the physical half, a fearsome warrior who crushes people between his mighty knees, is not (unless there's some slang of which I'm unaware) named after a penis, but Shiva is the procreator, and, in contrast to Saleem's impotence, there are 'legendary tales of the war hero's philandering, of the legions of bastards swelling in the unectomied bellies of great ladies and whores'.[6] Shiva thus stands for the body, the empirical, the *etre en-soi*, whilst Saleem stands for consciousness and the transcendental soul. The difference is illustrated in the rival positions they argue during the Midnight's Children's Conference: Shiva says '"Little rich boy, that's all just wind. All that importance-of-the-individual. All that possibility-of-humanity. Today, what people are is just another kind of thing."' To which Saleem replies '"But... free will... hope... the great soul"'.[7]

Peace, break thee off; look, where it comes again! For the first time in years, I had a plan, an idea, a project, a purpose, but whenever I sat down to write, to create, I was disturbed by the ghost of Broom. 'I'm phoning about Gulliver Broom'; 'further to my phone call about Gulliver Broom'; 'Dear Professor, I have tried to contact you on several occasions regarding the problem of Gulliver Broom'; 'Professor? Professor! I know you're in there, Professor.' There comes a point, does there not, at which ignoring a piece of work is more effort than doing it. My line manager explained that my mistake had been to enter oF instead of oN, which mark (oF) meant, as everybody knows, that Gulliver Broom had submitted a piece of work and achieved a mark of zero; whereas oN, of course, would have meant that Gulliver Broom had submitted nothing. According to my line manager, the Higher Education Funding Council for England (HEFCE) funds students who submit failing work (oF), but they do not fund students who submit nothing (oN), which is to say that if uncorrected, my error would have meant HEFCE would pay the university part of Broom's tuition fees in error. 'Is that all?' I said. 'If all you need to do is change one letter, why don't you do it yourself?' To this my line manager laughed raucously and said 'how on earth could I change that?'

---

[5] Salman Rushdie, *Midnight's Children* (London: Vintage, 1995) p. 39
[6] Ibid., p. 440
[7] Ibid., p. 255

Paragraphia, 2012, Vol.25, no.4

What are we to make of our contemporary novelists' obsession with cock? For Descartes, the mind and the body were hierarchically arranged, with mind 'higher' than body, but this hierarchy did not originate or end with Descartes: Aesop's master and slave metaphor argued that reason should be master, passion the slave; the dominant Christian view held that the spiritual side of men was of a separate and higher order to the sinful bodily passions; and in modern philosophy, as Diana Coole notes, 'Rousseau, Kant and later Mill all associate moral and intellectual activities with the control of a lower, appetitive self associated with desire and the body'.[8] (Ego-psychology, incidentally, reworks this dualism, so that id equals bodily desire, and ego equals mind and 'true self.')

Of course the dichotomy of 'mind and body' is a classic example of what the structuralists once loved to call a 'binary opposition.' Jacques Derrida inherited the structuralists' analysis of bicameral thought, arguing that the history of western reason had hitherto depended on a hierarchical ordering of opposites. His most famous example is the Platonic privileging of speech over writing, what he calls 'phonocentrism', which he claims is the necessary 'condition of the very idea of truth'.[9] Derrida develops this insight through complex readings of the philosophical canon, including his lengthy analysis of Plato's *Phaedrus*.[10] The attraction of the *Phaedrus* is that Plato's attempt to distinguish between the 'poisoning' and 'remedying' effects of written words, which is to say whether they accurately represent speech or not, involves using the term *pharmakon*, a word rendered indeterminate by its multiple meanings (it can mean both poison and remedy and Plato has recourse to both meanings), and avoiding the word *pharmakos* (scapegoat). Here, and elsewhere, Derrida's discussion is more elusive than his major insights: Plato may use *pharmakon* according to a specific intention, but its meaning is never present in a specific moment, but always dependent on its interpretative context. This is not a secondary problem of accurately interpreting the original meaning, because the system of signification that renders the status of *pharmakon*

[8] Diana Coole, 'The Gendered Self,' pp. 123-139, D. Bakhurst, D. & C. Sypnowich (eds), *The Social Self* (London: Sage, 1995) p. 126
[9] Derrida, *Of Grammatology*, Trans. G.C. Spivak (Baltimore: John Hopkins University Press, 1976) p. 20
[10] Derrida, *Dissemination*, Trans. B. Johnson [1968] (Chicago: University of Chicago Press 1981) pp. 61-172

Paragraphia, 2012, Vol.25, no.4

indeterminate is already necessary to that meaning. Similarly, Plato may avoid using the term *pharmakos*, but this word, too, is neither simply present nor absent; it exists in the text as a *trace*. What do we mean by this present absence?

Consider Derrida's reading of Rousseau's *Confessions*.[11] Rousseau condemns masturbation as 'that dangerous supplement'. But he contradicts himself: he argues both that masturbation allows a man to dispose of all women, and that masturbation allows a man to make any beauty his without the difficulty of obtaining her consent. The point here is simple: though masturbation is defined by the absence of one's object of desire, when I am masturbating I am thinking of whoever I want to have but cannot: I am thinking, perhaps, of the fresher who sits at the front of my Introduction to Enlightenment Philosophy class, whose name I do not know, but whose breasts I cannot help but look at, for they emerge from the lowest-cut tops, appearing to have been rubbed with oil or spray-tan or some other feminine secret. What I'm masturbating about is neither presence nor absence but the desire for presence; the girl is neither present nor absent but exists as a (honey-scented) trace. So it is with the word *pharmakos*.

Alas, poor ghost! The spectre was not yet at peace. 'Professor, the Gulliver Broom issue remains unresolved.' 'Professor, I won't tell you about this again.' 'Professor, you need to sort this today or I'm going to Gumthorpe.' 'Professor, I've spoken to Gumthorpe; he wants to know why this mistake wasn't spotted at the exam board on 28th May?' Did I attend the exam board on 28th May? It seemed unlikely, but after half-an-hour I tracked down the email and discovered that, according to the minutes, I was present and so was my line manager. 'Why didn't *you* correct the mistake,' I asked my line manager when next she phoned. 'I was there?' she asked, and then she started hyperventilating and shouting 'shit, shit, shitty shit. Oh fuck, oh fuck, oh fuck.'

Significantly, all the 'body' halves in these almost-brotherly dualisms are perceived as dangerous, fearsome, needing to be controlled. In *Waterland*, 'The Brainy one is hiding from the brainless one,' because 'the brainy one's scared'.[12] In *A Maggot*, Dick is described by a fellow traveller as having prayed to the moon in a 'lunatick fit', such that the man feared that he 'might at any moment turn and spring and tear me limb

---

[11] Derrida, *Of Grammatology*, op cit., pp. 141-157
[12] Swift, op cit, p. 33

Paragraphia, 2012, Vol.25, no.4

from limb'.[13] And Saleem says of Shiva that he is 'terrified of him'.[14] The two Dicks die (both are assumed to have committed suicide), whilst Saleem narrates Shiva's death then concedes he made it up. The similarities are neither coincidence nor conspiracy, neither chance nor necessity, but indicative of the western tradition's wishful belief in free will and transcendental self-hood. The Christian version of the binary is clearly expressed in *A Maggot*, when Rebecca says of Dick and his Lordship master:

> now do I see they were as one in truth, Dick of the carnal and imperfect body, his Lordship of the spirit; such twin natures as we all must hold, in them made outward and a seeming two. And as Jesus Christ's body must die upon the cross, so must this latterday earthly self, poor unregenerate Dick, die so the other half be saved.[15]

As in this Christian perspective, a Sartrean existentialism also requires that consciousness can emerge free from the determinism of physiology or the unconscious, which is to say, the body half has to be removed from the freedom equation: thus, Saleem's fear that Shiva will kill him is really the fear that he has no transcendental soul or free will. His attempt to narrate Shiva's death is the attempt to separate mind from body, and when this fails, it precedes his own ontological death as he cracks up and is swallowed by the crowd.[16] There is one problem with wishing the death of the body, which is to say that a disembodied consciousness becomes, like the ghost of poor Gulliver Broom, a spirit, an undead thing, a creature between life and death, a spectre, a ghost.

One woe doth tread upon another's heel! At the insistence of Gumthorpe, I contacted a man called Landcastle (it is a feature of the new university that it employs great numbers of people whose roles and identities are obscure to anyone not in management). 'Explain this to me again,' he said, after I had explained the problem at Length. 'Okay,' he said, after I'd explained it at length again, 'let me see if I've got this right. You've lost the cover sheet for a student with the improbable name "Gulliver Broom".' 'Nearly,' I said; 'good effort. There is no cover sheet for Gulliver Broom, there never has been a cover sheet for Gulliver Broom, because Gulliver Broom *does not exist*.' 'You're going to have to give me a minute.' Seven

---

[13] Fowles, *A Maggot*, op cit, p. 39
[14] Rusdhie, op cit, p. 443
[15] Fowles, *A Maggot*, op cit, p. 421
[16] Rushdie, op cit, p. 462/3

Paragraphia, 2012, Vol.25, no.4

minutes later, Landcastle informed me that everything was well; 'This Broom chap's in the system as having submitted, so I think we can all sleep easy on this one.' 'I see,' I said, 'and do you think, possibly, the system could have been deceived by human error?' 'Nope,' said Landcastle; 'it was all OK'd at an exam board on... let me see... May 28th.' Alas, poor ghost! It seemed Broom's haunting days were done.

It seems that now, on the occasion of my retirement, it is appropriate for me to pass comment on the education system I must leave to posterity. Mark Fisher has described the current mode of public service provision, with its market imperatives and bureaucratically-defined targets, as 'market Stalinist.'[17] I cannot improve on this definition. Targets have long-ceased to be a way of measuring performance and have become primary objectives: today's students will not attend a class that isn't directly related to the end of year examination, because the exam is no longer a measurement of learning; it is the reason for learning. The National Student Survey has become more important than the classes on which it ostensibly reports: here,

---

[17] Mark Fisher, *Capitalist Realism: Is there no Alternative?*, (Zero Books: Winchester & Washington, 2009)

Paragraphia, 2012, Vol.25, no.4

more effort is put into ensuring the surveys are completed than is put into any educational goal. Late-capitalism has inherited from Stalinism a preoccupation with the symbols of achievement at the expense of actual achievement. Mark Fisher cites an anthropological study of local government, which argued that 'more effort goes into ensuring that a local authority's services are represented correctly than goes into actually improving those services', and he compares this with Stalin's White Sea Canal project.[18] Stalin was so determined to create a symbol of industrial efficiency that the project was completed in a way that rendered it industrially useless. The rapid completion of the project *looked* very efficient, but the canal was so shallow that it was impassable to cargo ships.

In the market Stalinist madness of late capitalism, the ghost of Gulliver Broom continued to clang its chains. 'Dear Dr/ Professor, Re QAA audit. The auditors have requested to inspect physical evidence of submissions for students with surnames A-C on the following module(s): EL140 Understanding Shakespeare. Please send relevant mark sheets with evidence of submission dates and where relevant evidence of pre-submission extensions (MC1, MC2, MLE, and KKYs). Yours, etc.' I did not at first realise the gravity of the situation. Two days passed. After five further reminders, I sent mark sheets for Roberta Adams. Maria Augustus, John Archer, Duncan Billig, Cedric Charles, and Dominic Christie. The next day, I locked my office door, took the phone off the hook, and sat in total silence. Emails appeared soundlessly on my computer screen: 'URGENT! TREAT AS URGENT PRIORITY! Re: mark sheet Broom. And in the afternoon, colleagues started to bang my office door. 'Professor? Professor! We know you're in there!' 'Professor, we need a mark sheet for Gulliver Broom, Goddamn it!'

There was no mark sheet for Gulliver Broom, because Gulliver Broom did not exist, did not exist in any clear ontological sense, at least. However, since he'd been marked as oF, not oN, there *should* have been a mark sheet for Gulliver Broom. As a result of my error, the university faced failing the audit with consequent funding implications that, as Associate-Dean Fortburger put it, 'would threaten the very existence of this institution.' The following day, my line manager located the skeleton key and a coterie of senior academics forced entry to my office. Landcastle, a fat, comically bald man, dropped onto his knees and peered under my desk – 'we're here to help you look,' explained Gumthorpe – whilst Fortburger massaged

---

[18] Ibid., pp. 42/3

SCOPE

Paragraphia, 2012, Vol.25, no.4

his temples and yelled 'come on, man! Think!' Unable to withstand their presence, I feigned epiphany, put my hands to my head, and declared I remembered leaving Broom's sheet at home. Though this be madness, yet there was method in it: they wanted a mark sheet, and I planned to give them one.

Derrida has often characterised the whole history of western philosophy as the determination of being as presence,[19] accusing Hegel of asserting the 'self-presence of the subject' through equating 'the voice' that reflects with the proximity of being.[20] Where Derrida differs from Hegel can be understood if we return to Hegel's assertion that the first thesis of his dialectical system (being) depended on its negative (nothing). Derrida contends that the Kantian/ Hegelian 'revolution' consisted 'in taking the negative *seriously*. In giving meaning to its labor'.[21] This is not as complimentary as it sounds, which is to say that to Derrida's reading, Hegel's negative remains tied to its opposite, working to support meaning, as in the Master/ Slave dialectic where 'The putting at stake of life is a moment in the constitution of meaning, in the presentation of essence and truth'.[22] Derrida, *qua* deconstructionist, is interested in the supplementary 'play' of what is repressed in the construction of meaning, what cannot be sublated by the *Aufhebung*, what must be overlooked for presence to assert itself. So Derrida claims that Hegel blinds himself to the consequences of his own thought, and has to be 'followed to the end, without reserve, to the point of agreeing with him against himself and of wresting his discovery from the too conscientious interpretation he gave of it'.[23]

'Play,' in Derrida's early work, is what disrupts presence, the negative of a concept (what is absent for the concept to be present) that can no longer be called the negative because it is always dependent on additional plays of presence and absence, which is to say the movement of supplementarity. Thus presence is evident in phonocentrism – the idea that the voice (in consciousness or speech) corresponds exactly to being – because this way of thinking overlooks how the meaning of what

[19] Jacques Derrida, *Of Grammatology*, Trans. G.C. Spivak (Baltimore: John Hopkins University Press, 1976) p. 97; 'Structure, Sign and Play in the Discourse of the Human Sciences,' pp. 351-370, *Writing and Difference*, Trans. A. Bass (London: Routledge, 2001) p. 353
[20] Derrida, *Of Grammatology*, ibid., p. 12
[21] Derrida, 'From Restricted to General Economy: A Hegelianism Without Reserve,' pp. 317-350 in *Writing and Difference*, Trans. A. Bass, (London: Routledge, 2001), p. 328
[22] Ibid., p. 231
[23] Ibid., p. 328

Paragraphia, 2012, Vol.25, no.4

is spoken is upheld by its relation to other signs, signs deemed absent, signs necessarily involved in the production of meaning. Or as Derrida says in an unusually explicit statement:

> the word is lived as the elementary and undecomposable unity of the signified and the voice, of the concept and a transparent substance of expression. This experience is considered in its greatest purity – and at the same time in the condition of its possibility – as the experience of "being".[24]

Presence is impossible, then, because every transcendental in-itself moment of presence is actually dependent on its situation within a chain of concepts that can never be exhausted; every concept depends on what is not present, but that dependence means that the 'not present' is also not absent. So in *Specters of Marx*, Derrida finds the perfect symbol to defy the binary opposition between presence and absence, which is to say: the ghost. This is an extended pun on the opening of the *Manifesto* and the sense in which Marx has today become a ghostly figure, a 'revenant whose return so many raised voices today are attempting to conjure away',[25] but it also allows Derrida to ask the unanswerable question, 'What is the mode of presence of a specter?'[26]

The ghost is the deconstructive metaphor *par excellence*: it is neither present nor absent, but exists/ doesn't exist, between life and death, past and present, real and imagined, transcendental and empirical. In *Ghosts: Deconstruction, Psychoanalysis, History*, Peter Buse and Andrew Stott offer a summary of the deconstructive relevance of the 'revenant', which is worth here quoting at length:

> The relevance of a trope of spectrality to deconstruction is clear. Ghosts are neither dead nor alive, neither corporeal objects nor stern abscences. As such they are the stock in trade of the Derridean enterprise, standing in defiance of binary oppositions such as presence and absence, body and spirit, past and present, life and death (...) And so the liminal spirit, or to use Derrida's favoured term, *revenant*, the thing that returns, comes to represent a mobilization of

---

[24] Derrida, *Of Grammatology*, op cit, p. 20
[25] Derrida, *Spectres of Marx: The State of the Debt, the Work of Mourning, and the New International*, Trans. P. Kamuf (London: Routledge, 1994) p. 96
[26] Ibid., p. 38

SCOPE

Paragraphia, 2012, Vol.25, no.4

> familiar Derridean concepts such as trace, iteration and the deferral
> of presence."[27]

Ghosts occupy the indeterminable ground between action and circumstance, between what happens and the historical conditions that make such happenings possible. The ghost is the past intruding on the present, the tradition of all dead generations weighing like a nightmare on the brains of the living.

And so it came to pass that one of my final acts as a working man was to fabricate a mark sheet for an essay that had never existed, a very present absence, a very necessary fiction, an imagined reality which I now had to appraise. I clutched the pen, ape-like, in my left hand, and illegibly I scrawled Broom's name and student number. Then I restored the pen to my right hand and paused, unsure what to write. What feedback could I give that would justify a mark of zero? I waited a full twenty minutes before I knew what I had to do. 'This essay,' I wrote in my neatest hand, 'shows imagination and enthusiasm but does not meet academic criteria and fails to demonstrate attainment of key learning outcomes. I am glad to see that you benefitted from the lecture on Freudian responses to Hamlet, but I can't accept that merely typing the word MILF in giant block capitals is an adequate exploration of Oedipal themes. Equally, whilst I'm delighted to see that you've reflected on the class discussion of mimesis (the play within a play, the stage as a metaphor for theological determinism), I feel your discussion is again inadequate. You have photocopied the word MILF and then photocopied the photocopy and photocopied the photocopy of the photocopy... until, in the final pages of your essay, the word is faded, half-transparent, ghostly. This is an imaginative experimental comment on the role of 'The Mousetrap' within *Hamlet* and the role of Hamlet within subsequent culture. Nevertheless, your entire essay consists of one word – an acronym, in fact – which I understand to mean: Mum I'd Like to Fuck. This is not serious scholarship, and therefore I can award only a mark of zero, whilst demanding more matter, with less art.'

Exit ghost. I finished my post-dated mark sheet, persuaded the young chap down the corridor to sign as second marker, and sent it to a delighted Fortburger. The

---

[27] Peter Buse & Andrew Stott, 'Introduction: A Future for Haunting,' pp. 1-20 in Buse, Peter Buse & Andrew Stott (eds) *Ghosts: Deconstruction, Psychoanalysis, History* (London: Macmillan, 1999) pp. 10/11

Paragraphia, 2012, Vol.25, no.4

ghost had been exorcised, a new calm spread over the department, and I realised this was to be my last significant act.

I shall leave my last word to Derrida. In *Waterland* and *Midnight's Children*, as in most novels of the 1980s, characters are plagued by a void, hole, or chasm: in *Waterland* this void is the 'the dizzy void he can't get away from (...) this feeling of nothing'; this 'great vacuum inside him'; this 'emptiness'; etc.[28] In *Midnight's Children* it is the 'hole in the centre' of Saleem; 'a dark shadow like a hole'; a 'hole in his stomach the size of a fist'; a hole in the middle of him, 'the size of a melon', etc.[29] What we lack is the solid ground, the island, the fortress, some untouched transcendental originator of action that can escape the effects of history, of narrative, of the body, of the others, of *das Man*. In the most famous aphorism from *The Gay Science*, the mad man runs around shouting that he is seeking God – seeking the God we killed. Nietzsche asks, 'Is the magnitude of this deed not too great for us? Must we not ourselves become gods just to seem worthy of it?'[30] In a way we do, which is to say that secularisation demands new myths of transcendentalism, or, in the words of the medium in *Gravity's Rainbow*:

> Putting the control inside was ratifying what de facto had happened –
> that you had dispensed with God. But you had taken on a greater,
> and more harmful, illusion. The illusion of control. That A could do B.
> But that was false. Completely. No one can *do*. Things only happen, A
> and B are unreal, are names for parts that ought to be inseparable...[31]

And so the void is a paradoxical thing – the sign of a nothing that exists to replace the sign of a nothing, that still wants to anchor, in Derrida's words again, 'a system in which the central signified, the original or transcendental signified, is never absolutely present outside a system of differences. The absence of the transcendental signified extends the domain and the play of signification infinitely'.[32]

Adieu, adieu! All that lives must die, passing through nature to eternity. In the ghostly quiet of summer recess, I began to clear my office. What final words can I offer to the future? The world is infinitely stupider than when I set out to educate it

---

[28] Swift, *Waterland*, op cit, pp. 193; 202; 154
[29] Rushdie, *Midnight's Children*, op cit, pp. 192; 138; 55; 22
[30] Friedrich Nietzsche, *The Gay Science*, Ed. B. Williams (Cambridge: Cambridge University Press, 2001) § 125
[31] Thomas Pynchon, *Gravity's Rainbow* (London: Vintage, [1973] 2000) pp. 35/6
[32] Derrida, *Writing and Difference*, op cit, p.354

Paragraphia, 2012, Vol.25, no.4

nearly four decades ago. I have lived the life of the mind, but when the time came to leave my office, few were the books that seemed worth saving. Locke, Leibniz, Leavis, Lukács, Lévi-Strauss, Levinas, Lefebvre, even Lacan and Lyotard – I left them all. I took only a few volumes that contained some of my early writings. At the back of my shelves, furled in dust, I recognised a special edition of a now defunct journal, to which I had contributed an article entitled "'If Hamlet from himself be ta'en away'". The essay, presented as an historical investigation, defended Ophelia from the charge of suicide and investigated the forces responsible for her drowning. I was developing ideas that would eventually contribute to the great amphilogical breakthrough that so radically altered the direction of fin de siècle cultural theory; I remember that the final line asked 'Who was responsible for the death of fair Ophelia? You were, dear reader! It was you!' I cannot now remember what this was supposed to mean.

As I picked up this journal, thinking it would make an appropriate souvenir from a life-long career, there fell from between its pages a postcard. For a moment I thought to let it lie there, to spare my tired limbs and leave it be, but I was overpowered by curiosity. It had been sent to me from Cornwall by a woman named Barbara. I stood for a full ten minutes trying to recall life at the University of Southampton in the mid 1970s, but I have no recollection of Barbara, and no idea why she thought I might be interested in the Cornish weather. Yet I had carried her postcard from office to office, from job to job, hidden between the pages of an unread journal. The picture on the card was an image of concrete urban modernism, the sort of Le Corbusian town planning that had by then begun to decline in popularity. In the foreground, an elderly man sat on a bench; his walking stick had fallen beyond his reach and he seemed unlikely to move. The only greenery in the picture was a thorny plant that had forced its way through a crack in the tarmac. The plant was starting to wrap around the man's leg.

As I left the office for the last time, I paused, momentarily seized by an emotion that may have been nostalgia. Then I surprised myself by sticking the card to a stray lump of Blu-tack on the front of my office door. My last thought, upon leaving the academy forever, was to wonder how my colleagues would react to this mute farewell. What would they take it to mean? Then I realised that before anyone else saw it, the card would be ripped down by a semi-literate immigrant woman, whose pay has been frozen far below the poverty line, and whose performance, checked against targets, has been criticised in recent efficiency reviews.

F.K. Thrub, July 2012

Budapest, 1956

140

During the Hungarian Revolution, the people, lacking any other symbol, hacked the hammer and sickles from the hearts of their national flags, and from their windows they hung these empty-centred messages of freedom. We have modelled our vision of the human mind according to the logic of our governments. We believe there is, there must be, some central authority to order and adjudicate on the myriad processes of the brain. But there isn't. '[T]here is no single, definitive "stream of consciousness,"' writes cognitive scientist and philosopher Daniel Dennett, 'because there is no central headquarters, no Cartesian Theater where it "all comes together" for the perusal of a central meaner' (1993, p-253). 'In biology,' claims Dennett, 'we have learned to resist the temptation to explain *design in organisms* by positing a single great intelligence that does all the work. (…) We must build up the same resistance to the temptation to explain action as arising from the imperatives of an internal action-orderer' (ibid., p-251). If the breakthrough of modernism was to represent consciousness, the future of fiction is to recognise that consciousness is only one small part of an endless system of centreless causation.

141

Lempi and I hugged each other goodbye at Bristol airport, and I haven't seen her since. She returned to her family home in Dorset, and then, at the end of the summer, she flew to a new life in Arizona. At first we stayed in touch by email. She told me about the heat and the sand, and how the sun set on the Tucson Mountains ('the EKG of a dying day,' she wrote, quoting David Foster Wallace). She never mentioned Alfredo, but I don't know whether this was through tact or because he hadn't waited for her. As the months went on, as her new life grew busier, her replies became rarer and shorter, and then in December, when I wrote to ask if she was coming home for Christmas, I received a 'Your mail could not be delivered' message, and I realised that her Cheltenham University email account – the only address I had for her – had been deactivated.

As for me, I took advantage of my loneliness, and over the next year, I wrote the bulk of this thesis. Cheltenham seemed quiet without Lempi, and though I had learned to once again feel safe on its streets, besides occasional drinks with Robin, there was little to distract me from my work. Jez passed his viva in October, and soon after left to teach at a Bible college in Australia. Obi finished in March. New students arrived in the office. They decorated the room with conference posters and cartoons clipped from *The Guardian*. One day I arrived at the office and discovered that a pony-tailed linguist was sitting at the desk that had always been reserved for Samuel. Then, in July 2012, when six chapters of this thesis were complete, I realised it was the anniversary of the great research trip, and once again I thought of writing to Lempi. There was still something I needed to say – some apology or declaration I needed to make.

142

What would Elsie have felt had she encountered Ramón amid the Budapest crowds? He would have changed greatly, of course. His hair, beneath his fedora, had by then flecked white, and his face had been aged and hardened by years on the Asiatic Steppe. We are born to respond to faces – a 1975 study found that infants as young as nine minutes old will follow a moving face-like pattern (Hayes, 1998, p-39) – but exactly how we recognise faces in adulthood is unclear. Bruce and Young (1986) argued that we develop a 'face recognition unit' for people that we know. The spacing of features on the face of this aged man triggered such weight of memory and emotion that for a moment Elsie's brain was paralysed.

Consider how on a website one can 'tag' a post; for example, 'Anarchism and sexuality interview with Judith Butler' could be tagged 'anarchism', 'sexuality', 'Judith Butler', 'Queer', 'philosophy', 'gender studies', and 'interviews'. If you searched the website for 'Judith Butler' then you might find this article and a dozen more. Now think of everything in Elsie's life that had been tagged with Ramón's face. The feel of a hand supporting her head. The taste of olives. The clover-shaped taps on a washstand in a pension in Southern France. A recurring dream in which he swims to her, closer and closer, and when she can almost touch him, something pulls him under the water. A rash on her face from his stubble. The steps to the house in Valderrobres, worn into crescents by the feet of previous generations. A letter she has read a thousand times. The Spanish word for freedom. A feeling of emptiness that has connected with the word 'yearning'. The chorus of a song – *Prometemos resistir, ¡Ay Carmela! ¡Ay Carmela!*. The hum of cicadas. A hundred-thousand memories of hope and love and loss and fear and grief. It is not the case that she 'thought' any of these things – there was too much noise for any one thought to gain ascendancy – but all these things were present, driving the reactions that followed.

Her reactions upon recognising Ramón were, physiologically, inseparable from her reactions to imminent danger. There were people running, shouting from windows, dragging furniture and barrels into the street. Behind her, four men bounced a car, trying to turn it sideways to form part of a barricade. There was gunfire and artillery fire and the echoing chaos of the moment made it impossible to tell from which direction it originated. Nevertheless, even in her alarmed state, the facial recognition caused such a physiological overload that Elsie hunched as if absorbing a blow. Between when she last saw Ramón, and when she arrived in Budapest, this reaction of recognition had occurred 142 times. Each time it was corrected within three seconds, and the adrenaline and euphoria gave way to an empty feeling that linguistic consciousness variously labelled 'disappointment,' 'sadness,' or 'lovesickness'. Therefore the first word that now entered consciousness – which is to say, the first attempt at commentary – was 'no'.

Psychologists have attempted to differentiate between procedural and declarative memory. Procedural memory includes those familiar movements we sometimes call 'muscle memory'. For example, one can walk for ten minutes while thinking about, say, the ingredients one needs to make tiramisu. The brain ceases to commentate on one's walking, yet one neither stumbles nor falls. Some of these familiar movements were learned in childhood with great difficulty (for instance, many of us can remember learning to swim or ride a bike); others are internalised 'below' the level of conscious awareness (in what sense is conscious awareness 'above' other neurological functions? Why does this hierarchy seem to us so natural?). There was one movement that Elsie had performed a million times without a single commentary. She often placed her hand across her forehead and trapped her fringe between her index and middle finger; then she slid her hand sideways, combing her fringe, until her index finger tapped her left ear; at which point, she tossed her head, bouncing her short hair back to its starting position. She was not conscious of doing this.

The entire action took about 1.5 seconds. But it was, when one thinks about it, exceedingly complicated. Consider, examiners, just the hand and finger movements. The pronation of the hand and forearm depended on the forward rotation of the radius, directed by the anterior radio-ulnar ligament and the posterior radio-ulnar ligament in the inferior radio-ulnar articulation; and this had to be synchronised, not just with the altering position of the head of the ulna as the humerus rotated at the shoulder joint, but with the flexion, abduction, and circumduction of the radio-carpal as pulled by the lateral, anterior, and posterior ligaments; which actions, of course, were combined with those of the carpus: for example, the articulation of just the phalanges on just the index and middle fingers required the coordination of the dorsal and palmar ligaments with the synovial membrane and the transverse metacarpal ligament, which connects the inner metacarpal bones by transversely crossing the anterior surfaces of their digital extremities; as *Gray's Anatomy* helpfully explains, the transverse metacarpal ligament 'is blended anteriorly with the anterior (glenoid) ligament of the metacarpo-phalangal articulations. To its posterior border is connected the fascia which covers the Intorossei muscles. Its anterior surface is concave where the flexor tendons pass over it. Behind it the tendons of the Interossei muscles pass to their insertion' (1985, p-239). In addition to the movements of her hand and fingers, in this action she dipped her head, smiled, blinked, rotated her neck; she had to maintain her balance, breathe, pump blood, regulate her metabolism— to fully describe the muscular movements necessary for this short action would more than double the length of this thesis.

It is also difficult to explain *why* this action occurred. First, Elsie had since childhood favoured shorter hair. She used to have her hair cut by a neighbour, who had been a barber before the war, and who had no repertoire of feminine styles; thus, even in adolescence, her haircuts were longer versions of the short back and sides. In another era, this might have been disastrous, but Elsie was fortunate that her short hair was inadvertently consistent with high fashion's movement towards more androgynous, boyish looks: Elsie's short back and sides wasn't so different from Coco Chanel's bob or Louise Brooks' Dutch Boy look. There must have been a time when some discourse of femininity, crossed with the way men had started to look at her, generated some self-consciousness about her hair, such that she began to unknowingly touch it. To this we must add that Elsie loved movies and would appropriate gestures made familiar to her by actresses; when she touched her hair, men unknowingly responded to the gesture because it had symbolic value within a culturally-driven system of social signification. They spoke to Elsie in more attentive tones and were more likely to smile. This produced smiles on Elsie's face – initially just polite, somewhat nervous smiles, but smiles that were in turn reciprocated, until this warmth felt sufficiently good that the smiles appearing on her face were genuine smiles, during which the muscles around her eyes, the orbicularis oculi, contracted. Thus there was a period of training, in which, rather like a dog who learns to sit for biscuits, she came to subconsciously associate the gesture – which she still performed without commentary – with some positive outcome.

Now, for Ramón, the gesture was the essence of Elsie herself. It was uniquely hers, an action she performed without affectation, and in their short time together, it had often provoked him to laugh and kiss her forehead. Seeing it repeated in Budapest, he would stop, hold eye contact. There would be a moment of mutual recognition. By the time the commentary was being written – *It is him! ¡Es la niña Británica!* – they would already be walking towards one and other.

143

In July, knowing that Professor Thrub was soon to leave the University, I took the bold, reckless, decision to show him my near-finished thesis. I had, of course, an ulterior motive: Thrub had access to the University's student records system, on which would be listed – if not her new address in the States – at least Lempi's parents' address. Robin had dearly wanted to help, but his professional integrity had prevented him from furnishing me with confidential information. Thrub, however, could never be accused of suffering from professional integrity.

Even in the mid-summer heat, Thrub's corridor was dark and cave-like. The silence of the vacation-thinned department added to the ominous atmosphere, and the undead branched yucca looked more claw-like than ever. Predictably, Thrub did not answer the knock on his door, though I could hear him breathing on the other side. 'Professor?' I said, knocking again.

There was a pause of several seconds. 'What do you want?' he whispered from behind the door.

'I thought maybe I could show you my thesis?'

'Jesus fucking Christ.' The door opened a few inches and Thrub pulled me inside by my shirt sleeve. 'I thought you were something to do with this Gulliver Broom business,' he said, locking the door behind me. This behaviour, even by Thrub's standards, struck me as eccentric. His office appeared to have been burgled: books and papers obscured the carpet, and his shelves were gapped here and there like some dental calamity.

He had tied a hammock between the brackets on opposing walls. 'Well?' he said.

I passed him a wire-bound draft of my near-completed thesis – a document similar to the one you examiners are now reading.

'I don't have to read this, do I?' said Thrub, emphasising the weight of paper.

'No, of course not.'

'Thank fuck for that.' Thrub began to flick through the pages, pausing now and again to read a sentence or two. 'You've actually written it then,' he said. At one point he read for more than a minute, and I badly wanted to peek over his shoulder and see what page had held his attention. Then he resumed fanning the pages, as though I had laboured over one of those animated flick books. Finally, he scanned the bibliography and returned it to me. 'You do realise,' he said, 'that there's no hope in Hell they'll pass this nonsense?'

'I'm thinking the odds are about fifty-fifty.'

'An optimist, eh?'

'It's not finished yet.'

'And how will it end? Will whatsit and whatsit ride into the sunset together?'

'No, Elsie dies. But I know that Ramón's new family lived in Budapest in 1956, and at the end I imagine that Elsie and he meet up, and disappear from view, running through the streets hand in hand.'

'Ah, how very touching. And tell me; is this an allegory for your future with the lovely Miss Bridgette?'

'Lempi's left the University.'

'Really?' said Thrub, stumbling through the remnants of his office. 'I'm not going to face a final tribunal, am I?' He clambered over his hammock and took up position by the window.

'No, she finished her MA last year.'

'Really? How quickly the years pass.'

'She's in Arizona studying for an MFA.'

'Good for her,' said Thrub. 'And what about you?'

'Finish this and then who knows.'

'Yes, who knows.' Thrub turned towards me and extended his hand across the hammock: 'Best of luck for viva voce – God, you'll need it – and very best wishes for the future.'

'Thank you, Professor.' Thrub's hand was cold and bony. 'May I ask you one last favour?'

'Look, I'm not reading your bloody thesis.'

'No, not that. It's about Lempi. You see, I'd very much like to write to her but I don't know her new address. Even her parents' address would do.'

Thrub at first seemed not to follow, but then it dawned on him what I was asking. 'I see. You want me to look for her address on student records and then, in a clear violation of my professional obligations, divulge this confidential information to you, a seemingly unstable, potentially dangerous third party?'

'...Yes.'

Thrub gazed once more at the vacant quadrant lawn. 'And then you'll leave me alone?'

'Forever.'

He held the back of his computer chair and lowered himself, stair-lift slow. 'What the Hell,' he said. 'Consider it an old man's ode to young love.'

144

I cannot forget about a short film clip that I saw, several years ago now, during a visit to the Imperial War Museum in London. The reason for my visit was a temporary exhibition devoted to the 1956 Hungarian Revolution, and though I remember few other exhibits, I watched that video so many times that it is imprinted in my memory. The museum looped the footage, which lasts for only a few minutes, on a big screen suspended above a tattered, centreless, Hungarian flag.

It starts with grey-scale Soviet tanks smashing through a wall of barrels, through a railway wagon, crossing tramlines, rolling jerky and needle-scratched across an empty cobbled square. There are women clutching handbags. Husbands in long coats and Homburg hats, pressed still against the window of a pharmaceutical store. Cut. A five-pointed star topples from a fourth-storey rooftop, falling in slow motion, its points catching on the masonry, turning it in cartwheels. Cut. There are tanks on the boulevard, clumsy as daleks at such close range. Molotovs scatter fire across the road. The tanks pause, guns creaking towards the third floor. A Hungarian flag hangs from the window, hammer and sickle hacked out. There is white smoke, a silent *kaboom*, and a chunk of masonry lands with a crash of dust. The cannon levels – pause – *kaboom*. Cut. Young men and women push onto the pavement, impeding each other as they run. A boy with a flag. A girl with a rifle. A young man falls off his bike and scrambles to his feet and sees the bike and the tanks and pauses then runs. The film is jerky and fast, as though some ancient machine captured this section at sixteen-frames-per-second. The front tank bobs as it flattens the bike frame. Cut.

I remember seeing a woman, an older version of Elsie, her hair styled to a softer bob. In the film, she stands with a man, of whom one can see nothing except the brim of his hat and the sleeve of his coat; he is behind a police car, which must have been abandoned during some earlier incident; its doors are open and its windscreen is smashed. People are running and it is not clear why the couple remain so near to danger. Why don't they run? Why don't they run? And then they do. They hold hands and they run. They run, hand in hand, towards an unrecorded fate.

145

After my meeting with Thrub, I bought Lempi a copy of Ian McEwan's *Amsterdam*. I think it's an awful book, but I knew Lempi enjoyed McEwan, and the title seemed somehow appropriate. I wrote a cover letter to her parents, introducing myself as an old friend of their daughter's, and requesting they forward the parcel. Then, inside a separate envelope, I enclosed a long letter: an ode, an appreciation, an apology. At one point, recalling my churlish behaviour, admitting my romantic obsession, I quoted David Smail's *The Origins of Unhappiness,* which I was reading at the time. For David Smail, the 'whole of the psychotherapy industry' rests on a philosophical misconception of ourselves 'as more or less self-determining free agents' (2001a, p-VII). He claims that:

> The great error – one might even say the fundamental flaw – of psychology has been to consider individual meaning-systems as somehow belonging to and in control of the people of whom they form a part. Over and over again the assumption is made that things like beliefs and attitudes are located inside a person and that, while they may indeed be seen as guiding his or her conduct, they are also, in some way which is almost always left mysterious, subject to operations of his or her will. (2001b, p-82)

For Smail, there is never a central controlling 'self' or 'ego', or rather, what we experience as such an 'inner' process – while perhaps the 'defining feature of our humanity and the source of our greatest spiritual satisfactions' – 'in and of itself (…) has no *power*' (2001a, p-X). He goes on to argue that 'When it comes to trying to explain how and why people do things, what actually moves them to action, reference to interior processes (such as deciding and willing) has very little relevance' (ibid.).

In other words, examiners, I pled crime of passion. Then, in a rare act of maturity, I asked Lempi to pass on my best wishes to Alfredo. I reiterated my email and postal addresses, and I requested she write me back.

On the book's inlay card, I wrote Lempi a dedication: 'to my dear friend, with love.' And then, feeling these words were trite, as an afterthought, I asked her to imagine autumn leaves floating to the ground, drifting in the breeze, while saying to themselves 'Now I'll go this way... now I'll go that way,' an analogy I attributed to Wittgenstein.

I bubble-wrapped the book and posted the whole parcel first class to Dorset. I like to think that her parents forwarded it immediately, and I imagine Lempi opening it under the burning Arizona sun. I imagine her sitting below a parasol, pondering the meaning of my strange inscriptions. She is sipping from a tall glass full of ice. After a minute, she closes her eyes, reminisces, remembers.

But perhaps the parcel never reached her. At the time of writing, September 2012, two months have passed since I posted the gift, and I have yet to receive a reply. The summer is showing the first signs of tiredness – the edges of leaves are yellowing and curling, like documents from the past – but every day I await the postman, my heart beating with fresh hope.

146

Words flow out from the world. One starts a sentence with no idea what one is going to say, yet the words spell out with grammar and sense. Occasionally, when the words we speak sound, on reflection, inappropriate or discontinuous with our beliefs, we say 'I just blurted it out – I don't know why!' We wonder why nothing else in the world emerged to stop such words, to hold them back.

'Why did you leave me?'

Before I could reclaim the words, or put them to other purposes, I had typed them: Ramón and Elsie's last conversation: the conversation they had before her death.

But this reunion, this final interlocution, owes its existence only to hope. The couple I saw in the film are not Elsie and Ramón. Apart from anything else, the footage is almost certainly from the second Soviet intervention, by which time, I know from George, Elsie was already dead. So this reunion belongs to me and Elsie, and I imagine it started the way it always started in Elsie's mind: 'Why did you leave me?'

I imagine, too, that Ramón listened, taking a moment to separate these words from the distant clatter of rocks, the grind of engines, the explosions and cries; then he took a moment more to process this language that had become to him so unfamiliar. 'I did not,' he said.

And probably these words were the start of a fuller answer, an attempt to explain the years that had elapsed, to demonstrate that he had not left so much as been unable to return: the aviation school, the Novosibirsk transit prison, the Siberian nights that lasted all day, the frostbite and northern lights and the men with beards of ice. Maybe he would have told her of life in Karaganda: the digging and planting; the snow storms so fierce he thought he'd gone blind; the horses fighting mosquitoes – snorting and stamping and shaking – as if in religious observance. He would have told her about the Russian criminals and the Ukrainian soldiers and the Austro-Hungarian woman who became his wife. She would have asked, 'Do you love her?' And he would have said, 'Yes, Elsie, I love her.' Then, seeing the hurt on her face, he would have added, 'Elsie, she is the mother of my daughter.'

When Elsie's crying had subsided, he would have held her close and whispered that he named his daughter Elizabeth. Elizabeth, like Elsie. Elsie would have told Ramón about her family. 'I'm married, too,' she would have said. She would have described her husband as 'a good man' who 'always puts food on the table' and she would have felt great love for her son. Yes, she would have thought of little George – George who, far away in Manchester, had been knocked unconscious by a stone.

But there was no time for any of this. Elsie heard his words the way she'd always imagined them. She heard what he said as if he'd said, instead, 'I never left you, Elsie; you've been here in my heart every minute.' Like words and thoughts, like the waves on a beach, human movements are part of a ceaseless dance, which does not have a beginning or an end. In February 2011, a neurological study by Itzhak Fried et al. confirmed the findings of Benjamin Libet, who in the 1980s claimed that awareness of an action occurs after that action has been initiated in the brain. Fried et al. measured neuronal firing rates and discovered that related neural activity in the medial frontal cortex was evident prior to subjective awareness of the decision to act; in other words, when we feel we have decided to act, we are merely commentating on, perhaps reviewing, an action that has already commenced.

Now, one more note in time's chorus. In a shuttered room, a guesthouse mattress creaked with the weight of one more passer-through. Nearby, a gunshot fired pigeons flapping through smoke. On a torn newspaper report, unseen and kicked by running feet, Puskás and Kocsis clasped hands in celebration. Underground, a rat swam, where the roots of a weed had cracked the concrete. Overhead, a centreless flag saluted the breeze.

Subsumed in this ceaseless dance, two bodies prepared to extend two hands, and a second later three words were spoken.

Those three words were, 'I love you.'

ACKNOWLEDGEMENTS:

This novel was made possible by the help and brilliance of more people than there is space here to thank. I am indebted to Harriet Newton, Lucy Tyler, Martin Randall, and Martin Goodman; but the help I've received has been so great, and the helpers so many, that to adequately express my gratitude would double the length of this book.

Bibliography:
For a list of bibliographic and electronic sources, please visit ddjohnston.org/bibliography

Lightning Source UK Ltd.
Milton Keynes UK
UKOW03f1550300913

218210UK00001BA/9/P